Symphony of the Fallen Stars

Marie Lau

She got away from death, only to become indebted to the man ruling over it.

Symphony of the Fallen Stars.
A Symphony novel.
By Marie Lau.

Copyright ©2022 by Marie Lau, all rights reserved.

Developmental & Line Edit by Ad Astra Editorial (adastraeditorial.com)

Cover Design by Marie Grasshoff (marie-grasshoff.de)

Formatted by The Nutty Formatter (thenuttyformatter.com)

PUBLISHER'S NOTE: This is a work of fiction. Names, characters, places and incidents are either the product of the author's imagination or are used fictitiously. Any resemblance to real people, places, or events is entirely coincidental.

ALL RIGHTS RESERVED. No part of this publication may be reproduced or sold in any form, or by any means without the written permission of the author.

For more information contact: (authormarielau@gmail.com)

BOOK DESCRIPTION

He is Death incarnate, collector of lives. You only get to meet him once: the moment you die. But he makes an exception for Cassiana; instead of taking her soul, he saves it. But for what price?

Just imagine Death incarnate wouldn't kill, but save you. As crazy as that might sound, that is exactly what happens to Cassiana. All she's ever known is her desire to become famous. When she gets a chance to perform a play in front of the King of the fae, her breakthrough seems within reach. But what begins as a hope for her future becomes a nightmare when the fae King decides to kill her.

That is, until a man much worse than the King of the fae saves her: the Deathbringer. He is a creature as old as life itself. A man known not for saving, but for taking souls. He is ruler of the Dead, King of the Afterlife, and nobody has ever laid eyes upon him. At least, nobody living.

With his striking features, his mocking attitude, and that dark hair that shimmers like the stars of the night sky, he is nothing like Cassiana has imagined him to be. She's left wondering why he, King of the Afterlife, bothers to save her.
Whatever his reasons for saving her are, she owes him now. And what scares Cassiana most isn't the debt she needs to repay. It's the way she's looking forward to doing so.
The Deathbringer's darkness calls to Cassiana, begging for her touch, her affection, and her *love*. Will she be able to resist it?

***Symphony of the Fallen Stars* is a New Adult, sexy fantasy loosely inspired by the myths of Hades and Persephone.**

Either way, we are all going to die.

CHAPTER ONE

Sticky sweat clung to me like a second skin, the liquid slowly mixing with the makeup I'd spent hours applying. If not for the stickiness gathering in my clothing, it'd almost add to the glitter sprinkled over my body. I smoothed down the coarse fabric of the deep-red dress that hugged my curves in the most revealing way, forcing myself to take deep breaths, and slowly bringing my stomach to ease its tightness.

Four times. I had run four times to the bathroom, my body rejecting every single thing I'd had for breakfast. Which hadn't been much. The medication I had taken just before arriving to the theatre to quell my ever-crescendoing anxiety wasn't helping, either.

Soft murmuring started mixing with the sound of the orchestra checking its instruments, and candlelight illuminated the theatre in a soft glow, its brightness reflecting on the gilded adornments of the ceiling.

The guests had arrived.

I didn't know how many guests would attend the King's

birthday celebration. I couldn't check, either. The satin, deep-red curtains hid the stage on which I stood from the people entering the majestic theatre. But I knew *what* the guests were: fae.

The hairs on my neck stood. I couldn't explain the reason for it, but I had always been afraid of fae. There was something about them that seemed … off. It wasn't their perfect features, or their pointed ears peeking out from beneath their hair. Neither was it their flawless skin with their otherworldly glow that let them be recognized as fae from afar. It was the fact that they were too unpredictable. They kept to themselves, never mingling with what they regarded as lesser creatures.

This was also the reason for my theatre group's surprise when we'd been asked to perform our play at the fae King's birthday celebration. After all, my acting colleagues and I were humans.

I looked at the script I'd left on the table next to the makeup vanity.

My heart rate increased, threatening to beat a hole into my chest. I squeezed my eyes shut and forced myself to focus on my breathing.

Was it supposed to feel like this? The constant nausea before a presentation, the never-ending insomnia, the weight loss?

I scanned the faces of my fellow actors. Most of them were going through their lines, while others freshened their makeup in front of the full-body mirrors. They were nervous, yes, but they didn't seem about to have a heart-attack like I feared I would.

Shaking my head, I dismissed that thought. I wouldn't get a chance like this again. Today could be my breakthrough. Today could be my chance to prove to everyone that my acting was worth being cherished. That *I* was worth being cherished and acknowledged for my work.

"Cassiana!"

Fighting back a sigh, I plastered a tight smile on my face before I turned to my acting instructor, Mrs. Fitzgivens. She was a stern woman, the kind of instructor who'd notice the smallest mistakes, be it the minimal inclination of the head that contradicted a fictional character's behavior, or a failure in the posture. It was precisely her attention to detail that made her the best in her field. Her eyes took in my makeup before they lowered to my costume. Her brows knit together when her gaze dropped to the bracelet on my wrist. Instinctively, I crossed my arms behind my back, hiding the adornment from her reproving gaze.

Shaking her head, she clicked her tongue, making her sapphire earrings reflect the light. "What's this?" she demanded coldly, her intensifying wrinkles only adding to her displeasure.

"What do you mean?" I asked innocently, my left hand slowly working the knot tying the bracelet to my wrist.

My acting tutor's eyes thinned into slits. "Show me your arm."

Snatching off the bracelet just in time, I outstretched my arm. I didn't care that the bracelet wasn't part of the costume. It was the one thing I wouldn't leave off for long. Even if it meant displeasing Mrs. Fitzgivens.

My best friend Miriam's face flashed before my inner eye, her silvery gaze fixed on the small wristband she had given to me just yesterday. The white dots on it glittered against the black fabric like stars in a night's sky. *It's for luck and protection. Whatever happens, make sure to always keep the bracelet on.*

I'd be stupid not to accept Miriam's advice. She was well known for the magical bracelets she made. Not only could they protect you, they could also attract money, love, a better reputation, or new relationships. They were the reason she was the most famous witch in Washington, D.C.

Mrs. Fitzgivens eyed my wrist before tearing her gaze away from my unadorned arm and straightening her spine. I was sure it bothered her that her petite height couldn't loom over me in a threatening way. "Cassiana, I—"

The ringing of the small bell that indicated the play was about to begin cut her off. My tutor paled visibly. I was sure I did the same.

Her gaze moved away from me, hurriedly supervising how everybody rushed to their positions collectively. Spotting one of my acting colleagues having trouble fixing her hair, Mrs. Fitzgivens raced to her side.

As I scurried to my assigned position, I refastened the bracelet on my wrist.

I met eyes with Daniel, one of my acting colleagues, and flashed him what I hoped was a comforting smile. He didn't return it, his mind probably too nervous to notice my gesture.

I replayed the directions from the male fae who'd greeted us at the entrance of the theatre: do not speak or even look at the King unless spoken to, and in that case, he should be addressed as 'Your Highness.' The strong, suffocating smell of the rose fragrance he had made each of us put on still clung heavily to my nasal cavities. None of the actors had the slightest clue as to why the fae King had wished for our acting school, *Act as Dramatic as a Banshee,* to present the play he had picked. There were so many other acting schools he could've chosen. But we didn't question his preference. Maybe he'd gotten confused with a different school, maybe he'd chosen us consciously, but whatever his reasons, he'd given us a chance most actors could only dream of.

My hands shook as the rest of my acting colleagues began taking up their positions, all of us eager to make a lasting impression on the audience. And, of course, on the fae King. *Especially* on the King.

The heavy gold-embroidered curtains rustled when they were pulled open. I watched how the red satin glinted with the movement like the reflection of the moon on a river's surface. The spotlight immediately fell upon me, making my glitter-covered body shimmer under the weight of the countless watching eyes.

Sweat formed on my forehead at the heat cast by the artificial lights and at the emotions that threatened to overcome me.

I looked up at the ceiling. *God, please make this work.*

I wouldn't know until some time later that God must've been absent when I prayed for his help. For in his place, I'd be facing Death.

CHAPTER TWO

I had always been most calm at night. As soon as Mir was asleep, I'd crawl up on our apartment's rooftop, a blanket tucked beneath my arm, waiting for the stars to come out. I'd spent hours and hours there by myself, staring at the small glittering spots in the night sky and just … dreaming. Dreaming about a life that wasn't my own … A life in which people would acknowledge me for my work. A life in which I'd be seen, appreciated.

Maybe I felt that way because of the lack of love and affection my parents showed me throughout my entire life, or maybe I felt that way because I just wished to be famous. Whatever the reason, that deep, inner yearning was what initially led me to pursue an acting career. Little did I know how poorly that yearning was about to end.

The bell rang, and after a beat of silence, the orchestra began playing, giving way to the play's opening scene.

My vision blackened, my mind blanked, my blood pumped through my veins, keeping my body working through the countless rehearsed movements. I rushed over the stage, time flying past me like a dream. I wasn't me any longer. I *became* my character, letting my own personality slip away from my body—just like a snake shedding its skin.

There was no more sense of my gut knotting up. There was no more sense of my heart pumping powerfully against my skin. There were only the lines I had practiced day and night, all of them passing my lips as though a ghost whispered them to me.

I felt how I imagined hypnotized people must feel. Like being thrown into a vacuum of space, with nothing but my thoughts and the movements of my body to accompany me into the abyss.

I flew from one end of the stage to the next, never missing a beat, my steps never faltering, my lines never failing me. I was ignorant to everything happening around me. I wasn't aware of the gathered crowd watching the stage from their satin-covered chairs. Neither was I aware of the human waiters passing through the rows of chairs, offering the finest liquors to the fae King's guests. But most importantly, I wasn't aware of the ice-cold, glacier-white eyes watching every movement on the stage with absolute boredom and indifference.

I don't know how I managed to get through the play.

It felt as though I'd spent an entire lifetime onstage, but it couldn't possibly have been more than two hours. As soon as the curtains closed after the play's last scene, there was no more sense of my surroundings, no more thoughts clouding my mind. The only thing I felt was the adrenaline racing through my veins. Still high from anxiety, it took me several seconds to ground myself back to the here and now.

My gaze roamed over the happy faces of my colleagues.

We'd done it.

We'd actually done it! All the ongoing stress tensing my neck over the last weeks let loose all at once, as though it hadn't been there in the first place. I felt my lips stretch from the breadth of my smile.

The nightmare had finally come to an end.

Throughout my 26 years, I had never felt such a big inner sense of relief.

We rushed to the centre of the stage and lined up. We grabbed our hands, ready to receive the applause and congratulations from the audience. I took my co-actor Celine's hand with my right and Daniel's with my left, a happy, relieved grin plastered on my face. The sweat coating their hands mixed with my own. No matter how many times each of us had acted before a crowd, it was still something we didn't get used to so easily.

I stared ahead. My breaths were shallow, anxiety coursing through my veins hot as fire.

The curtains were pulled open again, revealing us to the gathered crowd. We lifted our arms in unison and bowed deeply before the audience.

A rain of applause fell upon us.

As we straightened again, I noticed some people had risen, clapping into their hands vigorously, cheering and waving at us excitedly.

I perceived everything as though a veil of euphoria had been draped over me, silencing the ongoing cheers and claps. The curtain call was my favorite part of the entire acting process.

Involuntarily, my eyes fluttered closed. I loved seeing the happiness and excitement radiating from the audience shining upon us. And witnessing the recognition of our hard work.

I blinked against the blinding brightness of the artificial light. My gaze raked over the colorful crowd. Their illustrious dresses and suits didn't leave any room to wonder whether they possessed the necessary riches to be invited to a King's birthday. The light of the candles floating throughout the entire theatre reflected on the sapphires and rubies adorning the women's dresses. Unsurprisingly, all of the guests were fae. Only the waiters were human. There was no trace of any vampire, witch, wizard, or werewolf whatsoever.

It was only after my heartbeat calmed that my gaze fell upon the man sitting on the majestic podium erected only for him downstage.

My breathing grew shallow as I recognized him.

King Silvan, King of the fae.

Out of all the six Kings, Silvan frightened me most.

He was too calm. Too unaffected. Almost motionless.

It was precisely this lack of interest that gave me the chills as I took him in. His crown was crafted of metal, its color bright like spun moonlight, just a shade darker than its owner's silvery hair. Everything about it screamed abundance, from the small rubies adhering on each peak, to the gold at the very tips of it. The way his hair had been gelled back drew attention to his pointed ears.

But it wasn't his physical appearance that made my blood turn to chips of ice. It was his eyes. His glacier-blue, calculating eyes. They seemed ... off. Somehow empty, like a shell without life; as did the power thrumming around him like a second skin. That cold, bone-rattling power for which the King of the fae was known.

King Silvan appeared to be in his early thirties, but his real age was closer to a thousand. While the Kings weren't immortal, they did have much longer lifespans than the average fae, vampire, witch, wizard or werewolf, who only lived up to one hundred years. There was only one King whispered about to be dead—yet, somehow, was still alive.

I had heard stories about the fae King. The Ice-King, they called him. And now I understood where he got that name. His arms were crossed in front of his chest, his eyes tracking how we bowed deeply before him and the audience. We might as well have been explaining our human tax system to him for all the excitement and interest he displayed.

He hadn't reacted to any of the other guests; neither did he cast a single glance in the direction of the two guards flanking his sides. The guards were serious, always alert to any potential threat to their King. A scabbard was fastened on the hip of one guard, while something made of leather was fastened on the other guard's hip. Squinting, I tried to make out the object, but I was too far away to recognize it.

Yet again, Daniel and Celine extended their arms into the air, tearing my attention away from the fae King and back to the gathered crowd. The applause and cheers flared up around us.

Glancing at Celine, I saw the way her eyes were lit in joy at the presentation's success. The exact same expression was written across the faces of all my fellow actors. I looked back at the audience, who barely managed to keep their enthusiasm in check.

Suddenly, a loud shatter interrupted the applause.

"How dare you!" A powerful voice boomed.

I spun my head to the noise.

My eyes fixed on King Silvan. His cold gaze blazed with rage.

A human waiter lay on the floor right in front of the King, picking broken pieces of glass from the marble floor and putting them on the tray next to him. His face was flushed, his hands trembling as he carefully hurried to pick up the glass. "I am so, so sorry. I stumbled. I am very sorry." He was so embarrassed, he wasn't even able to meet the King's eyes.

Oh, so very slowly, the fae King stood, his movements measured, calculated. "Don't you look at your King when you address him?"

All sounds grew quiet, the clapping easing to complete silence.

"Yes. I am so sorry." The waiter looked up to the King, his eyes swollen.

The monarch moved in front of him, arching a brow in annoyance. "Your Highness."

"I don't …" The waiter swallowed. Clearly, he was overwhelmed by the situation. "I don't understand."

"You ought to address me with my title." The King's dead eyes searched the young waiter's face, not a hint of his thoughts playing out in his facial expression.

Instinctively, I squeezed Daniel's and Celine's hands tighter. Why was he calling the poor kid out on this trivial mistake?

The waiter's eyes grew big. "I am sorry, Your Highness." He bowed his head in respect.

King Silvan didn't blink as he nodded to his guards. Both of them moved in unison toward the waiter.

Frantically, the boy's eyes darted between the two of them. "What—"

Before he could move, each guard had grabbed one of his arms and yanked him back against them. The gathered crowd began moving uncertainly, casting nervous glances at each other. No one seemed to know what to make of the situation. The boy struggled against the guards' unyielding hold. He looked back at the King, his eyes wide in dread.

King Silvan stepped down from his podium and began rounding on the boy, his arms crossed behind his back. "Not only did you trip in front of me, you also disrespected me by not addressing me properly."

He sounded casual, but there was an edge to his voice and a sharpness to his gaze that suggested otherwise.

The boy paled visibly. "I am very sorry." He looked extremely small next to the trained fae guards. "Your Highness," the boy rushed to add.

Silvan's eyes raked over the theatre. "You must see, I cannot tolerate this kind of behavior."

I felt my brows pucker. What the hell was the King doing?

The boy began shaking. "What do you—"

"You will talk when spoken to," the King's cool voice interrupted, his gaze coming back to the boy.

The boy closed his mouth, confusion and fear shining through his eyes.

Silvan straightened his spine, his eyes roaming over the gathered crowd. "Twelve."

The audience gasped collectively, and murmurs spread among the crowd.

Twelve? What the hell did he mean? Why was he manhandling the boy like this? What was going on?

Silvan extended his hands in the direction of one of the guards.

The object attached to the guard's belt elevated into the air of its own accord, slowly floating toward Silvan. I was too focused on trying to make out what the object was to truly notice that the fae King was using one of his infamous powers.

It was only once the King caught the object in the air and unfastened a strap holding it together that I understood.

Hissing, I staggered back, not wanting to acknowledge what my eyes clearly saw.

A *lash*.

The boy realized what the King wanted to do the same moment I did. He began to kick out and struggle against the guards' hold, but of course, he didn't stand a chance against two guards who'd likely toned their muscles since the very first day they had enrolled in the royal fae guard.

Slowly, my eyes slid back to the King. There was no way he was really about to do what I feared he would, right? In front of all these people? At his own party?

"Turn him around."

No, no, no, no!

"Please!" the boy screamed, tears wetting his rosy cheeks.

The King didn't even blink as the guards turned the boy around, completely ignorant to his cries and pleads.

"His shirt."

The boy's shrill shouts were so at odds with the King's calm voice. They grew louder as one of the guards held both of the boy's arms above his head, while the other ripped his shirt right open at his back.

The guard moved back to the boy. He kicked the waiter's legs out from beneath him, forcing him to kneel. The boy whimpered in fear of what was to come while the fae King watched everything with satisfaction. The guard stepped up next to the boy, once again grabbing one of his arms. Both of the guards held the boy on his knees, the boy's shirt falling open, ready for the King's lashing.

No, no, no, no!

King Silvan let the whip sizzle through the air before connecting it with the floor. Everyone jumped at the sound.

The boy's whole body trembled uncontrollably. "Please," he begged once more, panic shaking his voice.

The King laughed bitterly. "And you are still not addressing me properly. Don't you stupid humans learn anything?" His silver hair glittered as he rolled the sleeves of his shirt to his upper arms. "It shall be thirteen; fourteen if you don't keep your cries low." A disgusted expression appeared on his face when he took in the boy's shaking figure. "Don't be so fucking weak. You are a man. Act like one," he spat.

Before the boy could brace himself, the King lunged out, the whip swishing through the air and connecting with the boy's back.

The waiter screamed out, his body jolting forward from the force of the blow. He was only able to stay upright due to the guards' hold on him.

The hit immediately drew blood, a deep, ugly welt appearing on his back.

I was so shocked, I couldn't do anything other than stand on the stage dumbfounded, staring at the stream of blood dripping from the mark on the poor boy's back.

I squeezed my eyes shut as the King lunged out once more, the sound of ripping flesh making me nauseous.

Unable to grasp what was unfolding before me, I shook my head.

No, no, no, no.

This wasn't right.

I looked to the audience. Shock was plastered on most of the faces, but also silent acceptance of their King's behavior. Some didn't even seem surprised. Others had even drawn out their phones, trying to zoom out of here. But those who shocked me most were the ones who watched the lashing with … *fervor*. Those who didn't mind the King's punishment, but seemed to actually be … enjoying it.

And no one interfered.

The room started spinning around me.

Looking at the actors next to me, I saw the horror of what was happening shining through their eyes. I spotted Mrs. Fitzgivens peeking at Silvan, her body hidden behind the curtains. She was tense and her eyes were wide. She looked ready to flee.

No one moved. No one said a word. Everyone kept their positions. Everyone kept silent.

They are not going to stop him, I realized in complete horror.

They'd rather stand by and watch a boy get beaten than threaten their own safety. I stared at my colleagues in disbelief.

Why? Surely the possibility of fame from our performance and the King's favor must be a factor playing into their behavior.

The boy's screams cut through the silence. Each lash delivered to him made my body jerk as if I'd been the one beaten.

The sound of flesh connecting to flesh.
The sound of heavy breathing on my skin.
The sound of my whimpers.

Wrong.

This was wrong. This was wrong on so many levels.

I couldn't stand by and witness someone get punished for something he didn't have a chance to do differently.

The boy's body hung limp in the grip of the guards. He wasn't even able to hold his weight anymore. Blood streamed down his back and pooled at his feet.

Silvan had to stop.

"Stop." The sound wasn't more than a whisper, but it was enough for Celine to hear me.

"Be quiet!" she hissed through clenched teeth, fear turning her moss-green eyes darker. Fear of what the King might do. Fear of what she might lose if she grazed the King's bad will. We were already looking at what happened to those who displeased the King of the fae. She didn't wish to be on the receiving end.

I ignored her. "*Stop!*" This time, I screamed. The sound of my voice mixed with the sound of the boy's flesh being torn open.

All at once, the room became eerily quiet. Only the boy's blood dripping on the floor disrupted the silence.

King Silvan breathed heavily, his attention still fixed on the boy. Ever so slowly, he lifted his head and turned around to face the stage. Numbness marked his face. "Who dared to speak to me like that?"

Celine froze next to me and ducked her head.

I lifted my chin. "Me." I let go of Celine's and Daniel's hands and stepped out of the line. "Your Highness," I added, surprised at the bitterness in my tone. "Please have mercy and do not continue this," I begged the King. "It isn't right."

The crowd held its breath.

Silvan did not so much as blink. "How dare you question my will, human?"

Instinctively, I wanted to avoid his raging gaze.

But I didn't. "It isn't right," I repeated.

The King's eyes narrowed as he took me in. He cocked his head to the side. "Come here."

I swallowed as I obeyed, following the steps that led down the stage, walking right into the monster's reach. I felt the stares of Mrs. Fitzgivens and my fellow actors at my back, but I kept my head high, never looking away from the King. I was surprised I managed to walk up to him without losing consciousness. Everything about this felt like a game. A game I had no chance of winning.

The monarch cocked his head like a bird when I stopped a couple of feet before him.

It was hard not to recoil as I noticed the way the boy's blood had started to sprinkle the King's face with red dots. His white shirt was wrinkled from the movement of the whipping, and blood covered it.

The King stepped up to me, the lash dripping with the boy's blood. This close, I could see the countless small blue veins shining through his pale, almost see-through skin. When he searched my eyes, his dead expression sent chills down my spine.

But I refused to step back.

The irony! Even up close, there was no way to mistake his beauty. How unfair that someone as cruel as the King of the fae, was that good looking when he was the worst this world needed!

His gaze hardened when he recognized what must be in my eyes: defiance.

"Get her," the King commanded without taking his eyes off of me.

The guards immediately obeyed, letting go of the boy.

I cringed as he collapsed, his beaten body hitting the floor with a loud thud.

Should've interfered sooner.

I did not move as the fae guards grabbed my arms, kicking my legs out from beneath me and forcing me to kneel before their King. Manhandling me just like they had the waiter.

The King took a strand of my hair between his fingers, his touch leaving the boy's blood in its wake. When the back of his hand brushed my cheek, I couldn't help but flinch at the coldness of his touch and the warmth of the blood coating his skin.

Without tearing his eyes from me, he ordered to no one in particular, "Bring him away." Three fae guards I hadn't noticed before moved to the boy's broken body.

Swallowing, I stared at the boy. I just hoped they'd bring him to a place where they'd take care of him.

I jumped when the King suddenly closed his hand around my throat and forced my face up. His eyes gleamed dangerously as he let them travel over my face and body. "I have something better to play with," he murmured.

Locking my jaw, I forced myself to meet his gaze with the same indifference with which he watched me. Now, that I was kneeling in front of him, my chin held tight between his thumb and index finger, I saw an emotion flicker in his eyes.

Excitement. This excited him.

The recognition made my stomach recoil. He enjoyed inflicting pain and spreading fear.

His eyes gleamed even brighter as he looked down at me, his lips pulling into a frightening smile that sent shivers down my back.

I had no idea how I managed to stay so still as his hand began following an invisible path over my temple. Everything in me begged for me to run, to lower my gaze in surrender. But I refused to do so. There was a lot I'd do to get famous, but watching someone get beaten without interfering wasn't one of those things.

Suddenly, the King's earlier almost *caring* touches were replaced by him fisting my hair and yanking it forcefully back. "How dare you demand me to stop?" he asked, his hand preventing me from evading his gaze.

I locked eyes with him, my expression blank. "You cannot treat people that way. That boy did nothing wrong. Everybody trips. Even you, Your Highness."

I felt the King's fingers flex in my hair.

He leaned forward, and never taking his eyes off me, said, "Do you even realize you are talking to your King right now?"

"You are not my King." *Where the actual fuck am I getting this senseless boldness from?* I swallowed. "I do not answer to a King who rules by using fear to spread his power." I knew I should stop speaking, but I couldn't. My rage threatened to erupt out of me, and I couldn't rein it in any longer. Elevating my voice, I said, "So, to clarify, Your Highness." My voice had dropped to a sarcastic tone. "I will not obey any of your orders."

The crowd tensed at my words.

Silvan stared at me thoughtfully. Only the jump of a muscle in his jaw showed any indication of what was going on inside his head.

Even though I had meant every word exactly the way I had said them, my heart started beating faster and sweat formed on my forehead.

The King's eyes roamed over my face, lingering on my eyes. His left hand slid up my face, tracing the curve of my lips, while his other hand still gripped my hair firmly.

His lips quirked up.

Abruptly, he let go of my hair and stepped back. "Kill her."

CHAPTER THREE

I could still remember the first time I had come face to face with death.

My parents used to take me to the beach during our summer vacation. It had been at a time when my parents and I still had a good relationship. Though our "relationship" had never been like the relationships my friends had with their parents. Their houses had always been filled with love and affection. Maybe that was why I preferred going to their houses instead of inviting them to come over. I never understood why they blushed when their parents hugged them or why they rolled their eyes when they were reminded to be careful on their way to school.

My parents never acted that way with me. They always kept their distance, avoiding speaking to me or even looking my way.

On one of these vacations, they let me play at the beach by myself while they attended to whatever business they had going on at that time. I ran to the dock to refill the bowl I'd brought with me, wanting to build that sandcastle I had been dreaming about for ages—but I couldn't reach the water from the dock. It was too *far away, and my arms were too short. So, I climbed over the rocks near the water.*

But the rocks were slippery, and my small hands couldn't react fast enough.

I fell.

The ice-cold water stole my breath instantly. Desperately, I tried to get a hold of a rock, a helping hand, anything, to get out of the ocean. Except my hands kept reaching into nothing but water.

Even at that young age, I knew I had no chance against the mass of water that kept pushing me down. I tried to get to the surface, but my strength was leaving me quickly. Too quickly.

Back then, I didn't dwell on death. Death chose others. Not me. And, even if it would eventually choose me, I had been sure I was too young for it to be interested in that moment.

How mistaken and naïve I had been.

After all, death made no distinction between age, race, culture, or creature.

Breathing was never something I even thought about, but right then, when I gasped for air and filled my lungs with nothing but saltwater, the lack of oxygen fucking hurt. *The water not only took my breath away, but also dissolved the last of my remaining hope.*

It was precisely that moment when I knew it was too late for me. Too late for anyone to rescue me. Death was standing in the doorway, reaching a hand out to take me away from the world I had known until then.

And I grabbed it.

When I felt my eyes flutter and death enter my body, pushing the remaining energy out of its shell, it was nothing like I had expected it to feel like. I had expected it to be cold, frightening, even painful.

Instead, it felt like a sensation of sheer inner peace.

Even now, I couldn't explain how I managed to get out of the water that day. I could only remember that earlier peace being shattered the moment I caught my breath.

When my eyes peeled open again, I woke up on the beach.

Alone, with no one by my side.

When I finally gathered the strength to walk back home, my parents were chatting with friends. They didn't even glance in my direction. They didn't notice the tears streaming down my cheeks, the fluid mixing with the saltwater. Neither did their friends. I had gone to bed alone and forgotten about.

Dying had been a more welcoming sensation than coming home.

The promise of death did not feel as welcoming this time.

The only emotion I felt as the two guards released their hold on me and moved behind me was panic. Sheer and utter panic. There was no trace of the calmness or inner peace I'd felt all those years ago.

I choked on my breath as one of the guards drew a sword from its sheath with a scraping sound. I jumped when he pressed the cool, sharp edge against my neck.

I did believe in miracles—I myself had experienced one that day at the beach—but I also believed they occurred rarely. So rarely, it was impossible for them to happen twice to the same person.

I had gone too far. How had I thought King Silvan would accept my behavior? What had I expected to happen? That he would acknowledge the wrongness of his actions and apologize? Of course he wouldn't. And, as wrong as his behavior might be, I could even understand it. He had to make an example of me. He couldn't just allow a stranger to question him before his people without that stranger facing the consequences.

The cold metal against the sensitive skin of my neck brought back memories I'd long ago locked away. The guard behind me applied more pressure on the blade. A searing sting of pain made a trickle of blood run down my throat.

Suddenly, it hit me. Today was the day I would die.

I looked up at the King.

If I had expected him to look affected by what he had commanded, I would be disappointed. King Silvan's eyes showed no emotion at all as he stared down at me. I might as well have been a spider to crush on his wall, instead of an actual human being.

I let my eyes drift over the gathered crowd. I spotted some people who turned away to spare themselves the sight of my fate. Others looked at their feet, not able to acknowledge what their King had just commanded. But what made my stomach recoil were the ones who looked intrigued, as if they could not wait to see my head roll, staining the carpet in a deeper shade of red than it already was. They were the same people who had seemed to be looking forward to the boy's lashing.

My gaze came back to Silvan's. I only had one last chance to change his mind. "Please."

The word left my lips so softly, I almost wasn't sure the King had heard me. But as soon as I recognized the indifference laying in the King's eyes, I knew there was no hope—even if he *had* heard me.

Resigned, I stared at the palms of my hands. Careful not to injure myself further against the sharpness of the blade, I turned my head slightly, looking at the guard behind me. He was young. Too young to be ordered to fulfill this task. It would take whatever innocence was still left in him. He swallowed hard, not willing to look at me. When he finally gathered the courage to meet my eyes, I said, "Make it a clean cut."

He nodded, his throat bobbing.

I noticed the way his hands trembled around the sword's hilt. Locking my jaw, I turned around. *Poor kid.*

One last time I looked to His Royal Highness. I didn't know whether all the stories about ghosts tormenting the Living were indeed true, but if they were, I would make sure he regretted this decision and every chance he had to abuse innocents. Our gazes locked, and I was certain he saw the promise of revenge my eyes carried.

He tensed as I flashed him what I knew must be a scary smile.

I breathed in slowly before I let my head fall forward onto my chest. At least he was granting me a fast way to leave this world.

The spectators were quiet as I felt the guard lift his sword, aiming at my now perfectly exposed neck.

Defeated, I closed my eyes, hoping for the pain to be over quickly.

Suddenly, the wooden doors to the theatre burst open with a crashing sound.

I jerked my head up. People spun around to face the door and started putting as much distance as possible between them and it. I felt the guard behind me take a staggering step back.

And then … silence.

There was no sound.

No sound at all.

Nervous tension filled the theatre. I could almost hear my blood rushing through my ears in the silence.

The moment stretched out, the seconds ticking by painfully slowly, and then, all at once, I knew why everyone had gone so still. Goosebumps erupted on my skin as I felt it.

Power.

An ancient power that crept through the door and spread across the entire room.

It didn't feel right.

It didn't hold the cold, calculated energy Silvan's power had, nor did it seem to nurture itself from the energy of the surroundings.

It felt empty, dark and … *unearthly*. Like a vessel without content. At the same time, it felt so much more powerful than anything I had ever felt before.

The tension filling the room became palpable as my heart thundered in a forceful drum against my ribs. The flames of the candle lights flickered as if they were scared of the power asphyxiating them, lengthening the shadows of everyone and everything in the room.

I felt the temperature drop the moment the black mist began seeping into the room through the door. The King and everyone else moved farther away from it, pressing themselves as tightly against the walls as possible. From beneath the fae King, almost as though an invisible portal had been opened underneath him, white clouds began forming, surrounding His Royal Highness like a shield. At the same time, wind began flaring up. Air and wind—those were the powers Silvan wielded.

Nobody dared to move, and everyone seemed to be holding their breath, unsure of what to do. The King had frozen, too. His jaw was rock hard as his eyes remained locked on the door.

Even the guard behind me seemed to be holding his breath, the sword in his hand forgotten.

Too transfixed by what was going on, I stayed right where I was, still kneeling in the middle of the theatre.

The thick black mist crept closer and closer, getting thicker and thicker as it moved toward me, spreading through the entire theatre. Silvan's white clouds were pushed back by the darkness. I couldn't find it in me to move. It felt as if whatever power was creeping through those doors called to me, begging to be touched by me. Caressed by me. Worshipped by me.

I leaned forward, wanting to do exactly what it yearned for so deeply.

Enchanted, I held out my hand. The fog slithered toward it like a snake, ready to strike.

Suddenly, the sharp intake of breath from someone in the crowd broke whatever spell had been cast upon me. I yanked my hand back.

The floating candles flickered even more, obscuring the room in dim, glimmering light.

But still nobody moved.

Thud.

Thud.

Thud.

The sound of heavy footsteps broke the silence. Whoever was walking through the fog didn't seem to be in a hurry. In fact, the person appeared to have all the time in the world. The steps did not falter, as if the owner of the footsteps knew exactly where he wanted to go.

Then, abruptly, the steps stopped.

Everyone tensed, their breathing harsh. The air wavered, the fog began thinning in the doorway, and I watched the silhouette of a man begin to appear.

No more than a shadow was visible, his silhouette fuzzy.

Whoever this man was, he knew how to make an entrance. The fog seemed to swell behind him, almost as though it protected him.

The stranger didn't move at all for a couple of seconds. The anxiety in the room increased as everyone swayed nervously from one foot to the other. The stranger let his brightly shining eyes roam over the different faces until his gaze connected with mine.

My breath caught in my throat, and my heart might have stopped. His gaze upon me … it was like nothing I had ever felt before. With each passing second that we stared at each other, my heartbeat increased.

And then, the stranger stepped out of the mist into the dim candlelight.

I gasped for air, and I was not the only one. The entire theatre stared in shock.

The first thing I noticed were his glowing, moss green eyes. They glimmered like emeralds in stark contrast to his silken black hair that brushed his shoulders loosely. He wore a black tunic that had been fastened to his white linen shirt with a silvery pin on his right shoulder.

Blinking, I stared at him. The candles gave his face a sinister, almost devilish look. And his features … they felt so *familiar*, yet so unknown to me. Slowly, I let my eyes drift over his tall frame and his broad, defined shoulders.

He did not have pointed ears to give him away as fae, nor did he have the silvery eyes of a wizard, or the thick body hair of a werewolf. The sharp vampire's fangs were absent, too. Judging by the power he radiated, he wasn't human either. Whatever creature he was, remained unknown to me.

But the simple metallic crown resting on his hair left no doubt about his role.

He was a King.

And the King's attention was fixed on one person.

One person only.

Me.

He held my gaze as his sensual lips slowly curled up, turning his smile mocking. The power radiating from him increased as he strolled forward toward me, closing the distance between us. The flickering lighting accented his high cheekbones and the elegant curve of his nose. It was only him and me; alone in this room full of people.

Heat pooled low in my stomach. Dear God, who was this man?

A chill ran down my arms. The crown he wore was so much simpler than Silvan's. He didn't need to remind others of his power like the fae King did. His presence alone was enough to know the great extent of power he had. My attentiveness was unexplainable to me. How could I notice all these details about this man when I knelt moments away from certain death?

With each one of his mighty strides, my hands became sweatier. The power around him made crackling sounds, and the mist moved out of his way.

Shivering, I willed myself not to leap up from the floor and run. Although I didn't understand the reason for it, I wasn't scared of him; I was scared of the fact that I didn't fear him. How could I not be scared of him when everything about him suggested I should be downright *frightened*?

He walked up the stairs to the podium I was still kneeling on. Only a few steps parted us, and he seemed determined to close even that little distance. And then, right before the stranger reached me, King Silvan moved between us, efficiently breaking whatever spell had worked its magic. Both men stood so close to each other, their chests nearly brushed.

"Step away from this human right now!" Silvan hissed, lifting his chin. The white clouds at his feet raged, but were easily suppressed by the black mist.

Confused, I tore my eyes away from the stranger to stare at the fae King's back. The two fae guards watched what unfolded with attentiveness, but they didn't interfere. Probably because the newcomer was clearly a King, and because their King hadn't given them orders to act any differently.

My gaze came back to the newcomer, and I sucked in a shallow breath.

He hadn't removed his attention from me for a single second.

Silvan was tall, but next to the even taller and more broad-shouldered features of the dark-haired man, he seemed almost laughable.

Slowly, the newcomer tore his eyes away from me, and looked down at King Silvan. "Did you just give me an order, King of the fae?" he asked calmly.

That voice ... That sultry, rich voice of his. It touched something within me that made my knees go weak.

The promise of danger lay in his words. The fog flared up, building a wall behind him. His frame seemed to grow, making him even more intimidating.

Silvan tensed but held his position. "What is your business in the Land of the Living, Deathbringer?"

I froze.

Deathbringer.

The word echoed in my mind, making me shiver. I had heard it before. The name. Many times. It was a name as old as the world itself. A name feared by most.

And rightly.

His reputation preceded him, weaving stories around his figure that prevented more than just children from finding the peacefulness of sleep at night.

He was rumored to be dead—yet, somehow, was still alive. Never once had he been seen in the flesh. At least, not by the Living.

He who collected souls and brought them to the Afterlife, Land of the Dead.

He was King of the Dead.

Death incarnate.

And he seemed to have found an interest in me.

Staring up at the Deathbringer, I let my eyes take him in. *Really* take him in.

I had never imagined the Deathbringer to look this ... handsome. I had imagined the King of the Dead to look more ... well

... *dead.* A skeleton would be closer to what I imagined than this resemblance of sheer male perfection.

Slowly, the Deathbringer's eyes narrowed. His movements suddenly seemed predacious as he took in the other monarch. A dark smile spread his lips. It was a cold smile without any joy. The smile of a creature that could end one's life in the thrum of a heartbeat.

Claws scraped against the wall of mist behind him, faces forming in the shadows of the fog, begging to be let free, but as fast as they had appeared, they disappeared again, making me wonder if I had imagined them.

Rage radiated from the King of the fae. "Step away from her right now and answer me! What is your business in the Land of the Living?" he repeated, his voice rumbling over the theatre's high walls.

The Deathbringer cocked his head as he looked down at the King of the fae. "What makes you think I didn't come here to collect her soul?" he demanded calmly.

I froze. He had come here to ... take me to the Afterlife?

The thought of dying should provoke fear, panic in me. Instead, it filled me with a calmness I didn't understand. A calmness alien, yet familiar to me from that day at the beach.

Silvan shook his head vigorously. "You can't take her. I won't let you," he spat.

I wasn't foolish enough to think Silvan's interference had anything to do with his wish to protect me.

The Deathbringer arched a brow at the fae King. He couldn't have been more dismissive if he'd tried. "If I am not mistaken, by having her killed, you were just about to give her into my hands anyway." The Deathbringer's eyes dropped to the sword still held by the young fae guard. His jaw went rock hard, and a dangerous expression flashed in his gaze. The shadows on his face elongated, and his eyes began glowing unnaturally. Calmly, *threateningly,* he brought his gaze back to Silvan. "I'm done arguing. Now move."

Silvan yelped as he was dragged out of the Deathbringer's way by an invisible force that threw him across the room. The fae King cursed and raged, and the white clouds around him flared, but the Deathbringer's mist was much more powerful than the fae King's clouds. The Deathbringer didn't seem to notice the other monarch's outburst as he brought his attention back to me.

Now nothing stood between us.

It was frightening to have the full attention of those unearthly green eyes upon me. They seemed to see *everything*.

He extended a hand to me, addressing me for the very first time. "Shall we go, love?"

I squinted. *Love*? Why would he call me by that endearment?

About to ask him, I opened my mouth, only to close it again. There seemed to be much more pressing matters to attend to—namely, to get the hell away from King Silvan.

Swallowing, I stared at the Deathbringer's outstretched hand. He had delicate fingers. Fingers of an artist, rather than what society had declared him to be: a killer.

Maybe—no, most definitely—it was not the best idea to leave with the Deathbringer without knowing his intentions for me, but there was no fucking way I'd stay here with the King of the fae who had just attempted to behead me. Wherever the Deathbringer wanted to bring me, it couldn't possibly be worse than being murdered by a fae guard.

Hesitantly, I lifted my hand and brought it to his.

A sizzling feeling, similar to an electric shock, went through our joined hands. I looked back up at him. His expression hadn't changed. Apparently, he hadn't noticed the same thing I had. Or he didn't show it.

I let him pull me to my feet. My knees nearly buckled at his proximity. The moment I stood, he let go of my hand, turning away from me and moving toward the door.

Slowly, I went after him into the dark mist that moved out of the Deathbringer's way, making space for him and closing in behind me. He didn't glance back to make sure I was following him. He just seemed to *know* I would do so. Somehow, I wasn't scared of the creatures forming in the mist behind the Deathbringer. Maybe because I had a feeling that whatever those creatures were would leave me in peace as long as the Deathbringer was by my side. Or, maybe I was just incredibly stupid. Probably the latter.

"You will regret this!" King Silvan's voice rang to us through the mass of fog. I couldn't be sure whether he threatened me or the Deathbringer.

It might very well just be the Deathbringer's intervention that made the fae King angry. But I had a feeling there was more to it.

Before me, the Deathbringer snorted, amused. "Don't be so cliché, Silvan."

He halted, making me bump into his back. He glared down at me, saying loud enough for everyone in the theatre to hear, "Oh and something else." He let a beat of silence built up the tension while he kept looking at me. "I can take whomever I want with me. In the end, all souls belong to me. Even yours, King of the fae."

CHAPTER FOUR

As the fog around us began to calm, it slowly vanished, allowing our new surrounding to appear. I couldn't believe where the Deathbringer had brought me, and my legs began shaking, almost giving out beneath me. I did not know where I expected the Deathbringer to bring me, but it surely wasn't my bedroom.

How did he know where I lived?

As I stood in the middle of my room, letting my gaze slowly drift over my small space, the celestial wallpaper and the bookshelves that lined an entire wall, I felt tears prickle in my eyes. Miriam always advised me to get all the books out of my bedroom. She said they'd take up too much room, but I never wanted that. I'd rather live in a too-small room than give away my beloved book collection.

After everything that had happened, it felt surreal to be standing in my own bedroom, near my own familiar shelves. Somehow, I feared something might be different, but everything was just the way I left it.

I turned to the dark figure beside me.

Everything but *him*.

The Deathbringer's tall frame was so at odds with my small bedroom and its simple decoration and furniture. He was the only darkness in it, seemingly drawing the shadows to him like a magnet. His bright green eyes took in my humble home. He made no gesture that revealed discontent at its simpleness. In fact, he seemed totally unaffected by it. As he contemplated my room, I let my eyes roam over him.

He was handsome, beautiful even. Too beautiful to be human. His facial features were too sharp, his frame too wide. Everything about him proved his unearthliness, a constant reminder that he did not belong in this world. There was something about him that made me think I had met him before, but other than that inner feeling, I couldn't explain the reason for it.

"We are not in the Afterlife," I stated the obvious, breaking the silence.

His bright green eyes came back to me. "No, we are not." He didn't elaborate.

I swallowed, the sound resonating loudly. "Why?"

Questioning the King of the Dead was probably not the smartest thing to do, but I just had to know his reason.

He cocked his head. "Would you rather I take you there?" The way he asked was way too serious for my liking.

"No," I rushed to say, "I'm just ... surprised." *Surprised* didn't quite describe my emotions sufficiently.

"Ahh." His fingers traced the curve of the wooden chair at my desk. "I don't think it would be wise to bring you to the Afterlife after everything you've just witnessed," he said eventually, his eyes coming back to me.

Protectively, I crossed my arms in front of my chest as the images of the boy's beaten body resurfaced, his blood staining the floor red. The sound of the sizzling whip would probably haunt me forever.

Swallowing, I stared ahead. I'd be dead if not for the man standing in my room. Pretty ironic given the fact that it was the man responsible for death who had saved my life.

It was only once my attention came back to the man before me that I noticed the way he was watching me. Something far more dangerous than curiosity flashed in that lingering gaze of his, but as soon as I saw it, it vanished, leaving nothing but a motionless expression behind. "Be sure to stay out of trouble. I'll be back for you—even before your death."

I took an involuntary step back. He ... he wanted to come to me again?

A puzzled expression darkened his features. "Don't even attempt to run away. I'll find you. Wherever you are." His words hit me like a slap. I had come away from death only to get caught up in the hands of the man who ruled over it. I was completely at his mercy. And he was right, of course; where would I hide when he was able to locate all living and dead souls?

Clearly taking my silence as agreement, he tore his gaze away from me. "I set up a spell that will protect you from the fae. They won't to be able to find you in case they search for you." A muscle jumped in his jaw.

That was surprisingly ... kind of him. I tried not to read into it, but I couldn't quite help it. First, he had saved my life, and now he had cast a spell to protect me. Why? Why had he, the one creature who never gave but always took, decided to save my life?

He turned, coming to a sudden halt. "Oh, I almost forgot." His green eyes seemed to shine brighter as our gazes locked. "It would be wise for you to take a shower."

Bitch, what?

The Deathbringer leaned forward, whispering into my ear, "Underneath all that stinky rose fragrance King Silvan made you put on, I can smell something quite delightful. It would be a shame to let that disgusting smell the fae so deeply enjoy outshine your own."

He flashed me a wicked, wicked smile, and with that, the shadows around him crept closer, surrounding him like a lover's embrace.

I took a step forward. "Wait!"

The shadows halted. The Deathbringer raised an eyebrow.

Before my bravery had a chance to leave me, I said, "Why did you do it?"

He stared at me intently, his silken hair shimmering. "Do what?"

Wasn't it obvious? I shifted my weight. "Save me?"

He stared at me for so long I wasn't sure he would answer me. I was surprised when he did.

"There are mysteries in this world not even I understand."

I didn't believe him for a single second. After all, why would he just arbitrarily save a human girl? I wanted to press him, I truly did, but I wouldn't push my luck any further today. I was grateful enough to be alive as it was.

Clearing my throat, I brushed a loose strand of hair behind my ear. "In any case," I took a tentative step forward. "Thank you." I whispered the words so softly I wasn't sure he had heard me. My brows drew together. "If it weren't for you," I swallowed. "I'd be dead." It was hard to look truth in the face.

The Deathbringer's eyes gleamed like the sky's brightest star, filled with dangerous promises. He stepped closer to me, closing the space between our bodies. Even though my breath became ragged at his closeness, I forced myself to stand still.

"Careful, love. Do not thank me yet." I tensed when his warm breath caressed my skin. "You owe me now."

Dumbfounded, I stared at the spot where the Deathbringer had just disappeared into thin air. Without his presence, my room suddenly felt incredibly empty.

Dear God, what the hell had just happened?

Of course he wouldn't just save my life without wanting something in return. How had I not thought about that? I could still feel the coldness of the guard's blade pressed into my neck, only for it to be replaced by the softness of the Deathbringer's hand engulfing mine.

How the hell had he even known where I lived? If he knew where I lived, did he also …?

It took only a couple of seconds for the realization to hit me fully.

Shit!

"Miriam!" Still yelling, I crossed my room and yanked open my bedroom's door.

The apartment we lived in together was still the same one we had moved into four years ago. It was on the same street as the pub where we'd first met. We had become inseparable since, and now I was wondering if that inseparability may have caused my friend's safety or even her …

I refused to finish that thought.

Just because the Deathbringer knew where I lived didn't mean he had also tormented my best friend. I rushed down the hallway and entered the living room.

Sound emerged from the kitchen.

I halted. "Mir?"

"Cassiana?" The door to the kitchen was yanked open. Miriam stared incredulously at me. "You're back already? I thought you wouldn't get here for another half an hour." The countless rows of bracelets jiggled with her movements.

I let my eyes drift over her form. If it weren't for her silvery eyes, you wouldn't know she was a witch. She wasn't tall enough to be recognized as such; nor did she wear one of the bright necklaces that always gave witches away.

But most importantly: she looked *alive*.

She carried a cake in her hand. "How did it go? I wanted to surprise you." She gestured to the living room, where I spotted balloons decorating the walls. Miriam moved to the small table at the end of the room, putting the cake on top of it. "Tell me everything! How did it go? Were all the Kings present?" As she turned to face me, she froze, taking in my dejected expression. "Cassiana! What the hell happened?"

A low cry left my suddenly trembling lips.

"Oh my God!" Her bright eyes grew huge. "Cassiana! Is that ... blood in your hair?" My friend rushed to my side, her black hair bobbing with her movements. Tears began streaming down my cheeks as she hugged me in a tight embrace.

I held on to her as if my dear life depended on it. "I'm so glad you are okay," I said in between sobs.

"What are you talking about? What happened?" She paled visibly when she spotted the crusted blood on my skin.

My legs trembled, and hot tears ran down my cheeks.

"Oh, honey! Come here." She led me to our huge couch and pulled a blanket over my shivering body. "This calls for booze," she murmured. She whispered one of her spells under her breath, making two wine glasses and a bottle of Chilean wine appear on the coffee table in front of us. "What the hell happened?" she asked again. Absently, she rotated her left hand. The wine elevated, pouring itself into both glasses.

A wet cloth floated from the kitchen over to us. Miriam grabbed the fabric from the air.

A sob broke free from me. Sometimes, I really hated being human.

Carefully, she wiped the fabric over my face, cleansing away the boy's dried blood. She was very focused on the task at hand and didn't press me to open up to her. She let me cry while she took care of the physical evidence of today's nightmare. When my tears began ceasing, my friend handed me one glass, grabbing the other for herself. "Tell me everything!" she asked quietly, her melodic voice calming me.

And so I did.

She held my hand reassuringly the entire time, her grip tightening when I told her about Silvan. When I finally finished, her silvery eyes flashed. "King Silvan ordered *what*?" She didn't even try lowering her voice.

I grabbed another tissue out of its box and cleaned my nose with it. By now, we were surrounded by used tissues, and only the wine prevented me from starting to cry all over again. "He wanted to behead me."

Mir opened and closed her mouth, clearly not able nor willing to accept what I just told her. She shook her head. "And the Deathbringer …?"

"He just appeared and … teleported me home, I guess."

"You guess?" Miriam put her wineglass aside, a sign she was deadly serious. "Do you even know how dangerous the Deathbringer is? What have you gotten yourself into?" She pushed a loose strand of hair behind my ear. "How could you just go with him?"

I shrugged, finishing the rest of the wine in one big gulp. "What the hell was I supposed to do? I'm not sure if you heard me, but King Silvan wanted to fucking behead me." The memory of it pushed a sob from my throat.

"Fuck …." Miriam didn't curse often. She ran fingers through her black hair and looked at me cautiously. Fear and worry marked her beautiful features. "Did he say what he wanted from you?"

I shook my head. "He only said that I owe him now." Silence stretched between us. A thought, much more important than the Deathbringer pressed at my consciousness. "Miriam?"

She stared ahead of herself, clearly lost in thought. She was just as affected as I was by what I had told her. "Mm?"

"Do you … do you think the boy is all right?" I finally asked.

Bringing her eyes back to me, she exhaled heavily. "I don't know. I truly hope so. I really do."

I nodded and bit the inside of my cheek.

Miriam squeezed my hand before grabbing her phone from the table. Silently, she tapped something into the search before starting to swipe. Her brows drew together.

"What is it?"

She lifted a shoulder. "There's nothing to be found on the internet. Neither about the boy nor you. The news only congratulates the fae King on his birthday."

I sighed. This didn't surprise me. Of course Miriam wouldn't find anything. Just imagine how scandalous it would be for the fae King's reputation to be torn apart by information like this.

Miriam moved slightly away from me so she could face me better. Her eyes searched my tear-streamed face. "Cassiana. You did everything you could. You could have died." She shook me carefully. "Died." Her face was paler than I had ever seen it. "But you know what? I am fucking proud of you for standing up for that kid!"

I gave her a sad, resigned smile.

Bile rose up my throat as I remembered the way the rest of the audience had refused to help the boy. A new stream of tears rolled down my cheeks.

"Oh, Cassiana!" My friend closed her arms around my midsection and pulled me closer.

I twisted the bracelet she had given me before the play, watching how the white spots glimmered with the movement. "Your bracelet did not work," I mumbled.

The wine bottle stopped mid-fly on the way to refill her glass. "What?" She followed my gaze to my wrist.

"You said it'd protect me and give me luck." I didn't manage to keep the bitter tone from my voice. Today's experience surely didn't feel like luck. "It didn't work."

Miriam's eyes softened. "Oh, honey, but I think it did."

CHAPTER FIVE

A couple of days later, I lay on the rooftop, a soft blanket draped over me. I stared at the twinkling stars above me, but even the night's calmness that usually cleared my mind wasn't able to do so now. A sense of incredible numbness had taken ahold of me.

I had stayed at home since the day the Deathbringer had brought me back to my apartment, not daring to set a foot outside. I had cried my guts out and stared hour after hour at the white walls, too caught up with everything that had happened and had threatened to happen if the Deathbringer hadn't intervened. Each time I heard a sound, I flinched, thinking it was a fae coming to bring me to King Silvan, and when I closed my eyes, I heard the echo of the fae King's voice. *You will regret this.* Whatever protection spell the Deathbringer had put on me seemed to be working. There was no trace of a single fae in all those days I stayed hidden in my apartment. Or, maybe—more probably—the fae King hadn't bothered looking for me.

Each passing day increased my anxiety for what the Deathbringer might demand from me in exchange for saving my life. A cold chill ran down my back.

I made sure to call my fellow performers and Mrs. Fitzgivens to make sure they were okay. They were, indeed, okay. Tormented by what had happened, yes, but okay. I had learned that, after I left, Silvan cancelled his celebration and retreated to the fae realm. None of the performers dared to ask me about the man who'd come to my rescue. Understandably, they probably had been too frightened by who had saved me.

Mir wanted to spend the nights with me in my room so I wouldn't be alone, but I refused. In fact, I needed time for myself to get my thoughts in order and to process everything that had happened.

The day of the performance, after I had told Miriam what had happened, I showered. I cut the dress straight off my body, throwing it right into the trash bin. I did not want to see it ever again. It reminded me of the boy's unmoving body, lying in the theatre in a pool of his own blood. I grabbed body wash and rubbed it on thoroughly until my skin turned raw and I didn't feel King Silvan's cool hands any longer.

Over and over, I tried telling myself that I just wanted to shower because I wanted to wash the stress off of me. But the Deathbringer's parting words lingered in my head. *Underneath all that stinky rose fragrance King Silvan put on you, I can smell something quite delightful. It would be a shame to let that disgusting smell the fae so deeply enjoy outshine your own.* So, King Silvan had actually made us use the rose fragrance because he didn't enjoy humans' smell. Though apparently the Deathbringer did ….

After the shower, Miriam and I had stayed in a tight embrace until my tears eventually dried and the exhaustion of what had happened crashed upon me like a wave, calling me to let go of awareness and just drift to oblivion. I had complied happily.

As I came out of memories, I stared up into the night's sky. What was I supposed to do now?

Miriam had suggested going to the police and telling them what had happened to me, but neither King Silvan nor the Deathbringer were ordinary people. They were two of the most powerful, untouchable people on earth. There was a tiny, barely visible chance for the police to take me seriously and get in contact with the King of the fae. But then what? He'd just tell them that I had made up the whole story and the police ... they would believe him. Of course they would. They'd be fools not to. Silvan had connections everywhere. And now that I knew what he was capable of, I was certain that he wouldn't mind ending some police officer's life in order to protect his flawless reputation. Never mind that I couldn't count on the others present at the theatre to testify against their King. I had seen those people. Their fear of what the King might do them if they were to interfere. Their indifference.

No. They would not raise a single finger against their oh-so-beloved Highness. The lack of any news online was evidence enough that everyone attending the birthday celebration had kept quiet.

My heart skipped a beat at that thought. It wasn't surprising that strangers wouldn't stand up for the right thing, but what about my fellow acting colleagues? They hadn't even tried to interfere. Only Celine had tried to stop me; not for my sake, but for her own.

Even though I'd never recognized any of them as friends, the knowledge of their indifference stung. I had long ago learned not to let people get near me. Only Mir had managed to break through that shield—which was why my surprise at their inaction shocked me.

They all had been willing to witness the lashing of a boy, even though he had done nothing wrong. And why?

Bitterness exploded on my tongue. Because they had been too scared for themselves. Because they had been scared to endanger their chance for a breakthrough in the acting business if they dared to speak up. Was this the price we should pay for fame? Was success worth it? Losing one's morals? One's humanity?

The mere thought of going back to the agency and facing the others turned my stomach into knots.

Did I really want to keep practicing with people who were willing to let others suffer for their own sake and fortune? And was I willing to give up the dream I had been working toward forever because of this?

Just the thought of acting again made every fiber within me turn to ice.

I grabbed the invitation to the fae King's birthday I had brought up to the rooftop with me. The white letter weighed heavily in my palm. A golden stamp decorated the front of the envelope. The royal crest of the fae kingdom. It glimmered under the moon's light, drawing attention to its details. It depicted an elegant, decaying rose, some of its petals falling. I had always wondered why the King of the fae had chosen this symbol to be his crest, but suddenly it felt incredibly fitting for a King who rotted human society and morality by using our fears against us. I opened the envelope for the thousandth time, the moon casting just enough light for me to decipher the words printed on the white paper.

We welcome you to King Silvan's birthday celebration.

That single sentence and the date and hour of the celebration was everything the letter said. I remembered the countless times I had traced the delicate golden characters. How many times had I stared at that sentence wondering if the other Kings would also attend the fae King's birthday? A dozen times? A couple hundred times? How nervous I had been ... How *honored* I had felt that the King had chosen my academy to perform a play for him. That he had chosen me. I suddenly felt unbelievably young and naïve.

He had tried to take my life and thankfully failed, but he succeeded in taking what little respect I still felt for humankind. "Fuck you!" I spat, staring at the imprint.

Slowly, I took the lighter I'd also brought up here and held the flickering flame to the edge of the envelope. The flame licked at it, slowly burning the paper. As the heat almost reached my fingers, becoming unbearable, I put the enflamed paper on the concrete roof, watching the golden stamp bubble until the decaying rose melted.

My eyes drifted to the bracelet Miriam had given me, and I began toying with it.

Right after I had come home, she worked on the bracelet to strengthen its powers. My objections that the Deathbringer had already cast a protection spell had been futile. She said it was now the most powerful bracelet she had ever made. *If this will not keep you safe, a grown gorilla wouldn't either*, she'd added.

I pulled my knees to my chest and interlaced my fingers around them.

And what about *him?*

I couldn't keep myself from being in a constant state of heedfulness of my surroundings. Every shadow I saw made me tense, thinking it was the King of the Dead who approached me.

If the police weren't going to investigate King Silvan, they sure as hell weren't going to go after the Deathbringer. As far as anyone knew, he hadn't been seen for centuries.

Why did the Deathbringer intervene and save me? What interest could he possibly have in me to contradict his most basic nature: to take souls to the Afterlife? It all made no sense, and it made me afraid of what the Deathbringer might demand from me. Would the debt I owed him be payed off once I fulfilled whatever favor he wanted or would there be more?

I had tried researching him on the internet, but other than the obvious, namely that he was the ruler of the Afterlife, King of the Dead, and the incarnation of life's end, I discovered nothing.

There was only one other way for me to gain information about him: I needed to ask him myself, and I'd be doing that the moment he decided to show up.

A chill ran down my back, and I pulled the blanket tighter around me. Of course I had toyed with the thought of hiding from him, but the Deathbringer had been right: he was the King of the Dead. If he wanted to find me, he'd have absolutely no problem doing so.

But what scared me even more wasn't the favor I now owed him. It was the anticipation that came with the unknown.

"Cassiana!"

I jumped at my name.

"Are you up here, hon?"

"Yes! I'm here!" I turned to see Miriam pushing open the metal door to the apartment's rooftop. I blinked against the artificial brightness streaming through. The door fell shut behind my friend, the darkness overcoming the rooftop once again. Miriam's eyes gleamed in the night's blackness.

"I knew you'd be here." She made her way over to me, cursing as she almost tripped over a loose cable. "Why don't you put on the fairy lights I gave you last Christmas? I can barely make out my own hand," she scolded.

"They always draw in mosquitos." I leaned back, "And I can't see the stars if there's too much light."

Mir followed my gaze to the sky. Silence stretched between us as we contemplated the small lights illuminating the darkness.

I loved that our relationship had become that kind where we could spend time in silence with each other without it becoming awkward. We had spent so much time together that we instinctively knew when the other was bothered or needed to talk. For me, that was what our friendship was about. I enjoyed my friend's company. I had always been so fixed on my goals that I often forgot to just ... *live*. And enjoy life. Miriam reminded me of that.

She was the first to break the quietness we'd fallen into. "How are you feeling today?"

I sighed exhaustedly. She had been asking me that same question over and over throughout the last couple of days. "Okay, I guess."

She looked at the remains of the letter. Most of the ash had already been carried away by the wind. "I made some fortune cookies. Would you like some?" She sucked in her cheeks.

I didn't want any, but I knew it'd calm her seeing me have some so I flashed her a small smile. "Sure."

Relieved, she gave me her hand and pulled me to my feet.

Careful not to trip, we walked back to the door. I followed Miriam down the wooden stairs and let the door fall shut behind me with a loud clank. As we made our way to the kitchen, a familiar smell hit me.

"Oh Mir! How many times have I told you not to leave the sage burning so long?" I rushed to the windows and yanked them open.

My friend's head bobbed around the kitchen's doorframe before focusing back on the oven. "Sorry! I forgot. My last client wanted me to do an exorcism on him, and *boy,* did he have demons sticking to him." Miriam came out of the kitchen, a white tray with the fortune cookies, teacups, and a teapot in her hands.

Sighing, I collapsed onto the couch.

Miriam eyed me, worry written on her face. "How are you feeling?"

I glared up at her. "Stop asking me that." I grabbed one of her cookies.

She lifted a shoulder. "I'm just worried about you."

I cracked the cookie and unfolded its tiny paper. "I know you are," I whispered. I looked at her. "But I'm fine. Really."

She gave me a doubting look but seemed to accept my answer. For now.

I always got nervous whenever I opened one of Mir's magic cookies. She wasn't the one to put the letters on the small paper. She only cast the spell that would unfold the future on the paper.

Miriam pressed her lips together as she noticed that I left the cookie untouched. "You should eat, hon. You haven't eaten properly in days. You—"

"I'm not hungry," I cut her off before she could get started on my dubious eating habits. I didn't bother telling her that a cookie was definitely not a proper meal.

My friend eyed me cautiously. I knew she wanted me to talk and open up to her more, but she also knew that if she pushed me, I'd close down. Sighing, she leaned forward and poured us some matcha tea.

"How was your day?" I asked, desperately trying to change the subject.

She waved me off. "Oh. Same as always. Besides the exorcism, everything normal. Most customers just wanted some bracelets."

The amount of people willing to pay for those bracelets always astonished me. But, then again, Miriam always delivered quality products. Not only did Mir sell those bracelets, she also sold Ouija-boards, gave tarot-readings, offered trances, and had a huge crystal collection for sale. It had taken some persuasion to reassure Miriam that I was doing fine and she could get back to her clients again. And I was glad she had. I knew she only meant good for me, but having someone at my back throughout the day, watching out for me, did get exhausting.

I grabbed the cup my friend handed me and took a sip.

I put it aside, my attention coming back to the cookie's small paper. As Mir walked back to the kitchen, I unfolded it, watching how the letters slowly began to appear one by one.

Darkness calls to you.
But you mustn't be afraid.

For its call you will pursue.
And your burdens will fade.

The only bad thing about fortune cookies? They always came in riddles. You could basically read anything into them, and the words would still make sense.

"What did you get?" Mir asked as she entered the living room again and plopped on the couch next to me.

Sighing, I handed her the paper.

Her brows drew together as she read it. "Hmm."

I started biting my thumbnail. My thoughts drifted back to the man who had saved my life, to the way his tall frame had filled the door, to the way he had looked at me. No one had ever looked at me that way. As if he had been able to see through me. To what lay beneath my skin. Goosebumps erupted on my flesh at the mere memory of those unnerving eyes fixed upon me.

I felt Mir look at the way my skin pebbled. "Listen, I know you are scared, honey." She moved closer to me and patted my leg. "But you know what?"

I shook my head.

"You know it's cold outside when you go outside and it's cold," she said simply.

I blinked at my friend. "That makes absolutely no sense. What does that even mean?"

She shrugged. "Maybe you should just … wait and see what happens. I mean … it can't possibly be that bad if he hasn't killed you. The Deathbringer is known for collecting souls, which, let me remind you, in your case, he hasn't done." She took a sip of her tea. "Yet."

My friend sure as hell knew how to reassure me.

Without warning, I threw my arms around her.

She laughed, surprised, before wrapping her arms around me.

"Thank you," I mumbled against her hair.

She stroked my back in a friendly gesture. "What for?"

Snuggling closer to her, I exhaled. "For being here for me."

Her hand on my back stopped stroking me. Grabbing my hand, she looked at me. "Of course! That's what family's for." She gave my hand a loving parental squeeze.

"Are you up for a movie?" I asked Miriam, in a sudden mood to distract myself.

Her eyes lit up. "Hon, I was born to watch movies!"

But even as we closed the curtains and snuggled closer with a huge popcorn bowl Mir had made, I could not keep my mind from wandering off.

Back to *him*.

I couldn't get rid of the feeling that it was just the calm before the storm. And the worst thing of all: I was intrigued by it.

CHAPTER SIX

"Rise and shine, love!"

I cracked open my eyes, yawning as they adjusted to the day's brightness. The Deathbringer's face loomed above me.

Suddenly, I was wide awake, jerking upright. "Jesus Christ!"

He laughed darkly. "Not quite."

I stared up at him. The only resemblance he had to Jesus was the long hair, but the mischievous glint that promised the most delightful unholy activities negated that image immediately.

I ignored his comment and pulled the sheet up to my chin. "What the fuck are you doing here?" Probably not the best way to address the King of the Dead, but it was better to focus on annoyance than what I actually felt: a mixture of uncertainty, fear, and ... curiosity.

He turned from me and crossed the room, heading straight toward my wardrobe. "Don't you remember? We have a deal," he said, without looking at me.

I swallowed. So today was the day the Deathbringer had decided it was time for payoff.

Silly me had hoped he'd forgotten. Nobody had warned me that wishful thinking was just that: thinking.

I watched him open the closet and begin to rummage through its contents.

"Does this need to be today? I have to go to my acting lessons," I lied. I could at least try to get out of this situation. I clutched the bedsheets tighter to me.

"If you don't want to repay your debt by dying, then yes," he said simply, his focus on the clothing in my wardrobe.

Squaring my jaw, I glared at him.

He turned around and noticed the way I fisted the sheets. He rolled his eyes.

He actually knew how to roll his eyes? Not something I'd have expected from the King of the Dead. He had seemed too restrained and self-aware to do so.

He tsked softly. "Now, don't be shy. Don't you think I've seen enough human over the centuries?"

Pffff.

It wasn't my *human flesh* I didn't want him to see. Besides, he didn't even know how exquisite this flesh might be. But apparently, I was not suitable for the Deathbringer's appetite. I shot him a side glance. He was probably into rotten flesh, mummies, and skeletons.

He contemplated my clothing once more before grabbing a simple black dress. Judging by his own black-on-black clothing, it was his favorite color. What a cliché.

My breath hitched as he approached, his focus entirely fixed on me.

Those emerald eyes of his ... they were *old*. They held an

ancient, calculating edge, as if he had seen it all. The best and the worst of humankind.

He handed me the dress and crossed his arms. Watching me, waiting.

"Fine!" I gritted and stepped out of the bed.

His brows drew together in dislike. "Is that a Mickey Mouse nightgown?"

I had the weirdest urge to laugh. I looked down at my pajamas. *Nightgown*.

Deciding to ignore his comment, I grabbed the black dress and stepped past him, aiming for the bathroom.

The Deathbringer followed me, halting to contemplate a dead frog Mir had hung up next to the bathroom door. Don't even get me started on its smell.

He gestured to it. "Was this supposed to keep me out of the apartment?" Amusement shone in his eyes. "Did you really think such a simple, silly spell would keep me—death incarnate—away from you if I wanted to get to you?"

I crossed my arms. "No." Sarcasm dripped from my words. "It was cast to enhance my sexual abilities." In fact, the spell only served to ward off the nightmares I'd had since that day at the theatre. But I wouldn't tell him that. It was easier to act sarcastic than focusing on the second part of what he had said, because focusing on it meant that I actually cared for the fact that he sought me out.

Genuine interest shone in his twinkling eyes as he deeply chuckled. "What sexual abilities are you seeking to improve?" He took a step toward me. "I might be helpful in that matter."

"Oh, fuck off!" I said between clenched teeth, although his

words had produced quite the interesting reaction in the low of my stomach.

"I was planning to," he said, grinning broadly, his eyes alight.

I cast him an incredulous look as I squinted at him. Had he just made a sexual joke? Who'd have thought death incarnate would be so … feisty?

I shot him a doubtful look before I entered the bathroom and clicked the door closed behind me.

To my surprise, he granted me this privacy. I had almost been scared he'd decide to come in with me.

I mean, what did he expect me to do? I surely wouldn't bolt. As appealing as that thought might be, I wasn't stupid enough to think I'd succeed. And maybe, just maybe, I was also interested in what the King of the Dead might want from me.

Not wanting to keep such a dangerous man as the Deathbringer waiting for too long, I quickly changed into the dress and began combing my hair and brushing my teeth. I considered letting Mir know that the Deathbringer was in our apartment, but discarded the idea immediately. If there were any possibility that he didn't know about my friend, I wouldn't endanger her by seeking her out. Casting one last critical look at my reflection, I forced myself to take deep breaths before I stepped back into my room.

The Deathbringer was standing at the window that overlooked the main street, contemplating the passing pedestrians. He was so lost in thought he didn't notice my presence.

I eyed him curiously. It was such an odd feeling to have a creature as powerful as life itself in my small bedroom. His silken black hair was now held back in a man bun, accentuating the curve of his high-cut cheekbones. His body seemed to take up all the space, his presence making my breaths deepen.

There was no sign of the fog that had been around him like a second skin in the theatre, nor the bronze crown he had been wearing back then, but that didn't make him any less frightening.

My mind had come up with the wildest scenarios of what the Deathbringer might demand in return for saving my life, and shamelessly, some of those scenarios had made me blush.

I was staring at the Deathbringer like a complete stalker. *Pull it together, Cassiana. You are being a total creep*, I told myself, tearing my greedy eyes away from him. It didn't help telling myself that it was only his otherworldly beauty that kept my eyes wandering back to him.

I grabbed my phone from the nightstand and cleared my throat. "I'm ready."

He turned and assessed the dress. I tensed under his searching gaze. He nodded to my hand holding my phone. "You won't be needing that."

I furrowed my brows. "But … but what if I'm needed? And how am I supposed to call somebody if I need help?"

He shrugged. "I'm sure they'll survive. The place we are going doesn't have service anyway." My heart stopped a beat. There was only one place I could imagine without service …

The Afterlife.

A parallel universe where only war, power, and desire ruled. At least, that was what people whispered in the darkness of the night when the fear of death started creeping into their awareness.

He crossed his arms in front of his chest and grinned as his eyes smoldered. "And don't worry; I'm with you, so you won't be needing anybody's help."

I looked at him. Did the Deathbringer realize he hadn't eased my worries one bit? Resigned, I swallowed as I put my phone back on my nightstand.

When I turned around to the man himself, the Deathbringer seemed pleased, because he stretched out a hand to me. "Then let's go."

Nervously, I approached him. It was easy to keep a sarcastic attitude toward him when he stood a couple of feet away from me. But this close, I felt completely intimidated by him. It felt as if I were walking right into the predator's arms.

I stopped a foot away from him. I didn't want to ask him because the question would put my vulnerability and fear on display, but after everything I had experienced, I needed to be reassured. "Will we be coming back?" I held my breath.

The Deathbringer stared at me for a long moment. Then he nodded.

I exhaled. I didn't have a reason as why to trust his words. Over and over, I needed to remind myself of the fact that, ironically, the Deathbringer wasn't the one who wanted me dead but the one who had saved me.

I swallowed hard when I cut the remaining distance between us and laid my much smaller hand in his bigger one. He curled his fingers around mine and tugged me closer to him.

"So, where are we going?" I asked as casually as possible, all while I stared nervously at a point on his chest. I was so close to him, I could feel the warmth his body radiated, lulling me in like a blanket.

I tensed when I felt his words fan over my hyperaware skin. "You'll see."

Last time, when the Deathbringer had teleported me to my room, I had been too traumatized by the experience in the theatre to pay any attention to it. Today, I did.

I had always thought teleporting would make me nauseous. Everyone I knew who had teleported said so.

But as the Deathbringer's hand clutched mine tightly against his chest and the shadows crept in on us, building a wall of mist and darkness, cocooning us in calmness, I only felt the soft friction of the Deathbringer's skin against my own and the heaviness of his eyes on me.

I didn't feel the moment we vanished, nor did I notice how we appeared at a completely different location. As the shadows withdrew, they also withdrew the feeling of safety, making room for the coldness of the air, the Deathbringer's body being the only remaining source of heat.

Why the fuck had he chosen a dress for me? It was so cold each of my exhales formed small clouds. I let go of his hand and stepped away from him.

Slowly, I turned around to take in the surroundings.

If this was the Afterlife, it was just as I had imagined it to be.

Dreary.

That was the only word to describe the landscape unfolding in front of us. Gray rocks surrounded us. In the distance, I spotted a forest, but instead of leaves, only desolate branches protruded from the tree trunks. The trees looked more like skeletons than actual trees and the sky was nothing more than a single shade of gray.

Nothing moved. At all. Goosebumps erupted on my skin, and the hair on my neck stood. Nothing seemed to live here. No wind caressed my skin, no sound that would give away the place an animal was hiding. There was absolutely nothing. It was as though time had just decided to … stop. And, with it, all that was alive.

"Nice and cozy," I murmured, turning to the man himself.

He did not pay any attention to my words. His eyes were distant, and his head tipped to the side. He looked like he was listening to something only he was able to hear.

His next words made my breath hitch. "They await you."

"They?"

His face became grim as he turned around, clearly indicating for me to follow. "The Norns." All jauntiness had left his voice.

I stumbled over a loose rock. "The Norns?"

I stared at the Deathbringer's back. There was no way I had heard him right.

"Your ears seem to be working," he murmured, continuing his way toward a group of big, sturdy rocks. They lay in the opposite direction of the forest, just in front of what looked like the hillside to a valley.

"You mean the Norns, as in the Fates?" I nearly tripped over a branch. I caught myself just in time.

"Mm-hmm."

"What?" I shrieked. But the King of the Dead just kept on walking. "Wait! Why?" There was no freaking way I'd let him take me to the Norns. Biting the inside of my cheeks, I focused on my steps. After all, I didn't want to make the Deathbringer consider that killing me would be a much easier way to deal with me.

Of course, I had heard of the three women before. They were the ones to decide about a soul's death and reincarnation. The concept of it was pretty simple: every time someone died, that person's soul came to the Afterlife and a different soul from the Land of the Dead was reborn. It was a constant exchange between the Lands of the Dead and the Living. And the three women we were about to visit decided each soul's timeline. I shivered. There were many representations of them. Sketches, sculptures, and paintings. Each one more terrifying than the last.

I dug my feet in the ground and crossed my arms. "You cannot take me to the Norns," I declared.

The Deathbringer turned around. The brightness of his eyes and the secrets they beheld almost made me overcome my fear and follow him.

Slowly, he stepped up to me. He leaned forward so his looming presence invaded my personal space. I gasped at his nearness but refused to step back. "Have you forgotten, love? You owe me."

"Don't call me that!" I snapped as I crossed my arms in front of my chest. "And besides, I didn't ask for your help!" I hissed, referring to the day he had saved me in the theatre.

His eyebrows rose. "Would you rather I kill you now to settle your debt? Just say the words," he challenged.

I staggered backward. I didn't think for one second that he was bluffing. He didn't have anything to lose, while I had my entire life ahead of me.

"Fine!" I bit out. "I'll come."

I moved past him, not wanting to see the victory in his eyes.

His rich laugh sent goosebumps down my spine.

I came to a sudden halt as I stared at what lay in the valley beneath me.

This place looked like a freaking spiderweb and, sue me, but there was no way I would go down there. Thousands, no *millions*, of silvery threads were attached to tree branches someone must've brought here. The threads built a maze of lines, making it impossible to know the beginning and the end of a single one of them.

"Did you bring us the human female?" croaked a voice from the depth of the web.

"Took him long enough to get her here," another, all-too-similar voice murmured.

I couldn't tell whether the voices belonged to men or women. Their vocal cords seemed so out of use, each syllable came out almost indecipherably rasped.

"She needed rest. She has been through a lot already," the Deathbringer answered coolly.

It surprised me that the King of the Dead needed to justify his behavior.

I cried out in surprise as a woman, one of the Norns, appeared right next to me.

Her wrinkled, *naked* breast brushed my arm. "And a pretty one that is." She lifted a hand to touch my hair, but the Deathbringer suddenly grabbed my arm and yanked me to him. I bumped into his chest, but the appearance of the woman in front of me left me too deeply shocked to truly notice his gesture. Her hair clung to her greasy face, its strands matted. Her clothes were ripped, revealing the bony figure underneath.

Another voice cracked a dry laugh. "He seems to be quite possessive of her."

Another Norn ducked out from underneath the thick web, her white hair almost the same color as the silvery threads. "Well, well. Apparently, the King of the Dead knows what he owns."

I felt the Deathbringer freeze behind me.

Owns?

Were they referring to the debt I owed him? Or were they referring to the fact that all souls would belong to him once they died?

I didn't get a chance to ask.

The third Norn laughed at what her sister had said, the shrill sound making me shiver. I searched the end of the web for the last Norn and found her sitting in front of a big wooden spindle, her old, long fingers threading new threads through it. The ends of the threads accumulated on her feet in a tangle.

All three Norns looked exactly the same. There was no way to tell them apart and not a single one of the countless representations of the Norns did them justice. They were more horrifying than what people believed them to be.

I moved closer to the King of the Dead, unconsciously seeking his protection. He might be the most feared creature on earth, but he had torn me away from the Norn who had wanted to touch me. And these women were physically way scarier than the King of the Dead.

Apparently, the Deathbringer wasn't too keen on them, either. "Stop your games, Norns. You have called me." He paused. "Again. So, say what you need. I have matters that require my attention. Important matters." *More important than this*, he seemed to say.

I glanced up at him. He did not seem too happy about the fact that they had called him. Why had they demanded his presence before now? As far as I knew, the Norns enjoyed the presence of other creatures even less than the fae did. Having to judge the beginning and ending of every soul's life, they had more than enough to do. So why come here? And why bring me with him? Hadn't he even said they'd be waiting for me? But why would they?

The Norn in the middle of the chaos of threads turned, her empty, black eyes fixed on me. She began creeping closer, her worn out bones cracking with each movement. A thick line of threads blocked her way to me. She lifted a hand and cut through the thousands with her long, yellow nails. She ripped them apart without any sort of selection. I tried not to think about the volume of lives she had just ended by cutting all of those threads.

I shivered as she approached me.

The Deathbringer seemed to sense my body's reaction. He took a step forward so half of my body was hidden by his.

The second Norn joined her sister in front of me, while the last Norn kept working at the spindle, her attention fixed on us while her sisters approached me.

I wished the Norns hadn't come closer to us. They got scarier with each inch they closed. Their entire skin was marked with countless wrinkles from the years they had lived.

The right Norn cocked her head in my direction before she inhaled deeply. Her nostrils flared. A satisfied smile spread her thin, colorless lips. "That's her."

The other Norns nodded in agreement.

Shocked, I watched how she made to grab a heap of cut threads lying forgotten on the floor. She slowly brought it to her mouth and ... *ate* it.

Oooookay. I was outta here.

I took a step back, ready to run. The Deathbringer's arm shot out, encircling my waist before pressing me to his chest. I dug my nails into his forearm, but that only made his grip on me tighten.

"Wait for what they want to say," he murmured, bending his head low from behind me.

Shaking my head, I tried to wiggle out of his hold. To no avail. "I don't want to. They are ..." *Crazy, insane.* But I didn't finish. I didn't want to know what their wrath looked like. Especially not upon me.

I froze as I felt the Deathbringer lean in, his mouth brushing the shell of my ear. "Shhh." The feeling of his voice against my skin sent shivers down my spine. "If you let them speak out, we can leave immediately."

I didn't know why I listened to him. Maybe I recognized the logic behind the Deathbringer's words, or maybe it was his use of the simple word *we* that calmed me. Whatever the reasons, I relaxed against him.

The Norn standing to my right watched me closely while her sister kept eating the loose threads from the floor. "She's escaped death's hold twice."

I felt my eyes widen. "How did you ...?"

I stopped. Of course she knew. After all, they were the ones responsible for each life's end and beginning.

The first time had been all those years ago at the beach. Deep inside me, I had known I should have died that day. But I hadn't. Nor had death wanted me the day King Silvan had attempted to behead me in front of his entire court.

Still grasping a bunch of loose threads in her fist, the second

Norn tore her head up and said, "But to what price?" Her bones shimmered under her age-worn skin.

The Deathbringer growled, making me shriek. "Speak clear, Norns. Name the reason you have called us. As I've told you before, I have more important matters to attend, and I don't like repeating myself."

The three Norns started laughing highly, the sound more animal than human. "Impatient King," one of them reproved him.

"Brave Norn," the King growled, the sound vibrating against my back.

"You have done well by saving her," the Norn at the spindle sing-songed.

"But now you cannot let her go. Darkness calls to darkness." The second Norn looked up from the heap of threads, and leaning to her sister, fed some threads to her.

I grimaced at the sight. What the actual fuck was wrong with them? I was definitely going to need therapy after this.

"The one who beholds the power over the air and the wind is looking for her," one of the Norns hissed like a snake.

There was only one King who ruled over the air and the wind. "Silvan …." I shuddered as I said his name.

The Norns nodded in unison.

The Deathbringer seemed to sense that I wouldn't bolt and slowly let go of me, dropping his arms from where they had held me by the waist. "I know about the King of the fae. I have made sure he will not be able to get to her."

The Norn at the spindle giggled at that. "Naïve, beautiful King. The fae King has broken the wards you've set up around her house." She gestured in my direction.

I gasped. Ice-cold panic chilled my skin as one single thought overcame me instantly, making blood rush to my ears. If Silvan had found me, he had also found Miriam.

I grabbed the Deathbringer's arm. "We need to go back home!"

He glanced down at me before looking back at the Norns. The Deathbringer shook his head. His black hair glimmered with the movement. "That's impossible. I had—"

"But he did," the Norn to the left of us rasped out. Her whole ribcage was visible through her paper-thin skin.

I held onto the Deathbringer's arm. "Please! I need to make sure Miriam is okay," I begged.

The Deathbringer's jaw tensed as his eyes came back to me again.

One of the Norns managed to get nearer to me, running her fingers through my hair. I shrank back with such force, some strands of my hair were yanked from my scalp.

"The witch is safe. The fae King doesn't know of your relationship to her," she cawed. "But if you choose to go back to the Land of the Living, you'll surely bring his notice down upon her." The Norn looked at my hair in her fingers before bringing it up to her lips.

Some of the weight on my shoulders lessened. "How do I know you are speaking the truth?" I'd crossed into dangerous terrain by questioning the truth of the Norn's statement, but I needed to make sure Miriam—my best friend and only family—was safe.

The third Norn turned, holding up a silvery, glimmering thread. "The witch's life is safe. It will not be too soon this thread — her thread—will be cut."

Swallowing, I nodded. I had no other choice than believing

her. And why would she be lying?

I met the Deathbringer's thoughtful face. "What am I supposed to do now?" I whispered. "I need to get back. I have a job." A job I wasn't sure I wanted anymore, but still.

"You cannot go to the Land of the Living if you want to live," the three of them chirped at the same time.

My body began to tremble. "What am I supposed to do?" Fear roared through my veins like acid, burning me from the inside out.

My question was met with silence. Even the Norns kept quiet.

After what felt like an eternity, the Deathbringer's smooth voice broke the silence. "You are coming with me to the Village of the Dead."

I jerked my head up.

As he looked away, a muscle ticked on his jaw. Apparently, someone was not happy about his own offer.

The Norns nodded in agreement. They turned away from us and moved deeper into the maze of threads. They did it with such unconcern as though the Deathbringer's suggestion had settled the matter.

I stared at the Deathbringer as he calmly extended his hand to me once again.

A man feared by every living creature.

A man who ruled over the Dead.

A man who had saved my life and was saving me yet again.

If he wanted me dead, he'd already had more than enough chances to take me with him and make me part of his subjects. But he didn't act. *Yet*, Miriam's voice whispered low in my mind. I could only hope for King Silvan to stop looking for me soon so I could get back to my normal life.

Carefully, I lifted my trembling hand and, for the second time that day, placed it in his. He did not look down at me as he summoned the darkness, letting it surround us in mist and shadows.

CHAPTER SEVEN

I did not know what I had expected the Village of the Dead to look like, but this wasn't it.

The first thing I noticed were the stars. There were thousands of them, lighting up the entire night sky. How many times had I snuck out of bed as a child and tried spotting the stars through the sheen of smog hiding them from me? And how many times had I been scolded by my mother when she had found me curled up in a fetal position next to the window in the morning? But no matter how many times she got mad and reprimanded me, I had never stopped searching for the small lights in the night sky. The stars above us glimmered, each shining brighter than the last, casting everything around us in a shimmering light.

The Deathbringer had teleported us onto a balcony. I turned around to the imposing building looming behind us. It was a … *castle*. A vast, majestic castle built entirely out of stone. Towers raked high above us, and long flags were attached to them, the warm wind making them billow. Squinting, I made out the Deathbringer's crest imprinted on them. The royal crest of the Afterlife depicted the different moon phases in silver and the stars, sprinkled in a light golden glitter on top of the otherwise black flag, glittered beautifully.

Turning back around, I took a tentative step forward and rested my hands on the railing of the balcony to get a better look at the surrounding.

And what a surrounding that was.

Afar, a small village lay in a beautiful valley. Small rivers ran through it like veins, and lanterns adorned the passages, casting the entire hamlet in a beautiful glow. The stars reflected on the water's surface, amplifying the feeling that the village had fallen into a galaxy of its own. A small path led away from the castle toward the village, crossing over meadows outlying the castle.

I'd never thought I'd get to see what the Afterlife would be like before my death. I leaned forward to see more, but the balcony was too far away for me to be able to see any more the details of the small houses that were illuminated by the lights. I lifted my head to look once again at the sky. There were so many stars. More than I'd be able to count in a lifespan. Back at home, the stars hid behind a sheen of smog, and the city's lights shone brighter than the stars, making them almost disappear completely.

But not here.

I had never thought the Land of the Dead would be this similar to the Land of the Living. People had wondered over hundreds of years what life after death might be like. Somehow, I had always thought people were only worthy of a world resembling hell after their death. People were too cruel to deserve anything else. But evidently, I had been mistaken.

I was so caught up in the sight that I didn't notice the Deathbringer step up next to me until he spoke. "What do you think?"

His head was tipped back. I couldn't help but note how his silken black hair had the exact same color as the night sky he was observing.

"They are beautiful," I breathed in awe, looking at the moon that shone much brighter than the stars.

He nodded. "Indeed." He looked down at the village. "Welcome to Emoh."

His words channeled my attention back to reality: I was in the Land of the Dead. I swallowed nervously. "Thanks for letting me stay here," I said, meeting his searching gaze.

He gave a curt nod.

I could not believe that staying in the Afterlife would guarantee my safety... I honestly didn't understand why the fae King bothered chasing me. What interest could he possibly have in finding me? I wanted to ask the Deathbringer, but a question like that demanded a certain amount of trust for me to show my vulnerability and voice my fears to this man. So, instead, I asked, "What do we do now?"

The expression in his face made me retreat a cautious step. The small of my back bumped into the railing. His green eyes brightened, and a sly smile curved his lips. "As far as I know, we have some time to get to know each other better."

I flinched as his long, elegant fingers suddenly traced my collarbone, and his touch sending shivers down my spine.

I wasn't sure I liked all the promises in those few words.

He leaned forward. When he spoke next, his mouth brushed my ear. "And I cannot say that I'm not looking forward to it, especially given that you still owe me your life."

He turned on his heels, leaving me breathless and confused. "Make yourself at home. I'll send someone in who can help should you need anything," the Deathbringer said over his shoulder as he left the balcony through a door that was adjoined to the balcony.

As soon as he was gone, I traced my skin over the spot where the brush of his fingers still lingered. Maybe time in the Land of the Dead wasn't as colorless as I had expected it to be.

I stared down at the village. How the hell had I ended up here? And why the fuck was I so calm? Shouldn't I be freaking the hell out, demanding that my captor let me go?

But the Deathbringer wasn't my captor, was he?

He had saved my life in the theatre and had just saved me once again by bringing me to his realm, guaranteeing not only my safety but also Mir's by doing so.

I groaned. His realm.

Fuck.

The only thing the Living had been taught about the Land of the Dead was that it lay in a parallel universe. Its location was kept secret, but it was said that the Kings were the only ones who had access to that knowledge. Silvan had recognized the Deathbringer. That meant they'd met before. So at least those rumors must be true.

I looked up to the sky, realizing it wasn't that different from our own. How many times had I lost track of time as I had stared at the blackness, wishing to blend in with the darkness? Miriam had always made fun of me, saying that someday the stars might answer to my call.

I smiled at that thought. Miriam.

She'd never believe I'd joined the Dead.

Fuck. I didn't even know if there was a way to communicate with the Land of the Living to tell her I was all right, and according to the Norns, Silvan was supervising my home closely. I couldn't risk endangering Miriam by trying to reach out to her.

My hairs stood on edge. The Norns. They had implied the King of the Dead should've brought me to them sooner. I felt a sudden surge of gratitude toward the Deathbringer. If he'd brought me to them straight from the theatre after Silvan had tried killing me, I'd have lost my mind. I could only hope I wouldn't face them again too soon.

As that thought came up, I immediately regretted it. How could I think that after they had essentially guaranteed Mir's and my safety by warning me?

I walked across the balcony and stepped into the room connected to it. A huge bed stood in the middle of the big space, its cover looking so soft, I reached out and let my hands relish the feeling. The room was dark but still cozy. Floating candles illuminated the place in a soft glow. Judging by the lack of personal items, I came to the conclusion that it must be a guest room.

It surely wasn't the Deathbringer's bedroom. It felt too empty and lacked his presence.

The Deathbringer.

What were his motives for bringing me here? Why did he mind what happened to me and why had he saved me? Twice.

I shivered as I recalled the feeling of his touch against my skin.

What sexual abilities are you seeking to improve? I might be helpful in that matter.

My belly tingled at the reminder of his words, sending heat to my cheeks. It almost felt as though the Deathbringer were standing right next to me, whispering those seductive words in my ear. My eyelids fluttered closed as I pictured the way his broad shoulders filled out his loose linen shirt and the way his waist was tucked in.

What would it feel like to have all that power focused solely on me? Those lips grazing my skin... Those hands fisting my hair in a tight grip and drawing me closer... His body's heat pressing against me...

My eyes snapped open.

No, no, no, no, no!

The Deathbringer wasn't a man to be thought of in that way. He was known to be merciless and feared. People didn't conjure those kinds of stories without reason.

And yet ... he had allowed me to find refuge in his realm. That behavior didn't strike me as merciless.

I crossed to the door at the opposite side of the room and pressed down the knob. The door swung open, giving way to a long hallway. Frozen, I stared at it.

I wasn't locked in.

I didn't know why that surprised me. Probably because it, once again, contradicted everything I had heard about the man who'd brought me here.

Carefully, I stepped into the corridor. Just like in my room, candles floated everywhere, lighting the entire hall in a soft glow.

Hesitantly, I looked back to my room. Was I supposed to stay there? I could stay and wait for the person the Deathbringer had promised to send to me, but then I'd be left with nothing else to do than relive everything the Norns had told me and conjure up all the possible scenarios of Silvan getting to Miriam.

Should I really stay here and start crying, pitying myself? And over what? My friend was safe, and as long as I stayed away from her, it would remain that way. *Act as Dramatic as a Banshee* would be just fine without me. Either way, I didn't feel any need to attend the classes after the way everyone had reacted at the fae King's birthday.

And the fae King? Silvan would forget about me. Hopefully. He surely had bigger problems than looking for an unimportant human like me. And the Deathbringer had assured my safety.

So, I might as well keep my thoughts busy and explore the Land of the Dead.

Worrying at my bottom lip, I started walking down the corridor.

After only a couple of minutes, I halted, uncertainly looking around. I hadn't anticipated I'd get lost this quickly. Everything looked exactly the same. The same sturdy stone walls, the same floating candles, the same wooden locked doors.

But what surprised me most was that I didn't encounter anyone. At all.

Nobody seemed to live here.

I was about to turn at a different corridor when the floor led into a majestic foyer. Unlike the other corridors I'd passed, this hall had windows that stretched up the entire wall, opening a breathtaking view over Emoh. I drew an awed breath. It was *extraordinary*.

And the silence ... I hadn't noticed it before, probably because I had been too caught up in my thoughts, but now I did. There were no sounds of driving cars, no humming of electronic devices. Nothing. Just silence. My breathing almost seemed too loud for this place.

But instead of making me feel itchy, it made me calmer in both body and mind.

Slowly, I approached the windows and looked down at the small village. The castle was too far away to make out any details of the village. But there was movement. Lots of it. I pressed closer to the cool windows, trying to make out the moving silhouettes. Emoh was surrounded by a big forest that stretched over the tall, snow-covered mountains. I had the strangest urge to get to know the place. It seemed so pretty. At least from afar.

I stepped up to the door next to the window. Judging by its size and the red carpet laid out in front of it, it was the castle's main entrance.

"Where are you going?"

I jumped at the booming voice and turned toward the source of the sound. The Deathbringer was standing at the top of a staircase I hadn't noticed before, his frame cast in shadows.

"Oh my God! You scared the shit out of me!" I exclaimed, protectively putting both of my hands over my chest.

How long had he been standing there? Had he been watching me?

"Why so jumpy, love?"

I was sure I heard an amused smile in his voice, even though I wasn't able to detect it in the darkness.

"Don't call me that."

He stepped out of the shadows. There was a darkness looming in those mesmerizing eyes of his. A darkness that matched the darkness of every shadow. His lips twitched as he assessed me. "If you are trying to flee from me, I should remind you that you are free to go wherever you please."

I brushed a strand of hair behind my ears. "I just wanted to check out the village. It looks beautiful. I'll go nuts if I stay in one room. I'll just be thinking about all the possible ways for Silvan to get to Miriam," I admitted, fisting the fabric of my dress.

It surprised me how easily I shared my worries with him. Usually, I wasn't one to open up this quickly to other people.

Comprehension flared in his eyes. "I understand completely. I just thought you might need some rest after everything you've been through. I'm sorry I made your discomfort worse," he said.

I felt my brows draw together. That was surprisingly kind and considerate of him.

"Did you meet Kalira? I sent for her."

I shook my head.

"Mmm. She must be on her way." The Deathbringer descended the remaining steps and came closer to me. He moved into the light, candles reflecting in his green eyes.

I swallowed hard as he grabbed the door handle. His shoulder brushed my arm as his broad frame stepped through the door. He held it open for me and gestured toward the village. "I'll join you. Be my guest."

I narrowed my eyes at him. "You are not going to tell me that it's safer here or prevent me from leaving?"

He cocked his head. "Why would I? You are not my prisoner." He looked ahead. "And even if you were: I wouldn't need a single second to find you. After all, you are in my realm."

Just greaaaaaaaat. I didn't think he meant his statement to sound as threatening as it had.

I shot him a side-glance. "Don't you have stuff to do as King of the Dead?" After all, hadn't he told the Norns he had urgent business to attend to? Or had he just made that up to get away from them as soon as possible? While he had seemed familiar with them, he hadn't struck me as all too keen on spending more time with them than was absolutely necessary.

He laughed deeply. The sound made goosebumps erupt on my skin. "You see, being King of the Dead does have its advantages. Most people die without my help," he said as he winked at me. It was oddly weird and, at the same time, fascinating how casually he talked about death. "If I should be needed, I'll know."

I didn't know what to make of his cryptic statement. "Must be nice," I murmured, trying to ignore the way my heart was drumming as I stepped through the door.

"Mm-hmm." The door thundered as it closed behind us.

"I didn't see anyone in the entire castle," I blurted out after a beat of silence.

He nodded. "The staff works mainly in the morning. I enjoy silence throughout the rest of the day. And, of course, there are the cooks working below the castle."

I didn't know what to say to that, so instead I fell silent as the King of the Dead led the way. He followed the stone path I had spotted from the balcony in the direction of the village. Even from afar it was astonishing.

Golden lights danced in the town, reflecting on the countless windows of the small, but cozy- and inviting-looking houses. Each one was singular and beautiful in its own way. They were painted in different colors, flowers and rose bushes decorated the gates, and roses wound their way over the railings of the countless balconies. As we got nearer, beautiful music drifted over to us, infiltrating the air in sweet melodies. Laughter echoed from the countless little passages and stone walls.

"Emoh is known as the Village of the Lost Dreams," the Deathbringer said as his eyes roamed over the buildings.

"It's beautiful," I whispered, completely dazzled in awe.

We walked over a small bridge. The stream gurgled happily beneath us as I spotted the first people.

I stopped and stared at them. They looked ... normal. In fact, they didn't look different from the Living at all. Their bodies weren't transparent as I had imagined, nor were they decayed. A shiver rushed down my back as awareness scraped its claws against me. They all were really, truly *dead*. They had already left their lives behind.

I wasn't the only one staring. A gathered crowd cast curious glances in our direction. I spotted fae, witches, wizards, humans, and vampires in between them, and not one of them seemed to have a problem with the other creatures' presence. Their eyes jumped between me and their King, as though they were trying to understand his reasons for escorting me.

Welcome to the club.

"Why are they all looking at me that way?" I whispered nervously as I felt the Deathbringer moving closer to me.

"They are not used to the presence of someone who's alive."

Mmm. That made sense.

While there were some modern aspects represented in Emoh, it mostly had a medieval touch to it. As did the clothing. Some people wore dresses that hadn't been worn for centuries in the Land of the Living, while others were wearing loose jeans. Some even had piercings and tattoos adorning their skin.

The Deathbringer followed my gaze. "The shops sell the clothing. You can find anything you want from whatever century you wish," he explained.

Surprised, I turned to face him. "Shops?"

The Deathbringer nodded and gestured in the direction of a

small house. A human woman was leaning against the wall, smoking a cigarette. The smoke wavered in the air as the wind slowly carried it away. "We have everything the Land of the Living has to offer." He cocked his head. "Well, except electronics. That's also the reason why you'll mainly spot handcrafted goods."

As some of the villagers met their King's gaze, they immediately dipped their chins. The respect his people showed him with every glance demonstrated how highly they thought of him. None of them avoided looking in his direction as everyone had around Silvan. The living fae had been scared to get their King's attention for it was always linked with consequences. But here, people met the Deathbringer's eyes openly.

I glanced at the Deathbringer, noticing the nod of acknowledgement he gave to his people before everyone resumed their activities.

"Come now," he said over his shoulder to me.

I followed him, trying to absorb every single detail Emoh had to offer. The air was filled with the smell of different spices wafting from the small restaurants over to us. Each one of them was filled with people who clearly enjoyed their food. Some were sitting on the pavilions; others inside the small restaurants.

My eyes took in everything greedily. Children laughed, chasing after each other while a bunch of adults talked avidly and hugged each other.

How the hell had all those different gruesome interpretations of the Afterlife spread? A purgatory landscape; flames burning for eternity hunting the Dead souls …. This was nothing like they depicted.

I tore my eyes from the enormous water fountain that took up the biggest part of the village's plaza. People were gathered there, too, laughing and chatting. Their eyes drifted between me and the King curiously, but no one dared to approach us.

It was only then I realized the Deathbringer still wasn't wearing his crown— even among his people. It seemed as though he didn't need to remind them of his station.

"This is amazing!" I said as we halted in front of the water fountain. Coins glimmered on the bottom of it, making the water shine golden.

As I turned around, I noticed that his eyes were not fixed on our location with its cheerful people and gleaming lights, but on me.

"I'm glad you enjoy being here."

I nodded with vigor. "Totally! It is nothing like I expected it to be," I admitted as my eyes darted from the fountain to the restaurants around it. "I had expected it to be ..."

"Suffocating, bloody, dark?" he offered, a grim expression darkening his features.

I brought my attention back to him as I nodded slowly. I didn't bother hiding the guilt I felt for my assumptions. "How can this place possibly be called the Village of the Lost Dreams?"

The Deathbringer looked down at me, watching me closely. "It represents everything that could have been if not for the Land of the Living's society. Among the Living, people give up their dreams once they realize the reality they face. Here, they are allowed to live their dreams."

I recalled the two female fae I had seen kissing in a corner we had passed. Homosexuality and affection between the same sex was forbidden in the fae community. Even today. But here, in the

Village of the Dead, everyone who had been suppressed was able to live the life they wished.

I squeezed my eyes shut. What a horrible thing to only be allowed to truly live once death took you. If what the Deathbringer had said was true—which it was—I was looking at the proof of it right now; it meant that life was the only suffering one had to endure before being freed by death. If I looked at the seemingly perfect life in the Afterlife, I almost regretted the Deathbringer had saved me from dying. Almost.

I looked at the crowd of mixed creatures. Nobody gave a second thought about what creature the other person was, what their sexuality was, or their social status.

Death, the Great Equalizer.

"Tell me what you are thinking," the Deathbringer prompted, his attention still fixed on me.

This place is more beautiful than my most extravagant dreams

.

"It all is so ... surprising," I said as I turned around, trying and miserably failing to take in every single detail. Even though there was no sun, the colors were brighter than in the Land of the Living. The castle loomed on a hill above the small village, its darkness forming a striking contrast next to the star-lit sky. I brought my eyes back to the man who ruled over this fantastical world.

"Why does everybody believe the Afterlife to be so ... lifeless?" I asked, scared I might offend him with my question.

He lifted a shoulder. "Every creature prefers the liability of things known to them. The uncertainty of what they might encounter once they die scares them."

Thoughtfully, I bit the inside of my cheek. By the way he had answered my question without a second of hesitation, the Deathbringer had been thinking about this for a while himself. I guessed when you were dead for as long as he had been—and probably would be—you started getting to the existential questions of life. Or, in his case, death.

Propping his shoulder against a jamb, he crossed his muscle-defined arms in front of his chest. "Of course, there is a second reason for the Living's image of the Afterlife."

I lifted my gaze to meet his eyes. "Which is?"

"No one has ever left this place to talk about it."

CHAPTER EIGHT

The Deathbringer was accompanying me to a small marketplace when my stomach grumbled loudly, drawing his attention to me.

"You are hungry," he stated. "You should have said something."

I felt my cheeks flush. "Oh, yeah." Truth be told, I had completely forgotten to eat after what the Norns had told me. Additionally, my mind had been too occupied with the fact that I was in the Land of the Dead for me to notice the emptiness of my stomach. The townspeople were selling different colored spices and clothing while the sellers talked to one another happily and offered warm, broad smiles to their King as we passed their stands.

The Deathbringer turned around. "Come. I know just the right place."

I followed him through a passage filled with the smell of the most exotic flowers I had ever seen. The wall of flowers took up the entire side of a small house. The Deathbringer ducked as he entered a tiny, cozy-looking restaurant. I followed him. He chose a table for two at the very end of the room.

"Here, take a seat." He held out a chair and gestured for me to sit down.

As gentlemanly as a King ought to be.

"Thank you," I murmured as he walked around the table to his own seat.

I let my eyes roam over the space. The delicious smell of food and the rich smell of the flowers blooming outside filled the space. The other customers didn't mind us, and if they did, they only nodded in sign of respect before resuming their conversations.

The human waiter made his way to us. He didn't seem surprised by his King's presence. He took our orders with a welcoming smile. For myself, I ordered a spring salad, while the Deathbringer ordered a steak. After the waiter left, I cleared my throat. "So, how come there is food in the Afterlife?"

The Deathbringer looked at me through his thick lashes. The bright green of his eyes shone through them, making me so very aware of with whom I was lunching. "I try to make the Afterlife as pleasant as possible for everyone. That way I can make sure people feel as much at home as possible. Or, I try to, anyhow."

I nodded.

I pretended sitting here with the Deathbringer and talking to him about the Afterlife was normal, when it fucking wasn't. Otherwise, I feared I'd lose my shit, and since there didn't seem to be any danger coming from the man in front of me, my strategy seemed sound.

Drumming my fingers on the table, I let my eyes drift over the restaurant. "The Norns." I felt myself shiver at the mere thought of those three crazy women. "Do they also live here? In Emoh?" When we were with the Norns, our surroundings had been so different than the peaceful ambience of the Village of the Dead. Here, everything was buzzing with life, from the wind blowing through the flowers to the sound of the talking people and the gurgle of the small rivers. The liveliness of it all was almost comical given the fact that I was surrounded by the Dead.

The Deathbringer tore his eyes from the movements of my fingers back to my face. He shook his head. "They live on the outside of Emoh, past the Forest of the Lost Souls." His brows drew together at the mention of the forest.

"So does everyone who dies end up in Emoh?" I had already wondered how a village of such a small size could be home to all the people who had died.

He shook his head. "No. The Land of the Dead is much more extensive than you may fathom. I prefer keeping everyone in smaller villages. I just happen to live in Emoh; that's the reason why I brought you here. That way I can take care of all my subjects."

Control them was what he meant, surely.

I didn't know what else to ask, so instead, I fell silent and started staring at my nails that suddenly became so much more interesting than meeting the searching gaze of the man in front of me.

As we waited for our food to be brought to us, I felt the King of the Dead lean forward. I tensed as his eyes roamed over me. He cocked his head to the side, clicking his tongue. "What should I do with you now?" He interlaced his fingers on the table.

Something about that question gave me the chills. Maybe it

was his playful undertone or the way his gaze did not leave me for a single second.

I eyed him warily.

He rested his arms at the back of his chair. "What is your name?"

Surprised, I looked up at him. I had assumed he was acquainted with my name. After all, he had known where I lived. But maybe that had been too presumptuous on my part. I cleared my throat and wiggled nervously on my chair. "Cassiana."

"Cassiana." The way he said my name, each syllable rolling off his tongue with such an intensity, made me almost believe he savored the way it felt in his mouth. "That's an old name." He took a sip of his wine before adding, "A regal one."

I nodded. "My parents always wished for me to be something I was not." I didn't manage to keep the bitterness out of my voice.

"Mmm." Thoughtfully, he swirled the wine in his glass. "How old are you?"

I bit the inside of my cheek "Twenty-six."

"And you act for a living?" His legs brushed my feet as he crossed them beneath the table.

"Yes." This exchange started to feel more like an inquest than an actual conversation. I straightened my spine. "What about you? What is your name?" It couldn't possibly be Deathbringer. That was not a name. That was a description the Living had made up out of fear of him.

His moss-green eyes laughed at me. "That's not how this is going to work."

I felt my brows rise high. "What do you mean? You asked me a question; I get to ask one myself."

His eyes lit in anticipation. "Ohhh. So, you want to play a

game. I see." His deep voice rumbled over me, heating me up from the inside out. "A question for a question. I'm in." His eyes glinted with mischief as he extended his hand for me to shake.

I was not someone to back down from a bet, so I did not hesitate as I took his hand and shook it. Again, the sizzling sensation went through my hands at the connection of our skin.

"My name is Thanatos." Before I had a chance to ask, he continued. "My turn." The Deathbringer—Thanatos—leaned his arm over the chair's armrest. "What is your favorite color?"

Caught off guard by such an innocent question, I took a moment to answer. "Blue." I wondered why he wanted to know this but decided to focus on more important questions. "Why don't people call you by your real name?"

He answered without missing a beat. "People prefer to look at what someone represents, rather than who the person actually is."

Sadly, he had a point. I had never met someone interested in a person's character traits rather than their social status or what kind of creature they were.

Our questioning was interrupted by the waiter who made his way to us. He carried a tray with our food on it. He set down our plates in silence. I eyed my salad warily. It looked like a real salad. I had almost been afraid the Afterlife's food wouldn't be real food.

Thanatos waited until the waiter was out of earshot. His gaze settled on me. "Tell me about yourself."

"That is not a question." I pointed out.

He just stared at me, waiting for my answer.

Trying to gain time, I started picking at my salad with my fork and took a tentative bite. Yep, it was real salad. Ignoring Thanatos's waiting gaze, I chewed my food thoroughly. "What do you want to know about me?" I lifted a shoulder. "There isn't much to know."

"Oh, but I strongly disagree."

I cast him a glance through my lashes. How would he know?

Providing Thanatos with private information was a dangerous thing to do. After all, he was a dangerous man. But then again, I doubted there was much I'd be able to hide from him. He already knew about Mir.

"I work as a full-time actress," I relented.

I was aware that I was answering in the most superficial way possible and that Thanatos had already asked me this just mere minutes ago. But I still didn't know the Deathbringer's true motives for saving me, and I wasn't too keen on having him use the information I gave him against me.

It took some effort to voice my next question. "Why is Silvan looking for me?"

Thanatos's eyes darkened at the mention of the other monarch. He took a sip of his wine before he leaned forward. "It isn't so much about you. It's more about me defying him in front of his subjects."

I had a feeling there was more to it, but I didn't push him.

"He's trying to get to me by using you," he added.

"Me? Why me?"

Thanatos shrugged. "I saved you. So he thinks you are important to me." He shook his head, as though the idea alone was absurd to him.

Gee, thanks. "Why *did* you save me?"

Reproving, he lifted a finger at me. Right. It was his turn to ask a question. "Do you enjoy your profession?"

I shrugged. "It isn't the worst thing to be doing."

The Deathbringer eyed me curiously. "But …?"

I pouted. "That's already your second question in a row."

I decided to answer it anyway. As I searched for the right words, I let my eyes roam over the paintings on the walls, avoiding his scrutinizing gaze. The paintings pictured different houses and gardens, probably resembling Emoh. "I just feel like you need to be doing something that you love. You need to have something in your life, a reason for you to stand up in the morning. A reason to live. Something that makes you yearn to get to work each day."

Silence stretched between us.

"And acting isn't it?"

It was such an easy question. But it had such a complex answer to it.

"No. It's just a means to an end."

He leaned forward, making me tense. "And what end would that be?"

I shrugged. It always seemed so silly to talk about one's goals out loud—especially to a stranger—but the intensity with which the Deathbringer still watched me proved that he wouldn't let the subject go. "I want to become an actress. A real one. A known one. I want people to recognize me for my work. To appreciate me for it."

He tilted his head, his eyes reflecting the light. "Is that something you want or is it something society has made you think you want?"

Apparently, the Deathbringer was going all existential on me, and it still wasn't his turn to ask.

I took a swig of the wine that suddenly tasted incredibly sour. "What do you mean?"

"I can't possibly imagine you truly want that. Did you really order a salad because you craved it or because you need to look a certain way for society to accept you the way you are?"

He had ... noticed?

"Acting is something I always wanted to do." I was omitting the actual question, I knew that, but I couldn't give him an answer. Truth was, I didn't know what I wanted in life. Society made us think we had to have everything figured out. But I didn't.

I yearned for something that would make me feel fulfilled, and I *hoped* that acting would be it. But I would only know that for sure once I had actually accomplished a successful actor's life. Until that happened, it was nothing more than a dream, a hope, and now that I had witnessed firsthand what actors were willing to do to get famous, I wasn't sure I still desired that any longer. Of course, I was very aware that attitude wasn't limited to actors, but it did feel as though the industry made people more willing to cross any moral values than in other professions.

"Fame isn't as desirable as you may think. People make assumptions about you, and it's really hard getting rid of them," he said.

I lifted my head to the King before me. I couldn't help but think that he was talking about himself. He was, after all, arguably one of the most well-known people in the universe, and based off of the rumors about him, his fame wasn't really flattering.

I pressed my lips together. "I don't know ..." It did seem better than living the opposite side of fame. Like getting rejected.

Thanatos seemed to feel that I didn't have an answer to his question. He leaned back in his chair with a knowing, "Mmm."

I appreciated he let the subject drop.

"And what about you? Do you have something that quickens the beating of your heart?" I asked, desperately moving the attention from me to the Deathbringer.

His hobbies were probably stealing children's candy.

Thanatos was looking at me for so long and with such an intensely, it started to get uncomfortable. I shifted under his gaze. He was still staring at me when he finally answered, "Maybe now I do."

"What do you do in your spare time?" I asked the very first question that came to me after his last response. Anything to get rid of this suffocating, choking emotion I suddenly felt.

Thanatos watched the waiter refill our glasses. "You mean besides saving humans from the fae King and ruling over the Dead?" The corner of his mouth tipped up. "You might not believe me, but I honestly don't have time for much else."

It shouldn't surprise me, but it did. After all, he was spending his time with me right now, instead of ruling.

"My turn," he said after the waiter had left. I grabbed my glass and brought it to my lips.

His eyes gleamed sinisterly. "Do you have a partner?"

I choked on the wine and coughed loudly. "What?"

He looked totally unaffected. "Do you have a partner? A boyfriend, husband?"

"I know what a partner is," I bit out.

His mouth twitched at that. He seemed totally at ease, but there was an edge to the way he observed me.

I tried sounding as casual as possible. "Nope."

He nodded and took a big gulp of his wine.

"It's my turn to ask a question," I said, neither wanting nor willing to read into his question.

The Deathbringer smiled mischievously. "I am single, too, if that's what you are wondering."

Noted.

I tried keeping my expression blank. "That doesn't surprise me."

He arched a brow. "I should probably feel hurt by that statement."

"No—. I mean—" I wiggled nervously on my chair. I glanced at Thanatos. Great. He looked amused by my stammering. I forced myself to take a deep breath before I explained. "I meant that since you are dead, I'd guessed as much. I mean, who would want to date a dead guy?" Pointedly, I took in the way his broad shoulders filled out the linen shirt he was wearing.

"Mouthy little thing," he said, although his lips did curl. "So you have indeed been thinking about my sexual interests …." When I didn't reply, he leaned further forward. "So tell me. Would you be willing to date a dead guy?" His eyes were alight, noting every single movement I made. He was enjoying this way too much.

I snorted. "Sure thing, buddy." I crossed my arms over my chest.

The movement drew Thanatos's attention to my arm. His brows drew together as the smile on his face was wiped away. "What is that?"

"Uh, uh, uh. This is not how this is going to work." I echoed the Deathbringer's words. "You just asked a question. Now it's my turn. Why did you save my life?"

Ignoring me, the King of the Dead manifested right next to me and grabbed my arm.

"What the hell are you doing?" I tried jerking my arm back, but he didn't let me, his grip only tightening.

He turned my wrist around, eyeing it closely. "What is this?"

"What do you mean?" I asked, confused. I followed his gaze to my wrist. I searched my arm up and down for something that might've triggered his sudden outburst. "My mole?"

He traced the birthmark with his index finger. A deep growl emitted from his chest. "I am going to kill them." He let go of my hand before running his fingers through his hair. His eyes grew distant. "I have to go."

Baffled by his sudden change of mood, I stared up at him. "What?"

"I'll make sure Kalira finds you." He avoided my gaze as he summoned the shadows to him, his frame beginning to disappear. "I trust you can see yourself back to the castle?"

"Yes. But …"

Too late. He had already been swallowed by the darkness. Bewildered, I stared at the mole on my wrist.

What the fuck had that been about?

After finishing my food, I left the cozy restaurant. The waiter had assured me that there was no need to pay for the delicious meal. *Our King and his guests are always free to dine here whenever they want*, he had said.

Our. As if I'd already become one of his subjects.

I made my way out of the restaurant and began walking

aimlessly through the village. It truly was beautiful. It wasn't the round balconies and the countless little corners and passages that gave the place a homely feeling. It was the people. Their friendly eyes and the laughter echoing off sturdy stone walls filled the place with positive energy.

Leaving the small houses behind, I followed the irregular stone path that led to Thanatos's impressive, dark castle. It loomed over the village like a guardian. I walked past terraced fields with blooming flowers. I had never seen flowers blooming in the dark, glowing like thousands of fireflies. Their small leaves rattled with the soft wind blowing through them like a sweet caress.

I stopped and sat down on a large, flat rock to look down at the village. It was so peaceful up here. The wind carried the sound of the gurgling water to me, and the sweet smell of the flowers loosened the tension in my muscles. My gaze dropped to my left wrist, and I traced the small mole.

Thanatos. I didn't know what had gotten him to leave, but I was thankful for the time alone. Everything felt so incredibly odd. I felt completely overwhelmed by the last couple of days.

And powerless.

I listened to the stream of water gurgling its way toward Emoh. There was nothing I could do. I felt as though I stood next to myself, watching me, without having any way to interfere. Like I'd been caught up in a dream. And the weirdest thing? I couldn't explain it, other than having this *feeling*, but I somehow had the impression as though I had met the King of the Dead before.

I truly hoped I'd be able to get home soon. I longed to get back to everyday regularity, but I couldn't get rid of the sensation that my time in the Land of the Dead was only beginning.

I didn't know how long I stayed on the rock in the darkness, letting my thoughts drift freely, until a voice disturbed the silence.

"Cassiana?"

I lifted my head at the unfamiliar voice.

A petite woman stood before me, her cheeks dotted with freckles and her copper hair braided.

My brows drew together as I stood to face her. "Yes?" I was surprised that she approached as none of the other people I had met had done so.

"I'm Kalira. I'm supposed to help you around." She was wearing high-cut jeans and a floral-printed tank top. "The King told me your name," she hurried to explain at my confused expression.

I relaxed. Thanatos had mentioned he'd send someone to show me around. "Nice to meet you." I smiled at her.

She nodded, making her plait jump with the movement. "You too!"

Judging by her pierced nose and the tattoos covering her arms, she'd probably died in the 20th or 21st century. A deep feeling of sadness overcame me at that thought. It was easy to forget the reality of the Afterlife when everything in Emoh seemed so joyful, but the people here were indeed *dead*.

"Come on! I found such amazing clothing for you!" She looked at me, her eyes moving up and down my frame. "I hope it fits. You are taller than I thought you'd be."

I worried my lip as I followed her to the castle. "That's nice of you. I'm sure the clothes will fit just fine."

We fell silent as the castle's frame grew bigger the closer we moved to it. It wasn't a comfortable silence. I could basically feel the questions radiating from her.

She wasn't able to keep them to herself for too long, either. She shot me a curious side-glance. "So, you and our King, huh?"

Confused, I came to a halt. "What?"

She shrugged, picking at her chipped black nail polish. "You seem to have caught his interest."

"Why would you say that?"

She shot me a how-dumb-can-you-possibly-be look. "Because you are alive and he's brought you here," she stated as if it were the most obvious thing in the world.

I sighed. "It's complicated."

"I've got time. You know, being dead can get pretty boring." She looked at me with pleading eyes.

I chuckled at her expression. "He brought me here to save me from King Silvan, that's all."

Her eyes grew big at the fae King's name. "King Silvan?"

I nodded slowly.

She gave me a curious look. "Why did he save you?"

I tore my eyes from her, looking at the thick stone walls of the castle. "I wish I knew," I whispered.

Kalira leaned in close. "Maybe he hasn't gotten himself a proper lay in a while."

I tripped over the irregular path. Her baby-blue eyes smiled at me innocently. I did not buy it for a second. "I'm not interested if that's what he desires." My stomach clenched at my words.

I walked past her, wanting to get to the castle as fast as possible. Kalira's bluntness made me uncomfortable. Maybe because she faced me with my own thoughts.

Kalira caught up easily. "If that's what you think." I felt her eyes heavy on me, searching my face. "Maybe he likes women who play hard to get."

Narrowing my brows, I looked anywhere but at her. I wasn't playing hard to get. I was just not interested in the Deathbringer in any way other than what he was to me: my savior. I groaned. Why was I even thinking about this?

Kalira seemed to sense my reluctance. "What do you think he wants from you if not some sexual payback?"

When we reached the castle, Kalira pulled open the door. It surprised me that the Deathbringer left it unattended, but then again, who would dare to breach his castle?

Shrugging, I entered the castle, closely followed by Kalira. "I don't know. He just said that I owe him now."

Kalira murmured a knowing "Ahhhhh" and wiggled her eyebrows at me. "I should have chosen those red lace panties."

I stared at her back. *What was wrong with her?*

Choosing to ignore her comment, I followed her into the room where I'd first arrived. So, this was the place I'd be staying. My bedroom. The floating candles were still lit, and the room was exactly as I had left it save for the addition of a big trunk.

Kalira plopped on the bed, wrinkling the sheets with the movement. She gestured to the trunk. "There are your clothes."

Clothes. Right. I hadn't even got the chance to think about that. I swallowed audibly. The Deathbringer must anticipate that I'd stay for a while…

"Thanks," I muttered, walking across the room. I was skeptical of what Kalira might have chosen for me to wear, but I refused to start guessing wildly. So instead, I made to open the trunk. It was shod with metal, the top almost too heavy for me to lift.

Blue.

Most of the fabric inside was blue. I grabbed the top dress and turned to Kalira. "How did ...?"

She smiled at me before examining her nails closely. "Just before I had a chance to get them, the King appeared, wishing for this color."

So that was why he had asked about my favorite color. He must have sought Kalira out right after he left the restaurant, or after he had taken care of whatever business had been so pressing to him. After all, it had been a couple of hours since he had left me.

I looked at the dress in my hands. Thanatos had said everything in Emoh had been crafted by hand, and you could tell. The fabric was soft, delicate even. Almost too pretty to be worn.

"I guess the King wants to make a lasting impression," Kalira said from her spot on the bed.

I didn't know what to say to that. Clearing my throat, I looked at her ripped jeans. "How long ...?" Was it impolite to ask how long she had been dead?

She waved me off. "Ah, don't worry. You can just ask. I died in 2016. Fucking vampire on a high cornered me."

"Ohhh. I'm sorry to hear that."

I wanted to punch myself. People used that line for lost purses, not when someone revealed the way they had died.

Kalira seemed to notice my inner conflict, because she smiled as she jumped off the bed. "Did you see the bathroom yet?" She walked through a door I hadn't noticed before on the opposite side of the room.

I followed her and took in the space. Windows covered an entire wall, a huge tub set right in the middle of the open-spaced room. Although *huge* didn't do it justice; that thing was closer to a small pool.

I took a step forward. My shoulders relaxed when my gaze fixed on the bottom of the pool. The tub wasn't deep. Even after my experience at the beach, I'd never become afraid of bathtubs. As long as the bottom was visible, I knew I'd be okay. My gaze continued to roam over the lavish space. The lack of curtains surprised me, but then again, the tub didn't face any inhabited land from what I was able to see.

Kalira walked across the room and opened the closet drawer. "Do you want to bathe?" she asked me over her shoulder. She grabbed containers filled with shimmering liquid. "We have bathing essences. There's vanilla, lavender, rose—"

"Not rose," I stopped her, images of Silvan flashing before my inner eyes.

She gave me a quizzical look but put the rose essence back.

"Lavender is fine," I said, suddenly feeling incredibly worn out. Unsure of what to do, I watched Kalira pour some liquid into the tub—a.k.a. pool—and turn on the water. The lavender scent filled the space immediately, already beginning to calm my exhaustion.

"I'll get you your clothes."

"You don't have to. Really. I can do it."

She smiled warmly at me. "Don't be silly. That's my job. As well as helping you bathe, arranging your hair, and whatever else you might need."

"I am fine, really."

"I'll do what the King has commanded me to do."

I saw the determination in her eyes and slowly nodded. She wouldn't dishonor Thanatos's orders. I honestly didn't know why he thought it necessary to take care of me. He probably wanted to have someone watch over me at all times, but maybe— and this thought was way scarier than the former—he wanted to make sure I was okay.

While Kalira went to the bedroom to get the clothes, I let myself take in the bathroom's details. The bathroom's floor was entirely crafted of sand-colored marble and the floating candles had the softest whisper of vanilla. The door to my bedroom creaked when Kalira came back in. She carried gauzy clothing in her hand.

I nodded in the direction of the wooden door that lay parallel to my bedroom's door. "Where does the other door lead?"

Kalira followed my gaze, a playful smile tipping her lips. "To the bedchambers of our King."

"What?" I shrieked. "Our bedrooms are connected?"

Kalira's smile grew bigger. "Apparently, the King wishes you to be close to him." She put the clothing on a chair in front of the bathtub. When she turned around, she straightened her spine and looked at me. Her eyes were alight in amusement at my obvious shock. "Do you need anything else?"

I shook my head, still too shocked to do anything but stare at the other door.

The bedchambers of the King.

"All right. I'll see you tomorrow." She smiled sweetly at me. "Sleep tight, Cassiana."

As I was left in the quiescence, the only sound coming from the flicker of the floating candles, realization slowly kicked in. Thanatos and I shared a bathroom. Why would the King of the Dead want me this close to him? I could only imagine one reason.

My blood heated at that thought.

I woke to this feeling of ... awareness. I blinked my eyes open, realizing I had fallen asleep in the bathtub. The water had grown cold and the bubbles that had spread on the water's surface must have vanished long ago. Even the shadows the flames of the floating candles cast were longer than they had been when Kalira had shown me the bathroom.

I didn't know how long I had slept. I glanced outside, but the night's sky didn't give me any hint of time.

That's when I felt it. A presence.

I wasn't alone.

"I was just about to wake you," a familiar voice said from behind me.

My entire body locked down. The Deathbringer. Thanatos.

"I must have fallen asleep." I didn't dare turn to him, refusing to show my surprise at his presence. I glanced at the wooden door to his room. Was he here to ... collect my debt?

"I see you enjoy the view," he said.

I swallowed delicately. "I could say the same about you."

He chuckled, and I heard him stroll closer. "Yes, you probably could."

My whole body tensed as I felt him kneel behind me, his heavy gaze on the back of my head. His body radiated such power I felt as though it would physically push against my back.

I stared at the starry sky through the window. "I'm pretty sure it isn't polite to disturb a woman's bath." My voice trembled.

He chuckled again, the sound resonating on my skin. I jumped at the sudden soft touch of his fingers on my shoulder. "But I am sure it is, when the man has just saved the woman that was about to drown in a bathtub."

I snorted. I'd just fallen asleep.

"Cassiana."

The way he said my name... It made my eyelids flutter closed and my heart skip a beat. Every fiber within me heated, making my head buzz with— was it fear or anticipation?

From the spot where he knelt behind me, he wasn't able to see my nudity— at least, that's what I hoped—but the fact alone that I was indeed naked made me so very hyperaware of him.

"You room is connected to my bathroom," I stated, not knowing what to say or how to handle the Deathbringer's proximity.

"Mmm." I felt him lean closer. "So, tell me, love. Does that make you nervous?" His lips brushed the back of my shoulder. Suddenly, his fingers were in my hair, loosening the tie holding it up in a bun. He moved my mass of hair to the side, letting it cascade over my shoulder to my front.

"No," I lied, biting my lip.

"Mmm."

I could hear the smile in his voice. Not being able to see him made this moment so much more intense. The questions I'd had since the moment he saved me resurfaced. What had made him intervene at the theatre? Why had he saved me?

I was about to ask when he moved slightly forward. His arms slowly draped over the edge of the bathtub, coming to rest on its rim. Almost like an embrace. As he leaned even further forward, his face entered my peripheral vision. Words failed me at his proximity. I almost didn't dare to move my head in his direction. This close, I could see the two small dots at his cheeks where his dimples would show whenever he laughed. Thanatos was looking at me as if seeing me for the first time.

My breathing became ragged. Now, he only needed to lower his gaze to see my naked body through the water. But he didn't. His eyes remained fixed on my face. Not once did he lower his gaze to take in the rest of me. He was so close that I would only need to lean forward to press my lips against his.

He seemed to be thinking the same thing, his eyes dropping to my suddenly parted lips. The Deathbringer's hand brushed light as a feather over the skin of my shoulder. It moved toward my collarbone before tracing it the same way he had mere hours ago.

I couldn't help my body's reaction. My head fell back, coming to rest in the crook between his shoulder and neck.

"Thanatos," I whispered, my voice grown hoarse.

He froze.

His eyes jumped back up, his brows drawing together. He squeezed his eyes shut. "What am I doing?" he whispered. He drew back his hands and stood, stepping away from the tub.

"I am going to be away tomorrow."

Tomorrow? How did he even keep track of what day it was when the night was a constant companion in the Afterlife?

"Kalira will be with you. You are free to go wherever and do whatever pleases you as long as you stay within Emoh," he said, a sudden distance in his words.

"I thought I wasn't your prisoner," I queried, trying to ignore the thunderous beating of my heart.

Thanatos was fast to answer. "You are not, but there are creatures out there I wouldn't want you to meet." With those departing words, he left the bathroom through the adjoining door to his own bedroom.

I was left in the room alone, staring outside at the sky's darkness. Long after he left, I peered at the closed door connected to his room. What had made him leave so suddenly?

Despite the heat pooling in my core, I couldn't help but feel relieved. I didn't know what might have happened if Thanatos hadn't left, but I knew it was better this way. I couldn't risk letting him distract me from what I truly needed to do: find out his reasons for saving me.

CHAPTER NINE

17 years ago

My father invaded my personal space, his raging eyes burning on me. "If you ever even think about doing something like this again, I will end you," he spat. His fingers dug into my skin. I knew from experience his hold on me would leave bruises on my skin. Bruises I had to explain to my teachers. Not once had they questioned the truth behind my words. They hadn't noticed the way I had silently begged them for help. Neither had my classmates.

My father's grip tightened as he shook my body aggressively, making my head fly back and forth. He leaned forward, his rum-noted breath fanning over my face. "You do this once again, and I will end you. End you," he repeated.

I whimpered, my body shaking. Even though I should be accustomed to my body's reaction by now, I was still surprised as I felt hot tears streaming down my cheeks. The darkness around me hesitantly retreated, leaving me at my father's mercy once more. The loss of their company rattled me from the inside out. "I didn't want to do this ... I just ..."

He jolted me again, his anger coloring his cheeks in a deep shade of red. "I do not care. You are a fucking freak. A freak."

He let me go and stepped around me as he started to pace.

My body began trembling at his hateful words. I should know better than to glance at my mother for help; she just leaned against the kitchen counter, watching us in silence. I pleaded her with my eyes to intervene.

Her help never came.

Not when I needed help doing my homework. Not when I came home crying. Not when my father brought his fists down on me.

He left bruises not only on my skin but also underneath it. Mainly underneath it. Skin healed. But the deeper damage was a different story altogether.

He gestured to the place where I still stood trembling like a leaf. I wasn't able to meet his eyes. "That thing there is not my daughter. It's a freak."

Each word he spat carved wounds on my heart that would eventually scar but never heal completely, always reminding me of who my father really was. As he turned, hatred shone through his eyes. He trudged toward me. Then, he drew back his hand. I knew what would come next, but the knowledge didn't keep me from trying to protect myself from the blow.

The next morning, I curled in my bed and stared through the windows at Emoh.

After Thanatos had left, I had made sure to lock the door

adjoining our shared bathroom. I wasn't stupid enough to think that a simple lock would keep him from entering my room, but I didn't dwell on that for too long. A lock meant safety. At least that was what I tried telling myself over and over again.

Last night's encounter with the King of the Dead felt like a dream, his touch on my skin like a mirage.

Kalira had arrived in the morning to help me dress. When I'd asked her about the ongoing darkness, she had explained that, just like I had suspected, there was only night in the Afterlife. That wasn't a problem for me. I had always preferred the night over the day anyhow.

Kalira had chosen a flimsy dress with long sleeves and red frills. The fabric gathered in abundance on the sleeves and lacked near the cleavage. Kalira's taste in clothing definitely ran counter to mine.

"Does he do this often?" I had asked her casually after I found the courage to do so.

Her brows had knit in confusion. "Do what?" she had asked as she tied the backside of my dress.

"Save women and keep them in the Afterlife?"

She had looked at me over her shoulder, a smug expression lighting up her features. I almost regretted asking. I could basically see the wheels in her head spinning to conclusions. "No," she said as she resumed tying the laces. "Our King has never brought any woman here." She chuckled. "Nor any man for that matter," she added, not wasting the opportunity to wink at me.

It shouldn't make any difference to me. I should be thankful he had offered me a safe place and saved my life. Except it somehow did.

After that, Kalira had brought me breakfast, but I had barely been hungry. She had offered to stay with me and show me around, but I declined. I preferred to be alone to calm myself after everything that had happened over the last couple of days. When Kalira left, I had rummaged through the trunk's content, looking for something more adequate to wear. Something more … covering. In vain. Of course, I might've just asked Kalira for a different option. But judging by her enthusiasm for my current dress, I doubted she'd relent. And I didn't want to offend her taste.

A knock on my door tore me from my thoughts. It must be Kalira again. "Yes?" I called out as I sat up in the bed. What could she possibly want now? She had only left mere minutes ago. Had she forgotten something?

As the door opened, a tall werewolf-lady entered my room. "Good morning!" she said with that growling undertone that was typical for werewolves.

"Hi?" Absently, I let my fingers glide through my hair. I didn't want to look like I had already spent most of the morning in bed, and luckily, the braid Kalira had made still held my hair neatly together.

"I'm here to take care of your room," the woman explained softly. Compared to their male werewolf counterparts who had a tendency to let their hairiness grow wild, female werewolves kept their body hair cared for and trimmed. Yes, even the werewolves had their own gender standards.

"Oh, right. Come on in." I remembered Thanatos mentioning that the staff worked only in the mornings so he'd have his peace throughout the day. So *those* were the sounds I had heard moving around in the corridor for a while now. It had been the staff cleaning the entire castle.

She smiled at me as she moved inside my room.

Scrambling off the bed, I clasped my hands together. "Can I help you somehow?"

She smiled warmly at me. "No, thank you. We'll take care of everything."

"We?" I asked just as two more people followed closely behind her, both of them carrying cleaning supplies. They scattered, moving to the bathroom and beginning to do their jobs. They were so sure and fast in what they did, it was obvious this wasn't the first time they had to take care of this task.

"Are you sure I can't help?" I prodded.

The werewolf-lady looked up from my bed, which she was redoing. "No, it's fine. We are faster when we do it ourselves."

"Okay," I murmured. They seemed determined to finish their job as fast as possible, which was totally understandable having in mind the size of the majestic castle. I fidgeted uncomfortably with my hands. It seemed so rude to look at people cleaning while you just *stood* there. They didn't seem to mind me, though. They were so focused on their job, they didn't even glance up at me. I wondered if they speculated about me being here in their King's castle, or if they felt irritated by my presence in the Land of the Dead. I wasn't one of them, after all.

My gaze swept to the three people working. I was surprised by the speed with which they progressed. In the blink of an eye they had cleaned my room, the adjoining bathroom and were already packing their cleaning utensils back together.

"Have a good day!" The werewolf-lady said as she scurried out behind her two helpers.

"You too!" I managed to say before the door shut behind them.

I loosened a breath as I listened to the ongoing noise outside my bedroom before gliding to the armchair in front of one of the windows. I didn't know how long it took the staff to clean the castle, but eventually, the sounds in the corridor died off and the castle fell back to its looming silence.

Sighing, I walked over to the balcony overlooking the village. Soft music was playing from there, and I was even able to make out a couple of people dancing in the distance. I put my head back to stare at the sky. I didn't know how long I stood there on the balcony, trying to figure out the familiar stars' patterns from back home. I couldn't find any known constellations, and I knew a bunch of them. Even as a kid, I was obsessed with the stars, trying to learn as much as I could about them.

I wondered if Thanatos knew any of them, or if he only knew the constellations of his home.

Thanatos.

A shiver ran down my back at his name, at the memory of the heat in his eyes yesterday. If Kalira were right and Thanatos had brought me here to have sex with him, why hadn't he acted upon his desires? He had seemed willing to do so. And myself?

I swallowed hard.

Why the fuck was I even thinking about this? Shaking my head, I willed that train of thought to fade as I toyed with Miriam's bracelet. Miriam. She was the only person I had let in. It had taken us years and years to build our relationship to the point where it was now. I really hoped she was doing okay. I couldn't fathom what must have gone through her mind when I suddenly disappeared. The only reassuring thought I had was that the Norns guaranteed she was safe. I could only hope they had spoken the truth. I wished there were a way to get in contact with her. A sudden heaviness in my chest made me take a deep breath.

Unwilling to let my thoughts drift further in that direction, I moved through my room, aiming for the door. Maybe I could explore the castle a little more.

I stepped into the hall, its silence engulfing me immediately. This time I turned right, instead of left. The red carpet seemed to swallow every sound, drowning everything in complete silence. Yesterday's exploration had led me only to closed doors. Maybe today I'd find something to spend my time with. I could use some distraction.

I followed the candle-illuminated corridor, checking every door, but all were closed or opened only to more empty bedrooms. When I rounded the next corner, the carpet-draped floor gave way to slick marble. My steps, which had been barely audible just moments ago, suddenly pounded loud as a drum in the open-spaced foyer with its high ceiling. There was no window in this room, but the marble was *everywhere*. On the walls, the ceiling, the floor. I rounded a pillar that supported the ceiling.

I came to an abrupt halt.

Huge, serene, and ancient-looking statues stood before me. I had to crane my head back to get a better look at them. They resembled the Kings, I realized. The stone-carved statues were impressive. Standing much larger than the actual Kings, their stony eyes were focused on a point above me. They stood so close to one another their shoulders touched at their proximity. Involuntarily, I stepped closer, needing to contemplate the details.

One, two, three, four, five, I counted. My brows drew together. Why were only five of the six Kings included? Edward was missing. It wasn't a secret that the human King only had a representative role. Even though no one voiced it, it was widely known that the humans would be defeated first should it come to a war.

Maybe that was the reason for his statue's absence. Maybe the artist had deemed Edward as not important enough to be represented...

My gaze slid to the statue at the far left.

Cyril the vampire King's fangs peeked out of his stone-carved mouth, his lips tipped up in the playful smile so typical of the undead King. Next to him stood the statue depicting Lesmand, the King of all witches and wizards. He wore a floor-length cape, and in his palm, he held a small stone-crafted flame, the symbol of witchcraft. There was something about his expression that made him almost seem omniscient. On the far right, Helm, the werewolves' Alpha stood proudly, his hairy chest puffed out and his curly, long hair framing his broad face wildly.

When my eyes drifted to the statue next to the werewolf's, I took an unwitting step back. Goosebumps erupted on my skin.

King Silvan.

The artist had flattered the fae King with this representation. The statue's eyes didn't do justice to the cruelty that had shone through the real King's eyes. His pointed ears emerged through chiseled stone-hair, and his right hand rested on the shoulders of the fourth King. He looked as threatening as he did in real-life. But not as threatening as the statue next to him.

At first, I wasn't sure if the stone-sculpted man was indeed Thanatos. It had the same complex facial features as the King of the Dead and the same broad, muscled body structure, but this representation had *wings*. Beautiful, majestic wings. His wings were covered with thousands of stony feathers and the wingspan reached behind the backs of all the other Kings. Thanatos's gaze was fixed on Silvan, his stony eyes having a warm touch to them.

I stepped up to the sculpture, my height barely reaching its chest. Slowly, *reverently*, I let my hands glide over Thanatos's wings. If they were this beautiful carved in stone, I couldn't fathom how they would look in reality. They seemed so *powerful*. I'd bet they were ink-black, just like his devoted companions, the shadows. Would the feathers feel as soft as they promised to be? Or would they be coarse, hardly damageable?

I stepped back and stared at the statues of the Kings again. One last time, I let my eyes roam over their majesty. I couldn't help but feel intimidated by their unmoving silence that was only amplified by the quiescence of this room. I turned around, feeling their stony eyes rest heavily upon me as I left.

The castle was enormous. Literally. I felt sorry for its staff who had to take care of such a generous space. Yet again, I wondered how much time they must spend every day cleaning the castle. I stopped in front of a large door that caught my attention. It looked different than the other doors I had passed ... much more used.

Curious, I put my hands on the cool handle and pressed it down.

The door's wood was so compact, it didn't budge easily. I had to prop my entire weight against it to open it partly, letting warm air immediately surge forward. I wrinkled my nose at the smell. Even before I entered, I knew the room's purpose by that smell—one so impregnated in my memory I'd never be able to forget it.

Old paper.

I pushed harder against the door. Its hinges made a creaking sound as it gave way to the most impressive library I had ever laid eyes upon.

Rows and rows of books lined the entire space. The walls of the library were nearly thirty feet high. They supported the round glass ceiling that stretched above the entire library, letting the stars shine over all those thousands of secrets hidden and saved in between these countless, simple pages.

In wonder, I put one foot in front of the other and entered the knowledge-filled space.

Ladders rested against every shelf. Walking past them, I outstretched my right arm and let my fingers move over the spines of the books. Most were still leather-bound, while others, newer ones, had already replaced the leather with paperback covers. Plaques of each alphabetically-ordered topic had been fixed at the very top of each shelf: poetry, history of the 19th century, physics, the history of vampires, mathematics. You name it. Every topic I could think of was procurable. There was even an entire shelf labeled as erotica.

How magnificent it must be to have this kind of access to such an immense amount of wisdom at all times. I moved to the back of the library where I had spotted the romance section.

Silence so different than the quietness in the foyer with the statues engulfed me. It had a peacefulness only libraries retained.

Smiling, I pulled out a slim book with the absolute cheesiest cover ever. Just what I wanted. Something easy and fast to read that would shut up my mind. At least for a while.

Carrying the book underneath my arm, I moved to the library's center where I had spotted a huge circle of sofas ringing a mountain of cushions. I chose the cushions. The flames of a majestic fireplace in front of me emanated the most calming heat as I began reading, letting the story absorb me completely until it was impossible to distinguish between the images flashing before my inner eye and the black-on-white words before me.

Time passed like a dream. Before I knew it, I had finished the book about aliens that abducted human females to breed with them—which, to my surprise, wasn't as bad as I'd initially thought judging by the cover.

My limbs felt numb as I stood to grab another book. I moved back to the romance section, but nothing at eye-level interested me. I took the golden ladder that rested against the shelf and moved it in front of the romance section. Climbing it until I reached the middle of the shelf, I let my gaze move over the countless titles printed on the book's spines. Grabbing a navy-blue book, I flipped it to the backside and began reading the blurb.

"I see you have made yourself at home."

I lost the grip on the book and jerked around.

Just before hitting the floor, the book froze in the air.

My eyes darted to the opposite shelf to find the Deathbringer leaning against it languidly, his arms crossed as he watched me intently. His motionless face was cast in shadows. Only his eyes gave away his amusement.

Home.

I stilled at that word, but before he could notice my body's reaction, I climbed down the ladder and picked the book from the air without bothering to glance at him. I didn't want to give him the satisfaction of reading in my eyes how much he had startled me.

It was widely known that King Silvan could freeze objects and float them in the air. I hadn't known the Deathbringer had access to those powers, too. Maybe it was an ability all Kings possessed …?

As soon as my feet touched the ground, I looked at him.

"You scared me," I admitted. Cocking my head, I looked him over. If he felt rueful for his behavior, he didn't show it.

His gaze jumped to the plaque at the top of the shelf. When his heavy eyes came back to me, a sly smile lightened his expression. "I see I'm in the company of a romantic. Cute."

Ignoring him, I turned to the shelf and began looking at the spines without actually registering the titles. Biting the inside of my cheek, I stared down at my hands. The uncertainty of the Deathbringer's true motives and the possibilities of them made my stomach churn. Especially since Kalira had voiced her theories. I clenched my jaw and curled my hands into fists. Was Kalira right? Did Thanatos really want me to pay off my debt by sleeping with him? If that were the case, why hadn't he demanded it already? As much as I had tried to forget about his motives, I couldn't. Wouldn't it be better to just ask him straight away?

"When are you planning for payback to begin?" I asked as casually as possible, very well aware of his gaze still fixed on my back. I started pulling out books at random and looked at their covers— anything to avoid meeting those green eyes.

I swallowed. "I know what you want," I stated quietly as I put the books back in the shelf. You wouldn't notice the slight tremble of my voice if you didn't know me.

"Do you now?" Even without looking at him, I imagined that godforsaken smile plastered on his face. I heard his heavy footsteps approach and tensed as he outstretched his hands from behind me. He rested them on the shelf on each side of my body, effectively caging my body. My entire back radiated with his body's heat. "I am curious." His words fanned over my neck. "Tell me, love. What do you think it is that I want from you?"

My delicate swallow seemed incredibly loud as I let my hands slide from the shelf and ever so slowly, careful of not touching him, I turned to the man standing behind me.

My breath hitched at his proximity. His gaze was fixed on my face as he waited for me to answer.

I let my eyes drift over the curve of his eyebrows, over that sharp-cut jaw of his, over the elegant bridge of his nose.

What was he thinking? I searched his glimmering emerald eyes, but they gave away nothing.

He arched a brow and prompted, "Well? What is it you believe I wish as payback from you?"

My cheeks heated as I lowered my gaze. "Well … judging by the pretty *revealing* dress you chose—"

"Other than the color, I have nothing to do with the outfits Kalira has chosen for you." His eyes dropped, roaming over my body, making me shiver as if it weren't his eyes, but his hands moving over my skin. His heated gaze made me question whether he truly had seen enough human flesh as he had stated. His eyes lingered for a second too long on my extensive cleavage before coming back to my own gaze. He studied my features so intensely, I almost wanted to break the eye contact. My body locked down when he leaned forward and whispered conspiratorially, "But I must say: the dress does compliment you. Kalira has good taste in clothing."

Of course he'd think like that. Even the King of the Dead was a man after all.

I blushed at his bluntness but opted to ignore his comment and cleared my throat. "Well, based on the fact that you moved me to the room next to yours, and I am the only one here … And the shared bathroom …" My cheeks grew hotter and hotter with each spoken word. I didn't want to finish the sentence and, instead, let him come to his own conclusions.

He flashed me a smile as though I were the most entertaining thing in the entire world. "Come on, love. Speak your mind." Thanatos's grin turned mischievous, daring me to keep going.

I stared at a spot behind the King of the Dead. "I was thinking you might want to have …" *Just fucking get it over with.* "Sex," I finished, my face on fire.

Silence.

The moments ticked by painfully slowly as I waited for Thanatos to either confirm or deny my assumptions, but he kept staring at me, nothing in his face indicating what he might be thinking.

"Is that the way you wish for repayment to go?" he asked, his lips curling up just the slightest.

I narrowed my eyes at him.

His eyes widened in feigned shock. "Are you truly willing to pay such a tremendous price for your life?"

My instincts screamed at me to back away, but I refused because, one, I was still caged in by his frame; and two, I didn't want to show how much he intimidated me. "If it's not that, what else could you possibly want?" It was driving me crazy not knowing the Deathbringer's plans for me.

Thanatos smirked. "You'll see."

I could not believe him. Crossing my arms in front of my chest, I glared at him. "And why did you order my bedroom to be right next to yours?" I demanded.

He tipped his head to the side innocently. "Maybe because I

am lonely?" he offered, but the sarcasm dripping from his voice made me truly question that.

"Are you?" I asked, my breath rattling.

"Curious much, my love?" he purred.

"I am not your anything."

"Mmm …" He took a strand of hair that had loosened from my bun and curled it around his index finger. "Let's see if your presumptions about your payback are correct."

And, with that, he pulled away, his powerful strides aiming for the library's door. "Come, now. It has been a long day, and I am hungry," he said over his shoulder at me.

I just hoped his hunger involved food.

"So, what have you been up to today?" I asked absently as I watched dishes float into the dining room. Floating candles illuminated the great hall in a soft glow. The windows parallel to the table faced the village and the faraway lanterns elongated the shadows.

"Missing me already, love?" Thanatos asked from the opposite side of the long table. His eyes twinkled as he swirled his wine.

I snorted and eyed the food plate hovering in front of me. "Why do you call me 'love?'"

"Why shouldn't I call you that?"

I grunted. The Deathbringer sure as fuck was holding onto his secrets.

"Because it's creepy?" I grabbed the silverware, cutting through the juicy meat.

"You think so?"

I shot him a look over the rim of the food tray floating in front of me.

He chuckled. "*I* think it's cute."

Of course he'd think that. He was the King of the Dead after all. He probably thought all creepy things were cute. I didn't even want to imagine what kind of kinks he might like.

If he wasn't going to have a conversation with me and answer me properly, I surely wasn't going to try dragging responses from him. I took a bite of the meat and closed my eyes when the delicious flavor exploded on my tongue. Food in the Afterlife was amazing. It tasted brighter than anything in the Land of the Living. The flavor was so intense, I forced myself to eat as slowly as possible to relished the taste. I leaned back against the wooden chair with its elegant bow and looked at the way the tall windows reflected the moonlight.

Thanatos didn't seem too interested in the food for he never even spared it a glance. "Do you have family?"

My face crumbled at the mention of those people. "Not anymore."

I'm sure he noticed the way my entire body went rigid at his question, but he let it go. I was grateful he did. I had no interest whatsoever in talking about my family.

Deciding it was time to change the topic, I asked, "Which of the rumors about you are true?"

He rested his arms on his chair. I couldn't help noticing how his biceps bulged beneath his shirt with the new position. "Tell me which ones you have heard, and I'll tell you if they are true."

I took a bite of the salad as I considered carefully which rumors to ask him about. "Your touch can kill."

"True."

I eyed his tall frame over the rim of my wineglass. He had touched me many times, and I hadn't died. "Always?"

"Only when I will it to."

Nodding, I started picking at my food, my appetite forgotten.

"You haven't been in the Land of the Living for centuries." *Until now*, I wanted to add.

"True."

"Why?"

He lifted a shoulder. "I prefer being alone," he explained simply.

Given his profession, that insight into his personal life didn't surprise me. That should settle the question of if he felt lonely.

I decided to act on what Kalira had told me already. I just wanted to make sure she had been correct. "You have never brought a living person to the Afterlife."

"True," he confirmed.

I was sure the Deathbringer must've sensed all the questions lingering on the tip of my tongue, but he did not bother acknowledging any of them. I couldn't stop wondering about his untypical behavior: why had he brought me to the Afterlife if he hadn't done so with anyone else?

But I was too scared of the answer he might give if I'd just ask. So instead, I opted for a rumor well spread among the Living. "Your kiss drains the soul from the body."

His deep laugh rumbled through the dining room and made me shiver. He put his arms on the table. I tensed under his heavy gaze. Even though the table wasn't even remotely large enough for him to reach me, I leaned back in my chair, cautious of the seductive glimmer in his eyes. "Now, *that*, my love, you will have to find out yourself."

Heat spread on my cheeks at what he was insinuating.

Thankfully, the door to the dining hall opened and two cups floated inside, tearing our attention to the dishes. The desserts came down in front of each us. Curiously, I glanced at the dessert. It was a crème brûlée. My stomach rumbled at the sight of the golden-brown crust on top of the crème. I'd always had a soft spot for desserts. Thanatos didn't take his eyes off me for a single second. I avoided his gaze and, deflecting, I decided to ask him one last question. "Is it true you were born with wings?"

I recalled the huge wingspan of his sculpture and the way the thousands of stone-crafted feathers seemed to only add to his majestic features.

He nodded.

I was sure he noticed the delight written on my face. Never once had I met anyone with wings. I was just about to ask him to unfold them when two spoons floated in. I picked mine out of the air. Shifting my weight on the chair, I pushed the spoon against the crust, which made the prettiest cracking sound as it broke.

Carefully, I dipped the tip of the spoon inside the crème and brought it to my lips. I couldn't resist closing my eyes at the taste. It was just the right mixture of the sugar crust and the soft crème below. That was soooo good! Sighing, I put the spoon aside.

"Aren't you going to finish that? You clearly liked it," he noticed, pointing at me with his own spoon.

I shook my head. "Nah. I don't want to eat too much sugar.

It's not healthy." *And it has too many calories.* I looked through the window. Outside, a couple walked along the river.

Thanatos cocked his head to the side. "You will die anyway. You might as well enjoy your life."

Snorting, I tore my eyes from the view. Of course this was his approach to death. "I want to live as long as possible."

He cocked his head to the side. "Why?"

I laughed bitterly. He couldn't be serious. "Why?"

Thanatos nodded.

Wow. Apparently, he *was* being serious. "So I can make the most of it."

His elegantly-curved brows pulled together. "You want to make the most of your life by renouncing the little things that make life worth living?" He shook his head in disbelief. "You living creatures are so odd."

I wasn't sure whether I should feel offended by his statement.

"It is not a secret that your time in the Land of the Living is limited," he proceeded. "And yet, you choose not to enjoy it. Whatever you decide to do with your life, you will die. No matter what you do. You cannot change your destiny. Your whole life has been written in the stars before you were even born." He looked at his palm, tracing the lines of his hands. "The Living have always been so self-centered. Believing they can change destiny just because they will it." He laughed at that and shook his head.

I stared at him thoughtfully. He was probably right. Weren't we so self-centered we believed the universe circled only around ourselves when, in fact, there were so many things more important than us? But did we really not have a say in our own destiny? The sheer existence of the Norns proved he was indeed right. It wasn't us who chose our moment of death, but them.

But even so ….

"I just want to believe that I have at least some sort of control over my life, my choices. That we have a say in our own lives." My mind wandered back to the existence of the Norns, who decided our life's length. "Even if it's just an illusion," I whispered softly, my eyes fixed on the floor.

The Deathbringer watched me the entire time without saying a single word. His gaze dropped to the mole on my wrist before jumping up to my face again. He squared his jaw.

Suddenly, he stood, his chair scraping with his movement. His standing frame made me realize how tall and obviously inhuman he was. He cut through the space between us slowly, the sound of his heavy footsteps resonating in the big room. I swallowed hard as he stopped right next to me. My fingers clamped around the wineglass.

Extending his hand, he tenderly traced my jaw. "We do not get a choice in what happens to us, who we meet, or the reasons for it."

My breathing had become hollow, pushing my ribcage dramatically up and down with each inhale and exhale. Some of his hair had loosened from his man bun, tickling my shoulder at his proximity. "But whatever reasons destiny had to bring us together … I am more than excited about them."

CHAPTER TEN

The next couple of days were pretty uneventful. I spent most of my time in the library and reading, reveling in spending so much time alone. Back in the Land of the Living, acting lessons and castings had always kept me busy, and when I eventually got home, Miriam was there. God knew I loved her, but living with a roommate didn't grant me as much free time as I'd like.

I wasn't alone the entire time, though. Kalira was with me each day, making sure I got my daily dose of social contact and checking in on me on a regular basis.

I had barely seen Thanatos over the last couple of days. When I'd asked Kalira what he was up to, she'd shrugged and said he had business that required his attention. Immediately after asking for the King of the Dead I had felt stupid for wondering. Of course he was busy. He had important stuff to deal with. Much more important than me.

Eventually, after days spent in the library and my room, I got sick of staying in the castle.

I was just putting on my shoes to head out to Emoh when Kalira glared at me from across my bedroom. Her brows pinched together as she observed me closely. "This is not what I was expecting to get out of this job." She crossed her arms in front of her chest.

Ignoring her, I stepped past her, leaving my bedroom through the corridor. "What did you expect?"

I heard her reluctantly start following me, her feet dragging. "I don't know. Probably a little, spoiled princess who barely moves," she offered.

I shot her a side-glance. Why was she complaining? It was literally the first time in days I'd left the castle. "I am not a princess," I muttered.

"Clearly," Kalira murmured under her breath.

Obviously, she wasn't too keen on going to the village. When Thanatos had showed me Emoh, I hadn't gotten the chance to explore the adorable stands. Today seemed a perfect day to do so. I couldn't spend another day sitting around without having anything to distract myself with. Over and over my mind replayed everything that had happened since the day the Deathbringer had saved me.

But the worst thing about this entire situation was that I felt... *lost*. My entire life had been solely focused on becoming an actress. But now? My fellow actors' refusal to help the beaten boy at our presentation had shown me the true colors of my colleagues. All of them had been willing to give up their moral standards in order to become famous and succeed in their careers. I couldn't become like that. But if not acting, what could I possibly pursue? Without the one thing my entire life had been focused on for so long, how could I know who I was any longer?

And of course I was perfectly aware of the fact that I was dismissing an entire profession based on the experience I had from *one* acting academy, in *one* town, at *one* performance, but right now, I couldn't even think about getting back into that profession and figuratively prostituting myself in order to make a name in that industry. Not after that haunting experience in the theatre. A trip perusing Emoh's shops was just the thing to get my mind off of acting.

Kalira groaned as she followed me through the castle toward the main entrance, efficiently ripping me away from my thoughts. "Why don't you just ask our King to get you whatever you need?" She smiled slyly at me. "I'm sure he'll get it for you."

Lifting a brow at her, I kept striding down the path leading to Emoh.

Sighing, she struggled to keep my pace. "We had so much fun."

I cast her a glare over my shoulder. "*You* had fun." Kalira and I had spent the entire day playing dress up. Or rather, Kalira had. I had just needed to stay still while she fixed my braided hair in a circle at the back of my neck.

"Well, it was definitely more fun than *walking*." To underscore her words, she kicked a small stone out of our path.

Watching it roll away, I smiled to myself. Kalira was probably the laziest person I knew.

We passed the flower-covered hills until we reached the village. The air was heavy with the smell of food wafting from the restaurants over to us. I let my eyes drift over the small space. The market was set up in a round town square surrounded by small shops. A gurgling fountain sat in the middle of it. It was just now that I saw all the triangular flags hung up all around Emoh displaying the same royal crest of the Afterlife I'd seen at the castle. The moons on the flags vibrated in silver with the way the surrounding illumination reflected on them, and the stars on the crest glittered as though they were real stars, and not just gold-dust sprinkled on top of a simple, black fabric. I looked back at the shops. The stands stood closely packed, each one a simple wooden framework decorated with the most colorful fabric I had ever seen.

Awed, I approached the closest stand.

The stand's owner smiled warmly at me. "Welcome."

I blushed and smiled back at him. "Hi!" I wasn't used to people greeting me. People were much more reserved in the Land of the Living.

He wore a tight-fitting suit in the style of the 1960s. His gray mustache was well looked after, the two tips curled upward, almost touching his nose. I realized he was a werewolf as I noticed how hairy his forearms were. I should've noticed that before just by looking at his wide-built physique.

My gaze dropped to the table between us where dresses as flimsy and delicate as spiderwebs were outspread. I was almost afraid to touch them as fragile and yet graceful as they appeared to be. The fabric had been worked almost to perfection. I lifted one dress and examined the seam of it. Growing up, I'd hand-made much of my clothing so I knew from experience how hard it was to craft the fabric this impeccably. "This is the work of an artist," I murmured to myself in awe.

The owner's eyes lit up at my praise. "Thank you! If you have any questions or need any advice, just let me know," he said in a friendly, matter-of-fact manner.

"Thank you! I will," I promised, putting the fabric neatly back the way I had found it.

I moved on through the countless stands, eyeing their various offerings. The vendors were selling fresh vegetables, pearls, clothes, and soft fabrics. I was completely taken aback at the thorough work of the sellers. Everything they sold was handcrafted. All of them were true professionals in their fields. "This is gorgeous!" I breathed as I carefully threaded my fingers through the thin fabric of a scarf.

Kalira, who had been following me the entire time, leaned against a table and crossed her feet at the ankles. "Hey. Do you mind?"

I lifted my gaze to her. She wiggled a pack of cigarettes in front of me, nodding to the other side of the small market.

Surprised at her indulgence for not simply leaving, I nodded. "Um. Sure. Go ahead."

She left as she took a cigarette out of the small pack.

I looked back at the scarf.

"Can I help you?" A fragile female voice said.

My gaze came to the female seller who looked at me from across the table, a warm smile on her lips. She wore a big, coarse dress that seemed like it came from the 19th century.

I gestured to the scarf. "You made this by yourself?" I asked, reverence lightening my tone.

The woman nodded, the natural blush of her cheeks deepening. "Yes."

"It's beautiful!" The scarf was intertwined with thin, glittering threads that shone vibrantly underneath the light of the lanterns. I couldn't fathom how long it must have taken her to finish.

Her proud smile widened. "Thank you! It's—"

"Mom!"

Both of us turned to the high-pitched voice. A boy came running through the small passage between the stands. The resemblance to his mother was unmistakable. He had the same rosy cheeks and brown hair. Just like his mother, he also wore clothing from what must've been the 19th century.

"What is it, my cutie-pie?" The mother crouched down, easily picking up the boy. She gave him a small kiss on the top of his nose.

"Mom!" He complained, pushing against her hold on him. "Not in front of others," he whispered loud enough for me to hear.

She chuckled, letting him down.

I hid my smile, pretending to look at the different fabrics and tracing my fingers over the material to grant them some privacy.

How beautiful it must feel to be this cherished by your loved ones.

I shot a glance to the boy, my body suddenly growing cold. How old must he be? Five? Maybe six? My heart broke for him. He'd still had his entire life in front of him when he had died. How could destiny be so cruel? At least the boy and his mother had been able to rejoin in death. Despite my limited knowledge about the people living in Emoh, it still surprised me that families were able to live together in the Afterlife until it was time for their reincarnations. It somehow made the tension ease off my shoulders.

My stomach knotted up. Who'd wait for me? Would there even be someone waiting? And if someone did, would I actually *want* to meet them?

The woman knelt in front of the boy as she searched his eyes. "What is it, hon?"

The all-too-familiar nickname stung my heart, reminding me of the person I *did* want to see again. I really hoped Miriam was doing okay without knowing my whereabouts. She must be sick with worry.

"Another man went to the Forest of the Lost Souls today." The boy's voice was stammering from his running. He needed to catch his breath with every few words.

The mother looked shocked. "Again?"

The choppiness of his voice made it hard to understand him. "Yeah, and I saw him walking there. I wanted to stop him, but—"

"You what?" The mother screeched, her worry clearly detectable in her expression. "You shouldn't have done that. Everyone knows the dangers that lurk within that forest. It's each and everyone's own decision if they decide to take the risk to contact the Living."

My body froze.

It shouldn't surprise me, but it still did. I had not thought of the possibility that the Dead might also wish to contact the Living. Along with the bracelets she made, Ouija-boards and trances were some of Miriam's most popular items. I had always thought it was only the Living who wished to get in contact with the Dead. But apparently, it was also the other way around.

The child nodded slowly. His attention was fixed on his mother's hair. He glided his small, tubby fingers through it. "I know. But maybe he—"

The mother shook her head vigorously. "I don't want to hear it."

"There's a way to contact the Land of the Living?" I chimed in, not able to control my excitement.

The woman tore her eyes away from her son, clearly remembering that I still stood at her stand. After flashing her son one last lecturing look, she rose. "Pardon me?"

"Is there truly a way to contact the Land of the Living?" I asked again. My voice trembled with nerves.

She laughed nervously. "Oh no. Sadly, there isn't"

"But you just said—"

"I'm afraid you misunderstood." Her eyes dropped to her son. "Oh, James! Look at you! You ruined your shirt again." She reached down to James, lifting him into her arms, before turning back to me. "You'll have to excuse me. I have to take care of my son." She hurried away, leaving her stand unsupervised.

I stared after her.

If there truly were a way to contact the Living, I'd make sure to find it.

Kalira groaned as she followed me up the path toward the castle.

Amused, I watched how she forced herself up the alley. "You know you don't need to come with me, right?"

She caught up to me, her piercings reflecting the light. "I have my duties. The King wanted me to keep an eye on you."

"You didn't mind it when I wanted to be alone when I first arrived." I called her out on the day I had wandered alone through the castle and found the library.

"Yeah, well. Your lover sought me out."

I came to a sudden halt to stare at her. "What?"

Kalira's brows knit together. "He didn't tell you? He told me I shouldn't have left you alone that day. He commanded me to stay with you, or at least check in on you regularly."

That bastard. I had already wondered why Kalira bothered to stay with me all those days when I did nothing other than curl up on one of the library sofas. And those times I had been alone? She had checked on me frequently. And idiot me had thought I had spent most of my time in solitude, when in fact I had been supervised perpetually.

What had the Deathbringer said? That I wasn't his prisoner? Oh, that was rich of him.

Angrily, I yanked open the castle's heavy entrance door. Kalira's small figure had a hard time catching up to me as I rushed through the foyer.

"How dare he send you to babysit me!" I was perfectly capable of taking care of myself. As much as I may have come to accept Kalira's presence, I didn't need someone to check on me. "He has no right to do that. And besides," I smoothed down my wrinkled skirt, "he is not my lover."

Shrugging, Kalira gave me a side-glance. "If that makes you feel better …."

"He's not," I sneered. I was so caught up in my anger, I didn't notice the floating candles or the way the moonlight flooded inside the hall.

"Mm-hmm."

I narrowed my eyes at her. "What?"

"Nothing." She gave me a sly smile. "I know you probably don't want to hear it, but his entire demeanor says otherwise. First, he saves you, then he offers you the Afterlife as exile, then he moves your bedchamber next to his own, and now he's making sure somebody is looking out for you. Those are pretty solid indicators for the state of your relationship."

Clenching my teeth, I kept rushing through the castle. Even though I didn't want to listen or believe her, her trail of thoughts made sense. Which made me all the more angry.

Kalira's melodic voice drew my attention back to her. "But don't you ever wonder?"

"What?"

She rolled her eyes at me. "Oh, come on. Don't be so shifty." She nudged her elbow into my side as she wiggled her eyebrows at me. "Don't you ever wonder what it'd be like sleeping with him?"

"I'd ... I'd never do that. Or want that." I knew I sounded defensive.

Kalira's eyes became distant. "He's so tall. And you do have to admit he's handsome."

I mumbled under my breath. Why, out of all people, would Thanatos choose *her* as my babysitter?

"If his body is so big, I can only imagine what his di—"

"Where is he?" I interrupted Kalira through clenched teeth before she had a chance to start discussing certain theories about the Deathbringer's anatomy with me.

Kalira fell silent. She eyed me warily. "Why?"

"I have a bone to pick with him." The King of the Dead might think he had the right to set somebody up to look out for me. But he didn't. And I meant to remind him of it.

The double-doors to the dining room burst open as I pushed against it. They crashed into the walls forcefully.

My eyes zeroed in on Thanatos who sat at the head of the table, papers spread out in front of him. Calmly, his eyes lifted from them.

His mouth tipped up as he took me in. "Hello, love."

"How dare you?" I stomped forward. Kalira had wisely decided to stay in the foyer. Now, I was alone with the King of the Afterlife.

He reclined against his chair and lifted a hand. Silently, the doors fell closed behind me.

As soon as I reached him, I crushed my hands on the table's surface. Thanatos didn't so much as blink.

"Kalira," I sneered.

"The kitten has extended her claws," he murmured, delight flashing in his gaze as he watched me.

Moving into his personal space, I poked his chest with my index finger."You put a fucking babysitter on me."

His brows drew together. "Now, calm down. What is it that's bothering you?"

He pretended he didn't know what I was talking about. The audacity!

I threw out my hands. "Kalira. You told her she shouldn't leave my side. Why? I am not a fucking child." I felt every emotion I had been trying so desperately to suppress building to a crescendo."I am an adult. I can dress myself, I can bathe myself, and I sure as fuck can walk around by myself without needing to be leashed up."

Thanatos's eyes lightened as he leaned forward. "You don't

need to be. But do you *want* to be leashed up?" His expression turned pensive. "Didn't know that was your kink."

Incredulously, I stared at him. He. Could. Not. Be. Fucking. Serious. "What is it with you and your sexual needs?"

When he stood, his chair scraped against the marble floor. He stepped up to me, forcing me to bend my head back. "I told you. There's the possibility I have been lonely." Playfully, he batted his ridiculously long eyelashes at me.

Ohhh, I was done.

I shoved him away as hard as I could.

But in the same second that my hands connected with his chest, Thanatos grabbed my wrists. Before I could brace myself, he swirled me around. My back crushed against his hard chest. My wrists were tightly locked in front of my breasts by one of his hands.

"Uh, uh, uh, love. We do not work with violence. Words are the way to happiness," he reprimanded me cheerfully.

"Fuck you!" I spat, fighting against his hold on me.

He clicked his tongue and shook his head. "Not that kind of words." He sounded so *disappointed*.

"You can shove your words up your a—""

"You don't want to talk?" he interrupted. "Fine by me. Let's get to the fun stuff instead."

That shut me up good.

Breathing hard, I swallowed and squeezed my eyes shut.

I had forgotten.

I had forgotten who it was I lived with. Thanatos wasn't just a man. He was a powerful King who could kill me in a split second if he wished.

I forced myself to take deep breaths until I felt my body relax.

"Why did you tell Kalira to keep track of me?" I swallowed as I stared at a point across the room. "You said I'm not your prisoner," I whispered.

Suddenly stern, he answered, "You aren't. But I—"

"Then why did you order someone to look out for me?"

He fell silent, clearly weighing his answer. His voice grew lower as he responded. "I thought you might enjoy some company. To not be alone."

That was ... *kind* of him. But, even so, he didn't have the right to make decisions for me. "Stop assuming things about me."

My body had relaxed; his hold on me slowly loosening. His thumb was idly drawing small circles on the back of my hand. I wasn't sure if he did it to soothe me or if he did it unconsciously, but his touch *did* calm me.

I tried turning around once again, and this time, he let me. I gazed up at him, meeting his searching stare. "I prefer that you ask me."

He held my gaze before nodding. "You are right. I am sorry."

Surprised, I squinted. I hadn't expected him to agree so easily. Especially not after the way I had burst into the room. "It's fine," I said, accepting his apologies.

"Do you want me to send Kalira away?"

I shook my head. "No, it's fine." She probably depended on this job. "Just tell her that she may leave me when I want to be left alone, please."

He nodded.

"Thanks." Noticing how near I stood to him, I took a step back and cleared my throat. I peeked up at him cautiously. Should I ask him? Maybe I ...

He noticed my inner tumult. "What is it?"

"It's just …" I worried my lip.

His eyes grew impatient as he saw my struggle. "What is it?"

"When do you think King Silvan will give up searching for me so I can go back home?"

He stared at me, and I saw something in his eyes break; something so small and fragile, I'd almost missed it. A distant look grew on his features. He looked away, his Adam's apple bobbing. "I don't know," he admitted. "But I will keep you safe in Emoh until he gets bored of waiting."

Something about the fact that he was willing to protect me made my stomach clench.

"But the length of your stay doesn't depend on Silvan," he admitted, his voice hoarse.

Confused, I looked up at him. Hadn't he brought me to the Afterlife to make sure Silvan wouldn't be able to get to me? "What does it depend on?" I asked, suddenly nervous.

Silence descended on us, making the seconds tick by with painful slowness. My entire body sizzled with nerves as I braced for his answer.

Slowly, he walked back to the end of the table and grabbed his wineglass. He swirled the liquid before bringing his gaze back to me. A muscle in his jaw feathered.

"Me."

I slipped into my bedroom and closed the door behind me. Exhaling, I leaned against it, desperately trying to catch my breath.

The entire time I had been in the Afterlife, I had assumed Thanatos had kept me here to protect me from Silvan. But now?

This changed *everything*.

My stomach somersaulted at the knowledge of the Deathbringer's decision to keep me here with him. Then again, what had I expected? The signs were there. But I hadn't dared to read them.

I walked over to the balcony connected to my bedroom and approached the railing. I took a deep breath before I lay down to have a better visual of the stars twinkling above.

If it was the Deathbringer's call to decide when I left the Afterlife, there was no way to know when that might be. And that meant I needed to tell Miriam I was all right. Miriam and I had gone through hell together and survived only because we had been there for each other. I owed her the truth.

The Forest of the Lost Souls. If there were truly a way to contact the Living, I could talk to Mir. There would be no way for Silvan to know. You couldn't track magic. Mir would be safe.

A knock on my door made me jump. Was this finally the night my payback would begin? I stood on shaking legs and swallowed hard before smoothing out the wrinkled fabric of my dress. "Come in!" I called, bracing myself for the King of the Dead.

My shoulders dropped as Kalira opened the door and slipped inside.

Could this hollow feeling in my chest be ... *disappointment*? No.

"Hi! I just wanted to help you undress," she said, smiling.

I narrowed my eyes at her. That was the worst excuse for what she truly wanted: to know what had happened between Thanatos and me after I'd left her standing in the hallway and rushed to the King.

I opened my mouth to tell her I could undress by myself, but then I remembered the thousands of buttons Kalira had secured at my back before we'd left for the village. "Sure."

Kalira gestured to the vanity in my room and walked into the bathroom to get everything she needed.

Sighing, I took a seat in front of the mirror and exhaled slowly. My shoulders sagged as I heard Kalira's movements in the bathroom. It was sad, actually. Now that I knew Thanatos had ordered her to spend time with me, I knew she did so because she felt obligated. That it was her job. I mean, I knew from the beginning that Thanatos had asked her to help me around, but it was something different that he'd ordered her to spend her *time* with me … Even though she annoyed me most of the time, I had thought she stayed with me because she wanted to, not because the Deathbringer had told her to. It shouldn't make any difference, but it *did*.

Pushing those thoughts aside, I glanced at my reflection.

Since my arrival in the Afterlife, Kalira had always taken care of my hair and makeup, but not once had I bothered to contemplate her work. I didn't look tired. Her work hid it well. The smoky eyeshadow she had chosen made my eyes look bigger than they actually were, and the highlighter emphasized my facial contours. And even the dress Kalira had chosen for me didn't look as revealing as it had felt when I put it on earlier. It did emphasize some of my natural curves, but still left most of my body to the imagination. Only my eyes looked exhausted. They were missing their usual spark.

Kalira reentered the bedroom and began rummaging through

the small bag where she kept the makeup and her other utensils. She took out a hairbrush and moved behind me. Usually, I would tell her to let me brush my own hair, but I was too worn out to face the discussion that would happen if I told her so tonight.

Carefully, she started undoing the braid. "How did it go?" she asked innocently.

I ran a hand over my face. "Fine."

Kalira flashed me a curious look in the mirror. To my surprise, she didn't ask any more questions. Did I look that drained?

"So, what is it you do every day when you aren't gracing me with your presence?" I asked, knowing perfectly well the way she could drift off once she started talking. It was precisely what I needed. A distraction from my own thoughts and worries.

She clicked her tongue, making the piercing in her mouth click against her teeth. "I like to paint. Me and some other people in the village meet quite regularly to paint together. You are free to join if you want," she offered, focused on her task at hand.

I shook my head. "I can't paint."

She chuckled. "Neither can we. It's more like a social gathering. You know, to catch up with the local gossip. Some also sew or embroider clothing and other stuff."

"It must be nice," I murmured, watching Kalira unwind my braid. "I never thought the Afterlife was like this."

Kalira nodded in agreement. "No one did. But believe me: there are parts of the Afterlife you'd not enjoy seeing."

Surprised, I lifted a brow. I recalled Thanatos telling me how all the Dead live in villages. "Not everyone lives in the villages?"

"No," she said, stressing the word. Her copper hair shimmered like flames as she shook her head.

My brows furrowed at this new information. "Why? How do the rest live?"

"I don't know. Most of us live in one of the villages, but I've heard stories about other places ... I truly hope they are rumors, nothing more." She shivered.

Thoughtfully, I traced the bracelet Miriam had gifted me. And then, an idea began forming. "Kalira?"

"Hmm?" Her brows were furrowed as she removed the pins from my hair.

"What is the easiest way to get to the Forest of the Lost Souls?"

Her movements stopped. She lifted her head, meeting my gaze in the reflection of the mirror. "The Forest of the Lost Souls is not a place to seek out," she said, her voice thin. She dropped her head, focusing back on the braid.

Damn. I had never seen her close down like this. She wasn't going to help me. Maybe I needed to—

"The very last place I'd suggest you look for it would be behind the village. After passing the last river running through it. That is definitely the way I'd not ever choose to walk." She punctuated her words by tugging the newly loosened strands of my former braid. "But if you somehow, for whatever reason, should walk there, it would be wise to bring sage with you. It keeps the spirits at ease." As she spoke, she began opening the buttons at the back of my dress. "People go to that forest to contact the Living. They seek out the witches who live there." She shivered, opening the last of the buttons. "It is said they can be found at the very centre of the forest." She bent down, putting the brush back in the bag.

Relief flooded me when I realized what Kalira was saying.

She knew this information was important to me. And even though, she probably shouldn't, she was willing to share it with me.

Kalira's voice was cheerful as she met my gaze in the mirror. "You are all set." She squeezed my shoulders. "Sleep tight, Cassiana!"

And with those departing words, she moved out of the room, winking at me before letting the door fall shut behind her.

CHAPTER ELEVEN

8 years ago

My alarm went off on my nightstand. Slowly, I blinked my eyes open, trying my best not to look at the date on my calendar. I dressed quickly in a daze, not taking in my surroundings. I padded to the kitchen and froze dead in my tracks.

My father sat in the living room, his hands folded neatly atop the desk. I assessed him warily. Lately, he'd grown even more reserved toward me than usual. But today was different. I saw it in the way his eyes were distant. In the way his features turned stark when he met my gaze. My dad had always hated me. I never understood the reason for it, though. His feelings toward me had gotten worse since Mom killed herself.

"You look like her," he'd said to me on one of those nights when his drinking habits got out of hand and I had to carry him to bed. The words had stung. Not because my mom had been ugly, but because he had said those words with the intention of hurting me. Because he hated how I reminded him of her. I was a constant *reminder of the woman who had preferred taking her own life instead of living with a monster like him. She hadn't been able to stand the way he had treated me my whole life. That was what drove her to end her life. Or at least that was the reason I kept telling myself.*

I didn't dare think of the alternative: that she had hated herself for bearing a child so much, she had chosen to leave this world.

"Pack your stuff." His gaze was completely wiped of emotions.

I stared at him, the words barely registering. Once they did, my heart skipped a beat and a shiver coursed through my entire body, making me shake from the inside out. "What?"

He brought his gaze to me. It was only now that I saw the rage in his eyes. The determination. I knew there was no way to talk him out of this. I saw it in the stiffness of his body and in the way he looked at me with contempt. Even after all these years, it still shocked me. He was my dad after all.

I wasn't stupid enough to beg him to change his mind. I had learned the hard way that begging only amplified his distaste toward me.

"I have nowhere to go. I have no money," I whispered.

A muscle jumped in his jaw. "Don't you think I know? You have been living off my coin your entire life."

I flinched. Not once had I used his money except for food. I looked down at myself. My clothes were ripped, their color worn from years of wear.

I took a step forward. "Dad—"

He lifted a hand and cut me off. "Don't," the next words came out harshly, clipped, "call me that." He locked his jaw. "Leave."

The word echoed off the walls of our sterile kitchen, making them sound so much more final.

"But—"

He slammed his fists on the table, making the objects on it rattle.

I jumped at his outburst.

"You leave right now or you'll regret this day." My father's body was tense. He looked ready to charge. From his expression alone, I knew he was serious.

Deadly *serious.*

A sob threatened to tear through me. Protectively, I curled my arms around my body's midsection and nodded in resignation.

I walked back to my room and began collecting the things I deemed important enough to bring with me into my navy bag. Which, to be honest, wasn't much. It took me much longer than it should have to take the small plastic decorations off the ceiling. The adhesive tape had long ago dried, and it was nearly impossible to remove the small objects that over years and years had granted me comfort and solace from the wall.

Once I had gathered everything I needed, I turned around, assessing my room. It had never been filled with a lot of things anyway. But now that the few things I'd always considered important were gone, it felt as though nobody lived here.

Nobody does anymore.

I turned off the light and dragged my bag through the living room to the door. My father remained sitting in the exact same position I had left him, his eyes staring distantly at something only he was able to see.

Opening the door, I glanced back at my father. He had folded his arms in front of his chest, his back to me.

"Bye, Dad," I whispered.

His body tensed at the last word, but other than that small reaction, his body remained eerily still. He did not even glance back at me. At his own daughter, his own blood.

The sound of my sob mixed with the sound of the door falling shut behind me.

Weren't parents supposed to be the ones to reassure us? To be there for us? To love us?

My dad had chosen the very first opportunity he had to get rid of me.

Happy eighteenth birthday to me.

The next morning, Kalira joined me for a walk in the village. Thanatos must have told her to listen to me whenever I decided to be left alone, because today, she didn't complain like she used to when I was already dressed without her help and ready to get moving.

"Kalira?"

She tore her eyes away from a dancing couple and looked back at me. "Hmm?"

"Where would I get sage if I needed some?"

She gave me a sneaky smile. "Come with me."

I followed her through a maze of Emoh's small passages so hidden that I hadn't noticed them before. They connected to each other, making it impossible to orientate oneself, but Kalira seemed to know her way around because she didn't hesitate once.

We stopped in front of a tiny house. Whereas the houses in the centre of the village were all painted in the most vibrant colors and deeply cared for, this house was the opposite. Plants grew over it, hiding the windows and darkening it completely.

Smiling, Kalira moved a bunch of leaves to the side. She revealed a thick, wooden door and knocked on it twice.

As the door opened by itself, it groaned loudly, as though that simple act were enough to bring the house to its limits. Shivers ran down my spine as I followed Kalira inside. There would be no way in hell I'd enter this house by myself, but Kalira didn't seem nervous in the slightest.

The inside of the small cottage was as dilapidated as the outside. Drying herbs and crystals were set up and hung *everywhere*. The moon barely managed to illuminate the room, the plants in front of the windows too thick to let the light stream in. Some floating candles lit up the space, but the flames were too small to cast the house in sufficient brightness. The house seemed to absorb every sound, muting every breath and movement.

"That is a very powerful bracelet you are carrying, child," a woman's voice creaked from the backside of the cottage.

Startled, I spotted a woman standing in front of a cauldron. Her silvery eyes blinked. A witch. The resemblance to Miriam and her eye color drove a sting through my chest.

The woman was wearing a moss-green dress that complemented her long, gray hair she kept cascading over her back. She had kind eyes. Eyes that took me in with a little too much interest to be entirely casual.

I looked down at the bracelet Miriam had given me. "Yeah. I got it from my best friend."

The woman lifted her gaze to me. Her skin shone sweaty from the cauldron's heat. She moved away from the fire and grabbed a bundle of gray herbs. She weighed it from one hand to the other before moving to the opposite side of the room, searching for something in one of her wooden trunks. I shot Kalira a questioning side-glance, but she was too preoccupied assessing her nails to notice.

Holding an object in her hand, the woman stood. She approached me, and it took everything within me not to flinch away when she reached out to touch my neck.

I swallowed hard, my gaze flickering to Kalira, but she didn't seem alarmed by the witch's weird behavior.

It was only when the witch put more pressure on the side of my neck with her fingers that I noticed she was focusing on my pulse.

"Alive indeed," she muttered. Her silvery eyes paled when she tore her hand back. "Here you go."

Dumbfounded, I accepted the bundle of herbs she handed me.

"Sage to keep the spirits at bay and the nightcrawlers away," she explained, turning back toward the cauldron.

I stared at the objects in my hand. I didn't know what nightcrawlers were, but I chose not to dwell on it for too long. "How did you—?"

Kalira pushed herself away from the wall. "Minerva knows what everyone needs," she explained.

I nodded as though I'd understood.

"She's our healer," she elaborated.

Minerva smiled at me.

That was ... interesting. Why would the Dead need a healer?

"Thank you!" I said and followed Kalira back to the house's entrance.

"Of course, darling," Minerva said.

I was just about to close the door when her voice stopped me.

"Be careful out there. It would be a shame to lose the only pulse in the Afterlife."

And, with that, the door shut closed in my face with so much more vigor than it had opened.

Kalira led the way through the outskirts of Emoh to the Forest of the Lost Souls. The journey was not as long as I had first thought it would be. After passing the last river running through Emoh, it took us no more than twenty minutes before the Village of the Dead was no longer visible behind a small hill. The simple stone path we followed led us straight from Minerva's cottage to a trail junction. The wooden signs led the way either to Emoh or toward the Forest of the Lost Souls. At least, the latter was what I deduced when Kalira chose to head the direction of a dirty, washed out sign. Its letters weren't decipherable any longer, only chips of paint still stuck onto the rotten sign. The path, so much less cared for than all the small passages in Emoh, guided us over another meadow. After a while, far in the distance, I was able to spot the Forest. It looked like a wall of darkness, like a tsunami threatening to hit Emoh. The closer we came to it, the more barren our surroundings became. There was less flora and more and more dried patches of grass.

My spit got stuck in my throat when we came to a stop before the Forest of the Lost Souls. It stood like a dark force before us, the trees as unmoving as the the stillness of the stars above. The trees stood so closely to each other they swallowed all light, making it impossible to peek at what lay within.

I turned to Kalira. She had been quiet throughout the entire journey. Her untypical behavior did nothing to soothe my nerves. "Is it a stupid idea to seek out these witches?"

"It is." She didn't even try sugarcoating the truth for me.

I fisted the sage bundle as if my dear life depended on it. Which it probably did. Back at home, only the most powerful witches could contact the Dead, and they weren't always working with white magic. I guessed it was the same for the witches who contacted the Living. After all, there must be a reason for the reputation preceding them. I could still remember how worried the woman at the marketplace had been when her son mentioned the forest. "You are not being reassuring."

"I'm not trying to be." She took a step forward. "Cassiana, it is said that there are things in this forest that have turned visitors to stone just from the way they looked."

When Kalira had first mentioned the Forest of the Lost Souls to me, she had given me the impression that she'd already gone there herself. That had reassured me—at least to some degree. But now that I knew she hadn't, the thought of going in didn't seem as appealing as it first had.

Shivering, I stared at the forest's darkness. What had Thanatos said? That the Norns lived past the Forest of the Lost Souls. Which meant I already had a pretty solid idea of what might await me once I entered.

My gaze jumped to Kalira. "Why are you helping me?" I asked the question that had been pressing on me from the moment she had explained the way to the forest.

Kalira looked at the trees. "Because when I was still alive, I had a friend who died. She made sure to seek me out as soon as she could." Her eyes became distant, lost in thought as she clearly struggled to keep back her tears. "I wouldn't keep it from anyone to experience that kind of gratitude to know that the Land of the Dead cared for their loved ones."

Understanding spread within me. So, to some extent, she *had* experienced contacting the witches of Forest of the Lost Souls, only from the living side. "Did you meet her in Emoh?" I queried, my voice gentle.

Kalira shook her head. "No. I didn't have a chance to. When I died, her soul had already reincarnated."

I nodded. Reincarnation. Every time someone died, that person's soul came to the Afterlife and a different soul from the Land of the Dead was reborn.

Kalira lit the sage bundle. The smoke lifted in small circles into the air. "When you find the witches, they will make you appear where you want to go. You will only have a couple of minutes to get in contact with whomever you seek before you are drawn back to the Afterlife. Both of the universes are too far apart to prolong that time." She handed the sage bundle to me.

I nodded as I tried to process all the information.

Kalira searched my face and squeezed my upper arm. "I will be waiting here for you."

Even though I'd rather not go into the Forest of the Lost Souls alone, I couldn't bring myself to ask her to join me. If entering were truly as dangerous as everyone deemed it to be, I wouldn't risk her safety, too. Additionally, I didn't want Kalira to be present when I managed to talk to Miriam. I wanted to talk to her in private.

The thought of seeing Miriam's face filled me with new courage. I shivered as I took a step forward. My gaze raked over the trees. They grew in a perfectly straight, unnatural line, before giving in to wilderness. There was not one single leaf growing over that first invisible line. Taking a deep breath, I braced myself.

Before I could step over the tree line, Kalira's voice called to me.

"Cassiana!"

I turned around to face her.

Her gaze sharpened on me. "Be careful of the nightcrawlers. You will not notice them. They are creatures as dark as the night itself. As long as you keep that sage bundle with you, you should be fine."

I forced myself to flash her a reassuring smile before I stepped through the tree line.

As soon as I entered the forest, every sound was swallowed up at once. Shivers ran down my bare arms, and it took everything in me not to turn around and get back to the cozy village with its marvelous smells, people, and colors.

But Miriam needed to know I was all right. And I needed to know Miriam was all right. Especially if Silvan still kept an eye on things in the Land of the Living.

So, instead of running back to Emoh like I wanted to, I walked further into the darkness of the forest.

It is said they can be found at the very centre of the forest.

I crept as quietly as possible, keeping my eyes and ears open for any threat as I went further into the woods. It was probably just my imagination, but as soon as I put a foot in front of me, the surrounding, obsidian-colored darkness seemed to move further back, almost as though it'd purposefully enlighten my vision.

Trying to get rid of that absurd thought, I shook my head. My mind was already playing tricks on me.

Usually, I did not mind darkness, but this was different. This darkness seemed unnatural, almost threatening. As if creatures lived within the shadows waiting for me to get closer, so close they would need only extend their hands to grab me and snatch me to whatever horrific places they lived.

The sound of my swallowing made me jump. I laughed darkly at that. I was already growing mad. I continued my way faster and faster, the sound of my steps so incredibly loud.

This was probably the stupidest decision I had ever made, but the end result would be worth it.

Miriam putting two bowls of water on the floor. Miriam placing one crystal and one candle on the floor. Miriam murmuring her spell. Candlelight.

The images flashed before my inner eye. My memory of that day alone made me move faster, deeper into the forest. Instinctively, I knew it couldn't be very far now. The knowledge that I would soon talk to Miriam filled me with both guilt and anticipation. Guilt because I had let her wait so long, and anticipation because I could fix that now.

There were no paths, no trails to know my way around. There was nothing but me moving through the thicket of dead shrubbery and fallen branches. My hands clamped around the sage stick, my skin beginning to slicken.

I didn't know how much further I still had to go into the forest, but I was sure once I—

Something next to me snapped. I froze. I forced my body to take shallow breaths and listened.

Nothing. Nothing but the ongoing silence.

Had I imagined the sound?

Snap.

I jerked my head around. I felt the eyes on me even before I noticed them shining through the lingering darkness.

I stepped away from whatever it was that hid in the woods.

And that was my mistake.

I stumbled over a loose stone. Losing my balance, I fell. The impact whooshed the air from my lungs and ripped the sage bundle from my hold.

Desperately, I coughed, trying to get my body to work. I tried pushing myself into a sitting position as my attention was drawn to the creatures that had been watching me, hidden in the shadows. I drew in a staggering breath and shrunk back. I didn't understand what I saw at first—the bony figures, the ripped clothing—but when I did, a scream as horrendous as these creatures coursed through me.

If I had thought the Norns were scary, they were nothing compared to these things. The Norns at least bore some resemblance to humans. But these creatures?

They were born to feed nightmares.

Their pale skin looked as though it had been crafted out of bones, and their bald heads gleamed against the night's darkness. There was no way to tell how many there were. Their mad eyes raked hungrily over me, spit dripping out of their mouths. Black, ripped clothing hid their figures.

The nightcrawlers crawled toward me on all fours, their movements stiff and uncoordinated. Now I knew why these creatures had been given their name.

I backed away from them. "Stay away!" I demanded, my voice shaking.

My gaze jumped to the sage bundle I had dropped. It lay only a couple of feet away from me.

No, no, no, no!

I made to get a hold of the sage, but the nightcrawlers were too fast. They blocked my way, their long claws scraping over the hard ground.

As if it would do any good, I lifted my hands in surrender. Some of the creatures cocked their heads as they emitted clicking sounds.

As I backed away, I tried recalling anything that might help me, but the only thing I remembered was Kalira telling me to not let go of the sage.

My back hit a tree.

FUCK.

Cold sweat began coating my skin. In a new attempt to get to the sage, I moved to the side, but the nightcrawlers reacted quickly yet again, successfully caging me in. I searched their eyes, trying to find a flicker of humanity in them. But there was nothing. Nothing that would make them stop.

Never once had I thought I'd die like this: in a dark forest, surrounded by creatures whose appearance alone made my blood run cold.

Their ice-cold skin brushed my own, and their ripped clothing grazed against the soft material of my velvet dress, reminding me of a time when I myself had worn such ragged clothing as they did.

I pressed my back against the tree bark. I whimpered when their rotting smell hit me, almost making me gag. I kicked out to them, desperately trying *anything* to keep them as far away from me as possible.

But then, one of them grabbed my left leg. Before I even had a chance to brace myself, it yanked my body forward, almost ripping my leg out of its socket.

I cried out in surprise. Now it was only my head resting against the tree behind me.

Fuck. Fuck. FUCK.

Up close, their faces were even more gruesome. Their teeth were elongated like vampire fangs, and their white eyes missed their pupils. The screeching sounds they emitted made goosebumps break out on my skin. One of the nightcrawlers came closer to my face and stared down at me.

Tears prickled in my eyes. The creature bent down, as though it wanted to ... *kiss* me. Its leathery hands moved to my neck, applying pressure. Not so much as to cut off my air stream, but enough to make me realize it was the nightcrawler who was in control.

A low cry left my trembling lips.

The nightcrawler's mouth was exactly over my own. And then the nightcrawler inhaled.

I gasped for air as I felt an invisible hook smash inside my chest. At first, I didn't understand what was happening, but then I felt something inside me being torn out, transferring over to the creature looming above me.

Crying out in pain, I felt my energy slowly leave my body. I did not have the power to sob. My tears streamed down my cheek silently and into my hair.

My energy was just reaching the creature when, suddenly, from one second to the next, the creature crawled away from me, sending hectic sounds to the other nightcrawlers. Cocking its head from one side to the other, the creature lifted its nose in my direction, its nostrils flaring as it seemingly tried to smell me. I was too exhausted to be surprised when the nightcrawler hissed, "Part of darknesssssssss."

The rest of the nightcrawlers looked at each other, then at me.

My mind was bordering on a thin line between consciousness and oblivion when they all started backing away from me urgently, emitting panicked sounds, screeching, whispering, and whirring as they did so. I couldn't explain what got them to retreat. They seemed so *confused* as they backed further away from me.

Suddenly, the shadows around us exploded. They formed an enormous, thick shield of black mist around me. The guttural sounds of the nightcrawlers grew fainter behind that wall. Power slithered around me, mixing with my ever-crescendoing fear.

Then, a roar filled the air.

My entire body slackened against the tree in relief.

Thanatos was here.

CHAPTER TWELVE

The shadows around me wavered as though looking for any upcoming threat. If I'd have any energy left, I would have looked up. Instead, I stayed right where I was, my head leaning against the tree behind me.

Even before he appeared, I sensed him coming closer. The King of the Dead emerged right in the middle of the raging shadows, his hair as black as the darkness around him. His green eyes shone like emeralds. His gaze slid over the surroundings, obviously searching for something. Even from my spot, I saw murder in his eyes. The shadows swelled around him. Claws scraped against the surface, reflecting Thanatos's agitation and fury.

I'd have called out to him, but the only sound my beaten body could manage was a low whimper. It was enough to make Thanatos's head spin in my direction. As soon as he spotted my frame against the rough bark of the tree, his entire body relaxed.

In relief? I couldn't tell.

He manifested next to me and crouched down. His voice came

out as a whisper. "Cassiana. What were you thinking?" His gaze raked over me, clearly searching for injuries.

My body shook as tears began blurring my vision.

So very carefully, he turned me around, scanning my back for any external damage, the heat of his hands comforting me more than it probably should.

When he was satisfied, he bent down and searched my eyes. "Are you in pain? What happened?"

It took me a moment to gather my strength to answer to him. "Nightcrawlers." I couldn't find it in me to answer in a complete sentence.

Thanatos's entire body stiffened. "How …" He shook his head. "First, we need to get you home."

Home.

"What did they want from me?" I managed to croak out. At the mere memory of those cold, ink-black claws against my skin, more tears streamed down my cheeks.

The King worried his lips, clearly debating whether it would be wise to tell me. Tenderly, he slid his hands under my knees and behind my back. The fabric of my dress rustled as he lifted me effortlessly into the safety of his arms.

I winced at the pain shooting through my body.

Thanatos glanced down at me, his expression darkening with concern.

"What did they want from me?" I repeated my question with the little strength I still had.

He locked his jaw at the weakness of my voice. "The nightcrawlers feed from emotion. They drain everyone of whatever emotion they might feel, leaving only a vessel behind."

Then why had the nightcrawlers backed off before draining

me to death? And *before* Thanatos had arrived? They hadn't retreated because of the King of the Dead.

I wanted to ask him, but my body was too spent. I watched the shadows around us creep closer, ready to teleport us.

My eyelids fluttered closed and I felt my head fall back, but then there was Thanatos's hand, cradling my scalp against his biceps. A soft moan left my lips as his smell hit me.

Right before my body slackened in the Deathbringer's arms, I felt his hold on me tighten, drawing me even closer to him.

I wasn't sure whether I imagined the soft touch of his lips against my temple before everything around me gave way to blackness.

I woke to the sound of whispers.

Wearily, I blinked open my eyes, slowly taking in my surroundings. I was splayed on my bed in Thanatos's castle. The flames of the floating candles were dimmed, and somebody must have pulled the blanket over me.

My head hurt. My arms hurt. *Everything* hurt.

And then, slowly, my trip into the Forest of the Lost Souls came back to me. The images popped up in my mind incoherently. I wrapped my arms around myself as the grotesque faces of the nightcrawlers flashed across my inner eye. I shivered as I recalled the way their white teeth had reflected the little moonlight that managed to stream through the thickness of the forest.

"What happened?" Thanatos demanded coldly from the outside of my room. I had never heard his voice sounding so emotionless and so hard.

"She wanted to contact someone from the Land of the Living." Kalira sounded scared.

Wincing, I pushed myself into a sitting position. I tried my best not to puke when the room began swaying of its own accord. The nightcrawlers must have had drained more of my energy than I had expected.

"And did you or did you not know of the danger within those woods?"

"I—"

The Deathbringer's voice dropped to a threatening tone. "You knew. And you told her how she could get there."

I pulled my legs out from underneath the blanket. A sheen of sweat began forming on my forehead as I stood. My legs shook under my weight, making it so damn hard to reach the door. My vision blurred in and out with every movement.

"And even worse: you let Cassiana go into the forest by herself."

Bile rose up my throat, and I had to lean my body against the wall to stop the room from spinning.

The door was slightly open, letting in a slim ray of light. I squinted against it and tried to make out the two figures standing in front of each other in the hallway. Thanatos's back was facing the door.

"I made sure she had a bundle of sage," Kalira tried explaining herself.

"Even so." Thanatos took a menacing step forward. "You disobeyed my orders. It was your job to keep her safe. That was your one and only important task. And you failed."

Kalira flinched as though he'd just hit her.

"Stop." My voice was nothing more than a rasp, but it was

loud enough to draw the King of the Dead's attention. "It's not her fault." I knew Kalira had only wanted to help me. Despite the fact that our plan to contact Miriam had failed, she had been willing to help me and risk Thanatos's wrath if he found out. I wouldn't let Kalira get punished because of it.

I took a step forward, but I didn't anticipate that my legs would give out.

Thanatos reacted so fast, I didn't even see him move when he suddenly appeared next to me, catching my body before it could hit the ground. He lifted me in his arms as though I weighed nothing.

"You should be in bed." His usual mocking tone was missing. He stared down at me intensely, then back at Kalira. "This is not over," he promised and turned back around to face me.

Even though everything spun, I tried catching Kalira's eyes to give her a reassuring smile, but Thanatos's broad shoulder blocked my view.

Heat blossomed on my cheeks as he entered my bedroom and closed the door behind us. "Thank you for catching me," I mumbled, too embarrassed to meet his gaze.

Thanatos glanced down at me. "How are you feeling?"

"Good," I lied.

He snorted. "Yeah. That's why you almost fell."

I cleared my throat. "My head hurts. But it's getting better," I lied again.

Thanatos leaned forward to gently put me down on my bed. Even in my current state, I tensed when he removed his arms from beneath me, making me so very aware of him. He looked down at me. "That's expected. You are very lucky that the nightcrawlers didn't drain all of your energy." He sat down on the edge of the bed and reached out to a glass of water someone must have put on my nightstand while I had been unconscious. Our faces were only inches apart when he slid his left arm underneath my back and moved me into a sitting position. His eyes were guarded when he handed me the glass. He cocked his head, watching me drink the water greedily.

My stomach growled in protest at the sudden fluid invasion .

"How *did* you escape from the nightcrawlers?"

I wiped my mouth with the back of my hand as I tried to recall the moment the nightcrawlers had moved back from me, but the memory was drowned in a blur of smoke. "The last thing I remember was how your shadows built a wall around me."

But there was something else … something about the nightcrawlers' behavior … something the nightcrawler had said pe… Trying to clear my mind, I squeezed my eyes shut. But I wasn't able to put my finger on what had caught my attention.

"They just left?" He cocked his head. "Are you sure?"

I nodded, wincing at the pain immediately shooting through my scalp.

Thanatos's expression was pensive as he took the empty glass from me and put it back on the nightstand.

I watched in astonishment as it started to refill of its own accord. I cleared my throat. "What are the nightcrawlers exactly?"

Thanatos's jaw muscles spasmed. He slowly turned toward me. "When the Dead die, they become nightcrawlers. They are creatures with no soul. They have nothing, no memory that nourishes them. That's why they seek out intruders of the forest—to feed from their emotions."

I gulped. I hadn't known the Dead were able to die, too.

"Those who become nightcrawlers have no chance for reincarnation. They stay in their form forever, banned to the coldness of the Forest."

So that was the reason for the Forest of the Lost Souls' name.

He stared at me, a puzzled expression on his face. "It's just so odd," he murmured.

"What is?"

He ran his fingers through his silken hair. "That they stopped. They always finish what they start."

A shiver raked down my spine as I understood the meaning behind his words: they wouldn't have stopped until I died.

So why *had* they stopped?

My eyelids began closing slowly. I knew my body wouldn't be able to keep me conscious for much longer.

Without overthinking, I grabbed his hand. "Please don't punish Kalira. She wanted to help me."

Thanatos stared down at our joined hands for a long moment. "Her actions endangered you." He said it as though that were reason enough to castigate her.

"But I asked her to help me."

Thanatos shook his head. "Kalira can't—"

I gave his hand a squeeze. "Please."

The Deathbringer's eyes dropped to our joined hands, then they jumped back to me, his hard expression visibly softening. He squeezed his eyes shut and exhaled deeply.

When he opened them again, he nodded.

If I'd had any energy left, I would have hugged him in relief. "Thank you," I mumbled, completely worn out. My body began relaxing into the softness of the bed. The exhaustion demanded its tribute.

"Under one condition." His eyes raised to meet mine.

Everything in me froze. Of course any cooperation from the King of the Dead would have strings attached to it.

"You will not go anywhere outside of Emoh on your own again. Ever."

I stared at him suspiciously. That was his condition? "Okay." I fought against the sudden heaviness of my eyelids.

Before the darkness could take me into its embrace for the second time today, I asked the one question I needed answered. "How did you know where I was?"

"The shadows. They called me," Thanatos said, glancing down at me. An emotion I couldn't quite place flashed over his features. "Do you need anything else?"

I shook my head.

The King of the Afterlife rose. "Then I'll leave you to rest. You should sleep. You will feel better tomorrow. If you need anything, just call for me. I'll hear you," he promised.

I bit the inside of my cheeks and nodded. He shot me a searching look.

I grabbed his hand.

His eyes dropped yet again to our joined hands.

"Thank you." My voice was so very weak. Shyly, I smiled up at him.

His expression turned gentle and caring when he smiled back.

CHAPTER THIRTEEN

I woke to the sensation of a damp cloth wiping my forehead. Disoriented, I blinked open my eyes, sure I'd find Kalira taking care of me. It was the Deathbringer instead. His beautiful face loomed over me, his brows furrowed as he carefully cooled my forehead.

"You are awake," he stated. He turned around and wetted the cloth in a bowl of fresh water, then wrung it out before bringing it back to my skin. "How do you feel?"

I stared up at Thanatos. "Better." And it wasn't a lie. My body didn't throb anymore, and my head didn't hurt. I was surprised my voice didn't sound as raspy as I'd imagined it would.

I didn't understand. Why was it Thanatos taking care of me and not Kalira?

I tried pushing myself up, but the King of the Dead was there immediately, sliding his hands underneath my body to help me.

"How long was I unconscious?" I asked.

He spoke low, "You slept through the entire night." Once my back rested against my bed's headboard, he carefully withdrew his hands. The washcloth had fallen down on the bed, the wet fabric slowly soaking the mattress. He searched my eyes. "Are you hungry?"

I shook my head. Just the thought of eating made my stomach recoil.

"I'm glad you feel better." Thanatos looked at me through his coal-black lashes, his chiseled features turning hard. "You are lucky you got away yesterday." Suddenly, he didn't seem worried any longer. He looked *mad*. "How could you be so reckless?" I guessed he was done being careful around me. Before I had a chance to answer, he kept talking. "I understand perfectly well that you want to contact your friend, but why the fuck didn't you come to me for help?"

I felt my brows draw together. His help? How could he help me if not for—

"You can contact the Living?"

Thanatos grunted.

I couldn't stop staring at him. "I didn't know you could," I finally admitted.

"Well, now you do," he bit.

I scrambled to sit on my knees. The blanket dropped, revealing my nightgown beneath. I was too excited to wonder about my change of clothing.

"Careful." In an attempt to stop my hurried movements, he reached out to me.

I ignored him. "Will you help me?" The hope in my voice made it pitch high.

He glared at me. Obviously, he was still angry.

Oh well.

"Please?"

He looked at me for a long moment. Finally, he relented and gave a curt nod. Before I had a chance to get excited, he added, "But we will not do it today. You are too worn out after the nightcrawlers' attack."

I felt the blood in my cheeks withdraw at the mention of those creatures. Goosebumps broke out on the surface of my skin. Thanatos noticed it, too, his gaze dropping to my exposed arms. He leaned forward and gently draped the blanket over my shoulders. I was still too caught up on everything that had happened to be truly aware of his concern.

"Thank you," I mumbled.

"Mm-hmm."

I began squirming uncomfortably on the bed. "Umm ... I just need to," I nodded to the bathroom door.

Thanatos immediately stood. "Let me help you."

"No," I rushed. "I can do it myself." I gave him a tight smile to reassure him.

His brows pinched together. "Are you sure?"

Nodding, I lifted my feet out of the bed. It was a very kind offer from Thanatos, but I didn't know how to handle his kindness. Nobody had ever shown me how to accept the help of others. With the exception of Miriam, I'd had to lift up my broken body and soul by myself throughout my entire life.

His kindness? His care? His help?

I didn't know how to handle it. Any of it.

I stood. I was surprised I didn't get nauseous or that my feet didn't tremble like they had yesterday.

Thanatos's eyes watched my every movement, ready to help if needed.

I made it safe across my bedroom to the bathroom and slipped through the door. As soon as the door closed behind me, I exhaled slowly.

How the hell had my life escalated this quickly?

Just two weeks ago, my only worry had been attending to as many casting calls as possible. And now? Now, I was attacked by nightcrawlers and living in the kingdom of the Dead in its King's castle. With its King.

I shook my head. I winced at the sudden sting the motion provoked in the back of my scalp. I took care of my business and, once I finished, moved to the sink to wash my hands. One of the candles made a low, barely audible sound as the flame flickered.

Startled, I spun around. My heart hammered powerfully against my chest. I searched for the same grotesque faces that had watched me from the forest's darkness yesterday. I relaxed my shoulders when I couldn't find any. My eyes squeezed shut as I drew in a shuddering breath.

It's all right. They aren't here. The nightcrawlers can't hurt you anymore.

A knock on the bathroom door made me jump. "Cassiana, are you all right?" Thanatos's voice was muffled by the thickness of the door.

I forced myself to steady my breathing before answering. "Yes! I'm coming."

I opened the door, coming face to face with the King of the Dead. His gaze raked over my body as though I might have injured myself in those two minutes I'd spent unsupervised by him.

I flashed him what I hoped was a comforting smile before I moved past him toward the bed. I sank down on it and sighed deeply.

Thanatos still stood at the bathroom door. "I'll let you get some rest. Call to me if you need anything. I'll hear you." It almost felt as though he repeated yesterday's words.

I gave him a curt nod. He moved across the room in powerful strides.

The faces of the nightcrawlers flashed once again before me. I knew their horrendous faces would keep tormenting me if I didn't distract myself. Even though I felt better, I was in no state to roam the castle. So, there was only one option left.

"Thanatos," I called out to him before I could stop myself.

The King of the Afterlife halted. He was already at the door, his hand on the handle.

My bones shone through my skin from how tightly I gripped the fabric of the sheets. It required so much effort to voice my question. "Can you stay with me?" I asked, still sounding husky. I bit down on my lip as I felt heat spreading on my cheeks.

His body tautened, his muscles tense. Hesitantly, his hand glided from the knob as he turned to me very, very slowly. Our gazes locked. "Are you sure?"

Was I?

I didn't know. But I *did* know that I didn't want to be alone right now. Normally, it would be Miriam who stayed with me whenever I was in need of a distraction. But now?

"Yes," I whispered hoarsely.

He breathed out slowly, the tension of his body withdrawing. When he moved toward me, his eyes glowed like emeralds.

I watched him closely as he gently slid under the covers next to me. His slow, halting movements were so at odds with the way he usually moved. Shocked, I realized he was giving me time to stop him, to send him away.

But I didn't.

And I didn't know why, but it calmed me that he was here. With me.

His big, powerful body slowly eased back, his frame coming to rest right next to mine. I could feel the heat he radiated, even though our bodies weren't even touching.

Silence fell between us. Only our breaths disrupted it.

My body trembled.

"You are cold," he stated. He started to get up—probably to get me an additional blanket.

"No!" I grabbed his forearms. His eyes moved back to me, then down to the place where my hand held onto his arm.

"I'm fine. It's just …" *My body's reaction to you.* I shook my head. "Really; I'm fine."

He searched my gaze. Whatever he found made him lean back. My body still hadn't stopped trembling. He moved to lean on his side. He was facing me now.

As if he were afraid to scare me, his hand moved slowly to my arm, beginning to rub warmth and comfort into my skin. I smiled softly at him, but that only drew his attention to my lips. His throat bobbed as he swallowed before his eyes jumped back up.

He also smiled, making his dimples appear.

I could get lost in this side of him forever. This caring side of him. The one that wasn't hidden by his usual mockery.

Once again, we fell silent, too caught up in this moment to do anything other than stare at one another. It was truly so unfair how a man like him could possess such an unearthly beauty. Even though every single detail of his symmetrical face was cut sharply, as though his entire body had been crafted by an artist, his eyes didn't retain the same hardness. I could see it now.

Hundreds of emotions were hidden behind those beautiful eyes, making it impossible to catch and point out a single one of them.

"Do you want to know a secret?" I whispered, breaking whatever spell had worked its magic between us.

His hand, which had now reached my wrist, stopped before resuming his idle caress right over my mole. The gesture made goosebumps break out on my skin. He nodded.

"Sometimes, I'm scared in this room," I quietly admitted, watching how he let his finger circle over the birthmark.

The Deathbringer looked at me, a surprised expression written in those striking facial features. "Why?"

"I'm missing the stars." I bit down on the inside of my cheek. Why was I telling him this? Well, I wasn't going back now. "Back at home, when I was still living with my family," my skin puckered at the thought. Thanatos seemed to notice it, because he flattened his hands on my arm and drew me closer to him. I continued speaking, which seemed so much easier than thinking about the fact that I was … *cuddling* with the King of the Dead. "I had these small, fluorescent plastic stars. The kind that draw in day's light and gleam in the darkness. I used to look up at them and find comfort whenever I felt," a*lone, rejected, unloved*, "bad."

The Deathbringer's tall frame rested peacefully at my side, listening.

"I used to count them each day before falling asleep, scared they might have somehow fallen off the wall." But they never once left me. They had stayed near my entire life, always offering me comfort and peace. "As I grew older and moved out of my parents' house," bile rose in my throat at that memory, "I made sure to bring them with me. Exactly fifty-three. I counted them every day." I chuckled sadly. "This must all sound so dumb and childish. I'm sorry; I should ..." I made to stand, but the Death-bringer's arm snagged around my waist and drew me back against him.

"Not at all. It is hard to let go of the things you love, and there is no reason to be ashamed of the fact that you have something you love." His voice vibrated against my back as he spoke. "It is ... human."

I fell silent. My gaze slid over my room, never resting on anything. Now that I had revealed so much about myself, I suddenly felt silly. Like a small child unwilling to throw away a favorite cuddle-bear.

The timbre of his voice vibrated against my skin. "You wish to see the stars?" He asked, drawing me back from my train of thoughts.

I crunched my brows, not knowing what he intended, but I nodded anyway.

"Very well." He extended his right arm and formed his hand into a fist. All at once, the floating candles' flames died off. They left us in almost complete darkness. The only source of light was the moonlight streaming in through the windows.

"Ready, love?" He raised his left arm toward the windows, making a come-here gesture.

At first nothing happened, but then, a low, twinkling sound made me turn toward the open window.

My breathing stopped at what I saw

I pushed myself into a sitting position. Small dots of light moved in the night sky, slowly getting closer and closer to us.

I gasped as the realization hit me.

The stars ... they were descending from the sky.

"What—? How—?"

The small lights gravitated through the window toward us. Slowly, they illuminated the room in a bluish, shimmering light. They moved like thousands of fireflies as they spread evenly into the entire room.

I stood on shaking legs and turned in circles around myself. It wasn't possible to acknowledge every detail of the beauty this place beheld. "It's gorgeous!"

"It truly is," the Deathbringer said.

But, when I tore my gaze away from the glittering stars and met Thanatos's brilliant eyes, I realized he hadn't once been looking at the stars he had summoned. He had been looking at *me*.

I was too overwhelmed to be embarrassed by his attention. Tears threatened to leak from my eyes. "Thank you," I whispered, swallowing the knot that had started forming in my throat. "When I was young, I always imagined the plastic stars in my room to be real."

Thanatos stood and approached me. I had to tilt my head back to meet his searching gaze. A tear managed to escape out of the corner of my right eye.

He studied my face. "Do you know how stars are born?" Thanatos was still looking down at me when he cupped my cheek.

I shook my head, even while I instinctively leaned into his touch.

Thanatos watched the tear stream down my cheek. Lifting his hand, he caught it on his index finger. He furrowed his brows and studied it. Then, he formed his hand into a fist. The tear dropped into his palm.

"Stars are born," as he opened his palm again, a shimmering, solid light lay in his hands, "when dreams come true."

The light elevated from his palm. It slowly floated to the ceiling, joining the rest of the stars.

Thanatos's attention returned to me. "Thanks for sharing with me that you were missing the stars."

I couldn't form the right words, so instead, I just leaned forward, my face coming to rest against his frame. His body became rigid against me. He hesitated for a moment, but then he snaked his arms around my waist.

We stared at the star-covered ceiling in silence.

This felt good.

Too good.

Deep down, I knew perfectly well I shouldn't do this. I knew it. My life's experience had taught me that there was no point in building up a relationship only for it to be shattered. But, at the same time, it felt so incredibly *right*.

I snuggled closer to Thanatos. For once in my life, I didn't fight but accepted and welcomed a stranger's comfort.

CHAPTER FOURTEEN

4 years ago

"Let me know if you need anything else, hon!" *Miriam's bracelets made jiggling noises as she aimed for the door of our apartment. Cold winter air brushed into the room, reminding me to be thankful that today was Miriam's turn to do the grocery shopping. Even though Miriam didn't like this kind of weather either, she did prefer to do the shopping herself. She always claimed I bought the wrong products, and since she was the one who cooked, she preferred having the products she enjoyed most at her disposal. Now and then, I cooked too, but Miriam always found something she didn't like about the food. Witches ... always the perfectionists.*

"I'll let you know!" I grabbed the cereal box from the top shelf and poured its contents into a bowl big enough to satisfy my growing hunger.

It was strange not living alone anymore. Strange, but oddly comforting at the same time. I still didn't trust Miriam completely to tell her about my personal stuff. And I didn't know if I ever would. By now I was convinced I was incapable of ever bonding with people the way I watched others do, but the opportunity of paying less rent had been too appealing to pass up. Since my dad had kicked me out four years ago, it had been almost impossible to have enough money for food, let alone to pay for the ridiculous rents in D.C.

I had been lucky enough to get booked for a couple of stage plays where I managed to earn some money. Since an academy had started representing me, things had become somewhat easier. Act as Dramatic as a Banshee's reputation helped me a lot. But, even so, I couldn't just lean back and relax. I depended on every job, no matter how insignificant it might seem at first.

Miriam's hard work on her bracelets was really starting to pay off. She got more clients each day. I was happy for her, but I couldn't deny that it bugged me to still be struggling while her business flourished.

The door fell shut behind my roommate, the sound tearing me out of my thoughts. A shiver ran down my back, and I grabbed a blanket. I opened my computer to watch a new episode of Dark. God, I loved that series. It was so twisted, complex, and, well, dark. The actors were geniuses, too. The way they could control their bodies to show their discomfort or panic by the smallest of physical reactions was truly enthralling. I had learned most of my acting skills by watching movies and learning from some of the greatest actors of all time. These actors were acknowledged almost worldwide now. How it must feel ...

My gaze drifted from the computer's display to the window. Thick, black clouds cast the entire city in the darkest of light. The small snowflakes were barely visible against it. I hated these days.

As cozy as they might be, they were a pain in the ass in the rare cases I needed to attend casting calls. Sighing, I leaned back against the soft couch and let my thoughts drift while I watched the snowflakes fall faster from the upcoming wind.

Suddenly, a reflection in the window caught my attention. My breath hitched as I saw a dark silhouette moving behind me.

I spun around. But, by doing so, I lost my balance and fell off the couch. Fuck! If whoever was in my apartment hadn't noticed me before, they sure as hell must have now. My blood began pumping powerfully.

Heavy steps moved closer to me in a fast, hurried pace. I crawled backward, trying to get into a sitting position. What the fuck were you to do if someone broke into your house?

A shadow fell over me, and everything in me froze to chips of ice.

No.

No, no, no, no!

Impossible! This was impossible!

I backed away from the one man I'd been sure I had left behind for good. From the man who fed my nightmares almost every day.

The last time I had seen my father had been four years ago. The day he kicked me out. The day I had made a promise to myself to never see him again.

Subconsciously, I knew I should scramble to my feet and get the fuck out of there, but the confusion of seeing my father again shocked me so deeply I couldn't get myself to move. I was just lying there on the floor, staring up at him.

Time had taken its toll on my father. His skin that had once been stretched was now wrinkled and dry. He had gone bald and lost a lot of weight. He looked more like a skeleton than an actual human. Only his eyes hadn't changed. They still lacked every emotion like the dead shells I still remembered as they stared coldly down at me.

His lips twitched.

"Dad?"

I was aware of the mistake I made as soon as the word left my mouth. I had seen the expression on his face enough times to know I'd fucked up. It was the exact same expression he used whenever he punished me for things I still didn't understand his reasons for. His brows smashed together as his entire body moved forward to grab me.

"No! Stop!" I scrambled away from him. Suddenly, I didn't feel like the twenty-two-year-old I'd become but like the child he used to punish until bruises flourished on my skin. I turned around and pushed myself into a standing position.

But Dad had become fast.

He grabbed me by my neck and jerked me against him. I whimpered as he held me pressed against his chest. His other hand fisted my hair painfully. He yanked it back, forcing my head to tilt back. My hands went up, trying to ease the pressure he applied on my scalp. I stared into his emotionless eyes.

"You little bitch! How I have waited for this day." The hand on my neck let go of me, but the one in my hair still held onto me.

Tears stung in my eyes. He had never, not once, called me that. But the worst thing was that, even after all these years, his words still hurt.

Suddenly, something cool pressed against the skin on my throat.

A knife.

Too scared of the damage I might inflict myself, I didn't dare move. A whine escaped me when he applied more pressure on the blade. "Please stop." My chest rose and fell heavily with each breath.

I felt my father lean forward from behind me. His warm breath fanned over my ear. "Since I last saw you, I have been dreaming of this day."

I couldn't restrain the tears streaming down my face. I never cried. Ever. I knew it did not help to solve one's problems. But as I faced my father, memories began surfacing. Memories I had long ago tried to lock in the darkest place of my mind, hoping they would never resurge.

The sound of my father's hand coming down on my face.

The silence of my watching mother.

My unheard cries in my locked bedroom.

My father laughed at me as if I were nothing more than a bug dirtying his shoe as he crunched it. "Stop? Why should I stop when this is everything I have wanted for the last years?" He cocked his head, his voice falsely sounding soft and caring. A tone he had definitely failed to use when I was still a kid.

He had wanted to do this to me for the last couple of years? Did he only want to torment me, or ... kill me?

I searched his eyes, trying to find an ounce of humanity in them. "Why?"

He laughed right in my face. "Why?" He yanked my hair further back. My neck ached from overstretching. I could feel his lips touching my cheek as he next spoke. "Because you are the reason she's dead, you stupid bitch."

Struggling for breath, I felt my stomach recoil. Bile crept up my throat. I had no doubt he was talking about my mother. How many times had that same thought crossed my mind? Hearing it from the man closest to that woman felt like my insides were being ripped out of my body. My legs buckled, but the hand still fisting my hair prevented me from collapsing.

"I wanted to kill you all this time. But what kind of person would kill his own daughter?" He laughed humorlessly. "I should have killed you when I had the chance." My body flinched at his words. I smelled his rum-fanned breath as he applied more pressure to the knife at my throat. Something warm trickled down, and I knew it was my blood. But I didn't register the pain. The words my father had just said hurt more than anything physical pain he might inflict upon me.

He applied even more pressure on the knife. It was probably just my imagination playing tricks on me, but the shadows around me seemed to elongate. I leaned away from the knife, only to be stopped by his chest. He clicked his tongue loudly. The sound made me jump. "You think you can get away from me?" He chuckled. "No. You will not. I won't make that mistake again."

I knew I should struggle against him. Fight back. Do something *to get out of this situation. Even if it was just to spare time until Miriam came back or one of our neighbors noticed the untypical sounds coming from our apartment and decided to call the police. But I was so very* tired. *I was tired of fighting against him. And tired of being defeated by him over and over and over again.*

I felt my body relax in my father's hold, accepting my upcoming fate.

Suddenly, everything around me went pitch-black.

The light must have gone off. My father was yanked away from me brutally, his arms letting me go in surprise.

I cried out in shock. I still wasn't able to see anything. Something hit the floor with a loud thud. Probably the knife, given the sound.

"What the hell?" I turned around, but our entire apartment was imbued in darkness.

I heard a loud groan from the other side of the living room—my dad—before another thud hit the ground. And whatever it had been, this one was big.

"Hello?"

No response. My entire apartment was cast in silence, my heavy breathing the only sound to disturb it.

I didn't know what the fuck was going on, but I sure as hell couldn't just stand around and wait for the lights to turn back on, only so my father could come back and finish what he'd started. I might've been tired enough not to fight back against him, but now that I had an opportunity to get out of here alive, I wasn't going to waste it.

I couldn't see anything, and sweat began coating my body.

Trying to be as silent as possible, I put one foot in front of the other and moved toward the entrance of the apartment. My steps were hurried and resonated way too loudly in the silence of the darkness. I knew the door must just be a few feet away from me. When I was about to reach it, I stepped on an object lying on the floor. Halting, I crouched down, my hands carefully gliding over the floor's surface. I touched the cool object. My fingers curled around a hilt. The knife felt heavy in my trembling hands.

Swallowing, I tightened my grip on the knife. I didn't know what I planned to do with it, but I did know that I didn't want to run the risk of being unarmed facing my father—again. I extended my hand as I held the knife in front of me. I was careful to not walk against any object that might stand in my way. It was crazy how a place you thought you know perfectly well suddenly felt unknown in the darkness.

Softly, my hand bumped into an object. Letting my fingers trail over the material, I relaxed when I realized it was the couch. That meant the door was just a few feet away.

When I walked in the direction of it, I never stopped paying attention to my surroundings. But, other than the sound of my own steps, now muffled by the living room's carpet, the room stayed completely silent. I must have already crossed the living room halfway, when my feet suddenly crushed against an object. I stumbled over it and fell.

Crying out, I extended my hands in front of me in an effort to block my fall.

Air whooshed out of my lungs when I collided with the floor. From the force of my fall, the knife, still grasped tightly in my right hand, made a smacking sound as it imbedded itself into something beneath me.

It took me a couple of seconds before I realized that I had fallen into something ... damp. I let go of the knife's handle, and groaning, pushed against the thing beneath me.

I had to leave.

I had to leave before the lights went back on and my father had a chance of finding me. I pushed myself up, but as I took a step back, I fell over the same object again. What the hell? Did Mir leave her bag outside her room? I pushed the object away from beneath me but halted. The material was soft and ... warm.

Flickering, the lights went back on.

I stared down at the rigid face of my father. His eyes were

gazing unfocused into the distance. I had fallen right on top of him.

And then I saw the knife I had just held in my hand, jutting out of my father's chest. The weight of my falling body had rammed it straight into him.

I let out a scream and scrambled away from him.

I shook my head violently.

No, no, no, no, no.

This couldn't be true. This was all a bad dream.

No, no, no, no, no.

I had not just killed my father with a fucking knife. This could not be true; this was not true.

My breathing became ragged as I shook my head and crawled away from the body of my father until my back hit the wall.

Blood was leaking through my father's chest where the knife had pierced his skin. How the fucking hell could he even have gotten all the way over here?

A familiar jiggling at the door chimed through my panicked consciousness.

Miriam.

No, no, no, no.

If Miriam saw this, she would immediately think I had killed my own father.

You just did. Now you've killed both of your parents.

I pushed down the upsurging guilt and stared at the pool of blood at my feet. I needed to hide this before she came in. Frantically, I started to wipe the blood away with my hands. I only succeeded in rubbing the blood deeper into the white carpet.

Tears began streaming down my face. They mixed with the red liquid on the floor.

The doorknob turned.

Too late. I was too late.

Miriam tore open the door. She entered the living room, a frown on her face. Her gaze dropped to where I lay in a pool of blood, my clothing soaked in the sticky substance, before moving to the corpse in front of me. "What the fuck happened?"

I had never seen her this serious.

This was it. This was the moment my roommate realized what kind of person lived with her. I averted my gaze and stared at the blood crusted beneath my fingernails.

She didn't say anything for so long, I wasn't sure she was still here.

"We have to get rid of the body," she said calmly and matter-of-factly.

Horrified, I lifted my head and stared at her. Get rid of the body? What the hell was she talking about?

She moved around me to the head of the shell that had once been my father. "Get me one black candle and one aquamarine crystal," she instructed.

Miriam crouched down next to the corpse and put her hands on either side of my father's face. She closed her eyes and concentrated. When she opened them again, her eyes' silvery gleam almost looked unnatural. Yet again, bile crept up my throat as my eyes dropped to the knife jutting out of my father's chest.

I did this.

Miriam's gaze snapped back to me. "What the hell are you waiting for? Go. The longer we wait, the bigger amount of magic I'll have to use."

Her cutting voice made me jump out of the numbness that had taken hold of me. I hurried to her room and scrambled through the box where Miriam kept all her witchy attire and gadgetry. I grabbed the materials before running back to her.

Miriam had already put up two of her water bowls at my father's head and at his feet. She placed the aquamarine crystal on his left and the black candle on the right side of his body. She stepped back and assessed her work. Pleased, she nodded before taking her position at my father's head.

Closing her eyes, she focused. I knew better than to bombard her with all my questions. Witches should never be interrupted whenever they practiced magic, much less when they cast spells as powerful as this one must be. So I took a step back.

Miriam's eyes were flashing in a silver light as she began reciting the spell she had chosen. The candle lit up. Goosebumps began spreading over my skin. This was not the kind of magic Miriam usually used. This was dark magic. Forbidden magic.

I watched how the red pool of blood began shrinking with each word of her mantra. At the exact same time that the blood vanished from the floor, the two water bowls began turning crimson.

Shocked, I gasped for air as my father's body levitated from the ground. A powerful wind came up, making Miriam's hair fly wildly around her. She looked more like a fury than a witch. As her whispered words became louder and louder, the corpse slowly began dissolving itself into thin air.

The second the body disappeared, Miriam's words died off, the wind stopped all at once, and the water in the two bowls turned the deepest shade of red.

Miriam closed her eyes and breathed deeply. Only then did she look at me. "It's done. There is no evidence to be found in this room." With that, she knelt and grabbed the bowl that had been at the top of my father's head. I watched how the red water in the bowl started transforming back to its typical transparent, colorless shade. Now, there truly was no trace of what had occurred here mere moments ago.

I watched her warily. She trembled. The spell must have cost a lot of energy for her body to react this way.

I cast her a side-glance. "How did you know I needed help?"

She moved to the other bowl. "I had a warning spell put up in the house." The still crimson-colored water splashed as she lifted it, before that liquid, too, transformed back to its normal shade. Her nerves were just as irritated as mine.

I was still too taken aback to get my body to move. "Why are you helping me?" I asked as I stared at her uncomprehendingly.

She glanced my way. Her gaze dropped back to the place where the corpse had been. "Because everyone needs someone who'd go through hell to help them out."

We moved out of the apartment the day after the incident. Neither of us wanted to be reminded of the corpse that had been inside our living room. We moved into a different apartment on the same street as the pub where we first met. Not once did Miriam ask how my father had been killed. Neither did she inquire about his reasons for visiting me. But she made it a habit to cast protection spells in the house.

From that day forward, I trusted Miriam with my life.

CHAPTER FIFTEEN

It was late morning when I woke, and even though I had slept for countless hours, I felt exhausted. I hadn't dreamed of the nightcrawlers, but a feeling of unsettlement had constantly reminded me of the danger I had been in just mere hours ago. Groaning, I turned around and drew the pillow closer to me. The smell of musk and spice imbued it—Thanatos's smell.

I froze. Was he still here?

Slowly sitting up, I blinked against the brightness in my room. My eyes rose. Thanatos had left the stars on the ceiling, their shine blinking down at me and casting the room in the prettiest of silvery light.

Tears stung in my eyes at the sight of them. They were the proof that yesterday wasn't a result of my imagination.

I searched the room for Thanatos's tall frame. A sense of relief flooded my mind as I realized I was alone. Immediately, I regretted that sensation.

Thanatos had literally brought stars—*real stars*—into my room. He'd done that for *me*. How could I possibly feel *relieved* that he wasn't here? Guilt cooled my blood and made my swallowing hard. I shouldn't feel that way with him.

The problem with Thanatos wasn't that he was evil or that his behavior justified the rumors about the King of the Dead. The problem with him was that his actions *didn't* justify what people whispered about him. He was caring and ... *kind*. And all of it made me so confused. I didn't know what his actions meant. And, even less, how to interpret them. Was it just a kind gesture or was there *more* to it?

Closing my eyes, I could still feel the whisper of his strong arms encircling me, drawing me closer against him; the feeling of the steel-hard muscle beneath his shirt; the way his hair tickled me whenever it had touched my skin. I couldn't recall the last time I had fallen asleep this quickly. Neither could I remember the last time I had felt so safe, cared for, and *protected*.

I groaned. No, no, no. What the fuck was I doing? Hadn't I already learned that lesson many years ago?

Don't let people near you, or you'll get hurt.

It was as easy as that.

I had never, not once in my entire life, thought about someone the way I was beginning to think about the Deathbringer. Of course I had met some boys in whose bodies I had found pleasure. But this? Having someone cloud my mind when that person wasn't even present? Never.

My experiences with people told me they were creatures driven by their egoism. They enjoyed you as long as you contributed something to their own lives. Past that point, they let you down. Just take a look at my parents. If they had taught me anything, it was the fact that you should never trust people, no matter what.

They would always let you down. Always.

Except for Miriam, of course.

I wasn't going to experience that same deception once again with the King of the Dead.

My gaze locked on the star nearest to me. Was I allowed to touch it? Once I extended my hand in its direction, the star broke away from the ceiling and slowly started floating toward me. I held my breath when the small light came to a stop on the back of my hand. I was barely aware of its weight, its touch on my skin not more than a whisper. As it moved, it made a small tinkling sound. At the sound, a laugh broke through me.

"I wish I heard you laugh more often."

I jerked around to find the Deathbringer sitting languidly on an armchair on the other side of the room. Why hadn't I seen him? Or had he just manifested into my bedroom? Had he been watching me this entire time?

I let my left hand trail over my hair, trying to straighten the knots, while the star rested on my right hand's back. "Good morning."

"Oh, it's long past noon." Thanatos stood in a flowing movement and approached me slowly. His eyes were gleaming, and his jaw was accentuated by the lingering shadows on his face.

"Do you always stalk me when I'm sleeping?" I asked in a playful tone, even though I didn't manage to keep the tremble from my voice.

He materialized next to my bed. "How are you feeling?"

Guess we were going to ignore my question.

"Amazing."

Thanatos searched my eyes. When he didn't find any proof of a lie, he nodded.

"How are they so small?" I breathed, looking back at the tiny, glittering light on my hand.

His gaze followed my eyes to the star. "What you have in your hand is only a fraction of what would eventually form a star. It's stardust."

Stardust. Of course.

Thanatos straightened. "I'll have some food brought to you."

"No, I'm fine." I scrambled out from beneath the blanket. Thanatos's eyes dropped down to my exposed legs, tracing them extensively, before his gaze zoomed in on the mole at my wrist.

"Can we contact Miriam today?"

Darkening, his eyes jumped up to mine. "No. You have to feel perfectly well before I contact your friend."

"But—"

"No," he cut me off. "Today you will stay at home. I want to make sure you are truly okay."

Home. There was that word again.

Shyly, I glanced up at the Deathbringer's towering form above me. He wanted to make sure I was doing okay?

"Then we can and will contact your friend." The way he pronounced the last word carried a bitterness I couldn't understand.

Before I could stop myself, I jumped up and threw my hands around Thanatos's neck. He was so taken aback that he stumbled before catching himself.

My body was pressed tightly against his, but I didn't care. "Thank you. This means everything to me." I had to force my head back to meet his eyes. I couldn't wait to rid myself of this constant guilt and anxiety I'd felt since arriving in Emoh. I felt bad for not contacting Mir and not knowing how she was doing.

A muscle jumped on his jaw. "Of course."

Only once Thanatos's eyes became a heated glint did I realize I was hugging the King of the Afterlife tightly against me. My flimsy nightgown might as well be nonexistent.

I cleared my throat and took a step back. "Sorry about that," I whispered, avoiding his gaze.

A smile graced his lips. "No worries."

Since when had I become an impulsive hugger? So much for keeping my distance from others. "Um," I shifted my weight from one foot to the other, "I'll go take a bath."

It had only been one day since the incident with the nightcrawlers, but I hadn't had the strength to bathe since then, and I felt filthy.

Thanatos nodded and turned toward the door. "I'll call Kalira and let her know that you need her help." He didn't sound all too happy to call her.

Surprised, I stared at him. Did he trust Kalira again? Last I'd seen, he had been upset about her showing me to the Forest of the Lost Souls. Maybe my objection that she'd just wanted to help me had soothed him after all.

"I can take my bath alone," I interjected.

He puckered his lips, a playful shimmer brightening his eyes. "Damn. And here I was hoping you might offer."

I tried my very best to show off a strict expression, but the corners of my lips betrayed me as they glided upwards.

His gaze dropped to them, his smile growing.

"No, but honestly." I crossed my arms in front of my chest. "I can bathe alone, and I prefer to do so."

Thanatos took a step forward and crossed the distance between us.

He grasped my chin between his thumb and index finger, and he tilted my head back.

Surprised, my brows puckered as I stared up at him. What the fuck?

"I know you can bathe alone, but you have just been attacked by nightcrawlers. I don't want to take the risk of you fainting because of the heat." He was looking down at me with an emotion I couldn't quite place.

Swallowing, I stared at him. "Yes, but—"

He chuckled, the sound sending exciting shivers down my arms. "Why do you always try to argue?"

"Because I want to bathe alone, thank you very much." I didn't even try hiding my smug expression.

Thanatos shook his head, but I saw the amused glimmer in his eyes. "This is about your safety. It's either going to be Kalira or me who stays in the bathroom to watch over you." He leaned forward. His lashes brushed my cheek as he whispered. "I swear I won't look."

Yeah, right. His taunting tone suggested otherwise.

I glared up at him, my expression making him smirk.

His left brow arched. "Who is it going to be?"

I didn't hesitate. "Kalira, obviously."

He chuckled again as he let his hand drop from my chin.

Immediately, I missed the feeling of his skin against mine.

His eyes trailed down my arms. They were covered in goosebumps from his touch. "*Obviously*," he stressed, before disappearing.

A knock on my door tore me out of my thoughts.

Turning toward it, I put the book I had been reading on my bed next to me. "Yes?"

The door opened, and Kalira entered the room. "Hi! The King sent me to—" She stopped dead in her tracks as she took in my room. Her eyes darted incredulously to the stars lighting the entire ceiling. Her mouth gaped open. "So it's true …" she managed to say, her voice filled with awe.

I followed her gaze. "It's amazing, isn't it?"

She nodded, her eyes as bright as the starlight. Ever so slowly, her attention came back to me. "Our King put them there?"

I nodded, not managing to hide my shy, embarrassed smile. I could have kicked myself for my body's reaction. Since when had any man had this effect upon me?

"Well, fuck me." Kalira blew strands from her copper ponytail out of her face. She turned and assessed me. "How are you feeling?"

I looked down at my hands. How was I feeling? I couldn't say. On the one hand, I felt incredibly touched by Thanatos's care for me, but at the same time, I felt so unsure of the emotions his care brought up in me. Emotions I wasn't ready to share with Kalira. After all, I had basically just met her, and I wasn't sure I was ready to open up to her yet—or ever—so instead, I said, "A little bit unsure."

Kalira's back was turned to me as she searched the wardrobe for a new dress. "Where does it still hurt so I make sure not to touch you there?" she asked over her shoulder.

Confused, I stared at her. Hurt?

The attack. She meant the attack. "Oh." I laughed nervously. "I'm fine, actually."

She closed the door to the wardrobe, a deep-blue dress in her hands. "I'm glad to hear it. Let's get ya clean."

I shot her a side-glance when I scrambled out of bed. "You don't have to help me bathe. I'm fine, really." Even though Thanatos had basically ordered me not to bathe alone, I couldn't help but shoot one last shot. It always made me uncomfortable to accept other people's help. I made to grab the dress she had picked for me, but Kalira snatched it out of my reach.

"Nonsense. The King has ordered me to help you and so I will. The last time I failed to obey him didn't turn out so well after all."

She was right, of course. I had never seen Thanatos as wrathful as he had been that night before.

I followed her petite form into the bathroom.

As the tub began filling with hot water, I watched Kalira move to the other side of the room. She grabbed a sponge and some soap out of a cabinet.

While she still had her back turned to me, I took off my clothing and slowly eased myself into the water. I exhaled contentedly. The heat and the smell of the lavender essence Kalira had added to the water already soothed my tense muscles. I made sure the bubbles on the water's surface covered my body and rested my head back against the tub's rim.

Kalira pulled a chair next to the bathtub and moved behind me. She sat down and began to loosen the clasp that held up my hair. I sighed and let myself relax further against the tub. Her movements were unhurried and careful.

"Cassiana?" Kalira asked, her voice unusually high.

"Mmm?" My eyes had drifted shut, but I blinked them open at the uncertainty in her voice.

It took her a couple of seconds before proceeding. "I'm very sorry about the attack. I shouldn't have brought you to the forest. I should've just kept my mouth shut, but instead I put you in danger. If the King hadn't been there, I don't know what might've happened. Just imagine if you'd gotten hurt—that was stupid; sorry. I mean—of course you got hurt, but what if—" She was talking herself into a frenzy. Clearly, she had been blaming herself for the attack.

"Kalira," I stopped her. "It's all right. It wasn't your fault. I heard a woman talk to her son about the possibility of contacting the Living. If it hadn't been you who showed me the way to get there, I would've found another way. Believe me."

The reminder of the nightcrawlers made bile creep up my throat, but I didn't want to exacerbate her regrets.

"But you got hurt," she whispered from behind me, sorrow and guilt combing through her voice.

I forced myself to answer as calmly as possible. "It's fine. We shouldn't get too caught up in the past when it is only a fraction of our lives to which we have no access whatsoever any longer." It was something I had to remind myself every day over the last four years. Swallowing, I moved the bubbles on the water's surface in my direction. My hands glided over the rim of the tub. "I'm just thankful Thanatos was there."

Kalira drew in a hissing breath.

Alarmed, I stopped tracing the edge of the tub with my fingers. "What is it?"

Kalira hesitated before answering. "Nobody is allowed to call him by his real name."

Confused, my brows drew together. "Why?"

"It's just not done."

The townspeople don't call him by his real name? I tried remembering a single occasion where any of them called him by his true name, but he had only ever been regarded as 'King' or 'Deathbringer.'

I bit my lip. He hadn't told me not to call him by his real name, so it didn't seem to bother him that I did.

Silence stretched between us as Kalira combed my hair carefully. She grabbed a sponge and dipped it into the water. And, yet again, I was wondering about the Deathbringer's reasons for bringing me here. Who was I to him that he had saved me and cared for me the way he did? Why was I allowed to live in his castle and use his name so freely?

Kalira's soft, melodic voice interrupted my thoughts. "The townspeople talk," she said, drawing the words out cautiously. "They saw how the stars came flying from the sky into your room." She dipped the sponge in the water again and began scrubbing my back.

I tensed. "What are they saying?"

She moved the sponge over my back in slow circles. "They believe it's a sign."

I examined my nails, already bracing myself for the worst. "A sign of what?"

Kalira hesitated, taking incredibly long to rinse out the sponge. "A sign that our King has chosen his queen."

CHAPTER SIXTEEN

The next day, I stood on the balcony and stared down at Emoh. From my spot, I wasn't able to make out the details of the small village, but I did see all the movement. People were buzzing around with clear destinations in mind. Everyone seemed to know exactly what to do and where to go. My heart throbbed, my tongue suddenly tasting a bitter note.

I used to be like them. I used to know exactly what my goals were, what my dreams were.

Now that I no longer had the acting lessons and castings to occupy myself with, I did not know what to do with my spare time. After witnessing what moral boundaries my former acting colleagues had been willing to cross in order of becoming famous, it wasn't like I wanted to get back to acting anyway.

My parents had never approved of what I did, who I was, and what my dreams were. Maybe I had chosen an acting career because, subconsciously, I had always dreaded and hoped for the approval of the people around me due to the lack of my parents'. Even if it meant giving up the person I truly was.

It would certainly explain my nausea, anxiety and panic attacks before a play. Pills had always been a necessity for me to get through those experiences. God, I didn't even like attention to linger too long upon me.

And all those diets I had gone through … They had only ever served the purpose of helping me fit in. Of making the industry want me. Of making other people want a person who wasn't even me.

How pathetic I had been …

I had forced myself to get people to like me for so long that, now that I didn't have that pressure upon me any longer, I didn't know what it was that I wanted. Who I was. I had tried to get people to like me for so long that, eventually, I forgot who I actually was.

I had already lost count of the days I had stayed in the Afterlife, but the feeling of not knowing what to do was a constant reminder of the dream I had chosen to let go.

I let my eyes roam over the village. Couples had sought out the privacy of Emoh's outskirts and walked by the rivers, and a bunch of kids played hide and seek on a rock-covered field on the village's opposite side. Smiling, I watched how some used the small, curved stone bridges as hiding places. They were the smart ones. They wouldn't be seen easily in the shadows and the gurgling of the water would disguise their sounds.

My gaze settled on a tall, dark, very familiar figure of a man. He was apart from the rest of the people, walking alone over a field. Even before I saw how the shadows followed him like a loyal companion, just by the way he walked, I knew it was Thanatos. I watched how he walked seemingly aimlessly over the field by himself. He had promised to help me get in touch with Miriam. I was becoming more and more restless to do so immediately, but all my objections had fallen on deaf ears. He insisted on waiting until he was sure I was recovered fully from the nightcrawler's attack. Almost as though he felt me watching at him, he turned around and looked at the castle. It was probably my imagination, but his green eyes seemed to flash brightly when he spotted me.

My entire body heated. I lifted my hand hesitantly and waved at him. He didn't move, only kept staring at me. But the shadows behind him swelled to the form of a man. The dark figure of shadows lifted its arm and waved back at me at the same time Thanatos did.

I smiled.

The shadow-man evaporated at the same time that Thanatos aimed in the opposite direction of Emoh and began walking toward a dark forest with tree tips coated by snow.

I shivered as Kalira's words resonated in my head. *A sign that our King has chosen his queen.*

Shaking my head, I tore my eyes away from Thanatos's retreating form and turned to Kalira, who was curled up on my bed, a book lying open in front of her. Her rosy cheeks rested in her hands as her eyes flew from one line to the next. Since the attack, she made sure to always be by my side, even when I actually wished to be alone.

"Kalira?"

After all the time I had spent in the castle, my body and mind had once again become restless.

She glanced a peek over the spine of her book. One of her

brows arched as she saw my enthusiastic look. Sighing, she closed the book loudly. "What now?"

"Where are those social gatherings you told me about?"

The establishment where today's social gathering took place was hidden behind a wall of flowers in the backyard of a small, yellow-painted house. With its colorful walls and all the countless canvases decorating them, it looked absolutely lovely and welcoming.

A golden doorbell rang when we entered the narrow space. A low murmur of conversation filled the air in a friendly ambience.

I followed Kalira into the room.

Most of the women were invested in their work, barely glancing in our direction. A small group sat together in a circle, white canvases in front of them. Those who weren't painting, or pretending to be, had fabrics spread out and were sewing or embroidering dresses, bags, and clothing. I even spotted a spindle at the back of the room. It immediately conjured up the faces of the three Norns.

I looked back at the women. They were avidly talking and didn't seem to notice us. When I moved further inside, I also spotted men I hadn't been able to see before. Some practiced the same activities as the women, while others chopped wood or worked with big, heavy-looking metallic objects I couldn't make out from where I stood. Their deep laughter rumbled over the small space. Both genders sat mostly separated, but there were some individuals mixing with the opposite sex.

"Hi guys!" Kalira chimed as she approached the group sitting together in a circle. She sat down in the middle of the room, a white canvas already in front of her seat.

As soon as the people noticed us—noticed me—their conversation died.

I waved awkwardly at them. "Hi!"

They smiled at me, some muttering low greetings.

"Here, you can sit next to me." Kalira patted the chair beside her.

As I walked over to her, I felt everyone's curious glances settle heavily on my back. They looked at each other before prying back at me. Kalira handed me a white canvas and gestured to the different colors arrayed on a table. I did not know the first thing about painting. I knew which colors were acrylic paint and which were watercolor, but that was basically it. My gaze settled on the embroidery hoop on a table at the other side of the room. I bit the inside of my cheek. I knew how to sew and how to embroider clothing. Learning those skills had been a necessity when you lived with a father who didn't want to spend more money on his daughter's clothing than was absolutely necessary.

"Feel free to grab those supplies if you'd like."

I tore my eyes from the supplies and met a pair of hazelnut-colored, soft eyes. I wouldn't have known the woman who had spoken was a vampire if not for her two fangs peeking out from beneath her upper-lip.

Blushing, I smiled at her. "Thank you."

As conversations slowly resumed, I stood and crossed the room to the table where the different materials, such as needles, floss, scissors, and the different-sized embroidery hoops, were laid out. Awed, I let my fingers glide over the fabrics of countless trousers and dresses laid out to be sewn. They glimmered as though they had been crafted of stardust.

I chose a royal-blue dress. The waistline would look so pretty if I embroidered it with the golden floss I had spotted in between the rest of the materials.

Taking all the supplies I needed with me, I moved back next to Kalira. She was talking avidly to a werewolf-lady sitting next to her.

Placing the supplies on the desk in front of me, I let my gaze roam over the women sitting in the circle once again. Most of them were human, but I did spot two fae who were heavily occupied with their paintings on the other side of the room and only rose to get some new colors. Otherwise, they ignored the rest. Apparently, the fae didn't behave that much differently in Emoh than they did in the Land of the Living. At least here they didn't mind mingling with other creatures.

I recognized the men working with metal as werewolves. That wasn't surprising. Their strength didn't even require a fire to get the metal to bend.

Leaning forward, I took the dress in my hands. Eyeing the long sleeves, I wondered if I should also embroider them with the same golden floss, or if I should get back up and fetch the bluish floss I had spotted before.

"So, is it really true our King saved you?" The same woman who'd spoke to me before ripped me from my thoughts.

As soon as her question registered, I bit the inside of my cheek, noticing how everyone else had fallen silent, expectantly waiting for my answer. I didn't know how they'd come to know this. Was she referring to Thanatos saving me from Silvan or him saving me in the Forest of the Lost Souls? Apparently, there was also gossip in the Kingdom of the Dead. I lifted my shoulders, displaying more indifference than I actually felt. "Um, yeah, I guess so."

I knew perfectly well what questions they might have: *Why did he save you? What does he want from you? Why you?*

I didn't wish to be faced with these questions to which I had no answers myself.

The vampire nodded slowly, her brown hair held firmly in a bun. "Finally. It's time he found someone to open up to."

The others made approving noises.

I was surprised she didn't try to wring more answers out of me. I'd have loved to drop the topic now and get to embroider—after all, I had come here to distract myself precisely from the man this conversation was about—but her statement had piqued my curiosity. "What do you mean?"

A human with striking blue eyes glanced at me over the canvas through her thick, black glasses. "He never talks to anyone."

My brows knit together. "But I saw him walk through Emoh and eat at that restaurant at the end of the street."

The human nodded. "He always makes sure we are all taken care of, but he never wants to truly engage with us." Her statement wasn't so much a complaint as it was laced with sadness and concern for her King. Given the open way Thanatos talked and flirted with me, it was quite difficult to wrap my mind around the fact that, apparently, he acted so differently with me than he did with others. "He walks alone. Always alone," she said, worry clouding her gaze.

The image of him walking by himself over the field just before I'd decided to come here flashed before me.

"That is, until she came." The vampire-lady gestured in my direction with her brush. Water dripped from its tip, but she was too involved in the conversation to care.

Everyone nodded in agreement.

Kalira leaned forward as though she was telling them a secret. "The stars we saw moving in the sky toward the castle yesterday? We were right! It *was* him! He made them gravitate to her room."

The vampire's eyes grew big, and the humans drew in stunned and excited breaths.

"Kalira!" I met her gaze and shook my head. Why on earth would she tell them this? Of course, they didn't know the concrete reason for Thanatos bringing the stars into my room, but it still felt as though a very private, very *intimate* moment between the King and me had just been revealed to everyone gathered here.

She shrugged unapologetically. "What?"

I stared at her. She could not be serious.

She cast her gaze down as she saw the betrayal clearly written on my face. "I'm sorry. It just bubbled up," she said so low only I could hear her.

Clenching my teeth, I nodded, accepting her apology. She wasn't able to take back her words now either way.

The blue-eyed woman threw her hair over her shoulders. "I guessed as much." She fell quiet, playing with the brush in her hand. "I've never seen him talk so much and for so long to anyone."

I couldn't help but feel somehow special at that comment.

"I'm just glad he's not alone anymore," someone murmured.

"I was so worried about him. It's not healthy being alone for so long. People need others in order to have a chance at happiness. Without others, we risk losing contact with our shared humanity and will suffer the consequences."

Everyone nodded. They all seemed so *relieved*.

"Finally he has found himself someone who speaks to him, to whom he can open up," the vampire-lady said. She stood and moved behind me. I tensed when she put both her hands on my shoulders. "Thank you for taking care of him."

I laughed nervously as I felt my cheeks flush. "Oh, um ... I don't think—"

"You don't have to say anything, sweetheart. Just know that we are thankful for your help."

I glanced behind me. She looked at me with so much gratitude and joy that I couldn't tell her how mistaken she was—all of them were—to put their hope in me.

So, instead of correcting her assumptions, I nodded.

When she moved back to her seat, I grabbed the needle on the table. Trying to fumble the embroidery floss through its hole, I couldn't help but think that they were wrong. Thanatos didn't open up to me. We connected on a deeper level than I did with most people, yes, but he was still a stranger to me. As soon as Silvan gave up searching for me, I'd be back in the Land of the Living and all this would be nothing but a long-forgotten dream. And, even if their hope of making Thanatos open up was rightfully placed, I wasn't sure if I was the right person for this. I was too broken to make anybody open up to me, let alone be worthy of their trust.

As the conversation drifted away from the King of the Dead, I got lost in my work, barely listening to the women's ongoing gossip. When I grew up, sewing and embroidering had always taken my mind off of things I didn't wish to occupy myself with any longer. And today was no different. It was easy to forget everything around me in the way the needle pierced the soft fabric of the dress, slowly creating an interwoven pattern on the waistline that ended in a low bow in the front.

I was so focused and occupied with my work that I didn't notice the way the conversation around me had started to slowly die off until Kalira spoke.

"Are you ready?"

"Hmm?" I asked, reluctantly shifting my gaze from the dress to Kalira.

"Everyone already left. Or do you want to stay longer?" she asked.

I was surprised when my eyes drifted over the now empty space. I hadn't even noticed everyone leaving. How could I possibly be so unaware of my surroundings? I looked outside. When only darkness greeted me, I shook my head. It was still a habit of checking for the sunset even though they didn't happen in the Land of the Dead.

"No, I'll come." I put everything I'd used back on the table at the end of the room. One last time, I let my fingers reverently glide over the golden embroidery on the dress before moving back to Kalira. She let the door fall shut behind us. I noticed how she didn't check if it was locked. Emoh seemed to be so safe; nobody had to protect against robbery. I inhaled deeply, letting the cool, fresh air fill my lungs to their fullest as the light wind caressed my skin.

Embroidering had helped me relax, and once again, I took in

the beauty of the Kingdom of the Dead. Floating lights illuminated the stone-crafted paths that wound through the countless small houses. Flowers blooming on the walls emanated a sweet scent that mixed with the smell of herbs coming from the plaza. I followed Kalira there. People sat in the cafés or relaxed on the benches set out in a circle around the water fountain. I spotted the boy who had talked to his mother about the Forest of the Lost Souls playing with a group of other kids. They sat together on the border of the fountain. The boy leaned over it and held a bowl beneath the water's surface. When he assumed a sitting position, his gaze settled on me.

Smiling, I winked at him.

His smile grew bigger. He said something to his friends before moving toward me. He balanced the bowl, careful not to spill the water.

When he was close enough to hear me, I bent down. "Hey there, young man. What have you—"

Before I could brace myself, he drew the bowl back and splashed its contents right into my face.

Kalira sucked in a hissing breath. All at once, every sound died off. The people stopped eating and speaking. Only the four of his friends began giggling, holding onto their bellies as laughter shook their tiny bodies.

"David! How dare you do this to her?" His mother yelled from a bench where she sat. She hurried to stand and snatch her son away from me, but I held up a hand, which made her stop immediately.

Everyone stared at me, seemingly holding their breath.

Kalira's gaze jumped nervously from the boy to me. "Cassiana!"

I ignored her. Water was dripping down my face, wetting my dress.

The boy smiled wickedly at me.

He wanted to play? I'd give him something to play with.

I glared at him, which only made him giggle more. "Oh, you just wait until I catch you!" Laughing, I fisted the skirt of my wet dress, and before David could answer, I began running toward him. Screeching, he turned around, starting to flee from me.

Chuckling, I ran behind David and tried to catch him, but that boy was fast. Everyone relaxed and watched us or moved their attention back to whatever it was they had been doing. Eventually, I managed to catch him and, as soon as I did, I picked him up and began turning him in circles, holding him high in the air. His lighthearted laughter filled the streets, and people pointed at us, warm smiles lighting their faces.

"Please, let me down!" David screamed in between laughter.

"Oh, you sure about that?" I teased.

"Yes!" David said still giggling.

I stopped turning. David exhaled a relieved breath, but as soon as he stood on his own two feet, I began tickling him.

I laughed with him as his small body jolted from sheer joy.

"I give up! You win!" He screamed, joyful tears streaming down his face.

I didn't budge, tickling him under his small armpits where he seemed to be most sensitive. "What was that?"

"I—" He gasped for air, trying to wiggle out of my grasp. "Give up!"

I smiled at him and stopped tickling him.

He collapsed on the ground, exhausted, his cheeks a shade of deep red from the play. Smiling, I offered him my hands and drew him to his feet.

"That was fun!" he said, his voice still breathless and his eyes alight.

I smiled at him and stroked his hair. "We'll have to repeat it then," I said, winking at him. "As long as you don't splash me again."

He nodded vigorously.

Suddenly, the voices around us hushed, a nervous energy filling the marketplace. David got serious and rushed off to where his mother stood. I didn't need to turn around to know who that powerful, sizzling energy belonged to.

"I see you are enjoying yourself." His deep voice rumbled loudly over the plaza.

Righting my clothing, I turned around.

The sight of Thanatos alone sent tingles down my spine. He was wearing a simple white cotton shirt with long sleeves. It was tucked into his trousers loosely. His dark hair was held up in a man bun, and his expression was soft as he looked at me almost … lovingly.

"Very much." I felt the curious glances on us as I approached him. Somehow nervous, I tried smoothing out the wrinkles of my skirt and wiped the remaining water off of my cheeks.

His eyes traveled the length of my wet body, making me shiver as I approached him. When I stopped in front of him, he bent low until it was only me who could hear his hushed voice. "You would make an extraordinary mother." He straightened his spine.

I felt my face flaming, but I didn't have time to process his words properly before he asked his next question.

"How are you feeling, love?"

The gathered people drew in stunned breaths at the public endearment.

I cupped my cheeks, hoping that my hands' coolness would chill the blush. "I'm great," I mumbled, weirdly touched by his presence.

Thanatos nodded, his seafoam eyes bright. "Good. So, we can contact that friend of yours first thing tomorrow morning."

CHAPTER SEVENTEEN

I walked through the empty corridors of the castle. Next to me, the Deathbringer was quiet, his brows furrowed. He had sent Kalira home, so it was only the two of us making for our rooms. It was really mindful of him to go to the village to fetch me.

A sign that our King has chosen his queen.

I swallowed hard at the reminder of the townspeople's hopes and forced my mind away from that topic. It would do no good wondering over rumors. Usually, the truth behind rumors wasn't remotely enough to worry about what people were whispering about. *Usually.*

I came to a halt in front of my bedroom and glanced up at Thanatos's profile, but he seemed completely lost in thoughts. He didn't even seem to notice that we had already arrived at my bedroom. He had been quiet since the second he'd picked me up from Emoh. Something was bothering him.

I wanted to ask him what he was brooding about, but I didn't feel entitled to do so. Who was I that he would share his problems with me?

Finally he has found himself someone who speaks to him, to whom he can open up.

Clearing my throat, I willed the woman's voice to fade and grabbed the door handle. "Well, have a good night."

Thanatos nodded.

After casting him one last glance over my shoulder, I slipped through the door. Just before it fell shut, his left foot darted out, preventing it from closing.

I pulled it open again and arched one eyebrow in question.

Thanatos's eyes drifted over my room. They came to rest for a split second on the stars on the ceiling before his attention came back to me. He extended his arms and rested them on the doorframe at his sides. His muscles stretched his shirt at his posture and made him seem broader and more intimidating than he already was.

His body seemed relaxed, but his eyes weren't.

Sucking the inside of my cheeks, I wondered what it could possibly be that was occupying him this much.

A long moment passed in which neither of us spoke.

"Are they happy?" he finally spoke.

Happy? Who?

It took me a moment to realize that he was talking about the people in Emoh.

I stared at him incomprehensibly. Did he not see how ridiculously happy they were? To me, his people's happiness didn't seem in doubt at all. Why would he even wonder about what was so obviously before him?

I nodded. "Yes, I think so." I watched him closely before asking, "But why don't you ask them that yourself?"

He swallowed, the motion making his Adam's apple bob. "I

do." He stared outside the window at the village. "But as I'm their King, I'm worried they might not be telling the truth," he admitted.

Chewing on the inside of my cheek, I reached up to my hair and loosened the bun holding it up. My hair cascaded freely over my shoulders.

Thanatos watched me silently, never taking his eyes off of me.

I was procrastinating, but I didn't know how to address this. Neither was I sure if it should be me who voiced what I was about to say. But if what the villagers had said was indeed true, and Thanatos barely talked to them as freely as he did to me, I was the only one with enough access to tell him this. I inhaled deeply. "They worry about you."

He frowned. "They—?" He straightened his spine, clearly caught off guard by what he'd just learned. He leaned his waist against the right side of the doorframe and crossed his arms in front of his chest. "Explain," he demanded.

Apparently, we were doing this. "I didn't have enough time to speak to them sufficiently, but they said that they worry about you, because …" I fidgeted with my fingers. "Well …"

"Because?" The King of the Dead was growing impatient.

I forced myself to speak before I could get a chance to overthink. "Because they say that you are always alone and that you need company."

There. I had said it.

He watched me closely before averting his eyes. A muscle flexed on his jaw, but he kept quiet. "Thanks for telling me."

Accepting his thanks, I nodded.

I was surprised when he spoke again. "I just tend to keep to myself. It's better than taking the risk of trusting the wrong people."

At those words, I felt a sudden rush of connection to him. I knew perfectly well what Thanatos was talking about. He feared that the people around him might be dishonest and might want to take advantage of him. So he thought that it was better to be alone. But choosing a life in solitude wouldn't help anyone. Before Mir came along, I had tried just that. It hadn't worked out. And despite knowing this, I still didn't live according to this wisdom either. I didn't go out into the world with open arms, welcoming everything and everyone into my life. I had Mir, and she was the person who broke my solitude. And for me, she was enough.

I spoke softly next. "You don't need to explain yourself."

He tried to appear so unaffected, when he obviously wasn't. "But I do. What King wouldn't talk sufficiently with his people just because he had trust issues?"

I let my eyes roam over him. Suddenly, I wanted to know his reasons for preferring to keep his distance. I knew what *my* reasons for that behavior were. But what about *him*? What had happened for him to become this way?

My gaze dropped to the hem of his shirt, which had bunched up with the way his forearms were crossed in front of his chest, revealing his muscle-defined, cream-colored skin beneath. I tore my eyes away from it before my mind had the chance to drift to any inappropriate thoughts.

But, of course, the Deathbringer had noticed. The right corner of his mouth lifted, making his small dimple appear. He was way too observant for his own good.

"See anything you like?" he asked as he wiggled his eyebrows at me. Sue me, but that man didn't lose an ounce of his attraction by wiggling his god-damn eyebrows at me. There was no trace of his prior earnestness to be found in his expression. Talk about having priorities.

Crossing my arms, I puffed out a breath. "You wish."

His eyes were openly laughing at me. "Mmm …."

Narrowing my eyes, I straightened my spine. "What?"

"You want to know what *I* think?"

With the way his voice was laced with insinuating undertones, I was almost too afraid to ask.

I didn't need to anyway.

He pointed in my direction. "*I* think that you find me attractive."

I laughed at that, but the tone was too high-pitched, too nervous. "Sure thing, buddy."

He pushed against the doorframe, his body languidly moving toward me.

Sweat began forming on my skin, but I refused to take a step back and reveal the effect he had upon me.

When he stepped so close to me that he invaded my personal space, my arms fell to my sides. Instead of it becoming suffocating, his closeness seemed to let me take deeper breaths, almost as though I hadn't breathed properly in a long time. My neck hurt from how far back I had to tilt it to look at him.

His eyes lingered on the crimson flush of my cheeks. "Oh, love. How your body betrays your words."

I was very thankful he couldn't detect the flush his presence alone provoked on other body parts of mine.

He seemed to sense the path my thoughts had taken, because

his eyes began glimmering mischievously as they briefly dropped to my cleavage.

I crossed my arms protectively over my chest. As his heated gaze returned to my eyes, my lower stomach tightened and heat pooled in my core.

He stepped forward, and I had to force myself to keep still. Somehow, he seemed to always know when I was okay with his presence. With having him this close. How would he know that? Obviously, I wasn't vocalizing my discomfort or pushing him away. But still ...

An idea began forming in my head.

"Can you smell arousal?" I asked before I could stop myself.

Thanatos drew back, his brows pinched in confusion. "What?"

"Well, can you? You know, smell arousal?" I balanced my weight from one foot to the other. I knew that werewolves could. That was also one of the reasons why Miriam was so fond of them. She did not need to say what she wanted. Her scent alone was enough to give them the right idea.

The King of the Dead stared at me intently. When he realized what I was asking, he threw back his head and laughed at me.

"What is it?" I asked.

He was still openly laughing at me.

Anger filled my veins. Why was he laughing about what I said? It was a justified question. "What's going on?" I demanded again with more fury than I had intended. The shadows in the room seemed to waver at my outburst, though that was probably just my imagination.

Thanatos's laugh died off, and his eyes found mine. They were so heated that I took a cautious step back, but he was immediately there, cutting through that won space, coming to a stop right in front of me. He stood so close our chests brushed with each inhale. Instinctively, I pushed against his rock-hard chest, but he did not budge. Instead, he leaned even closer; so close that his breath fanned over the skin of my flushed cheeks.

"I cannot smell your arousal, love. But your body's signs are easy to read," he purred. He pulled away a little to look at me. "Your cheeks are red, your pupils dilated." His fingers traced over my left wrist, right over my mole, in the lightest touch. "And your pulse is racing. All signs that you are aroused," he concluded, his purr never leaving his voice.

I snorted. At least I tried to. The sound that escaped my mouth was came closer to a low moan than a snort.

Thanatos also seemed to notice because his dimple showed. "Did I read you right? Are you aroused?" He asked, his voice so sweetly innocent.

"Stop saying that!" I grumbled as I took another step back.

Suddenly, his hands circled my midsection and drew me against him. My breath fled my lungs as my body collided against his. Shocked, I realized his chest wasn't his only hardened feature. There was also something else entirely pressing against my lower abdomen.

Shocked, I looked up at the King.

I was definitely not the only one *aroused* right now, and that knowledge alone—of my effect on the King of the Afterlife—did the strangest things to my most feminine part.

He tilted his head as he contemplated me. Slowly. Taking his time.

Carefully, he lifted his left hand.

I held my breath as his fingers traced the curve of my eyebrows before making their way over my temples to my chin.

My nipples stiffened as I felt his hands trailing down my neck to rest on the hollow of my throat.

Thanatos flashed me a self-aware, male smile as he noticed my body's reaction to his touch.

"We should stop," I breathed.

"Should we now?" He tilted his head, his gaze slowly moving to my parted lips.

I felt myself nodding, even though my body seemed to have a mind of its own when he leaned forward.

"What if I don't want to?" He challenged, the brightness of his eyes dimmed with lust. He slid his right hand through my hair and cupped the back of my head in the most exquisitely possessive way.

My hands—which had been about to push him away—formed themselves into fists, pulling him closer to me.

My tongue darted out, wetting my suddenly dry lips. His eyes followed the movement, something deliciously wicked swirling the tones in his eyes into a molten light-green.

"I don't think … that I'd mind," I admitted. *Not minding* was an understatement. I *burned* for the electricity his touch evoked.

He growled. Yes, g*rowled.*

And then I was not able to stop him anymore. And nor did I want to.

His body was swallowing mine up, pressing into me, backing up, until I felt the hard wall hitting my back. The shadows in the room flickered with excitement. I moaned at the feeling of all that power fixed solely on me.

Thanatos swallowed the sound as he pressed his lips against mine. It was not a sweet kiss you might expect to receive as the very first kiss from a person.

No. This kiss was something else entirely.

We weren't Romeo and Juliet. We were the rest of the Capulets and Montagues, fighting over who'd bring the other to their knees.

Thanatos's tongue didn't ask for permission; instead, the second I gasped for air, it plundered into my mouth.

I didn't know what I was thinking. Probably because I wasn't.

I gave myself over to the feelings the Deathbringer's touch provoked within me. It felt as though my entire body lit from the inside out.

His hand still held my hair in a firm, but never hurtful, grasp. He applied just enough pressure to let me know that he did not intend to let me go anytime soon.

His knee bumped into my thigh, and my legs spread for him of their own accord.

As he slipped his knee in between my legs, nudging them farther apart, I couldn't help but moan at the friction it provoked whenever it touched my groin. I felt him smile against my lips at the sound. Flattening my hands on his chest, I marveled in the defined muscles beneath the fabric.

His left hand found its way to the low of my back, pressing my body as tightly as possible against him. When he held me like this, I realized just how unbelievably *massive* he was compared to me. His body was so broad, it covered my own entirely.

He brought his lips down on mine again with such force that our teeth crushed together. My stomach somersaulted at the intensity. The only sound in the room was our heavy breathing, my occasional low whimpers and his deep rumble. I couldn't help but move my hips in slow, entirely unintentional, circles over his leg and moan at the delightful feeling the movements created.

Eventually, at some point, our touch began slowing down.

Both of our breaths were harsh when Thanatos slowly, reluctantly, pulled away. He withdrew his knee from between mine, leaving a throbbing and entirely too-empty feeling behind. I kept my eyes closed, still feeling the touch of his lips on me.

"No is the answer to the question you once asked me," he said.

Still high from the kiss, I blinked, not knowing what he meant. "What question?"

He smiled down at me. "My kiss does not drain the soul out of another's body."

He leaned closer, brushing his lips against my forehead. "Sweet dreams." He exited my room but stopped at the door. A sly, mischievous smile tipped up his lips as he looked at me. And then he left.

When the door fell shut behind him, I wasn't sure if he had been right with his answer. Because as I stared at the closed door, it did feel as though the King had drained me of something. I felt this empty ache in my chest, and I knew only one person could alleviate it. And that person was sleeping in the room next to mine.

Lifting my hands to my face, I let my fingers carefully trace my swollen lips.

I had just kissed the King of the Afterlife.

I stared at the closed door. I almost hoped he'd come back and finish what he started.

Almost.

CHAPTER EIGHTEEN

I stared at Thanatos's back as he led the way through the countless corridors of the castle to the object he referred to as the 'shadowmirror'. Although the inside of the castle looked very similar wherever you went, I was sure I hadn't come across these halls before.

As excited as I was about finally getting the chance to talk to Mir, I couldn't help but worry about last night. What the hell had I been thinking? Kissing the King of the Dead? Freaking *rubbing* myself against him? Heat spread on my cheeks at the mere reminder. I stifled a groan. God, he ruled over the freaking Dead.

What the hell was wrong with me? He was a dangerous man. A man who could kill you in the blink of an eye with his mere touch if he wished.

But mostly, and more importantly than *who* I had kissed, was that I feared I might get too attached to him. The sheer fact that I was replaying yesterday's kiss instead of forgetting it was reason enough to get some distance between us to keep me from replaying how he had held me; how his hands had fisted my hair;

how his body had pressed against mine, drawing the most embarrassing noises out of me; how he had looked so—

Stop it!

I forced my mind to focus on the fact that I finally got a chance to talk to Mir instead of the man next to me. We walked past a majestic stairwell. The prettiest celestial designs I had ever seen had been painted on it. I made a mental note to come back here and look at its details. Right now, I had more pressing matters to attend to. I had trouble following his quick pace. I glanced at his back. I had to stop this—whatever it was—before it got out of hand.

"Cassiana." He slowed down so it wasn't as hard for me to keep up.

I focused on maintaining my blank face, instead of on his lips. "Yes?"

"Be sure not to take too long." We stopped in front of a door to a room I hadn't entered before. "I know how anxious you must be to contact your friend, but the shadowmirror doesn't allow interactions longer than a couple of minutes." Thanatos put his hand on the doorknob. The doorframe was arched, and there was no light streaming into the corridor from beneath it.

I nodded. "All right." I made to push the door open, but the King moved in front of me and blocked my path. My brows raised in question when I blinked up at him.

He looked serious, his face stony. "Whatever happens: do not, under any circumstances, touch the mirror."

"Why?"

"Don't question me on this."

I searched his eyes and, when I realized how deadly serious he was, nodded again.

He seemed content with my answer and moved to the side. He pressed the handle down and the door swung open.

The room was dark. So very, very dark, the only source of light being the moon. On the ceiling was a huge, circular window, and the moon shone right above it. Since there was no lunar orbit in the Afterlife, the moon's location never changed, keeping an everlasting glow on the only object in the entire space.

A round mirror.

It had a golden frame and was laid out on top of a table. But that wasn't what caught my attention. Where the mirror should reflect the moon and the night-sky, it was black. Pitch black. It didn't reflect the walls or the windows. Its surface was completely dark, so dark, it seemed as though it'd swallow up the light. Even without Thanatos's warning, I could feel the power radiating from it.

I didn't notice Thanatos move until he stood next to me.

"Are you ready?"

Tearing my eyes from the mirror, I cleared my throat. "Yeah."

"Very well then." He gestured toward the mirror. It rattled on the table before it slowly began elevating and moving toward us. The Deathbringer let it angle itself until we would have been mirrored if not for the darkness within its depth. "Your image will appear to your friend almost as though you're standing in front of her. Because of the great amount of magic contacting the Land of the Living requires, she will be able to tell that you aren't physically there, but that she's seeing an image." He looked down at me. "Do you understand?"

My hands trembled as I dried them off on my dress and nodded.

"Good." He looked back at the object before us. "Move in front of the mirror," he instructed.

I did as he instructed.

Thanatos stood behind me, his presence making my back tingle. It was truly interesting that my body was almost more aware of the man standing behind me than the powerful mirror before me. It did calm me more than it probably should that he was here with me.

"What do I do now?" I asked, nervously shifting my weight.

"You look into it and start imagining your friend. See her in full clarity, and the mirror will show her to you."

I focused on the swirling darkness of mist within the mirror and began picturing Mir. Because of my nerves, it took me some time to concentrate, but eventually, I managed to visualize her silvery eyes gleaming in kindness, her black hair that she usually kept in a bun, her colorful clothing, and the jingle of all the bracelets lining her forearms. I smelled her almond-milk perfume she was so fond of and heard her melodic voice. I imagined how she threw her arms around me and drew me in a tight embrace.

"Cassiana?" Miriam's voice ripped me out of my concentration. I opened my eyes, not realizing I had closed them.

Tears immediately began forming as I saw my friend standing inside the mirror. "Mir!"

"Oh my god! Where are you? I've been looking everywhere for you! Are you all right?" she cried out.

The mirror didn't show me where Miriam was. It only displayed her body. My eyes took her in. She looked exactly the same as she always did. There was no trace that something bad might have happened to her. My legs buckled and almost gave out in relief.

I nodded. "I'm fine." Wanting to be closer to her, I took a step forward, but Thanatos immediately put his hand on my shoulder.

He inclined his head to me. "Don't get closer."

Mir's eyes were fixed on the King of the Dead. "Who's that?"

I was sure she must realize who the man behind me was, but apparently, she was too shocked to be able to grasp it.

"It's the Deathbringer." At her hissing intake of breath, I rushed to explain. "He's the one who saved me from King Silvan. The Norns told me that Silvan was searching for me."

She stared at me. "Silvan? The Norns?"

I shook my head. "It's a long story, and I don't have that much time," I said, remembering Thanatos's warning words.

Miriam seemed to realize how serious I was about the time issue, so she didn't question it.

"Are you okay?" I asked, watching her closely.

"I was out of my mind with worry! But I am fine. I don't understand why I couldn't find you. None of my searching spells worked."

"It must be because I'm in the Afterlife," I murmured. If my best friend, a powerful witch, wasn't able to locate me that also meant that Silvan shouldn't be able to either. A sense of relief washed over me.

"What?" Miriam didn't even try to hide her panic as she stared at me, her eyes huge.

"Yeah …" I could imagine how confused she must be at the revelation, but I wouldn't explain everything to her just now. I only had a couple of minutes, so I'd have to save some stuff for later. I straightened my spine. "Mir. I was so worried about you, too; you have no idea! Did Silvan do anything to you? Are you truly all right?" I wouldn't put it past her to lie to me just to ease my worry.

Her brows knit in confusion. "Silvan? The fae King?"

"Yes?"

She cocked her head. "Why would I have seen him?"

I opened my mouth, only for it to fall shut. "Didn't he … Didn't he search for me at home?"

She slowly shook her head. "No. All my wards are still intact. If he entered the apartment, I would've known …."

"He … he did't come by?" I verified.

Mir shook her head again.

But the Norns … they had said—

I felt Thanatos inch closer to me. "Your time is running out, love."

Miriam's eyes widened at the endearment, but for once, she kept her mouth shut. She bit the inside of her cheeks. "There's something I need to tell you about."

There was an undertone in her voice that immediately caught my attention. I saw the conflict in her gaze. Stepping closer to the mirror, I asked, "What is it?"

I watched my friend roll up the sleeves of her pink sweater. "I didn't want to tell you, but something's going on in the Land of the Living."

I cocked my head. "What do you mean?"

Mir started fidgeting. "I can't explain it, but there's a certain tension in the air. I feel that something is happening. I can't put my finger on it, but something is definitely going on. The creatures are behaving very oddly. Especially the fae. I haven't seen a single one of them since you left."

It wasn't unusual for the fae to keep to their realm, but Miriam not spotting *any*? How long had I been here? It must've been at least a few weeks. Even for the fae, that was a very odd behavior.

"Can't you ask your tarot deck?"

She shook her head. "I tried. But the cards keep the future hidden."

I glanced at Thanatos. He had his arms crossed in front of his chest. His expression serious and pensive.

"Has this ever happened before?"

Miriam lifted her shoulders. "Not that I know of."

"Cassiana."

I looked at Thanatos.

"You really need to hurry. The shadows are becoming restless."

I looked back at the mirror. The shadows within the black onyx surface were indeed flaring around Mir's contours.

For a split second, Mir's gaze flashed to the bracelet on my wrist that she had gifted me. Her shoulders relaxed slightly at the sight. "Can I do anything for you, hon? Do you need anything?" she asked, clearly aware of the time-pressure. Her worry almost brought tears to my eyes.

Softly, I smiled at her. "I'm fine."

She watched me silently, weighing her next words carefully. "When are you coming home?"

Home.

Glancing over my shoulder at the imposing frame of the King of the Dead, I lifted my shoulders. "I don't know."

"Why did he bring you to his realm anyway?" She jerked her head in Thanatos's direction. "Are you in trouble, hon?"

I forced myself to laugh. "No. I enjoy it here. I want to stay here."

I felt Thanatos's eyes settle heavily on my back. Truth was, I didn't want to worry Mir by telling her that I was hiding from Silvan in the Afterlife. I didn't want to concern her any more than she must already be.

Her eyes darted between the Deathbringer and me, clearly jumping to conclusions. A knowing smile tipped her lips up.

I wouldn't correct her assumptions. If I did, I'd have to explain the real reason for staying here: that apparently it was up to Thanatos to decide when I'd be free to go.

I'll pass.

I had absolutely no idea why my stay depended on Thanatos, but I wouldn't linger on that when I only had a restricted amount of time to talk to Mir. Trying to get rid of those thoughts, I cleared my throat. There was just one last thing I needed to sort out. "Can you do me a favor and tell Mrs. Fitzgivens that I will no longer participate in her lessons?" I wanted to make sure my acting tutor was aware that I wouldn't come back for a while—or ever for that matter.

Miriam became serious, her posture rigid.

Immediately, I knew that something was wrong. "What is it?"

My friend looked at me, clearly unsure of what to tell me.

"Mir? What is it?" I pressed.

She dropped her hands. "Mrs. Fitzgivens has not once asked about you since you left. Neither have the other actors. They didn't even care that you went missing," she whispered the last sentence while avoiding my gaze.

They ... they hadn't even cared that I went missing? When was the last time I had talked to any of them? The day Thanatos had saved my life by taking me away from Silvan's birthday celebration, I had called them to make sure they were okay. But after that? They hadn't even cared to so much as contact Mir to make sure *I* was all right?

Hurt shallowed my breathing at their indifference.

Thanatos inched closer, talking low enough only for me to hear. "Time's up."

I forced myself to focus back on my friend and not on people who weren't part of my life any longer. It was Miriam who was here after all. And that was all that mattered. "Mir. Apparently, time's running out. Please take care of yourself, will you?"

She nodded and smiled at me. "You too. I love you."

I smiled back at her. "Love you, too."

Not a second later, the darkness in the mirror intensified to the point that I couldn't see my friend any longer. I kept my back to Thanatos as I watched the mirror gravitate back onto the table.

When I turned to him, he was observing me, a pensive, wary expression on his face. "Are you all right?"

I sighed deeply. "I need a drink."

CHAPTER NINETEEN

As soon as the door to Thanatos's library closed behind us, I clapped my hands. "What are we drinking?"

Thanatos flashed me a wicked smile. "Don't drown your worries in liquid, love."

I huffed out a breath and collapsed onto one of the couches set up in the middle of the room.

"What is bothering you? Aren't you happy you spoke to your friend?" Thanatos asked over his shoulder as he moved to the liquor cabinet hidden by a shelf at the end of the room.

The image of my former acting colleagues flashed before my inner eye. "People are jerks, that's all."

Thanatos pulled his shoulder-length hair up into a bun. I couldn't help but notice how it accentuated the sharp cut of his jaw. "Can't argue with that."

My gaze settled on the fireplace crackling peacefully as I replayed my encounter with Mir. I was so glad she was all right. All the worry and anxiety about her well-being that had settled heavily in the pit of my stomach over the last couple of weeks started releasing. Thank God, Silvan hadn't gotten to her.

I wondered why the fae were behaving so strangely in the Land of the Living and withdrawing to their kingdom. Granted, they lived so secluded from society that there was no way to predict and understand their behavior. But the demeanor Miriam had described was alarming either way. For Mir not to see a single one of them...

And Silvan—

Silvan ... Why hadn't he checked my home for me? God knows I was grateful he hadn't, but the Norns had been so *convinced* that he was searching for me. And finding me would be child's play for him. So why hadn't he? I really didn't understand. Could it be that the Norns had been wrong about him? That he had never been looking for me in the first place? But that made no sense. As far as I was aware, the Norns knew about everything going on in both the Lands of the Dead and the Living. There was absolutely no possibility they might've been wrong about Silvan.

All these thoughts were starting to give me a headache.

I looked back at Thanatos. I watched him open a shelf underneath a small table. He pulled out a set of tumblers and bent down again to grab a rum bottle. After filling both glasses with the amber-colored liquid, he headed in my direction.

"Bring the entire bottle!" I commanded.

Thanatos arched a brow but didn't lecture me on my poor life choices. Instead, the rum bottle elevated into the air and flew toward the set of couches. When it reached the small coffee table before me, I caught it mid-air and put it right next to me.

"I have a feeling that this night is going to escalate fairly quickly," the King said with that deep, rich voice of his. He put the tumbler down on the coffee table before us and sat right next to me.

My eyes darted over the three other couches (perfectly unoccupied, I might add) and the mountain of cushions in the centre of the couch-circle, but I didn't bother reminding him of their availability. I was too fixated on the liquid to care. I took a big gulp straight from the bottle. I coughed when it burned its way down my throat.

"Easy there, love," Thanatos said, watching me in amusement. "Lightweight?"

I shook my head before admitting, "I never drink this heavy stuff."

He looked at the way my right hand was fisted around the rum bottle as if I were scared someone would snatch it away from me. "That's what all alcoholics say," he murmured. He took a sip from his glass, and it looked so damn elegant I almost wished I cared for my manners.

Oh, well.

"It must be easy for you," I said, taking another big swig from the bottle. "I mean, you are a King for fuck's sake. I'm sure you've never felt like you didn't matter in your entire life," I mumbled, staring at the bottle.

He swirled the rum in his glass. "No. That is something I indeed haven't had the chance to experience." His voice turned harsh.

"It must be so empowering," I mumbled.

Thanatos grunted.

Surprised, I lifted my head, seeing how bitterness coated his eyes.

"Do you know what it's like being feared your entire life? It's not empowering." He inched closer, his legs pressing against my thigh beneath the table. "It's lonely," he whispered.

My gaze jumped between his eyes, and the pain I saw in them conveyed the truth of his words.

I had never considered.

I had never considered the possibility that the King of the Dead was actually suffering under the weight of his crown.

He leaned his arms on the backrest, his fingers lightly brushing my shoulder. His muscles bulged beneath the material of his shirt. "And the people who at first seem trustworthy are actually only with you because they benefit from the power you hold."

I cocked my head. "Who were those people?"

He shook his head, a sudden distance turning the shadows on his face darker. "It doesn't matter."

I brought the bottle back to my mouth and took another big swig. "Why precisely *do* people fear you?" I probably knew the answer to this already; after all, I myself had feared him throughout most of my stay in the Afterlife— and even before that. But I wanted to get to know *his* point of view.

"They fear not me, but what I stand for. The promise of death, the awareness of dying someday, that everything you are currently experiencing and owning will eventually come to an end. That is what frightens most."

"What do you think about that?" I asked carefully. I felt the liquid beginning to heat my insides.

Thanatos considered for a moment. "The awareness of looming death can be incredibly encouraging to get you to stand up for what you really wish and desire. If people had indefinite time at their disposal to pursue their dreams, do you really think they would get up and do so? They wouldn't. People need something to push them. And the knowledge that their lives will come to an end does that.

"Death is not only good or bad. For a person who has been suffering for a long time, it can be incredibly freeing, while for the person who just lost a loved one, it can become suffocating." He took the rum bottle from me and refilled his glass before handing it back. After a beat of silence, he said, "It's sad, actually."

"What is?"

"That it's not so much the Dead that the Living mourn, but rather the fact that they have lost someone dear to them. That they have lost a companion." He exhaled heavily. "In the end, that mourning's nothing more than self-pity."

At what point had we started discussing these existential questions?

"You are right," I agreed while I brought the rum bottle to my lips. Just like he'd said, it was sad. Who was it people felt pity for? The person who had passed away, or themselves for losing someone and, with it, being reminded of their own death? A sudden bitterness exploded on the back of my tongue. What did people actually feel or do that wasn't driven by their self-centeredness?

Astounded, he lifted his brows. "That's it? You will not fight my pessimistic view?"

"I think you have been around death long enough to know how it works and what drives people. You probably know the answer for your question better than I do."

He stared at the fireplace, his mind clearly distant. When he spoke again, his voice was so low, I almost missed his next words.

"Sometimes, I just wished to be mistaken. To have some more hope."

I squinted at him. "Hope for what?"

Startled, he lifted his head, almost as though he had forgotten I was still here and had heard his hushed words. "Hope for humanity."

The rum bottle was already empty when I reached out to it. Only three drops made it into my glass. Making a face, I put the bottle aside.

Thanatos's deep chuckle rumbled in the large room. "I have never seen such a disappointed look on you."

"Life is dull without booze," I lectured him, my voice entirely too sarcastic to be taken seriously.

Thanatos leaned forward. "I'm worried. With that attitude it would be wise to seek out a psychologist." He was sitting very close to me. Too close to be appropriate. My gaze dropped to the way his muscles filled out his shirt. The alcohol was already taking a toll on me.

I snorted. "Says the man who kills people for a living."

Thanatos's eyebrow arched up. "Did you see me kill someone?"

I gave him a look over the rim of my glass. "Nope. But that doesn't mean anything."

Thanatos huffed out a laugh. "If you say so."

"So, tell me, *Deathbringer*," I stressed his title.

He lifted a brow.

"I imagine now that we know that Silvan isn't looking for me,

I am free to go home?"

If I weren't so drunk in that second, I might've caught that sudden dark expression flashing over his face like a cloud blocking the sun. It didn't match the lighthearted tone with which he answered. "Have you forgotten, love? Your stay doesn't depend on the fae King, but on—"

"Yes, yes, I know," I cut him off, rolling my eyes. With a single hand, I painted imaginary quotation marks in the air. "It depends on you."

I swirled the rum—all three drops of it—in my glass, lamenting again over the small amount.

His eyes followed my gaze to the glass. He moved in closer.

Under any other circumstance, I might feel nervous at his proximity, but the alcohol had dulled that feeling.

He outstretched his hand. "Let me."

I passed him my glass and watched him tap on it three times. Astonished, I observed how it refilled itself. When he handed it back to me, I took a sip, confirming it was indeed rum.

"Maybe you are Jesus," I pondered. A hot Jesus for that matter.

"Jesus turned water into wine, love. Not air into rum."

He reached for his own glass that rested on the coffee table next to the sofa. In doing so, he had to lean over the couch's armrest.

I watched the way his trousers accentuated his butt with the movement. Gesturing in his direction, I took a sip of my glass. "See? You are even better than Jesus."

Thanatos arched a brow. "I take it you are an atheist."

Rather completely drunk for that matter.

I shrugged and leaned forward. "So, tell me: how come you,

the most powerful of the Kings, gets drunk?"

Thanatos crossed his legs. "I'm barely tipsy. And besides, I'm not the one drooling," he pointed out, a smirk across his features.

Was I? Shrugging, I dismissed the topic. "You are too hot to be Jesus anyway."

Thanatos flashed me a mischievous smile. "So, you think I am hot." He wiggled his eyebrows at me.

Rolling my eyes at him, I snorted. Only a blind person would disagree. "Oh, fuck off!"

Suddenly, he materialized *right* in front of me.

I gasped for air and shrieked back.

He braced his hands on the couch's backrest, efficiently caging me in. My lips parted at the hooded intensity I recognized in Thanatos's raging eyes. His gaze dropped to my parted lips. My hair stood on end as he leaned forward, and my breathing became shallow when his cheek grazed my own. His smell encircled me in a soft shell, making me forget everything but his presence.

His voice had become deeper, rougher when he spoke next, his lips pressing against my ear. "Careful, love." My eyes fluttered closed at the sensation the rumble of his voice provoked within me. "Or I might make good on that offer."

He drew back a couple of inches. Neither of us moved as we stared into each other's eyes. His eyes dropped to my breasts, which were pushed up with my exaggerated breathing. He ran a hand over his mouth. But, except for that gesture, did he not move.

I was perfectly aware that the burn of the rum had loosened my tongue, but that was no reason to stop now. I looked up at the King of the Dead through my lashes. "Maybe I want you to."

Thanatos stared at me. There was no sign he had heard me. Only his dangerous, gleaming eyes gave away the turmoil within him. He searched my face for a sign that would call my bluff.

But he just knew.

He saw the hungry look in my eyes, and a savage smile spread those beautiful lips that always seemed to draw me in, making me lean forward, wanting to touch them, wondering if they would feel different than they had yesterday.

He smiled. That wicked, wicked smile of his that promised trouble.

And, boooy, I was down for whatever trouble the Deathbringer wanted to make.

He seemed to sense it, because he stepped up to me, forcing me to tilt my head further back to meet his gaze. "Shall we play a game, love?" he purred with that deep, rich voice of his, rumbling through my entire body. His breath fanned over my sensitive skin.

I should say no. I knew I should say no. But that question of his and that heated look in his eyes just ... promised.

Promised something dangerous. Something that would be ... fun. Something that would make me forget about life's reality.

"You'll like it," he promised, leaning closer. His lips brushed my earlobe at his next words. "So, what do you say, love?"

My eyes opened leisurely, settling of their own accord on the Deathbringer's lips. When had they fallen shut? "What game did you have in mind?" I asked, my voice becoming breathless.

No, no, no. I shouldn't even consider this.

His eyes lit like the sky on a stormy night. He already knew I was down for whatever game he'd choose.

"We, my love, are going to play hide and seek."

Incredulously, I stared up at him. This game was definitely not one I'd pictured playing with the King of the Dead. I felt my brows knitting together. "How old are you again?"

He chuckled deeply. "I lost count." He tucked a strand of hair behind my ear. The soft touch awakened my body to molecules of fire.

"Aren't you supposed to be all wise and, well ... mature?"

"Ouch," he said dryly. He was so close to me I was able to detect the small sprinkles that dotted his irises. "Believe me when I tell you that the things I plan to do with you once I find you are very much *mature*."

Sexual tension heated my blood.

"Okay," I heard myself say, my voice grown hoarse.

Wait, what?

The Deathbringer stared down at me, those striking green eyes fixed entirely on my face, and then his lips turned into a smile. A real one. One that made my core clench in anticipation.

He closed his eyes. "One."

I stared at him.

"Two." Now that his eyes were closed, I allowed myself to take him in. *Really* take him in. He was beautiful. My eyes roamed over his captivating facial features. His sharp-cut cheekbones cast long shadows on his face, and his ink-black lashes touched his cream-colored skin in an enthralling contrast. He looked like a fallen angel coming to earth only to remind us of our imperfections.

His voice cut through the silence, making me jump. "You'd better hurry, love. I can still hear the beating of your heart."

He didn't have to repeat himself.

I felt like a giddy girl as I got up from the couch and turned around. I ran out of the room, trying to find a place to hide.

Suddenly, the fog of alcohol clouding my mind was replaced by the feeling of utter excitement. I rushed down the corridor, heading for the staircase to the second floor. Hurrying up the stairs, I halted as my eyes flew over all the places I could hide. A small bench, an even smaller table …

No. These hiding places were too easy. What would the Deathbringer assume I would do?

Run to my room.

But what he wouldn't assume is that I'd choose his own bedchamber. A proud smile spread my lips as I aimed for the wooden door to his room. As soundlessly as possible, I pushed the handle down and slipped through the door. I closed it behind me and leaned my back against it.

Silence.

My heart accelerated when I took in the space. I was in Thanatos's personal bedchambers.

The room was furnished spartanly. There was only a bed, a nightstand, the door connecting to our attached bathroom, and a desk overlooking Emoh. Other than that, the room was completely empty. The only sources of light were some floating candles and the window facing Emoh. It was identical to the window in my bedroom.

The air …. I drew in a shuddering breath and let my eyes close. It smelled like Thanatos. Like a night spent under the night sky in the company of oneself.

My eyes darted to the satin, deep-red bedcovers. Would they feel as soft as they looked? Would they also smell as promising and comforting as their owner?

The things I plan to do with you when I find you are very much mature.

The reminder of his words triggered a feeling unknown to me. It wasn't only anticipation, but something more profound, something that should definitely worry me.

Did I actually want him to find me? Did I want to find out what those things he'd talked about were? Heat pooled in my core.

Yesssss, hissed a voice that wasn't remembering everything I had experienced throughout my life.

I moved past the bed and let my fingers glide slowly over the covers. Turning around, I aimed for the big, floor-to-ceiling mahogany-toned curtains. They rustled in the softest of sounds when I pulled them back. The material was opaque, making it my perfect hiding place. I moved my body behind the curtains and let the material slide back. The curtains hid my body successfully.

Just in time.

The door to the King's bedroom was pulled open, and heavy steps entered the small room.

It had taken the Deathbringer no time at all to find me. Apparently, I was that predictable after all.

The window at my back was ice-cold as I pressed further against it.

Please don't let him find me, please don't let him find me. I repeated the mantra over and over in my mind.

Please find me, please find me, the same voice begged simultaneously.

"Come out, come out wherever you are!" His voice thundered dangerously.

I held my breath as I heard him slowly circle the room.

"I know you are here."

My heart skipped a beat when I heard his steps stop right in front of me. I tried evening my breathing as I carefully lifted my hand to draw the curtain back a couple of inches. Just enough to glance at the King. He was standing mere inches away, his back facing me. My heart pounded against my ribcage so furiously I was sure he must be able to hear its attempts to jump out of my chest. He only needed to turn around, and he'd be able to see me.

He turned around.

I pressed my eyes together, stupidly begging not to be seen. My breathing sounded incredibly loud, and my entire body was pent up in anticipation.

Nothing happened for a while, and I slowly blinked my eyes open again. Thanatos had turned around once more, checking the other side of the room. Just before he should've been able to spot me, it had become darker around me, a shadow—most probably a cloud—blocking the moon's light. The darkness had embraced me just in time to hide me from Thanatos.

Slowly, I let the curtain fall back, hiding me yet again behind the fabric. I hadn't anticipated the low rustling sound it made by the movement.

A startled cry escaped me as the curtain was yanked back, revealing Thanatos's tall, muscle-defined body looming powerfully over mine.

He cocked his head, tsking as he assessed me. "I found you," he declared. "Now tell me, love. What do you think would be an adequate prize for winning this game?"

"I don't know," I stammered. Did they have Snickers here?

"Oh, but I do." He reached out to me, his hand cupping my face gently.

"You do?" My eyes slid to his lips.

"Mm-hmm." Ever so slowly, his right hand moved down my

throat, gliding softly over my collarbone. Each one of his touches was complete torture. They were too light, so light they drove me mad. It felt as though he didn't touch me at all.

All at once, I realized how small I was compared to him. It wasn't only his height that made me feel small, it was also his presence that managed to intimidate me.

My breathing became hollow as his fingers reached the neckline of the dress Kalira had chosen that morning.

I had always had cleavage that attracted men's attention. Usually, I hated that, but for once, I enjoyed the fact I could show it off.

"What prize would you deem adequate?" I asked, looking innocently at the King of the Afterlife.

"I think ..." Thanatos leaned forward, pressing his head against my own before he inhaled deeply. "I think it's time to make good on that offer of yours."

Thanatos grinned at the shock on my face. He pressed his index finger to my throat, exercising just the whisper of pressure. His eyes lit at the fast beating of my heart. His other hand traced an invisible path up the right side of my body until it grazed the swell of my breast. At the small, feather-like touch, my eyes immediately fluttered closed.

Why the hell had I told him to fuck off? I couldn't possibly want this, could I?

If my off-rhythm heartbeat wasn't a big enough indicator, the heat in my core surely was.

"Would you like that?" His hand glided over my bodice, reaching lower and lower. "Would you like to make good on your offer?" He advanced so slowly, he gave me more than enough time to stop him.

But I didn't.

When he reached the thick fabric of my skirt, right over my core, he applied the slightest pressure, flattening his hand against the place I most desperately ached for his touch. A soft moan escaped my trembling lips, and my eyes had already drifted shut at the question. I felt the Deathbringer lean forward, his body pressing mine harder against the window.

"Tell me, love. I need words."

I blinked open my eyes, scanning his mesmerizing, beautiful face. Should I let him?

My body seemed to talk before I had even made up my mind. "Yes."

He smiled.

Oh, fuck.

That smile promised danger. That broad, victorious-looking smile he flashed me, and the look he gave me ... I had never seen him so keen on doing something. "Your wish is my command." With a savage smirk, he eased himself down my body onto his knees.

"What are you doing?" I asked hoarsely as I watched the King of the Afterlife kneel in front of me.

"You'll see." And, with a wink, both of his hands found their way to the hem of my skirt, pushing the fabric up my legs. His hands glided higher and higher. His touch electrified my skin when he pushed the skirt slowly over my knees, up to my thighs, and even higher. My core pulsed with need.

"Thanatos." The way I rolled his name on my tongue ... it sounded like a sinful plea. My breathing deepened, pushing my breasts heavily up and down. He hadn't even touched me properly, and I was already a complete mess. My body quivered, my skin prickled, and my heart pounded in my chest like thunder. My hands found their way into the thickness of his hair.

He looked up at me and the sight was just so ... regal. Even when he was on his knees, a gesture of surrender, he did not lose his royal presence.

His hands pushed my skirt up the rest of the way until he held it bunched at my waist with his fists.

At this point, I was a shivering mess. Both his hands spanned the side of my hips. He stared at my exposed skin for a couple of seconds, and then he leaned forward and pressed a feather-like kiss on the skin right under my navel.

I sighed contently and felt Thanatos smile against my heated skin. When his lips withdrew, both his index fingers hooked into the last piece of clothing that stood between him and my most intimate part. My breathing stopped completely.

He removed my panties painfully slowly. Too slowly.

He dragged them down my thighs, over my calves, and when they reached my ankles, I lifted first my left foot, then my right, stepping out of the thin fabric. The Deathbringer stood, and before I could brace myself, he had lifted me into his arms and carried me toward his bed.

He was looking down at me, either oblivious to the deep-red flush I was sure had spread over my cheeks onto my cleavage, or choosing to ignore it.

Carefully, like I was the most treasured thing in the world, he put me down on the satin that felt incredibly cool against my hot skin. I watched him moving around, coming to a stop at the end of the bed. He climbed onto it, once again pushing my skirt up.

I swallowed hard as he moved it completely over my waist, my core now exposed to his searching gaze.

Except, he wasn't looking at my centre. He was looking at me, observing each small reaction that would indicate to him that I wanted him to stop.

It was a good thing I didn't.

Only once he noticed that did his gaze drop to my sex.

"You are marvelous," he said, before adding, "and drenched for that matter."

Under any other circumstance, I'd be completely mortified by my body's reaction, if not for the satisfied, entirely pleased, male look I recognized in Thanatos's eyes.

"Spread those pretty thighs for me, love."

Heat pooled in the low of my stomach at his commanding words, igniting a fire unknown to me. Hesitantly, I did as he asked.

"Good girl," he praised, his voice sounding pleased and much deeper than I remembered it being.

I had never been shy around men, but Thanatos's entire being was made for this. The way his body moved so self-assuredly, the way he was so aware of the effect he had upon me, the way power surrounded him like a second skin. It all made me so very aware of who it was I was letting close to me. Literally and figuratively.

He pushed my legs farther apart, his strong body sliding between my parted thighs. His movements weren't hurried. On the contrary: he seemed to relish every second.

My left hand reached down to him and traced his temple. Thanatos grabbed my hand and, for a split second, stared at the mole on my wrist. A puzzled expression flashed across his features.

Why was he always looking at my mole like that?

Before that thought had a chance to take root, he let go of my wrist and his hands were suddenly *there*, gliding over my calves toward my thighs.

My lips parted, expelling a gentle sigh.

And then, without giving me a second to anticipate what he was about to do, he slid his strong hands underneath my butt cheeks and gave a strong pull toward him.

I squeaked as my body was yanked forward, hard though never painful.

Thanatos now kneeled in front of the bed. Even having alcohol heating my insides, my face burned as I realized his face was eye-level with my core, and I was sure he was able to see every single drop of proof that I was totally turned on by this.

And, sue me, but for once in my life, I wasn't embarrassed by it in the slightest. Maybe because of the Deathbringer's longing I recognized in the depth of his eyes, or maybe because this just felt incredibly right.

My entire body jerked as his hands moved over the inside of my thighs, aiming for my centre. Every small brush of his skin against my own kindled a desire within me I couldn't understand.

His hands paused at the apex of my thighs.

I glanced down at Thanatos. He was watching me closely, a wolfish smile spreading those sensual lips. My breathing had become ragged, my breasts pushing heavily against the bodice of my dress. Thanatos's eyes dipped to them, watching the way they heaved, before coming back to meet my eyes. His gaze grew so intense, I almost came apart beneath it.

Ever so slowly, his eyes dropped to what was laid openly in front of him.

And then he stopped staring.

At the first touch of his hands on my mound, a low moan escaped my trembling lips.

His deep laugh at my body's reaction sent heat right to my core. His fingers moved past my lips to my entrance.

I fisted the sheets, my breath panting as he slowly inserted one digit inside me.

"Mmm …" he said thoughtfully as he watched me squirm. "I think you do enjoy this game."

A moan was my only answer.

When he pulled out his now damp finger, I almost cried out at the loss. But then he found that small, sensitive, little nub of my body. He coated my clit in my own dampness before tracing idle circles around it.

But it wasn't enough. He didn't put enough pressure on it to help me release the tension that had gathered in my body at his touches and caresses.

"Please!" I breathed.

His movements stopped. "What is it you want?"

I growled in frustration. He couldn't be serious. I blinked my eyes open, only to find him looking at me with those flashing green eyes, his lips curled up.

He was totally mocking me. And he was enjoying the hell out of this.

I glared down at him. "Stop teasing."

He laughed at that, and then, he didn't mock me anymore. No, he got damn serious.

He lowered his head.

The first stroke of his tongue against my core made me gasp for air, crashing my head back against the bed. My fingers found their way into his silken hair. He lifted his head once more. He stared at my centre as if in amazement.

My grip on his hair tightened, drawing him back.

He got the implicit message. Before I could brace myself, he was on me, lapping at my core. He growled at my taste, the sound kindling my own need and arousal. At first, his touches were playful. His tongue circled my clit in small circles, making me move without control against his face, trying to apply more friction on the spot where I needed him. He locked his muscular arms around my hips, preventing me from squirming any further.

I panted.

Suddenly, I felt his teeth scrape against my clit, carefully nibbling at it. Now, I couldn't restrain the desperate moans escaping me. I panted Thanatos's name like a prayer, needing him to put more pressure on me.

And he obeyed.

He spread my legs wider apart as his right hand moved from the place he was holding me trapped against the bed toward my core, inserting two fingers at once.

My orgasm crashed upon me like a thunderstorm, making me scream out Thanatos's name, my body bucking under his touch.

He smiled when he slowly eased his fingers out of me.

I flinched at the sound that only proved my desire. I stared in complete astonishment at the man nestled between my thighs.

Thanatos looked utterly satisfied with himself. Like a predator, he moved up my body. He locked his arms around my waist and turned over, changing our positions.

I ended up cradled on top of his chest.

My breasts pressed against his upper body with my heavy

breathing. Even with him still wearing his shirt, I felt his rock-hard chest through the material.

As my breathing eased back to its normal pace and my skin cooled again, I pushed against his hold on me.

He drew me back against him, murmuring into my hair, "What are you doing?"

I looked at him through my lashes. "I thought you won. Shouldn't it be *me* who rewards *you*?" I asked, surprised at my unusual boldness.

His face lit in shock as I slowly moved down his body, taking my time, and swinging my hips seductively with my movements.

His desire-ardent eyes tracked every action. "You don't have to. I did what I did to please you, not because I wanted something in return."

"I want to." When I reached his waist, I stopped crawling down his length.

Usually, my shyness might get the better of me, but right now, my body was still buzzing with the feeling of pleasure—and loads of rum—discarding all other thoughts. Taking my time, I opened his trousers. I smiled as my gaze landed on his shorts. He was already rock-hard for me. I freed his cock and stared at it. Even his length was unearthly in every single one of its details. It was too thick to be entirely human, too long to be in any sense average, and definitely too beautiful.

I lowered myself onto my forearms and reached out to him. The skin around his shaft was smooth, even silken, and precum had gathered at the tip. I traced my thumb over the essence, spreading it over the shaft.

Thanatos watched me the entire time, not once rushing me or demanding that I stop. He seemed content just looking at me.

I smiled sweetly at him before descending on his member.

He jerked at the very first touch of my mouth against him. I dragged my tongue over his saltiness before taking him in completely. It was a challenge to swallow him whole. But it was a challenge I was more than willing to accept. I had to open my mouth as wide as possible for him to fit. He did fit, though.

Barely.

I rolled my eyes back at him, bobbing my head up and down on his thick length.

"Fuck," he cursed under his breath, staring at me. His pupils were dilated in sheer bliss.

I laughed around the thick mushroom of his member, making him jerk up into me. Who'd have thought the King of the Afterlife was acquainted with foul language?

I enjoyed the way a thin sheen of sweat began coating his body; his breathing increased, and the veins on his cock began to thicken.

Not once did he look away from what I was doing as I worked him until I felt him grow bigger. I knew he was about to come. His curses were just an additional hint. I reached out, grabbing his heavy balls, slowly rolling them while my head kept bobbing at his length.

"Fuck!"

Before I could brace myself, his seed pumped into me. I made sure to swallow everything.

As I let his spent cock slip out of my mouth, he pulled me up against him, kissing me savagely. "Thank you," he whispered, his lips pressed against my temple.

That night, I fell asleep on top of the King of the Dead. Sated, held against him, and overall, happy.

CHAPTER TWENTY

When I woke the next morning, I purred and stretched like a cat. It had been way too long since I had last slept this deeply. I yawned and turned around.

Thanatos was lying on his side next to me, his arm loosely draped over my torso. I suppressed a scream.

Fuck.

The memory of what we did yesterday came back to me like an avalanche, its weight threatening to pull me under.

No, no, no, no. What had I done?

Careful not to wake him, I moved Thanatos's arm away from my body. Then, I pushed myself up and eased my body quietly out of the bed. My panic was so overwhelming, I didn't even bother to look back at Thanatos as I rushed out of the bedroom into the corridor.

The things I plan to do with you once I find you are very much mature.

No, no, no!

Why had I let him do this? Fuck.

Images of Thanatos's face buried in my core flashed behind my eyes, and my tongue still seemed to taste the saltiness of his essence. The cool air in the corridor hit me as I let the door to the King's bedroom fall shut behind me.

I jumped at the soft sound. Had I woken him?

Heart thundering, I pressed my ear against the door and listened. No sound came from the other side of the room. Slowly, I exhaled in relief. I didn't know what I'd do if he had woken and I'd had to face him.

Dread clenched my abdomen as I stared at my bodice that had fallen loose throughout the night's activities. I grabbed behind my back and tried to fix the ties as tightly as possible. Usually, Kalira would help me with a dress like this one, but it must have been so early in the morning that she was still at her home, sleeping peacefully. That, or she couldn't find me in my own room. My blood ran cold at what she might be guessing. At the truth behind her assumptions.

When I somehow managed to secure the bodice, I scrambled forward.

I knew I was having a panic attack by the way my heart pumped against my temples and by the wetness gathering on my palms. I hadn't had one of these in ages. And I knew the only thing that would stop it.

Air.

I needed air.

I raced down the stairs of the main hall, making sure my skirt was out of my way as I did so. The handle to the castle's entry was comfortingly cool as I pressed it down. Outside, the wind blew violently. When I stepped out of the castle, it tore at my loose hair aggressively. I welcomed its coolness.

I ran the way leading to Emoh , but stopped as soon as I saw some people walking in the city. They ducked their heads as they hurried through Emoh, trying to protect themselves from the outburst of the weather.

Without thinking twice, I turned left toward the small stone bridge I had seen before. My hair was flying wildly behind me, and my skirt was ripping with my hectic movements.

The bridge became bigger as I cut through the distance to it. Once I reached it, my breathing was jagged. I leaned against its ice-cold stones and struggled for air.

Last night shouldn't have happened.

Why had I done this?

Why had I let Thanatos get this close to me?

I was old enough to differentiate between a casual fuck and what we had done yesterday. I pressed my back further against the stone wall. Slowly, I let my body glide down until I was crouched down. The stone was hard and wet against my back, but my skin felt numb and I wasn't able to feel anything besides the deep, all-consuming anxiety pumping through me.

My hands fisted my hair, and I bowed my head. My stomach was fighting against what little I had eaten yesterday.

It was the rum. You got drunk. You didn't know what you were doing. You only acted the way you did because of the alcohol.

It means nothing. Nothing at all.

But the problem was, that wasn't true.

"Oh God!" I squeezed my eyes shut, forcing myself to take deep breaths. I was hyperventilating. I needed to get as much oxygen into me as possible. But the more I tried forcing air into my lungs, the more my throat seized, blocking my airstream.

I had become intimate with Thanatos, but that alone wasn't

the bad thing. I had slept with a fair number of men before, and it had never provoked this reaction from me. The rum hadn't conjured up these feelings. It had made me act upon what I truly desired and stopped me from pretending I didn't want it.

And that was just wrong, wrong, wrong.

I leaned my head back against the wall.

I shouldn't desire Thanatos. Fuck, I shouldn't even think about him at all. I should leave the past behind. But I couldn't. Yesterday, it wasn't only about a physical attraction. It hadn't just been a harmless fling. I had been ... attached.

FUCK.

People weren't there so they could help you. So that you may find joy in each other. No. People only wanted to take advantage of relationships for their own benefit.

Why hadn't I learned that by now? My own damn parents had taught me that lesson.

It wasn't so much what we had done, but rather the feelings behind it. I had *wanted* that. It had been important to me. And that scared the shit out of me.

Tears blurred my vision, and I began shaking uncontrollably.

I also damn well knew that the townspeople had been right about Thanatos: isolating oneself wouldn't help anybody. And I knew they were right. I *knew* it. But wasn't Mir enough? Did I need to open up to another person when it was the one thing that scared me the most?

All these emotions were so damn confusing. All of this would be so much easier if I didn't feel what I did for Thanatos. Yesterday would just be a one-night stand with no emotion attached to it. But it freaking wasn't.

My heightened emotions threatened to weigh a pit in my stomach.

The wind was whipping at my clothing, but I refused to go back. I couldn't. Not after what had happened between Thanatos and me.

I began rocking back and forth. I still held my hair fisted to the point of pain. I wasn't sure if it was the raging weather or my mind starting to pass out that made black dots cloud my vision.

Suddenly, I felt a soft palm pressing against my neck. "Breathe."

I recognized who that soft touch and soothing voice belonged to immediately. I wanted to rip his hand away from my skin so I could make sure I was safe, but at the same time, I wanted to lean into the touch, forgetting everything bad that had ever happened to me and just get lulled in by his comforting body heat.

It had always been easy for me to blend in with the darkness. Whenever I didn't want to be found, I just chose to stay hidden by the shadows. And no one would find me. It should have been nearly impossible to find me on the bridge, hidden by the obscurity. But, of course, Thanatos had found me. After all, he ruled over the darkness.

The King of the Dead lowered himself to his knees. "Cassiana. You need to breathe." When I still didn't comply, he gently took my chin between his thumb and index finger and forced me to meet his eyes. "Look at me, love. You have to breathe."

It was as though my body listened to Thanatos of its own accord. Air began filling my lungs. I gasped for it like a fish on the dry and sagged forward in exhaustion. Thanatos's arms slipped around my waist immediately, preventing me from hitting the ground.

I still shook with silent sobs.

"Shhh." His left hand stroked reassuringly over my back. He rested his chin on the crown of my head. "Everything is going to be all right, love. Trust me. Whatever it is. We can work it out."

I exhaled a pained breath. Why? God, why? Why was my body relaxing the second it was held by him when he was the cause of its tumult in the very first place?

I began thrashing in his hold. "Let go of me!"

He didn't. He just kept stroking my back. "It's all right. I'm here."

New tears began forming. "No, you are not! You will only be here for me until Silvan finds someone else to mess with. Oh right, he hasn't even searched for me. So, you don't have to keep me here any longer. And once I go back home, you will forget me like everyone else! You are no exception!" My yelled words were barely understandable with the sobs interrupting them.

His arms fell away as if I had burned him. "What?"

I did not want to show him my vulnerabilities. So instead, I rose and began walking away from him. Telling him what I was feeling would only mean that he'd manage to get even closer to me.

He manifested right in front of me, blocking my way and causing me almost to crash into him. Surprised, I jumped back.

"You will not just walk away from me like that," he declared. "What is wrong?" His voice became soft. So very soft, warm, comforting, and kind.

I wished it was hard, demanding. Then I wouldn't have difficulty pushing him away.

"Nothing." I forced myself to smile and rushed past him. I tried my very best to avoid his gaze.

Before I could react, his hands were on my cheeks, cupping them. "Goddamn, Cassiana! What the hell is wrong?"

"Just leave me alone!" I cried out, trying to turn away again, but his hold on my face, even though it was gentle and tender, prevented me from doing so, forcing my eyes to meet his.

"Do not lie to me. You ran out of the room and almost passed out. I see the paths your tears have left on your cheeks, and I see the way you avoid my gaze. Stop lying to me and tell me what's going on!" His right thumb followed the curve of my jaw. "Whatever it is, we can work it out together. You're not alone. If you choose to walk away, I will walk beside you."

A low sob left my trembling lips at his words. Because they made everything just … worse.

His high arched brows drew together. "Hey. Hey." His hands left my cheeks only to curl under my thighs and lift me up effortlessly. He carried me to a nearby bench and sat down. He rearranged my body in such a way that I was now straddling him.

"Let me go!" I demanded, but the whispered words sounded much more broken than I intended. Even when I began sobbing, I pushed weakly against his chest, achieving nothing by doing so.

"It's all right," Thanatos murmured, resting his forehead against mine. His hand left the small of my back and began stroking my hair.

Against my inner will, I felt myself slowly relax against him.

Why? Why did I start to feel something other than fear for the man holding me?

He held me the entire time, never ceasing to stroke my hair or wipe away the stream of tears leaving my eyes like a waterfall.

Eventually, my tears began to subdue, my body becoming too exhausted to suffer any longer.

"What happened today?" He cleared his throat, and I felt his hands slightly tremble as his fingers combed through my tangled hair. "Did I ... did I do something wrong yesterday? Did I hurt you?"

I felt his Adam's apple bob against my temple. When I looked up at him, I saw his face crumble in uncertainty for a split second. "Do you ... do you regret what we did?"

I thought my crying had ceased, but with his worry, a new, stronger sob rocked my body. It wasn't a pretty cry. My gaze dropped to the wet spot on the Deathbringer's shirt. Whether it originated from my tears or my snot, I couldn't tell.

"What did I do?" The Deathbringer pulled away to look me in the eyes, and the softness, the vulnerability, I found in his gaze almost made me break.

Shaking my head, I took deep breaths, trying to pull myself together. "You did not do anything wrong. At all. You are perfect." *Too perfect for me*, I wanted to add.

The Deathbringer's hand stopped before resuming the light caress on my cheeks. He was giving me space, waiting for me to open up to him.

And God ... that alone was exactly why I had started crying in the very first place. Because his actions provoked feelings within me I had long ago sworn to never share with another person, except for my friendship with Miriam.

I gathered my courage and, not meeting his eyes, admitted, "I'm just so fucking scared." I had spoken so low I wasn't sure he had heard me.

His hand dropped to the small of my back, and his thumb began painting small, reassuring circles on it. "Of what, Cassiana? Tell me. Nothing will harm you. You are safe here with me."

"But I am not safe *from* you."

I felt his entire body freeze beneath me. He looked as shocked as I felt for telling him.

"What? I... I would never hurt you," he rasped out.

I could make out the pain in his voice that matched my own. I couldn't bear to be this close to him when what I was going to tell him was so important. I stood.

This time, he let me.

I began pacing. "It's not what you think. It's just …." It was so freaking hard to tell him why I was so devastated. I felt the Deathbringer's eyes heavily on me, tracking my every movement, but always waiting, never pushing me. Searching for the right words, I ran my hand through my hair. "It's just … my parents never loved me the way parents should." I wasn't saying this to get his pity. I was telling him this because I owed it to Thanatos to tell him the truth. He had taken care of me. He had saved me. The least I could do was be honest with him. "My mom never interfered with anything my dad did to me. Mothers are supposed to be the ones to guard their children from harm. She never did. She never once even tried." I swallowed hard.

Thanatos's body had grown still, his expression darkening with every word.

"Maybe they even did me a favor." I laughed humorlessly. "Maybe by showing me humanity's worst, they prepared me for reality."

I did not tell him about all the times my father had locked me up in the closet for hours and hours letting me think that he had forgotten about me. Nor did I tell him of the countless times my father had said that I was losing my mind. To hear something so cruel as a child had nearly broken me. Especially coming from my own father.

Neither did I tell him of that windy night my father had come for me in the apartment I split with Mir. I wasn't ready to share this with Thanatos just yet. It still felt too intimate.

But his look clearly indicated he felt there was more.

I couldn't grasp how thankful I was that he kept quiet and didn't start digging into my past. That he let me set my own pace.

It took me some time until I found the courage to proceed. "I'm just so fucking scared of being … left. Miriam is the only one I have. I am so scared of being cast aside. Miriam has stood by my side in good and in bad, and I know she won't do that and that I can trust her. But with others … I am just scared for my trust to be …"

"Exploited," the Deathbringer filled in for me, his eyes sad. So very sad. "And I understand. God, Cassiana, do I understand."

I turned to him. "Do you? Do you truly?" I didn't manage to keep the bitterness from coating my voice.

When he stood, the shadows around him flickered uncontrollably. He stepped up. "You have no idea. I understand more than anyone what you have been through." He leaned forward and pressed his forehead against mine.

I closed my eyes, relishing the feeling of his skin against my own.

He swallowed hard. "I used to walk the earth." His voice was distant, caught up in the past. "There was a time when I didn't enjoy my own company more than anyone else's. There was a time when I actually sought out the company of others."

I became completely still, feeling that the Deathbringer was about to open up to me, talk to me, lowering his shadows to uncover a small part of what was hidden behind them. His memories.

"Of course, when you are predestined to live over thousands of years, you seek out the company of like beings." The Kings. He was talking about the Kings. "There was a time when all the Kings met on a regular basis. Me included. We had ... fun." The word sounded sour as it left the Deathbringer's lips. "But, as all good things do, the time inevitably came to an end."

He stopped, his breathing becoming heavy. The memory of whatever it was he was about to tell me still hurt him. Deeply.

Tentatively, I reached up, caressing the soft skin of his cheek. He leaned into my touch, and his eyes began fluttering. When he kept talking, his voice had dropped, sounding rough and exhausted. "They were my friends. Best friends for that matter." He laughed, his voice missing its joy. "I had never been as happy as the moment I realized the Kings wanted to be friends with me," he swallowed, "only for that hope to be shattered into pieces. I am not sure if I'll ever be able to hope again."

He ran a hand through his hair. "I've never told anyone about this." He straightened his spine, visibly trying to regain his composure.

Seconds turned into minutes before he was able to keep going. "The Kings had organized a meeting at the Kingdom of the fae."

I felt myself stiffen at the mention of the kingdom.

His eyes met mine. "My real name—"

"Thanatos," I whispered.

He nodded. "It derives from Greek mythology. The winged personification of death. I am sure you have seen the statues?"

When I nodded, I felt his power swelling around us, and I

glanced behind him, seeing how the shadows closed in on him and began forming ...

I gasped for air.

They formed *wings* at his back. Huge, majestic, black wings.

They resembled his statue. I remembered the day when I had seen the statues of the Kings. I had seen Thanatos's statue. Its gaze had been fixed on Silvan's sculpture, which rested its arm on Thanatos's shoulder. The artist must've made the statues in a time when all the Kings had still been friends. And Thanatos's wings ... the way his stony wingspan almost managed to curl around the other five Kings. I remembered wondering how they might feel beneath my touch. How it must feel to let the wind whip around you as they elevated you into the air.

Slowly, Thanatos put his hands at the small of my back and pressed me against him. I had a feeling it was a gesture more about emotional connection than physical. His voice came out in a rasp. "That's right. I used to have wings."

My breathing stopped. *Used to.* Past tense.

I opened my mouth, only to close it again. "How—"

"As we've discussed, almost everybody is scared of death. Only the brightest people are not. The Kings are no exception. They had also been scared of dying." Surprised, I looked at the Deathbringer. While the Kings had a much longer lifespan than any other living being, they were just as mortal as the rest of us. Only Thanatos was dead, yet somehow, still alive. I had never considered the Kings' own fear of death. Thanatos's gaze was distant, lost in memories. "We held regular meetings. But at one of them, they decided, foolish as they are, to take me hostage."

Oh my God. The shadow-formed wings behind him jerked. I

ripped my gaze away from them and looked back at Thanatos in disbelief.

"They wanted me to make them immortal. They found a holy vow that would force me to oblige." A shadow flashed over his face. "And they had their ways to try to force me to make that vow."

I shook my head in shock. "Thanatos …"

His eyes grew distant as he avoided mine. A muscle jumped on his jaw. "When I refused to make the vow, they took my wings."

My stomach dropped at his words, and my heart broke for him. It broke for the hope and the friendship he'd thought he'd found in the other Kings.

"They organized everything just perfectly. First, they drugged me, and once they managed to hold me down, they started chopping them straight off of my back." His grip on me tightened.

I knew there must have been more to it, but I was sure he didn't want to succumb to the memory any more than necessary. So, I didn't press him.

"Sometimes, when I give in and dream at night, I can still feel the hot dribble of my blood running down my back, gathering in a pool on the white marble floor in that godforsaken throne room of Silvan's. But my wings didn't make it easy on them. Even being held down, they tried working against that razor-sharp blade. They were powerful." Wistfully, he lowered his lashes. "The bones didn't break easily." He swallowed as he stared ahead. "It took three Kings to tear them off."

I squeezed my eyes shut. I didn't dare let my mind wander to the sight of three powerful Kings yanking with their inhuman strength on Thanatos's wings ….

"Little did they know that I couldn't grant them their wish. I can only take life once the target's time has run out, but I don't hold the power to make someone immortal. Only the Norns have that kind of power."

Now, I finally understood why he always teleported instead of choosing to fly. I had just assumed it was easier. But now I knew that, even if he wanted to, he couldn't.

Not anymore.

"But the worst nightmares aren't the ones where I dream of that day. The worst are the ones where I remember how it felt to fly. There is no feeling more perfect than elevating into the air." His eyes grew distant. The expression on his face proved how dear his wings had been to him. "The wind caresses your skin, and when you are up there, above the earth, you almost feel untouchable."

He shook his head. "They ripped off my wings and with them my hope and trust in others." He laughed darkly. "It truly is a pity that I am dead already. After all that pain and deception, I'd have loved to die that day. Fate's truly a bitch." He was talking lightly, but I recognized he was only trying to mask the hurt within him.

"Oh Thanatos ...." I hugged him closer. His arms circled me in from behind my back. What had happened to me—the way my parents had pushed me aside, even detested me until I preferred to be alone—had been awful, but what had happened to Thanatos ...

I couldn't fathom.

I'd never have thought he had endured something like that. He always seemed so self-assured ... It had never occurred to me that he had the same difficulties as I did in opening up to someone.

I wasn't sure if his eyes remained closed because the memory still hurt him so deeply or because he did not want to show his vulnerability in front of me.

"And you know what angered me the most?"

I shook my head.

"Once I managed to break free of them, I couldn't take their lives. And, God, did I want to. Such malice does not deserve to live. But even *I* need to follow life's rules. The Norns didn't see fit for the death of any one of them at that moment, and so I left without being able to … see any one of them off. I swore to myself to never trust anyone again. Ever."

So that was the reason why he had turned his back on humanity and preferred to stay alone. Now I finally understood the reason why I had never met any of his friends. He didn't have any. And his preference for the staff to leave in the morning … He wanted to be alone.

It was only then that I realized I had never seen the Deathbringer talk to anyone other than me at length. And to Kalira after the nightcrawler's attack. He kept his distance even from his own subjects. He preferred to watch from afar rather than get attached to people who might hurt him.

He pulled slightly away from me, just enough to look me in the eyes. "So, yes, Cassiana. I know exactly what you mean."

He turned away from me, as if unable to bear my gaze on his skin. I was shocked. The way he behaved with me in the Afterlife had given me no reason at all to think he carried this with him.

And if someone would be able to understand his behavior, it was me. Maybe he flirted and talked openly about everything with me because he had somehow felt this connection between us, and contrary to my own reaction, had accepted and acted upon it.

My voice was raspy and hoarse. "Why do you keep the statues?"

His swallow was loud when he answered. "All the Kings are bound to have them in their kingdoms. It's a sign of acknowledgement of the other reigns." A bitter expression turned his features grim.

I couldn't imagine what it must have felt for him to see those sculptures each day. It was a constant reminder of his friends' betrayal. Of his pain.

I wanted to say I was sorry for everything he'd been through. I should. But from my own experience I knew saying it wouldn't help him. It would only make his pain hurt even more, because he'd get the feeling of being broken, a lost cause.

What did he do to deserve the misfortune of being betrayed by the people closest to him? A tear slipped out of the corner of my eye.

Before I could prepare myself, he leaned forward to kiss it away. My knees buckled at the doting action.

He reacted instantly, lifting me up and pressing me against his strong, protective body. He squeezed my hip as he sat down back on the bench.

It shouldn't be me who was crying. It should be him. But I no longer cried for myself. I cried for him. For what he had experienced. For what he had lost.

I dug my head into the crook of his neck and slid an arm around it. "How did you endure it?"

A beat of silence. Then, "I never said I did."

I didn't know how long we stayed like that, just staring at one another, before Thanatos stood, bringing me to my feet with him.

"I want to show you something."

Confused, I furrowed my brows. "Now?"

He nodded and extended a hand to me. I stared at it. It reminded me of the very first time he had offered me that same hand. Despite the fact that he had saved my life, I had been so distressed to take the hand of a man society deemed a killer. But now? I looked up at him, meeting those old eyes that gazed down at me with the softest expression I had ever seen.

My fingers trembled slightly as I accepted his hand, letting him pull me toward him. When he drew me to him, his hands circling my waist, I looked up at him. A strand of his hair had loosened out of his man bun. I lifted my hand and tucked it carefully behind his ear.

His eyes softened. I cracked a shy smile at him, which he returned.

We remained like that, looking at one another even as his shadows around us crept closer, making us disappear.

My breath caught as our surroundings reappeared.

I let my arms glide from the Deathbringer's chest and took a step back. I turned around in circles, drinking in the beauty of what I saw.

A very dark forest— almost as dark as the Forest of the Lost Souls— built a stark contrast to the enormous lake that lay within it. The lake …

The sight alone almost made me fall on the ground. It shone in the most intense shades of blue and seemed to glow from within. The lake stretched for miles and miles, the end of it not even visible from the place Thanatos and I were standing. The stars reflecting on the water's surface only added to its brightness. It shone as brightly as the moon itself, casting the surroundings in the most beautiful glow. There was no trace of Emoh, making me suspect that this lake was far from the Village of the Dead.

"What is this place?"

"This is the Lake of the Fallen Stars."

At Thanatos's voice, I turned to the man himself.

The King of the Dead was facing me. "Just like you have found such joy looking at the stars on your bedroom's ceiling, I find joy in this." He crouched down on the shore, running his hand through the water. "The lake is made entirely of stardust." He brought his hand back out of the water. It was covered in glittering powder. "The stardust comes from the stars that have long ago fallen in the Land of the Living. I collect them." He stood, staring down at his stardust-covered hands.

I took a step forward and reached out to touch one of his hands.

Thanatos watched me closely as I let my fingers run over his palm through the sparkling powder.

Astonished, I stared at how the dust began clinging to my own skin, coating it in glitter. "Why do you collect them?" I asked as I rubbed the glitter between my thumb and index finger. It made the softest noise at the friction.

"Because they mean something."

I drew my eyes from my fingers, taking in Thanatos. His emerald eyes reflected the brilliant lake, making them shine like the water's surface on a star-clear night.

"I collect them because they are dreams." Thanatos turned away from me. He stared at the calm surface of the lake. "People look up into the sky every day, choosing a star and addressing their wish to it. Sometimes, they choose a star because it symbolizes a loved one. Before those stars fell, each one of them symbolized a dream to thousands of people. The moment the star falls, their dreams die with the star."

New tears began prickling my eyes.

"Their existence reminds me that despite everything I went through, there is still hope in this world. I keep them because, no matter what, dreams should never be forgotten. No matter how unapproachable the path might seem, every dream is accomplishable as long as they are believed in. We should never forget that. After all, dreams are what anchor us to our happiness."

I noticed the struggle written on his facial features. He wasn't only talking about the dreams of strangers. He was also talking about his own.

I had never been as happy as the moment I realized the Kings wanted to be my friends, only for that hope to be shattered into pieces. I am not sure if I'll ever be able to hope again.

I squeezed my eyes shut at the pain lacing his voice when he had told me those words.

"That's why I keep them here, making sure they are never forgotten."

I stared at the man in front of me. For everyone else, he was this powerful, dangerous, and untouchable person. But, in reality, he was just as broken as the rest of us. The only difference was that he had learned to hide his pain behind masks. He hid his hurt with the mockery in his tone; he hid his hurt by showing his power, by reminding the people of his role, when in reality he needed someone to care for him just the same as I did.

I lowered myself into a squatting position in front of the lake. The stardust made the prettiest twinkling sound whenever the waves rolled against the shore. I felt Thanatos's eyes watching me as I submerged both my hands elbow-deep in the water. When I stood, the stardust clung to the skin of my arms. It looked like I wore sparkling gloves.

Thanatos watched me cut the distance between us. His entire body locked down, his muscles tense as I approached him.

I *make him this self-conscious.* I *make him so aware of himself.*

I swallowed nervously at his penetrating gaze. Moving up to him, I only stopped once our chests were almost touching. The King of the Dead stared down at me, his expression unreadable. He had put up his guard again.

Up close I could see every single detail of his chiseled contours. Ever so carefully, as though scared of him flinching away from my touch, I lifted my hands and cupped his cheeks. I needed to get up on my toes to touch him there.

Thanatos watched me silently, remaining unbelievably still. The only sound surrounding us was the rolling of the stardust against the shore's sand.

"Thank you for sharing this place with me," I whispered. I moved my fingers over the softness of his skin up to his eyebrows. Gently, I traced his outlines.

Thanatos's breath became heavy, but never once did he withdraw his eyes from my face. The stardust clung wherever my fingers touched his skin, creating a map of affection.

"You must come here often," I whispered, moving my hands over his throat to the back of his neck, the stardust clinging to him like a lover's embrace.

"What fun would it be coming here if I couldn't share this place's beauty with anyone?" Thanatos's voice had grown coarse.

"But now you can," I murmured. My hands moved to the back of his head. I found the leather band that kept his hair tucked up and loosened it. It cascaded free, framing his face beautifully. I smiled up at him and brushed a strand of his hair away from his face before I reached my fingertips to his lips and grazed them.

It felt unbelievably odd to be this affectionate with him mere moments after my breakdown, but what he had told me about his past had provoked a feeling of partnership within me: he had experienced the same deception in humankind as myself.

Leaving aside Mir, he was the very first person I had told about my past, and instead of walking away from me, he had opened up, granting me an insight to his own inner workings. If he had opened up to me the way he had, I'd try my very best to do the same. I wouldn't push him away because of my trust issue.

The King of the Afterlife reached out to me. His fingers flexed against the flesh of my hip.

I applied the lightest pressure on the back of his head and tilted it down to me.

Thanatos obliged immediately and dropped his chin.

Desire had made his pupils dilate. My gaze moved from his eyes to his lips, then back up. Sometimes, just like now, it felt as though I had known Thanatos forever.

I tipped my head back at the same time as Thanatos dropped his face down. This time, I knew perfectly well whom I was kissing. I wasn't driven by alcohol or desire like yesterday. I was driven by the feeling of emotional kinship.

Our lips met.

At their very first caress, every single molecule within me heated.

Thanatos growled against my lips. His hands on my hips

squeezed me tighter, pressing our bodies together. Every hard part of him collided with every soft part of me.

I panted against his lips and buried my fingers in his hair, trying to press him even closer to me. The stardust that still stuck to his lips passed onto mine, tasting like the sweetest sin.

This kiss. It was hard for us. So very, very hard for us. Because it wasn't just a kiss with which we shared our desire for each other. It was a kiss shared between two people who had been so deeply hurt in their lives that they understood one another without needing words.

Thanatos's smell swathed me like a blanket on the coldest of winter nights, granting me not only heat, but also protection. At the soft touch of his tongue against my lips, I opened up for him. His tongue slipped inside, caressing my own tongue ever so carefully. When he felt that I didn't resist the touch, he pushed further into me. And then the kiss became something else entirely.

We kissed like two people drowning and tasting air for their very first time, and in a way, we were.

When our movements began slowing down, we disconnected our lips reluctantly. Our shallow breathing mingled as we gasped for air.

I kept my eyes closed, even when I felt Thanatos lean forward, his forehead coming to rest against my own. I wanted to hold onto this intimate moment for as long as possible.

Never once, not one time in my entire life, had I felt this deep connection to another person. This connection that went further than two bodies seeking out sexual relief. I never wanted to let go of this moment. I wanted to keep it as close to me as possible. And I knew I would.

When I finally opened my eyes, I saw that Thanatos, too, had his eyes closed. I lifted my hand to his face and traced his jaw. I smiled at the sight of the stardust smeared all over him.

He opened his eyes and met my soft gaze. We stared at one another in complete astonishment.

We stayed there for a long time, sharing this intimate moment together. Neither of us wanted to get back to the castle. So, we stayed, listening to the stars in the lake twinkle as they moved under the water's surface.

Listening to the symphony of the fallen stars.

CHAPTER TWENTY-ONE

The next couple of days passed unbelievably fast. After we had contacted Miriam and assured her of my safety and well-being, I was able to enjoy more of the Afterlife without constantly worrying about her.

After what Thanatos had told me, I recognized more and more the patterns in his behavior that indicated the way he maintained his distance. Whenever he was in Emoh, although he greeted everyone with a curt nod, he never did approach any of his subjects. He was always watching them from afar, making sure everything in his realm was working the way it should, but never trying to get to know his people. I truly hoped that would change over time.

I snorted at that. How hypocritical of me to encourage the Deathbringer's socialization when I myself hadn't managed to open up to anyone but my best friend.

And, now, Thanatos.

I didn't know what that made him to me. We hadn't repeated what we had done the night I had gotten drunk, but we had shared casual interactions here and there, like him brushing his palm over the small of my back whenever I passed him, or me casting shy looks at him whenever I thought he wasn't paying attention to me.

Of course, every time I did, he turned around and caught my stare.

These small, non-sexual intercourses felt so much more important than everything we had done in liquor-induced intimacy. I had stopped locking the door attached to our shared bathroom. It somehow felt safer to have it unlocked and know that Thanatos could enter whenever I needed him. It felt good to have someone to talk to, who understood me without needing me to explain.

The only thing that still gave me a severe headache whenever I thought of it was the fact that, according to Miriam, Silvan hadn't been looking for me in the Land of the Living like the Norns had said. But the Norns were the ones who should know. Could they be wrong? Or had they maybe lied? But why on earth would they lie? It made absolutely no sense. The easiest thing would be to ask Thanatos if he could contact the Norns, but every time I opened my mouth to discuss it, it fell shut again. I feared that, by asking him, I'd also be faced with the other question burning in my mind since I talked to Miriam: what were Thanatos's motives for keeping me here in the Afterlife? Twice, he had said that the span of my stay in the Afterlife depended on him. But what did he need me for? Thanatos didn't seem to want to bring me back to the Land of the Living any time soon, and it wasn't like I wanted to go home right now, especially not after Thanatos and I had opened up to each other at the Lake of the

Fallen Stars. I did wonder, though, about his reasoning for keeping me here.

A knock on my door ripped me out of my thoughts. I put the book I had been staring at on my nightstand before turning toward the sound. "Yes?"

The door opened, and Kalira entered the room. Despite her questioning me several times in the past, I hadn't shared the details of Thanatos's and my budding relationship. It was *our* relationship after all. She had no business in getting to know everything her King and I talked about. But even without giving her those details, it was obvious Thanatos and I had become more and more affectionate with one another. The people of Emoh seemed to have noticed so, too, judging by their pleased smiles and approving looks whenever Thanatos and I passed.

Kalira looked at me and said, "The King wishes for you to come."

Not wasting a second, I stood, letting the blanket fall from my lap to the floor. Thanatos never let Kalira summon me. Usually, he was the one to fetch me whenever we wanted to spend time together. So, there was only one other possibility: something bad had happened.

"Where is he?"

"In the foyer."

"Thanks." Rushing past Kalira, I hurried downstairs.

What was the reason he had called me to him? Was he all right? Had something happened? Was there an attack? I didn't want to think about all the countless possibilities.

I spotted Thanatos standing at the end of the staircase, looking as royal as ever, watching me come to his side. "Somebody is eager to see me," he said as a way of greeting, a broad smile plastered on his face.

"What happened?" I asked breathlessly and looked up at him.

His eyes twinkled. "*We* are going swimming today." Trouble sparkled in his eyes.

My body grew incredible still at his words. "Um." I brushed a loose strand of hair out of my face. I needed some time to calm my nerves again and wrap my amped-up mind around the fact that everything seemed all right. "You want to go swimming?" I prompted, my voice failing to hide its worried tremble.

Nodding, he put his hand on the low of my back and maneuvered me toward the door.

Desperately, I tried to find an excuse, something I had to attend to today, *anything* so I wouldn't need to go for a swim, but my mind had become completely blank.

Once outside, I started fidgeting with my hands. "What are—"

I shrieked when he suddenly grabbed my arm and spun me around. I ended up plastered to his chest.

The shadows around us swallowed us whole. Apparently, we were teleporting. I couldn't see anything else other than darkness. Funny, how I never once had been scared of the shadows.

Closing my eyes, I focused on the way Thanatos's hand pressed on the small of my back, keeping me close.

When the shadows withdrew, I didn't need to look around to know where they had brought us. The twinkling sound of stars being washed ashore gave it away immediately.

The Lake of the Fallen Stars.

"I don't have a bathing suit," I tried to object lamely as I took a step away from the shore.

Thanatos's lips curled up. "Oh, love, didn't you know that swimming doesn't require any clothing at all?

Usually, his comment would've made me smile. But not today. Biting my bottom lip nervously, I looked at the lake. The stardust glistened under the water's surface in stark contrast to the dark forest and the obscure night sky.

I brought my eyes back to Thanatos. "I'm not getting in the water naked," I declared.

"Who said anything about getting naked? Cassiana, what kind of a man do you think I am?" he asked angelically.

Apprehensively, my eyes darted back to the shore. "I mean it, Thanatos."

He lifted his hands. "Okay. Then neither am I." A devilish smile spread his lips. "Let's get you wet!" There was no mistaking his double meaning with the way his eyes sparkled, but this time, his words didn't provoke even the slightest spark of excitement. He made to grab my hand, but I took a step back and shook my head.

"What is it?" Thanatos looked down at me, only now realizing I was not in a playful mood.

"I can't swim," I blurted out.

Thanatos paused.

There. I had said it. There was no need to lie.

Ever since that day on the beach, I avoided swimming by all means. Walking by the beach or a lake was fine. It was also fine for me to get into bathtubs. I could still see the bottom, and I *knew* it wouldn't be deep. But *swimming* in a lake? No.

There was nothing that would ever get me to overcome that deep-rooted fear. I had tried countless times to swim, but every time I put on a bathing suit and attempted to get in, something in me froze to ice. The feeling of that indescribable mass of water pressing down on me, pulling me deeper and deeper into the ocean's depth …

Thanatos was silent, calmly watching me. "Why?"

It was an easy question. But answering it would force me to relive that day. And that was something I wanted to omit by all means. Trying to be as truthful as possible, I said, "I'm scared of swimming …"

He moved closer into my peripheral vision. "Then maybe it's time to change that?" He outstretched his hand.

I stared at it and bit the inside of my cheek. How could I tell him that it wasn't as easy as he thought without telling him about that day at the beach?

As much as I wanted to, I couldn't reject his offer after we had opened up to one another at the lake.

So, there was only one option left.

I met his gentle gaze when I took his hand. "I should probably take this off." I motioned to the bodice of my dress.

His eyes twinkled. "I thought you didn't want to swim naked."

I shook my head. "The fabric sucks." It was hard enough to undress when it was still dry. I didn't want to find out how long it would take me to remove it when wet.

Thanatos nodded.

I made to open the strings at my back, but suddenly Thanatos moved behind me. "Let me." He said, with that raspy voice of his. His words felt more like a command than an actual request.

Nodding, I let my hands fall to my sides.

Gently, he began undoing the straps. Underneath the bodice, I wore a plain-white shirt that had been tucked in the skirt.

And it was thin.

Each time his knuckles brushed it, he also brushed my skin. Even though we had done far more than this, it still felt so intimate. Maybe because both of us had opened up to each other and knew this wasn't something either one of us did on an ordinary basis. When his fingers reached the very last of the laces, I felt the bodice loosen completely.

Thanatos let it fall to the ground. Then, he moved in front of me. "Are you ready?" he asked, his voice raspy as he searched my face.

I nodded. Both of us got rid of our shoes and moved to the water's edge. Nervously, I glanced at the water.

Suddenly, Thanatos's hand moved slowly from my arm down to my hand.

My hand shook slightly when I took his.

It felt so damn hard to do this. To trust.

And I had to remind myself that it wasn't easy for him, either. Even though Thanatos just made the first move, it was still both of us who had been hurt deeply and to whom it was an obstacle to show this kind of physical and emotional approach.

Holding tightly onto his hand, I let him lead me toward the water. As soon as my feet touched it, I stopped and looked at Thanatos. "I can't believe we are going to swim with our clothes still on," I said in an effort to loosen the tension.

He smiled. "Well, I already made clear that swimming doesn't require it, so …"

Laughing, I poked him with my elbow to his side.

"So aggressive," he murmured, his eyes alight.

It was easier to joke than panic over what lay before me.

As we began wading deeper into the water, I clutched his hand tightly. The sensation was … breathtaking. I felt the stardust rubbing against me, tinkling like the lightest laughter with every movement. The stars' light that illuminated the entire lake somehow made it easier to get in. It felt as though I moved into the galaxy's Milky Way rather than water. I smiled as the stardust tickled underneath my feet. Slowly, I let my hand glide into the water and watched how the stardust clung to my skin when I pulled it out.

"Is this deep enough to start?"

I had been so caught up admiring the water, I hadn't even realized it was already reaching my waist. When I looked at Thanatos, his attention was solely focused on me.

I nodded slowly.

"Good."

It was such a simple word, but my entire body grew still at it. I was about to do this.

Thanatos stepped closer, not once looking away from me. While the water reached my waist, it only lapped at the Deathbringer's hips.

"We'll start with something simple." Before I knew what he had in mind, he slowly dropped to his knees. Shocked, I took him in.

The King of the Dead kneeling in front of me yet again.

With him kneeling, I was now taller than he was. He looked up at me. "Can you try easing into the water? I'll hold you," he promised, that deep, rich voice of his serious.

I saw genuine truth shining in his eyes. But it still wasn't easy.

Forcing myself to take deep breaths, I began to lower my body slowly into the water. But as soon as the water reached my chest, I stopped, shaking my head vigorously. "I can't. I … I …"

Water pressing down on me, getting into my lungs, making my breathing hard.

"Shhh ... I'm here. You are doing great, love."

I hadn't noticed the Deathbringer moving to my side. His hands rested on my hips, and his body pressed into me from behind.

"You are almost in."

When I looked down, I was surprised to realize the water was already reaching my shoulders. I was so thankful that Thanatos didn't ask for the reasons for my panic and rather just accepted it.

Feeling his hands on my hips granted me some sort of security, and I eased in until I submerged just above my shoulders.

I let my eyes drift over the water's surface. "What now?"

"Now, you are going to lean back and float." He must've felt how my body tensed beneath his touch and said, "I'll hold you." One of his hands moved from my hip to my left wrist. His fingers began to circle the mole on it reassuringly.

Haltingly, I reclined until my body floated on the water. I exhaled deeply, feeling how the water brushed the back of my scalp.

Thanatos moved to my side and slid his hands underneath my back.

I looked up into the sky, spotting all the countless stars that built constellations that were so different than the ones back in the Land of the Living and yet felt so familiar.

"They are beautiful, aren't they?"

I knew perfectly well he was trying to distract me from the fact that I was currently floating in the water, my fear of it constrained only by his hands. "They are." Swallowing, I stared at the small sparkling spots lightening the sky. "So, what are the next steps to become a professional swimmer?" I asked jokingly.

"First, you have to feel safe in the water," he explained.

We fell silent as Thanatos held me. Gently, the King began moving in circles, letting me get used to the feeling of the water supporting me. He withdrew one of his hands from beneath my body and kept the other on my back. His hand moved to my head, slowly starting to follow my hairline with his index finger.

I drew my gaze away from the night-sky to look at the King.

He was gazing at his hands moving over my scalp.

"What are you smiling about?"

"Your hair." His fingers moved further up my head, combing through my wet hair beneath the water's surface.

"What about it?"

His smile widened. "The stardust clings to your hair. Now it looks like it was spun out of moonlight." His eyes became peaceful. Unguarded.

I looked up at him, into those mesmerizing green eyes that always managed to enthrall me. My eyes darted between his. I felt the same inner connection I had felt for him since the very first time I laid eyes upon him kindling around us.

And, suddenly, I knew why I had all these unexplainable feelings toward him. It wasn't his physical appearance, nor was it his power that had drawn me in from the beginning. I was able to spot the looming darkness in the corners of his eyes. It was a darkness I should've recognized immediately. Because it was my own.

Pain. Deception. Fear.

It was the same darkness I had spotted in my own reflection for years.

A bitter taste exploded on my tongue as I recognized the hidden emotions. Both of us had learned to dampen the hurt, the pain. But I saw through that now. I saw the true man behind his masks. In front of his subjects, he was this unapproachable yet caring King. In front of Silvan, he was someone to be feared. And in front of me, he tried dissolving his discomfort by hiding behind his mock.

I cocked my head and looked at him. My attention slowly settled on his lips.

The last time we had kissed was here, at the Lake of the Fallen Stars. Would his lips still feel the same?

I didn't know where I gathered my courage from, but I rose from the water.

Thanatos was watching but not stopping me as I moved out of his embrace. He hadn't walked deeper into the water, so I was still able to stand with the water reaching my waist. He was completely motionless. He didn't even blink.

He only watched me very, very calmly.

He still knelt in front of me, so when I moved closer, it was him who needed to tilt his head to look at me.

Feeling brave, I didn't hesitate as I lifted my trembling hands to cup his cheeks. Thanatos watched me through his raven-black, thick lashes. Swallowing, I let my eyes narrow in on his full, sensual lips. Ever so slowly, giving him space to pull back in case he didn't feel the same way, I bent down. My hair fell forward, creating a curtain of glittering silver around us.

Suddenly, his hands were there, moving over my waist down to rest on my backside. He pulled me closer to him.

I inhaled sharply when he pressed my soft body against his hard one, leaving no question about his arousal.

Heat pooled in my core.

There was absolutely no way to hide how turned on I was right now with the way my nipples pebbled, becoming visible through the transparent, wet fabric adhering to my skin and pressing against Thanatos's chest.

My hands had dropped to his shoulders, fisting the fabric of his shirt. His muscles jumped beneath my touch. The effect I had on him made my blood run hot. I couldn't help but feel so empowered by it. The mighty King of the Dead was affected by a simple human girl.

Slowly, my attention still focused on his mouth, I bent further, until only a few inches separated our lips. Our breathing was shallow, mixing in between us at the anticipation. When I met his gaze, his eyes were dulled with lust.

Before I could stop myself, I pressed my mouth against his.

His arms immediately wrapped more tightly around my body, as though he didn't want even the slightest distance between us.

He sighed deeply at the first shy touch of my tongue against his lips. Suddenly embarrassed by my boldness, I started to pull back, but he tightened his hold on me and then he got straight down to business. His mouth cut off my airstream.

I gasped, and he took the advantage to swipe his tongue inside my mouth.

Any reservations I might still have at that point melted away. As did my body, becoming a soft mass of desire against his. How ironic my body's reaction was. After all, we were still in a lake, a place that usually provoked fear and panic within me. But, at Thanatos's presence, those initial emotions I first had gave way to nothing but molten longing.

My core pulsed in unison with the beating of my heart.

Thanatos's right hand moved farther south.

"What are you doing?" I breathed against his lips.

"What I should have done the moment I brought you to the Afterlife."

I moaned when he pulled my skirt up and held it to my midsection. Before I could brace myself, he stood and brought me to stand with him. My legs wrapped around his waist instinctively, pressing our cores together.

I shivered when I felt the result of his lust for me pressing against me.

He drew back, just enough to look at me. "Tell me you want this." I knew that we wouldn't stop where we had last time. There was so much hope in his eyes that I couldn't reject him.

Neither did I want to.

I nodded. "Yes."

He bent down, *devouring* me. And then—

He stopped.

Confused, I blinked my eyes open. "What is it?"

He pulled back and looked at a spot behind me. His eyes turned to an unsettling green of angry waters. There was no trace of the lust and desire that had shimmered in his gaze just seconds ago.

"Thanatos?"

He didn't look at me when he answered. "Someone has entered the Afterlife."

"What—" Before I could even finish speaking, he had teleported us to the lake's shore.

He set me down and looked toward the forest's tree line.

I followed his gaze but didn't see anything suspicious. "Thanatos? What is it?"

As if he had heard something, his body froze, turning alert.

A tremor wracked my body. It was the first time I'd felt cold since I had arrived in the Afterlife.

I followed Thanatos's gaze. And then, I saw it.

Out of the darkness of the forest, a figure—flanked by two others—stepped into the moon's light. The lead man was tall and stood proudly. Even from afar, I recognized his ice-blue, unaffected eyes.

I staggered back.

Silvan, the fae King, stood before us.

CHAPTER TWENTY-TWO

Panicking, I turned to Thanatos. The crown on top of his head reflected the moonlight. He must have just materialized it. His expression was dark and distant. The shadows around us became alive as they began crawling closer to us, creatures growling within the mist of darkness.

Thanatos straightened his spine. "Fae King."

"Deathbringer." Silvan's cool voice resonated over the lake. He looked just like the last time I had seen him. His silver hair was paler than the moonlight.

Based on the two swords sashed to their sides, the two fae accompanying Silvan were his royal guards.

Silvan's calculating gaze slid to me.

Suddenly, I became so very aware of the see-through fabric clinging to my chest.

Thanatos moved in front of me, effectively blocking me from the other King's view.

I stared at his back. No one had ever tried to protect me like this.

"What do you want?" The Deathbringer asked, deadly calm.

Silvan clicked his tongue. "I see you still keep your little plaything."

Even with Thanatos's broad frame blocking me, I couldn't help but grow still at Silvan's attention. After all, the last time I saw him, he tried having me killed.

"Answer the question," Thanatos demanded in a tone unfamiliar to me.

I stared at the nape of his neck. Suddenly, I was wondering if I had just imagined the nice, gentle side of Thanatos. Because there was no sign of the broken man beneath the crown any longer. He had locked that man in a safe place, where he couldn't get hurt by Silvan again.

This is the version of Thanatos that is feared, I realized. *The side of him for which he is known.*

"Aren't you going to welcome me? Seems appropriate given my status." Silvan didn't even need to straighten to draw the attention to his own crown.

Thanatos balled his hands into fists. Still blocking my body from the fae King's lingering gaze, he growled dangerously, "Leave."

I'd have wetted myself at the venom in his words. There would be no way I'd disobey him.

But Silvan took a step forward. "Make me," he challenged.

Thanatos's body went rigid, his breaths deepening.

Silvan's lips curled up. "Oh. That's right." He ran a hand over his chin, his eyes gleaming triumphantly. He clapped his palms in euphoria. "You can't." He began pacing calmly.

I spoke, low enough for only Thanatos to hear. "What does he mean?"

"Hush!" Thanatos hissed back at me over his shoulder.

I jerked at that. He had never talked to me in a tone like that, and even though I couldn't be certain, I was sure he did so to keep me safe from Silvan.

Silvan explained the question anyhow. "You can't make me leave because I am King. You wouldn't risk a war between our courts over a harmless, casual visit from one of your friends, would you now?" he asked sweetly.

Thanatos's entire body gave a slight jerk at the mention of their former relationship, but just as fast as his body had reacted, he regained his control, his body becoming hard as steel. "What do you want?" he growled yet again.

"Maybe," Silvan stressed as his fingers traced the curve of a wooden bench near the lake's shore, "I want to get to know your little human."

His eyes met mine. Shivers, so different than the shivers Thanatos's touch provoked within me, spread over my skin.

"I'm sure she makes the most delightful sounds when her legs are wrapped around you, does she not?" the fae King provoked. He gestured at our wet, stardust-clinging clothing. "Or did I interrupt you before you had a chance to find out?"

Thanatos moved so fast, I didn't even anticipate it.

He manifested right in front of Silvan. The shadows around him were raging when he grabbed Silvan's shirt, crumpling it by doing so, and stared down at the other King. He poked his finger into Silvan's chest. Hard. "I will not stand for you disrespecting her. You talk about her like that again, you are dead." He poked his index finger into Silvan's chest again. "Consequences be damned," he hissed.

"Thanatos, stop!" I shrieked. The surrounding shadows flared up at my scream.

It wasn't worth getting into war over this. For whatever reason, Silvan's only goal was provoking Thanatos.

The two fae guards were watching the confrontation between the two monarchs, but they wouldn't interfere without their King's orders. Silvan arched a silvery eyebrow and laughed. The most dangerous creature on earth was menacing him, and he was laughing. "Thanatos, huh? Didn't know your slaves are allowed to know your name. You know her this closely already? Or are you just an emotional fuck, Thanatos?"

The Deathbringer lunged out and punched Silvan right in his face.

"Thanatos!" I screeched.

A crunching sound resonated over the water like thunder before Silvan was thrown away by the force of the punch.

Calmly, Thanatos watched Silvan. "You are only alive because you disrespected *me*. If you disrespect *her* again, you are a dead person, no matter what the Norns may still have in store for you." His voice made my stomach flutter in the most bizarre way. Thanatos unclenched his fists. "And do not ever address any of my subjects as slaves. Because, unlike you, I don't keep slaves."

I stared at Thanatos's back. The day Thanatos had saved me, he had seemed so calm and unaffected by Silvan. But now? His behavior seemed so at odds with that last encounter.

The two fae guards rushed to their King's side and helped him. Blood was dripping from Silvan's nose, but when the guards pulled him up, his bleeding began to fade. Blood was coating his teeth in the most satisfying red color when he spoke next. "You have grown balls, I see." Red dots sprinkled his white shirt, reminding me of the waiter's blood in the theatre. He ran his hand over it, smoothing out the wrinkles.

"And yours will soon be cut off if you disrespect her again."

Okaaaaaay then.

Silvan shrugged. He straightened his spine and became serious. "I need a word with you."

Thanatos crossed his arms. "About?"

Silvan looked around. "Not here."

Thanatos and I exchanged a glance, before nodding. As Thanatos summoned the black shadows to teleport us back to the castle, Silvan summoned his white clouds, the colors of both powers building a stark contrast against each other.

I didn't know what Silvan wanted, but whatever it was, it couldn't be good for the fae King to come to the Afterlife.

CHAPTER TWENTY-THREE

After changing into new, dry clothes, I hurried to Thanatos's study where he was waiting for me with Silvan. I stopped when I heard voices wafting from the study through the hall.

"So, your old, stone heart has at last softened. For a human girl." Silvan didn't even try to keep the amusement out of his voice.

Thanatos didn't bother answering. "Why are you here, fae King?"

Straightening the wrinkles of my dress, I walked around the corner. Both of Silvan's fae guards stood at the door, but they didn't so much as glare at me as I hesitantly knocked on the study's door.

"Come in," Thanatos said.

When I entered, he gave me a look that clearly stated he didn't want me to be there. He wanted to keep me safe, tucked away from Silvan.

But I wasn't going to leave the two of them alone. Ignoring

his burning eyes on me, I moved across the room and sat next to him on the couch. The heavy smell of rose fragrance infiltrated the small space, almost making me gag.

"She's already allowed to attend royal discussions?" Silvan, who sat leisurely on a couch opposite ours, asked incredulously.

"Get to the point, fae King. Cassiana is her own person and is free to do as she pleases."

Silvan arched a silvery brow. "Oh. Is that why you keep her here? Because she is free?" Silvan laughed, taking a swig from his wineglass.

I felt my body tense at the questions that had been popping up in my own head. Now that Mir had told me that Silvan had never been looking for me in the Land of the Living like the Norns had said—which, given Silvan's surprise at my presence in the Afterlife, must be true— there was no reason that I knew of why Thanatos would still keep me here. Hearing the question out loud made a weight press on me from all around, forcing me to swallow.

Thanatos reclined his forearms on his knees and stared at the other monarch. "I'll ask you one last time. What do you wish here? If you don't have an answer, I'm afraid I'll have to leave. More important matters demand my attention."

Silvan's eyes thinned into slits. "Do you dare call my matters unimportant?"

Thanatos leaned back, his right arm slouched over the back of the couch behind me. He seemed calm, unaffected, but the way his fingers drummed behind my back gave him away. "If you don't tell me your worries, I'm left thinking that they don't matter as much as you'd like me to believe."

Silvan folded his hands neatly in his lap. "Very well. I need you to contact the Norns for me."

I inhaled deeply at the mention of the three crazy women.

Silvan continued, "You are the only one who is able to contact them, and the issue that brought me here is very dear to me."

Thanatos didn't even blink. "What is your issue precisely?"

A spark of fear—the very first emotion he had shown since I'd met him, aside from his joy for cruelty—flashed over the fae King's face.

He doesn't want to tell us, I realized. But he had to. Because, apparently, he needed Thanatos's help.

"My powers. They are fading." His muscles spasmed, and he avoided our gaze.

The fae King was known for the power he held over the wind and the air. I bet the sugar-coated stories about the powers weren't as close to reality as I might have thought before meeting the fae King.

Thanatos kept silent for a moment. "Why?" The fae King had the Deathbringer's attention.

Silvan shrugged, a desperate expression deepening the shadows of his face. I could basically see him grinding his teeth. "That's what I've tried finding out. I ordered all my subjects to search for a possible solution, but every single hint led to a dead end."

So that was why Miriam hadn't seen a single fae in the Land of the Living since I had left.

Thanatos calmly nodded. "I see."

"I need you to ask the Norns what's going on and how to stop this."

Thanatos rose, downing his drink in one single gulp. "I'll take care of it straight away. I wouldn't want to keep you away from your kingdom for too long." He said it as though he wished the best for the King, but everyone present knew that he just wanted the other emperor gone.

Surprised at Thanatos's eagerness, I looked up at him. Why on earth would he want to help the fae King after everything the other monarch had done to him?

Thanatos bent down to me and nodded toward the door. "Come on, love. Let's go." He spoke so low only I was able to hear him. I, too, rose, and walked next to him toward the door.

Before we reached it, I stopped. I had kept quiet this entire time, but I couldn't hold back my next question. "Wait." I swirled around to face the fae King. "The boy. What happened to him?"

Silvan's unaffected, bored eyes stared at me. "You shouldn't speak this freely to me ...." His gaze slid to Thanatos, who stood behind me. His jaw locked when he looked back at me. "What boy are you talking about, human?"

He didn't even remember? Squaring my shoulders, I tried looking as confident as possible and not to reveal the slight trembling in my voice. "The boy you had lashed the day of your birthday?"

Thanatos touched my arm lightly. "Let it go, Cassiana," he muttered under his breath.

Silvan's eyes dropped to the place where Thanatos touched me. "Oh, *that* boy." He shrugged, dismissing the topic altogether. "He's dead, of course."

The moon shone down on the balcony connected to Thanatos's room. I looked at the village of the Dead. It was buzzing with life, completely oblivious of the visit of another monarch in its kingdom. The shadows in Emoh seemed to be more dense than normal, creating a securing force around the village. I didn't dare let my mind brood about what Silvan had said about the boy and, instead, I focused my entire attention on Thanatos.

Thanatos gave me a chaste kiss on my forehead. I cupped the back of his hands that held my face cradled tenderly and looked up to him. "Don't go."

We had just shown the fae King to his chambers (as far away from ours as possible), and Thanatos was getting ready to meet the Norns. I wouldn't put it past Silvan to trick Thanatos into an ambush. I didn't trust that bastard of a King, and I didn't understand why Thanatos let him stay here. I had wanted to go with Thanatos, but apparently, he was the only one allowed to visit the Norns. Why I had been allowed to meet them back when he had saved me was a mystery. According to the Deathbringer, they were the ones to tell him who'd be welcome. Apparently, the impression I had made hadn't been too good.

"Are you scared for me?" he teased, a playful smirk plastered on his face.

I wasn't in the mood for his cockiness. "Yes," I said without a second of hesitation.

Thanatos's eyes softened. "I have to," he whispered. His lips moved against my skin as he spoke.

"Why do you let Silvan stay here?" Swallowing, I pushed against him, but he didn't budge. "He was the one who hurt you so deeply,"

Thanatos tucked a curl behind my ear. "I know, love. I know." He tilted my head back, forcing me to meet his eyes yet again. "I can't risk a war between our kingdoms just so I can defend my pride. What good would defending your pride be if thousands of innocent lives would be threatened?"

I remembered what Thanatos had explained to me once: while the people in the Afterlife were already dead, there was always the threat of dying again in the Land of the Dead. That was the worst fate anybody could experience. By dying, they'd lose their chance of reincarnation and become nightcrawlers forever, doomed to abide in the Forest of the Lost Souls. A war would increase that threat exponentially. Of course Thanatos would try evading that by all means.

I dropped my gaze to his chest and began tracing invisible patterns on the soft material of his tunic. I couldn't imagine what it must be like for him to have to welcome those in his home who had hurt him the most. "You are way too selfless for your own good," I mumbled.

Thanatos watched me silently as he played with the tips of my hair. "Maybe."

"How did Silvan manage to get to the Afterlife? I thought only the Dead are welcome?" And me, apparently.

"The Kings have access to all Kingdoms," he explained simply.

Nodding, I let the silence stretch out between us. "Take me with you," I tried changing his mind again before I could stop myself. "Please, Thanatos." My hands fisted in his fabric, unwilling to let him go.

Thanatos shook his head. "I can't. They wish to see me alone."

I bit the inside of my cheek and nodded.

"I shouldn't be gone that long." He paused, letting the silence envelop us. "Can you promise me something?"

Forcing myself to meet his gaze, I straightened my spine and tilted my head back. "Anything," I breathed. I let my eyes rake over the Deathbringer's marble-crafted face, memorizing each dip and curve that had drawn me in from the very first second I laid eyes upon him.

He smiled. "You should never promise that when you don't know what I will be asking from you."

"But I trust you." I dropped my gaze. I hadn't planned on admitting this.

Thanatos's mouth closed in stunned silence before he swallowed audibly. "The same goes for you."

Shyly, I looked up at him through my lashes. When had I become so self-aware around the King of the Afterlife?

Thanatos returned the smile before it dropped again. "Promise me to stay away from Silvan."

I nodded lightly. "Sure."

He grabbed my chin in a firm grip. He didn't grab it hard enough that it would hurt me, but just enough to clarify his seriousness. "I mean it, Cassiana. Promise me not to get in his way. No matter what happens."

I gave him a reassuring smile. "Okay."

He watched me cautiously and, when I didn't seem to give him any reason to worry, he sighed deeply and drew me closer to him. "I'll be back soon."

I breathed in the musky smell of him, letting the rumble of his voice vibrate through my body. "Be careful."

I felt him nod against the crown of my head.

After what felt like the blink of a second, Thanatos stepped away from me and, gently, let go.

He gave me a reassuring smile as he called upon the shadows

that crept from every corner in the room, enveloping him in a weave of mist and darkness. Even from here, I could see his worry about Silvan's news and request.

I stared at the spot where my King had disappeared for a long time before exhaling a shuddering breath. I could only hope that this wasn't a setup from Silvan and that Thanatos would return safely.

CHAPTER TWENTY-FOUR

The next day, I walked down the main stairs toward the foyer. Kalira had just helped me get dressed but had excused herself for the rest of the day because she said she had something important to do in the village. My night had been horrendous. I had thrashed in sleep from one side of the bed to the other. Each time I had tried closing my eyes, the body of the boy Silvan had killed seared across my vision. I couldn't wrap my mind around the fact that he was dead now. When I had awoken, my body tired and sore, I hoped to find Thanatos already returned from his visit to the Norns, but when I knocked on his door, no one answered.

When voices drifted up to me, I halted mid-stairs and leaned over the railing to get a look at what was happening in the foyer. When I spotted the fae King, a cold shiver ran down my back. Silvan stalked toward the door of the castle. Leaving aside his crown, he wore simple black attire. His two guards followed close behind, their concurrent steps resonating over the smooth surface of the castle floor.

My brows knit together. What did he have in mind? I had presumed he'd just wait in the castle for Thanatos to return.

Careful not to catch Silvan's attention, I fisted my skirt and rushed down the rest of the stairs. Remorse made my tongue taste bitter as the promise I'd made to Thanatos resurfaced. I didn't want to break that promise. But at the same time, I didn't trust Silvan and I was scared of what he might've planned.

I watched Silvan's determined strides as he aimed for the castle's main door. The guards were watching the surroundings closely, always ready to pounce on any threat. One of them opened the door for his King. Once outside, they followed the path leading to Emoh.

Locking my jaw, I started following them.

I made sure to stay behind so they wouldn't see me.

The soft wind blew laughter and pieces of conversation from the village in our direction. It carried a sense of peacefulness and joy that only the Village of the Dead retained this extensively.

I watched the fae King closely from afar. Unlike Thanatos, he made sure to always wear his crown. He was lean, but not as broadly built as Thanatos. Everything about him screamed power, but it wasn't the natural authority Thanatos carried. It was a cruel, threatening authority earned by reminding people again and again that he was in charge.

Thanatos.

I could only hope he hadn't been set up by Silvan.

When Silvan crossed one of the small bridges and entered Emoh, I made sure to keep myself hidden. It was only when he had walked around the corner that I stood and followed him.

As soon as Silvan entered the village, its entire energy convulsed. It was as though someone had abruptly drained the positivity from Emoh. Where there had once been glee and happiness in the eyes of the townspeople, fear made room for caution and mistrust.

I mixed with the gathered crowd, making sure Silvan wouldn't be able to spot me. A cold smile played on the fae King's lips as the crowd parted to let him pass. I clenched my jaw. His walk was the walk of a man used to getting whatever it was he desired. He wasn't behaving as though he were a guest to this realm but as though he *owned* it.

When he reached the marketplace at the main plaza, his steps slowed. The triangular flags that had been hung up all around Emoh seemed to dull their color at the presence of the other monarch. The moons and the stars of the Afterlife's royal crest that was imprinted on the flags didn't shine as brightly as I recalled them to. Silvan eyed the colorful products laid out for sale with boredom.

"Can I help you?" A man asked in a friendly tone from the spot behind his table. Dresses and jackets were laid on the table. The man wore simple clothes but a broad smile. I had seen him before. Although I hadn't talked to him yet, his kind eyes had always stood out. "They are all made out of wool. My wife makes them," he said proudly. "And I take care of selling them. She always says the market is too early for her to wake up and sell her work." He laughed lightly at that.

Silvan's eyes narrowed into slits. "How dare you speak to me without being spoken to first?"

The seller's eyes flashed up to Silvan's crown, and he paled visibly. "Oh, um, I'm sorry, my King! I hadn't been informed about this," he stammered. He added a slight bow when he saw the anger in Silvan's eyes.

The seller's subservient attitude seemed to soothe Silvan. His eyes raked over the seller's fabric. "Tell your wife she's wasting her time. There's no punishment as bad as forcing someone to wear these rags." He looked at the products in disgust.

Approvingly, the two guards laughed at their King's words.

The seller nodded, pain and hurt flashing in his eyes.

I clenched my jaw. How dare Silvan treat the townspeople like this? I was certain Thanatos would not approve.

Silvan resumed his walk toward the fountain. I followed him.

When I passed the old man's stand, I halted. His eyes flashed in surprise when he recognized me.

"Don't listen to him. Your wife makes the most beautiful clothing in the entire kingdom." And it wasn't a lie. The fabric shimmered in the brightest colors. It was hard to choose which piece was the most beautiful. I grabbed his hand and gave it a squeeze. "We can be proud to have such a talented woman like your wife in Emoh."

He returned my smile proudly and nodded. "We can, can't we?"

I smiled warmly at him. "I'll come back," I promised before I rushed after Silvan.

The fae King was just walking around the fountain when he paused mid-step. "What's this?" He gestured in the direction where two female fae leaned against the wall, holding hands.

The two fae looked at each other in sudden alarm. The red-haired fae let go of her girlfriend's hand and took a step forward. "Your Highness." She bowed deeply, and the fae behind her followed suit. They knew how to behave before Silvan. After all, they'd spent time under Silvan's regime when they still lived in the Land of the Living.

They maintained their bowed posture while they waited for Silvan to speak to them.

"Why were you holding hands?" Silvan demanded.

Nervously, I stepped from one foot to the other. I knew homosexuality was a concept forbidden in the fae realm, but Thanatos had made the saying 'in death everyone becomes the same' literal and had allowed his subjects to live their lives as they wished.

The two fae glanced at each other nervously. The brown-haired fae sucked the inside of her cheeks.

Her girlfriend was the one to speak. "We are dating."

Of course she would admit the truth. And why wouldn't she? She was allowed to choose whom to date and love freely in Emoh. She didn't have any reason to fear. After all, she had Thanatos's consent for her actions.

But Thanatos wasn't here.

Silence stretched out while Silvan eyed the fae girls. "Rise." His voice was filled with authority, not leaving any room for protest.

The girls stood but kept their heads lowered.

Bile crept up my throat. What must the fae kingdom be like if, even in their death, Silvan's subjects behaved like trained puppets?

Anger flared up inside of me. How dare he question the townspeople— people over whom he had no authority whatsoever?

Silvan began circling the two females. The brown-haired girl had hunched her shoulders in an effort to duck away from the attention of their former King.

"You dare dishonor my orders?" Silvan asked casually. He remained as calm as the first time I'd met him.

"Our King has authorized our bonding." The red-haired fae spoke up. "We love each other."

There was no fear to be found in her attitude. Only determination. And why would there be fear? She had been oppressed by Silvan her entire life.

She had literally needed to die in order to be allowed to live her true nature and desires.

It was clearly visible: she wouldn't budge from the right Thanatos had given her only to please a King who had no right to order her around any longer.

Silvan laughed, the tone too high-pitched. "Love? What you are doing isn't normal."

With each passing second, my hatred for the fae King heightened.

Silvan's almost-white eyes raked over the two girls in revulsion.

While the brown-haired fae took a step back, the red-head's face flushed, matching her hair color. The bold one took a threatening step forward. "Do you know what's not normal? Acting like you're still our King."

Silvan didn't so much as blink at her outburst.

"You have absolutely no say here. Because, listen carefully, *King*," she mocked him. Her eyes were bright with hatred. "Here, you are nothing. Your powers are nothing. Compared to our King, our true King, you are powerless."

A slap silenced her.

Her body was thrown to the side from the force. She collapsed with a loud thud on the cement pavement.

The assembled masses gasped for air, unable to grasp what had just happened.

Silvan had struck her so fast the blow hadn't even been visible. The fae girl was kneeling on the ground, complete horror written on her face. Her left cheek already blossomed in a deep red color. Silvan approached the woman with slow, measured steps before he came to a stop, hovering over her threateningly. "How powerful am I now?"

The two guards watched him silently, and the townspeople were so shocked, they were frozen on their spots.

He drew his foot back, ready to kick her.

"Stop!" I felt like I had déjà vu as I scrambled forward. The masses parted for me willingly.

Once again, I came face-to-face with the fae King. Silvan's face brightened in delight as he recognized me. Besides the fear when he spoke of the loss of his powers, it was the first genuine emotion flashing over his features since he had entered the Afterlife. It sent cold shivers down my back. Last time I had seen him this happy, he had ordered me to be killed.

He cocked his head like a bird. "Well, well. Look who it is." He flashed me a sly smile. "History seems to repeat itself."

I ignored his comment. My eyes were glued to the fae woman who was shaking like a leaf on the ground. "Let her be, and her girlfriend, too."

Silvan shrugged. His gaze dropped to the woman at his feet. "Off you go."

Shocked, I looked at Silvan. Was he being serious?

The fae woman looked at me uncertainly. Even though I wasn't sure what Silvan had planned, I gave her an encouraging nod. As soon as both female fae had run off, I exhaled heavily.

"Cassiana—" My attention was caught by Kalira's copper hair within the watching crowd. She tried moving through the crowd toward me, but one of the sellers stepped forward and locked his arms around her waist. She struggled against him, but he didn't budge. Catching his gaze, I gave him a thankful nod. I didn't want Kalira to be involved in this mess. Understanding, the seller nodded back at me.

When I looked back at the fae King, his attention was fixed on my face.

I crossed my arms over my chest protectively. "What is it you want?" I knew perfectly well he hadn't let the girls go without strings attached. My entire body locked down when Silvan took a step forward. He was so close to me I could see that his irises were practically nonexistent. I felt his breath on my skin, but I refused to step back. I refused to remind him of my vulnerability.

"I might not be able to kill you with the Deathbringer's protection over you, but there are other ways to make you pay for getting in a King's way." His eyes gleamed dangerously. "This time, there will be no savior for you."

I leaned away from him, but one of the guards rushed to my side and prevented my movement.

"Apparently your dear King wants you alive." I felt Silvan lean forward when he whispered, "It's good there are things worse than death." He clicked his tongue in anticipation. "It gives us more scope to have fun with one another. Don't you agree?"

He didn't wait for my reply and, instead, gave two curt nods at his guards. Before I knew what was happening, each grabbed one of my arms. They pressed down on me, forcing me to kneel on the rough cement pavement in front of their King.

And then a cool, metallic object pressed against my back.

"What—"

I sucked in a breath. The strings binding my corset together were ripped open from behind, and the fabric loosened around my body.

I thrashed against the guard's hold as I realized what Silvan planned to do with me. I had witnessed what he had done to that poor boy. And now it was my turn to face that same fate. Today, it would be my blood running down my back. I clawed and kicked at the guards, but my efforts were in vain. Some of the townspeople drew in hissing breaths, while others seemed paralyzed with horror. Some children began crying as their parents carried them inside the surrounding houses.

I tried clutching the torn fabric against my chest, but with my hands being held apart by the guards, my efforts were fruitless.

Silvan put a finger under the fabric of the bodice, slowly letting it expose my back to him. I swallowed hard, trying to blink away my tears.

I felt his eerie eyes rake over my exposed skin.

Before I could even start hoping for something—anything—that would end this nightmare, Silvan crouched down next to me. I watched him put his hand into his boot. When it came back up, he held a lash in his hand. I cried out in panic, tears blurring my vision. He'd probably hidden it there knowing that Thanatos would demand that he surrender it. Silvan smiled at me. It was a cold-hearted smile without compassion.

"You are nothing more than a slave." His breath smelled like his rose fragrance, making me gag. "He only brought you here to make a statement."

A statement? What was he talking about?

He walked out of my vision.

I forced myself to listen to my breathing. It was the only thing grounding me. The only thing that would keep my panic at bay.

Breath in, breath out.
Breath in, breath out.
Breath in, breath out.

"This is going to be fun," Silvan predicted cheerfully.

Then, the sound of the lash hitting the paved street resonated on the high walls of the surrounding houses, making my body jerk forward with the mistakenly anticipated blow. Those gathered screamed in surprise.

It was so dark that, at first, I thought I was drifting to unconsciousness from fear, but then I realized it wasn't my sight that had darkened. It was the surroundings.

That was the moment I felt it.

That ancient, indomitable presence I'd become all-too familiar with throughout the last couple of weeks. A roar cut through the air. Still being held down by the guards, I glanced behind me.

"Let her go!" Thanatos growled, fuming mad, his voice booming over the place.

Every fiber within me froze to ice. I exhaled a shuddering, relieved breath.

Thanatos was here. Everything was going to be all right.

Silvan will pay for this. I'm sure of it. At the thought of retribution, a sick feeling of happiness heated me from the inside out.

The townspeople seemed to be holding their breaths as everything around me had frozen.

Thanatos stepped out from behind the shadows next to a small restaurant. He stood with his legs spread apart. The darkness surrounding him contrasted the blooming, colorful flowers that grew over the stone walls of the restaurants as the shadows crept closer and closer. His green eyes were glowing in wrath as he approached us.

The townspeople looked noticeably relieved at the sight of their King.

Thanatos's eyes dropped to the place where I knelt on the ground, my back exposed. A muscle ticked on his temple as he balled his hands to fists. His knuckles strained his skin white. He lifted his head so very, very slowly to the man still standing menacingly behind me.

The creatures in the mist behind him roared soundlessly, their claws scraping against the darkness, their teeth trying to break through to the man standing behind me.

I glanced behind me. Silvan was staring up at the Deathbringer, fear coating his eyes. He paled visibly at the sight of the creatures in the mist.

"What's the meaning of this?" Thanatos spoke calmly, coldly even. He had never talked like this to me before. Anger radiated from him in waves, cooling the air until my breath became visible in small clouds. He wore his crown proudly, not missing the chance to remind the fae King of his authority.

The fae King didn't miss a beat. "She attacked me."

The people who had been watching gasped in shock.

"What?" I shrieked, jerking in the hold of the two guards. How dare he lie about what had happened in order for his actions to be justified?

"Is this true?" Thanatos asked calmly, not breaking Silvan's gaze for a second.

"It's not!" I jerked my head up to the King of the Dead. "Thanatos, he's lying! He wanted to hurt two fae."

The townspeople started murmuring approvingly. Some even began shouting at the fae King in anger.

Thanatos lifted a hand, efficiently silencing the agitation around us.

"She needs to be punished for her behavior," Silvan stated simply, the sweet innocence of his voice making my stomach convulse in repulsion.

The Deathbringer watched me before his eyes jumped back to Silvan. "Let her go," he demanded calmly.

Silvan yelled, "What? You'd rather believe a slave than me? A King? She needs to be punished for her actions. She—"

Thanatos stepped forward. "I will take the punishment instead of her."

Silence boomed like thunder around us.

"What? No!" I thrashed against the guards, but their strength was so much superior to mine.

I stared at the Deathbringer, not able to comprehend what was happening. "Thanatos! Look at me!" His eyes found their way to mine. He wasn't showing an ounce of doubt. I shook my head, silently pleading with him. "Don't," I whispered.

Silvan moved into my peripheral vision. An excited glimmer had entered his eyes. He cocked his head to the side. The guards immediately reacted, pulling me to my feet and dragging me away.

"No!" I screamed. I put up my best fight, bucking, kicking and pulling against them as hard as possible, but it did nothing to stop them.

"I didn't do anything! There's no reason why any of us should be punished!" I screamed at the top of my lungs.

Thanatos squared his jaw. Horrified, I watched him remove his shirt and reveal his toned skin beneath.

In my complete terror, I stumbled over a rock. Not anticipating the sudden movement, the guard on my right let go of my hand. The second guard caught me before I could hit the ground. I tried scrambling away from him, but he wrapped his arms around my midsection, caging me in successfully, his hold restricting my movements completely.

Aghast, I watched Thanatos walk toward Silvan. He kept his chin high, not letting any emotion show.

Silvan's smile was callous as his eyes followed the King of the Dead. He drew his lash back, letting the end smack against the ground.

No, no, no!

This couldn't be happening.

He shouldn't punish the Deathbringer for something I didn't even do, and Thanatos shouldn't be willing to take my punishment for me. Why had he offered it anyway?

"Thanatos! No!" I screamed, squirming under the hold of the guard. My blood ran cold as ice when panic started seizing me completely.

Thanatos's striking green eyes flashed in my direction. He smiled reassuringly at me, but it missed its usual cockiness. "It's going to be all right, love." He turned toward the townspeople who had begun to squirm nervously as if unsure of how to handle this situation. "Nobody interferes. Do you understand?"

Some townspeople nodded reluctantly but obeyed and took a step back. The werewolves in between the gathered crowd flashed their teeth at the fae King and his guards, but they, too, obeyed their King.

Thanatos exhaled heavily and turned around, bearing his exposed back to the gathered crowd. Horrified murmurs emerged from his people.

It was only when he knelt that I caught sight of Thanatos's back. I drew in a staggering breath.

His back was covered in scars. They had the form of a V, running from his shoulder blades down to the small of his back, bulging against the rest of Thanatos's smooth skin.

My body shuddered. Suddenly, I knew what those scars were and understood the reason he had kept his shirt on when we went into the Lake of the Fallen Stars. They were a souvenir the other Kings had imprinted upon him when they turned on him; when they had ripped out his wings.

Even kneeling, Thanatos did not show an ounce of fear. His entire attitude was mocking the fae King.

"How noble of you to sacrifice yourself for a slave like her," Silvan said, gesturing in my direction.

Thanatos squared his shoulders. "Don't you dare call her that. It was more than enough that you attempted to hurt her. Don't even get me started on your attempt to kill her at your birthday." A beat of silence. "Your *failed* attempt."

Although I respected Thanatos for it, I wished he wouldn't pick at Silvan's ego like this. It only guaranteed that his upcoming punishment would be even more brutal.

Silvan squared his jaw, starting to open and close his fist around the whip's handle. He'd probably wished for Thanatos to shake like a leaf at his mercy.

"If you insult her once again, I'll end you. Consequences be damned," Thanatos repeated the same threat he had made when Silvan arrived at the Lake of the Fallen Stars. Even from his spot, looking up at Silvan, Thanatos still had more authority than his opponent. His words evoked a nervous flutter in my stomach. "Now stop speaking and get it over with," the Deathbringer bit out.

My heart might have stopped at his demand. Everything within me seized together, and I couldn't help the tremors wrecking my body when everything around me started spinning.

A cruel smile played at Silvan's lips. "As you wish."

"No!" I screamed, starting to buck against the guard's hold on me.

Silvan nodded in the direction of the guard who wasn't holding me. He ran over to Thanatos. Appalled, I watched him grab Thanatos's arms. He extended them in front of the Deathbringer and held them there together. It wasn't so much to restrict Thanatos as to humiliate him in front of his subjects. Thanatos didn't even try to protest.

Tears began blurring my vision.

My gaze jumped to Silvan, who was watching the scene with satisfaction. When the guard had secured Thanatos completely, Silvan stepped up to Thanatos and grabbed the crown on his head. "We wouldn't want this to get dirty, would we?"

The sound of metal hitting the ground made me flinch.

It was just another blow at Thanatos's pride.

The fae King moved around the monarch who knelt in front of him, his eyes fixed on the Deathbringer's back.

His fingers trailed over Thanatos's bulging scars. "I still remember when I ripped those wings from your back. How we chopped them off. Chop, chop, chop." He laughed at the memory.

His touch was almost gentle but for the hardness in his eyes. "Those feathers covered in blood were such a beautiful sight. I'll never forget it. Ahh, and the way you screamed ... it was the most beautiful symphony I've ever heard."

The townspeople froze, completely unaware of this part of their King's history. A bloodcurdling cry from the crowd made my breathing more difficult.

Without giving Thanatos a chance to brace himself, Silvan poked his thumb into the scar. He pressed into it harder and harder until he drew blood.

Thanatos groaned in pain but remained in his posture.

"Please, please, stop! I beg you!" Tears streamed down my face, but Silvan didn't so much as glance in my direction, and Thanatos held his head bowed, not meeting my eyes.

Silvan laughed loudly when Thanatos began sweating. "Let's get started, shall we?"

I exhaled in relief when he withdrew his hands from Thanatos's skin and stepped back.

But then Silvan drew the whip back.

It cut through the air, and I watched—repelled—as the end of it connected with Thanatos's back. The Deathbringer's body pushed forward from the force of the blow. He would have collided with the ground if not for the guard steadying him. Not a second later, blood began trickling from the welt Silvan's whip had left behind.

Silvan didn't grant him any time to recover, landing the second blow just a little higher than the first.

"Please! Please stop this!" I cried out.

I did this. I did this. I did this.

I stared at Thanatos, shaking my head vigorously. Suddenly, I wished I hadn't intervened with the two female fae. *Anything* was better than seeing Thanatos get punished for an insult no one had actually committed.

The blood looked grotesque as it streamed down Thanatos's cream-colored skin. I squeezed my eyes shut when the whip collided with his back once again.

I heard the sound of the lash cutting through the air over and over and over again. Worst of all, I could do nothing to stop this madness. The sound of Thanatos's ripping skin and his painful groans almost made my body give out.

"Look at him, princess. Your oh-so-noble King, bent down just for me," Silvan prompted me.

My sobs became heavier as I squeezed my eyes tighter. My body jerked forward with each strike as though I were the one getting beaten. And I should be.

All around me, the townspeople cried and sobbed, but everyone listened to their King's orders and stayed back.

"Look!"

I didn't want to, but I was scared for Silvan's wrath to increase if I disobeyed. Fighting my tears, I forced my eyes open at Silvan's command.

Thanatos was covered in his own blood. His entire body trembled from the energy it must take him to stay conscious. His weight was only supported by the guard who still held Thanatos's arms extended in front of him. Hugging each other or looking at the ground, the people around us averted their eyes from the abominable sight in front of them.

But no matter how many blows Silvan lands, the Deathbringer can't be killed. That thought was the only thing keeping me from a panic attack.

Silvan smiled the smile of a sadist when he assessed his handiwork. His shirt was dotted with the blood of Thanatos. He had used Thanatos's back like an artist would use a canvas. Welts were marking Thanatos's skin, and the blood streaming from the wounds made the welts' pattern undetectable.

Why didn't Thanatos fight back? He was so much more powerful than Silvan.

I can't risk a war between our kingdoms just so I can defend my pride. What good would defending your pride be if thousands of innocent lives would be threatened?

It was hard imagining the stakes of a war for people who were already dead, but after Thanatos had shared with me that if the people of Emoh died, they'd become nightcrawlers and lose their chance of reincarnation, I understood.

I hated seeing Thanatos like this. This seemingly defenseless shell of a man. That wasn't him. And he did all this for me and for his people. He chose to bow before Silvan's will rather than risking his people's safety by questioning the fae King. Silvan crossed his hands in front of his chest. He cocked his head as though weighing his options. "What do you think? Ten more?"

I shook my head frantically. "No! This is enough! He can't take anymore!"

Silvan chuckled. "Eleven it is."

This time, I knew better than to respond.

"Make sure she's watching," he ordered the guard at my back.

The guard grabbed my chin, forcing my head in the direction of Thanatos.

Silvan took his position. His lash was already tinted red. He looked over his shoulder at me. "Count."

I felt my eyes grow big. I shook my head and opened my mouth, but before I could voice a single word, Silvan chirped in.

"Shall it be twelve?"

I shook my head again.

Silvan smiled kindly at me. It made bile rise up my throat. "Then count."

At my first attempt, my voice failed me, but then, somehow, I managed to speak. "One."

Smack.

Thanatos began trembling. With effort, he blinked his eyes open slowly and met my gaze. "It's all right, love."

Tears began streaming down my face.

"Count!" Silvan bit out.

"Two."

Smack.

A sob left my mouth, and Thanatos squeezed his eyes shut at the pain exploding on his back. How dare he tell me everything was all right when it was him who was being lashed to the point of almost falling unconscious?

Silvan laughed at the parting sound of Thanatos's skin, his face so very, very pleased.

My terror began turning into wrath, fueled by each one of Thanatos's groans. It was an anger I had never felt before in my entire life.

How dare Silvan come into a realm and act as though he owned it? How dare he treat the people who lived here and wished only good like this? How dare he make up lies about the Deathbringer in order to provoke fear and pain within the people? And for what reason? Just because hundreds of years ago Thanatos couldn't grant him immortality.

My eyes swept over the aghast faces of Emoh's inhabitants. And those weren't Silvan's only wrongdoings. He'd also killed an innocent boy at his birthday for fuck's sake. And he'd almost killed *me*.

My breathing became labored. Silvan had inflicted so much pain …

"Count!" The fae King demanded.

He had cut off Thanatos's wings. He suppressed his own people and found joy in others' pain.

And it was enough.

Silvan turned around to face me. Thanatos's precious blood coated the fae King's face. Now he looked like the King he was: a monster King.

I felt something within me awaken. A power that had been asleep for years and years, and although it should have frightened me to death, it calmed me. It hammered against my skin, begging to be released.

"Count!" Silvan screamed at me. His usual white face reddened in anger.

He should have shut up while he still had the chance.

"Fucking start counting!" he hissed when I still didn't start.

I flashed him a smile, making him rear back at the sight.

My smile turned broader. "Three," I whispered.

Something in me snapped, and darkness lashed out from within me.

The thickest darkness I had ever seen boomed out of me like an atomic bomb. The surroundings became pitch-black. The shadows swarmed so thick I wasn't able to see my own hands in front of my face.

And, suddenly, I felt set free. I laughed.

I knew I probably should be panicking over this, but I just felt like coming home. Like suddenly becoming myself.

The guard who had held me had been thrown off by the force of the shadows hitting him. Startled gasps emerged from somewhere in the darkness, but I didn't mind the people's tumult. I had one goal in mind. One single goal.

Reaching Thanatos. Helping Thanatos.

Blackness streamed at the ground from underneath my fingernails and pooled around me menacingly, waiting for my orders.

"Show me," I demanded, and the darkness obeyed.

It moved out of my way, growling as it did so, but I knew it wouldn't harm me. Only those I deemed a threat.

I followed the short path toward Silvan and Thanatos.

My eyes fell on Thanatos, who still knelt on the ground, too weak to stand. He stared at me in complete shock. In any other situation, I'd have laughed at his expression, but my wrath for the man standing behind him was too powerful to ignore.

So very slowly, I met Silvan's gaze.

Silvan still held onto his lash. As though it would be any help. How pathetic.

The shadows around us flared up, leaving only me and the two Kings in a bubble. Scales, talons, and nails scraped at the shadows. I felt their hunger.

The shadows were always present. In every room, no matter time or space. They had seen all the atrocities committed by this tyrant of a King.

And they demanded *death*.

Silvan shook his head. Horror had amplified his devilish features. "It's not … this is not … it can't be." He took a step backward and tripped. His lash fell to the ground.

I looked at it and cocked my head. Thanatos's blood was coating it, and I had the strongest desire to grab it and whip the King of the fae with it. He had started lashing Thanatos for a reason he made up, just because he found pleasure in it. I wouldn't stop until his skin loosened from his body and I could tear it off him so slowly he would scream in agony.

"Please," he drew my attention from the whip back to his face.

That was probably the first smart decision he had ever made.

I took a threatening step forward. In a desperate attempt to get away from me, Silvan summoned his white clouds, but as soon as they started flaring up, they were swallowed by my shadows. Power hummed around me as I imagined putting my hands around the pale skin of his throat and squeezing.

Squeezing until he'd died.

The shadows caging him in from behind suddenly moved. Two hands of shadows formed and wrapped around his throat.

Silvan jumped and tried to move away, but they were already holding onto him tightly. He thrashed against them, but how could you hurt darkness?

I flashed him an eerie smile.

His glacial-blue eyes jumped to me. "What are you doing?" he growled. "I am King. You can't do this."

I laughed. It was a high-pitched sound that gave me the chills. I walked the last remaining steps forward. Silvan tried hiding his emotions behind anger, but I recognized the glimpse of fear underneath.

Thanatos may be bound to politics, but I sure as hell wasn't. I wasn't queen. There would be no consequences for Emoh if it was *I* who acted against Silvan. He might want to punish me, but he wouldn't punish Emoh. And I would not hesitate to repay him for hurting the only person besides Miriam who had stood up for me in my entire life.

The fae King seemed to sense it, too. I did not know what he saw in my eyes, but whatever it was must have been frightening enough for him to shut up.

Leaning forward, I stared him down. "You will leave now. You will take your guards with you. You are no longer welcome here."

Putting some distance between our faces, I patted his cheek. Hard. "If you don't obey, they will take care of you." I nodded in the direction of the shadows. They growled approvingly.

Silvan jerked at the sound.

"Are we clear?" I asked sweetly.

Thanatos stayed silent. He probably was too shocked to do anything other than stare. Or he was just too weak to act. Probably both.

Silvan nodded.

"Great!" I said cheerfully. My smile disappeared. "Now leave."

The shadows let go of him, and he stumbled forward. He caught himself just before he falling. The shadows made room for his guards, who looked like they would be ready to fight.

"We are leaving," Silvan snarled. The two guards, who hadn't been able to see what happened between the three of us, exchanged surprised looks, but other than that, relented to their King's orders.

"You will pay for this," Silvan promised as his white clouds began forming around him and the guards.

Then they disappeared.

I exhaled heavily before turning to Thanatos, and then I realized that his eyes were closed.

All at once, the power that had kept me on a high evaporated. I rushed to Thanatos's side and grabbed his hands. They were cold as ice and didn't squeeze mine back. "Thanatos?" Gently, I stroked his cheek, but he didn't react. Bile crept up my throat as I realized I was standing in a pool of his blood and was able to see the detached pieces of his skin.

Slowly, the mist of darkness around us dissolved, making our surroundings reappear. The shadows had hidden everything from the townspeople and, now, they were trying to put the missing pieces together as their gazes flew over us.

"He needs a healer!" I yelled to no one in particular, my fingers trembling uncontrollably. I could only hope Emoh had a healer. Hadn't Kalira mentioned one?

My voice seemed to rip the townspeople out of their shock.

They began moving and rushed to my side. "We need some space!" someone shouted.

Reluctantly, I moved away from Thanatos. I watched in a trance as the townspeople hurried forward and carefully laid their King on a stretcher someone must have fetched. My entire attention was completely focused on Thanatos. Everything but him was blurred around me. The townspeople laid him on his stomach so his back wouldn't be further injured. When his body was secured, they began moving.

As I followed them, I stared down at my hands.

I had summoned mist and darkness.

And it had answered me.

CHAPTER TWENTY-FIVE

I was sitting next to the bed where Thanatos lay. The torn back of my dress was held loosely together by pins. Minerva, the witch who had given me the sage for the Forest of the Lost Souls, turned out to be Emoh's healer. She had managed to stop the bleeding on Thanatos's back with a spell and had put herbs and crystal powder on the open wounds. Witches were known for their healing attributes, and Thanatos's back had visibly improved within minutes.

It had been hours since Silvan left, but Thanatos still did not wake. I held his hand, which was slowly regaining its natural warmth. The townspeople had decided to stay with their King after they had carried him to the small bed in Minerva's cottage. They were waiting outside for their King to wake. Thanatos probably wasn't even aware of how much his people valued him and how loyal they were to him.

"How long will he be unconscious?" I voiced the question burning on my tongue.

Minerva glanced back at me from where she stood next to the

cauldron. "As soon as his fever has lowered and his body doesn't feel the pain of the lashing any longer, he will wake. My spell will help," she promised for the thousandth time since I had set foot in the cottage.

I respected the witch for not losing her patience with me.

Sighing, she moved away from the kettle. Her brows knit when she lifted a patch of herbs from the Deathbringer's back and glanced beneath it. "He should wake fairly soon. The wounds are almost healed. See?" She lifted the patch enough for me to see the skin beneath. The welts were glowing an angry red but looked much better than a couple of hours before.

I nodded. "Thank you."

She smiled warmly, flashing her yellow teeth at me. Her body was voluptuous, and her eyes kind. When I first met her, I had felt scared by her appearance and her home, but now, as I saw how kindly she cared for Thanatos and how respected she was within the community of Emoh, I glimpsed more and more of her gentle nature. I had learned she was the one everyone sought out whenever something was needed. She made potions, sold herbs, and made herself available for the people. So not only was she Emoh's healer; she was also, of some sorts, the local psychologist of the Kingdom of the Dead.

We fell silent again, Minerva focusing back on her work, and me pursuing my thoughts. The crackling of the fire beneath the cauldron and the voices outside the cottage were the only sounds besides Thanatos's deep breathing.

I stared down at my smaller hand holding Thanatos's bigger one. The white spots on the bracelet Mir had gifted me glittered like the stars of Emoh's sky.

The feeling of empowerment I had felt back at the plaza had

vanished, leaving me an exhausted mess. I wished I could lie down next to Thanatos and let my consciousness drift away, too. Preferably with my memories.

But I couldn't. I wanted to be awake when Thanatos woke.

Light as a feather, I traced Thanatos's fingers. Weirdly enough, touching him seemed to rein in my emotions.

Over and over, my mind replayed what had happened in the plaza with Silvan. For the very first time in my life, I had felt the desire to hurt someone. And, although that thought scared the living crap out of me, what scared me more were the shadows, the darkness.

How the darkness had exploded from within me. How it had *obeyed* me.

Looking at the sleeping man on the bed, I swallowed audibly. The shadows. The darkness. They had felt so familiar ... I only knew one person to have access to those powers.

Thanatos.

They were Thanatos's powers.

After all, he was the one who ruled over the shadows. Not me.

So why the hell had those powers answered to me as though they were my own?

A gentle squeeze on my hand ripped me out of my thoughts. My eyes jumped from our joined hands up to Thanatos's eyes. Every single thought I had vanished. He was finally awake!

Careful not to startle him, I whispered, "Hi there. How are you feeling?"

His gaze darted restlessly over the room, clearly trying to put together the missing pieces of his memory.

"Where is Silvan?" He pushed himself up, ready to face any threat.

"It's all right." Gently, I pressed his shoulders down. "He left."

Exhausted, his body collapsed. It was as though he only allowed himself to rest when he was sure his realm and its people were safe.

His gaze became calmer. He looked at me, his eyes searching my body for any injuries. "Are you okay?" he rasped, his voice exhausted.

I smiled down at him. "I'm fine."

His shoulders slumped in relief.

Minerva approached him, a bowl filled with water in her hands. "How are you feeling, darling?" She was the only one I knew who wasn't addressing him as King.

Thanatos smirked at her. "Like a newborn, thanks Minerva." But his voice was too worn out to believe him.

Apart from Kalira, Minerva was the only person I had seen Thanatos exchanging contact with. And I couldn't help jumping to the conclusion that he did so because she was there for his people, helping and caring for them whenever she was needed.

She smiled back at him and put the bowl next to the bed. She handed me a cloth. "Make sure his back is clean, and don't let the cloth get too wet," she instructed, "or the water will reopen the wounds."

I gave her a curt nod and accepted the cloth.

"I can do it myself," Thanatos said, weakly trying to snatch the cloth away from me.

I glared at him and yanked the cloth out of his grasp. "Don't be ridiculous. You can't reach your back by yourself." I put the cloth in the warm water, feeling the King's eyes on me. I met his gaze. "Let me take care of you," I whispered, hoping he'd let me.

Squaring my jaw, I noticed his gaze was missing its typical glimmer.

Thanatos didn't say anything, but when I lifted the herb patches from his back, he didn't protest.

I knew how hard it was for him to surrender to someone else and let me take care of him. He himself had told me how hard it was to trust others. For him to relent and let me do this was a huge step for both of us.

"I have to get something. I'll be right back," Minerva murmured under her breath. The wooden door fell closed behind her, leaving only Thanatos and me alone in the cottage.

The fireplace crackled as neither of us spoke.

Thanatos kept silent as I removed the last remaining patches and assessed his back. It was looking way better than it had a couple of hours ago. The welts were slowly fading, but dried blood still crusted on his skin. The two grotesque-looking scars where his wings used to be hadn't disappeared, though.

I wetted the cloth and wrung it out. As Minerva had instructed, I was careful not to leave it too wet when I touched Thanatos's skin with it.

Thanatos inhaled sharply.

I jerked my hand away. "I'm sorry. Does it still hurt?" I whispered, my voice husky.

His head was leaning to the side, watching me while I took care of him. "No. Not at all. It's your touch."

Biting the inside of my cheek, I didn't know what to say to that. So, instead, I began to carefully clean the blood off of his body. When I dipped the cloth back in the water, it turned crimson red.

"I didn't attack him," I said softly, hoping he'd listen to me.

He inhaled deeply. "I know." Defeat clung to the sad hardness of his face, proving how worn out he must feel.

I looked down at him. His eyes had closed again. His body needed rest, and each second he spent awake was energy he needed to heal.

"Then why didn't you stop this? All of this could have been avoided," I said all while I gently traced the bloody scars with the washcloth.

"If I'd questioned the truth behind his statement, it would have incited a war simply for the fact of believing someone who isn't royal," he confirmed my earlier assumption.

I nodded in understanding. Thanatos was smart enough to try to avoid a war. At any cost. He'd rather get punished for something he didn't do than threaten the safety of his kingdom because of a dispute between two Kings.

"That was very noble of you," I whispered.

It was so much easier to let your emotions reign. To let wrath, hate, and fury get the better of you. But stepping back? Thinking before acting? Letting the one person you hate from the depth of your heart willingly hurt you? Just so you could secure the safety of your subjects? That was unheard of, and it showed how deeply he cared for his people.

He closed his eyes and sighed. "When I saw you kneeling before him with your dress ripped, I wanted nothing more than to kill him. That would have been noble." His muscles tensed. "And what did I do instead? Let him get away with it. Again."

I put the washcloth back in the bowl and leaned forward. "Thanatos," I breathed his name as though it were the most treasured secret and cupped his cheek. "You sacrificed yourself to prevent a conflict. I don't know what would have been more noble."

He pressed his lips together in a tight line, clearly unsure of what to say. He didn't know how to handle compliments, I realized. After all, he had been faced with hatred his entire life.

He looked at me thoughtfully. His eyes were coated in exhaustion. "The shadows answer to you."

I tensed. So he remembered.

Staring at the bloody bowl of water, I nodded.

"Everything's going to be all right, love. We'll figure this out. Together." He looked up at me with endearment.

I nodded, again reaching out to the washcloth. I didn't know why, but I believed him. I wanted to ask him what he had found out when he visited the Norns, but it wasn't the right time. He needed to rest. I could see it in the shadows on his face. Gently, I scrubbed the remains of the dried blood away before dipping the fabric back in the water.

"You should have listened to me and stayed away from him."

Did he feel hurt that I broke my promise? I glanced down at Thanatos. He watched me carefully. His eyelids fluttered heavily, and I knew he was about to give in and fall back asleep.

I swallowed and refocused on his back. "I couldn't just stand by and watch how he hurts others."

The King of the Afterlife sighed deeply, his eyelids falling shut. He grabbed my left wrist and, circling the mole on it, whispered, "That's why I love you."

CHAPTER TWENTY-SIX

I was held by a cocoon of warmth. Lovingly, something brushed my arm up and down. I sighed contently and snuggled closer to the warmth beneath me.

"Morning, love," a deep, male voice rumbled, the sound resonating underneath my body.

Lazily, I blinked open my eyes and stared at a pair of twinkling, moss-green eyes. "Thanatos?"

His smile turned wicked. "The one and only."

Fuck! Had I fallen asleep?

My eyes darted around the room. We were still in Minerva's cottage. The fireplace crackled peacefully. Plants covered the windows densely, only letting a fraction of the moonlight illuminate the small space. Minerva was nowhere to be seen.

To my horror, I realized I had fallen asleep *on top* of Thanatos. What the hell? When had I crawled into the bed the villagers had carried him to? He was injured, for fuck's sake! I pushed against his chest to get up. Against his *naked* chest.

Oh, well ….

Thanatos smirked at my obvious horror. "You were drooling," he said, a wide grin tipping up the corners of his sensual lips.

I had not been. Had I? Horrified, I lifted my head and searched his skin for any spit-leftovers.

His body shook with laughter.

My eyes narrowed when I realized he had just been teasing. "I assume you are feeling better?" I stood with as much dignity as one might have when one has fallen asleep on top of a King who's just been lashed.

"Yeah," he murmured, also standing. His movements were fluid, no longer impaired by the pain he had endured yesterday. Whatever spell Minerva had used to speed his healing process must have worked magic, because he didn't seem to hurt anymore at all.

Now that he wasn't injured any longer, I let myself contemplate his body. He was lean, his muscles defined. The trousers he wore hung loose on his slender hips, accentuating the stark v-cut of his muscles. The sight evoked the most bizarre flutter in my belly. In an effort to get rid of the sudden feeling, I swallowed hard.

Discreetly, I brushed my hair out of my face and righted my clothing.

His waist was tucked in, and his shoulders were taut with muscles bulging beneath the skin. He reached to the belt the townspeople had taken out of his trousers' loops to tend his injuries.

Heat spread on my cheeks as I recalled the words he had spoken to me yesterday just before he had fallen asleep. I turned away from him and hid my shyness.

They had been the words of an ill man. The fever must have loosened his tongue.

They didn't mean anything.

Right?

When I turned to the King of the Afterlife again, he was already dressed, his scars hidden beneath a white linen shirt with long sleeves.

Clearing my throat, I asked, "Why did he do this? What did he get out of this?"

Thanatos stopped fastening his belt. "Revenge." His expression darkened as he resumed his movements. There was no trace of his usual cockiness.

I tipped my head to the side. "Revenge for what?"

Thanatos ran a hand through his hair. "For intervening in his plans to kill you. And for not granting him the immortality he came for when he took my wings."

I jerked back. "What? But that's crazy! How can he still be mad about something that happened decades ago? He can't keep punishing you for that! You don't even have the power to make him immortal." It almost felt as though I were repeating some of my earlier conversations with Thanatos. But I just couldn't understand how Silvan could feel this way.

Thanatos chuckled darkly, a dangerous expression flashing over his features. "I never said the King of the fae was sane."

I snorted. He sure as fuck wasn't.

I couldn't wrap my mind around the fact that Silvan had lied and said that I had attacked him. How could a person be this dishonest?

"Did the Norns tell you what's to be done about the loss of Silvan's power?" I truly hoped they hadn't. Even if that thought made me a bad person, I'd be relieved if a ruler as malicious as Silvan didn't have access to more power.

Thanatos's body grew still. "Yes."

Damn. "So, what did they tell you?"

He looked around, making sure no one could eavesdrop into the conversation. When he seemed satisfied, he slowly said, "They said that a member of the council has awoken."

I leaned my back against the wall next to me and watched Thanatos. "The council?"

He straightened. "The Council of The Great Old Times." Noticing my confused look, he explained, "There was a time when the Kings worked alongside some very carefully selected people. Those were the members of the council."

I had never heard of this. It must've been a long time ago for the stories about the council to die off. "To do what, precisely? What were their roles?"

"They attended the Kings during the most important political decisions. Their influence guaranteed that an objective decision could be made without the personal interests of the Kings interfering in the matters."

Without the Kings deciding solely upon what was best for their own reign, was what he meant. "What happened?"

Thanatos exhaled deeply. "That's the thing. Nobody knows. The council members suddenly disappeared, and the Kings didn't bother searching for them. Without needing the council's approval of their decisions, they got a taste of full autonomous power. And, of course, they didn't want to lose it again."

I nodded in understanding. Of course they wouldn't. Who would want to search for people who'd diminish one's influence?

"Why didn't *you* search for them?" I couldn't help but wonder this. Not for a single second did I think he shared the same reasons as the other Kings. Thanatos didn't strike me as someone as power-drunk as the rest of the Kings, and as he spoke of the council, I got the feeling that he thought its existence had been useful and good. So why hadn't he searched for the members when they disappeared?

Thanatos's jaw slackened. "As soon as the council disappeared and the Kings learned of their benefits as autonomous rulers, they wanted to maximize their power." He inhaled before proceeding. "It was around that time that the Kings took my wings."

So, the Kings had wanted not only to be as powerful as they were but also to make it last for eternity by becoming immortal.

Thanatos avoided my gaze, shame and guilt for his own behavior clearly weighing down on him.

But I understood why he had acted the way he had. He'd had more than enough on his own plate back then to do something about the council. He didn't need an additional problem to solve.

"And, apparently, one of the council has awoken." He scratched his neck. "Whatever that means."

"I don't understand. What does the council have to do with the loss of Silvan's power?"

His gaze roamed over the inside of the cottage before coming to stop upon me. "Silvan isn't just losing his power. It's being transferred to the member."

I let that sink in. So that was the reason why Thanatos was so serious. There was a big threat looming in the shadows of not knowing who the member was and why all the power was transferring to them. And most importantly, there was no way to anticipate what the member planned to do with that kind of power and why they had awoken in the first place.

"It's dangerous to have a person with that kind of power running around freely," Thanatos voiced my own thoughts.

"So, is there a way to stop the member?"

His eyes flashed to me. "You."

I shrank back. "Me?" I couldn't possibly imagine how *I* could be helpful in that matter.

He nodded. "The Norns said that you are the key to stopping the member."

"What? Why?" There was no way I'd just heard him right.

Thanatos looked at me, a puzzled expression written on his face. "I don't know either … maybe it has to do with the powers you now have."

I felt the blood rush out of my face.

The shadows, the darkness.

The same emotions I had yesterday came crashing down on me all at once. My lungs seized together, making it hard to breathe.

The shadows had listened to me … how the hell was that even possible?

Noticing my shift of mood, Thanatos came up to me. "Hey. What's wrong?" He grabbed my hand.

I tipped my face up and met his preoccupied gaze.

"Nothing." I forced myself to smile.

Thanatos shook his head and took a step forward. He was invading my personal space, and I had nowhere to go. The wall was already digging into my back, and he was in front of me, his body caging me in.

Thanatos looked down at me with narrowed eyes. "Don't do this. Don't cut me out. Not after everything."

I looked away from him and swallowed. He was right. I had to open up to him. If anyone would know what was going on with me, it was him, who ruled over the darkness. My hands became sweaty. "The shadows, I just … how?"

His expression gentled. Ever so slowly, his hand reached out and traced my jaw. "I don't know, love. I don't know … but we'll figure it out," he repeated yesterday's words. His eyes searched my face. Whatever he may have found in my gaze made him add, "I promise."

Biting my bottom lip, I nodded. It felt so incredibly unfamiliar but so damn good to have someone who'd help me figure everything out.

I was surprised when he leaned forward, resting his mouth on my forehead. "Cassiana …" The way my name resonated over my suddenly hyper-aware skin sent shivers down my back. My eyes closed of their own accord as I breathed in his musky, soothing scent, drawing it as deep into my nostrils as possible. I loved the way my name sounded on his tongue. The way he savored every vowel, making the most of my name's touch in his mouth. It felt like the waves of the Lake of the Fallen Stars caressing the sand and leaving only the stardust at its shores.

The end of his hair tickled my chin. I leaned a couple of inches back and brushed it behind his ears.

Thanatos's hands rested on my waist.

There was so much depth in his intense gaze that I braced myself inwardly for his upcoming words.

"Cassiana. There's something else they told me …"

The door to the cabin swung open and a happy-looking Minerva entered. She was carrying a basket filled with all kinds of greenery, most of it unknown to me. "I'm back," she announced. She set the basket on the top of the counter before she spotted us.

Minerva took in the closeness between our bodies. Her eyes softened visibly. "You two lovebirds have people waiting for you in the plaza."

Thanatos walked out of the cottage first, his imposing frame barely fitting through the doorway.

I rushed to his side. "Are you sure you are feeling up for this? For facing everyone?" Even though his back looked fine, I wouldn't be surprised if his injuries still hurt him internally.

He peered down at me. The village's light reflected in his eyes, giving them a devilish glimmer. "Oh, love. I'm already up for all kinds of physical activities." He winked at me.

His humor had returned. That should be a good sign.

As we walked through the village, aiming for the plaza, we didn't meet anyone. Judging by the silence and the lack of people, it felt as though nobody lived here.

My eyes darted to the plaza. Murmurs and low whispers flared up from there.

Thanatos's body grew rigid, alert for any danger.

Suddenly, as we walked around the next corner and came into view, excited cheers erupted from all around us.

Thanatos stopped dead in his tracks. "What's this?" he demanded.

Everyone living in Emoh was gathered around the plaza.

Some were holding flowers, and others threw glittering confetti at us.

My stomach knotted as I looked at the spot where Thanatos had been lashed yesterday. Someone had already taken care of the blood on the pavement and scrubbed it away. It was as though last night had never happened. Cautiously, I checked if someone was looking at me strangely, but the villagers' attention was entirely fixed on their King. Nobody cast worried or terrified glances at me. They must not have seen how I had commanded the darkness. My shoulders relaxed.

My eyes darted over the countless joyful faces. Everyone was wearing their finest attire. Some even had glitter sprinkled on their skin, and I spotted some children holding balloons with the Afterlife's crest painted on them.

A smile danced on my lips as I realized that all of Emoh has gathered here to celebrate their King's well-being. I stepped up to the King of the Dead, who didn't seem able to grasp what was happening.

Gently, I touched his biceps. "They are here to welcome you," I whispered to him.

The King's eyebrows were knit in confusion. "What, I—"

The people calmed as one of the townsfolk stepped forward with slow, measured steps. He was carrying a red cushion in his hands, a small object lying on top of it. He bowed when he reached us. "My King."

Thanatos seemed frozen, not able to do anything other than stare.

The villager, an old man whose neatly combed grayish hair reached his shoulders, said in a clear voice, "We waited eagerly for you to heal so we could finally approach you." He spoke up, loud enough to be heard from everywhere. The crowd had silenced, listening to his words. "We have all witnessed that Cassiana did not attack the fae King."

Agreeing murmurs rose.

"And we all know that you—our King—took that punishment upon yourself to save us. To avoid a war. To save those lives that are innocent." He stopped, tears of gratitude glittering in his eyes.

Thanatos kept silent and warily watched the man standing before him.

The man struggled to regain his voice, but once he did, he proceeded proudly. "And in the name of your entire kingdom, I want to thank you."

Cheers and clapping erupted around us. The faces of Emoh's inhabitants were lit with glee and joy. But most importantly, they radiated a deep-rooted gratitude.

The man reached for the object on the pillow. Only now did I realize it was Thanatos's crown that Silvan had thrown away. It shone as though it had been freshly polished for its owner.

Slowly, the man walked up to Thanatos, the crown extended highly in front of him. He stopped before his King and smiled at him. "If you weren't already our King, we would make you ours."

The Deathbringer's eyes widened in shock as his hands began to tremble visibly.

The old man had to stretch his arms high in order to reach Thanatos's scalp. Oh, so very carefully, he placed the crown on Thanatos's head, the silver reflecting the moonlight brightly against the raven-black hair of the King.

The man took a step back and nodded in approval. Then, he sank down on his knees.

And suddenly, all at once, everyone followed suit, getting down on their knees and bowing before Thanatos.

Thanatos swallowed hard, the movement bobbing his Adam's apple.

Smiling, I contemplated him. He was uncomfortable. Yet again, he had braced himself for people's worst. But this? Earning his people's trust? No. This was something he hadn't foreseen.

And how could he? He was used to the opposite.

I spotted Kalira in between the masses. She was smiling broadly at us. Minerva knelt next to her and observed everything with a satisfied smirk.

My smile widened as I, too, fell down on my knees and bowed my head in acknowledgement of the King.

Thanatos looked at his people on their knees before him of their free will. His eyes met mine, and he mirrored the joyful expression plastered on my face. I had never seen him this happy before.

The main difference between Silvan and Thanatos was that Thanatos wasn't only a King by birth. He was a King because he acted for the sake of the people, and today, the people had demonstrated they'd act for his.

CHAPTER TWENTY-SEVEN

The next evening, Thanatos and I walked by the shore of the Lake of the Fallen Stars. It was late, and the wind carried a sweet note of hibiscus.

Yesterday, Thanatos had tried finding out if anyone had witnessed my powers. But, apparently, only Thanatos, Silvan, and I were aware of them. That knowledge had calmed me to some extent.

I let my eyes roam over the lake's surface. The King of the Dead wanted to resume my swimming lessons. His idea came surprising, especially given the Norns' implication for me to stop the council member. There were more than enough problems we needed to fix, but both of us wanted to stay in our small, happy bubble for a little longer.

To say that I wasn't particularly fond of Thanatos's idea on *how* we'd spend that time was an understatement. "Do we have to do this today?" Why couldn't we just, you know … Netflix and chill? Not that there was Netflix here, but just sprawling out and relaxing after everything that had happened sounded damn tempting. Though with Thanatos, I couldn't be certain it would involve as much relaxing as I might think …

Thanatos nodded enthusiastically. "Of course! What else would you want to do?"

I was about to suggest chilling, but he cut me off.

"I think exercising is the best thing we can do to soothe our minds."

I closed my mouth. I had no retort to that. He was right, of course. As alluring as relaxing might sound, it did nothing to prevent our minds from wandering off to places neither of us had any desire to go.

Thanatos slowly opened the buttons of his golden-traced jacket. "What do you say, love? Are you feeling up for it?" he watched me closely, ready to go back to Emoh if I wished.

Shrugging, I began toying with the bracelet Mir had gifted me. Just because we had gone in waist-deep last time didn't mean I felt any more comfortable doing so a couple of days later. "Don't you think that the—ah!" I went down in a cry of pain. My body collided with the twinkling sand.

Thanatos spun around, instantly manifesting at my side. "Cassiana? What's wrong?" His eyes laid bare his worry for me, while his hands slid over my body, searching for any visible injury.

"I don't—ahhhh!" I cried out as pain tore through my scalp all at once. My body curled inwardly at the all-consuming agony.

Thanatos cursed under his breath. "Talk to me, Cassiana. Now! Where do you hurt?"

My vision began blurring. "Everywhere …" I couldn't finish whatever it was I had been about to say before my body contracted in yet a new wave of agonizing pain. The last thing I saw before everything went black was Thanatos looming over me, his eyes pained in distress.

I was surrounded by darkness. It was so dense, I couldn't make out where I was. The shadows around me raged furiously, but never once did they reach out to me.

A small path lay before me. A path of shadows.

The way the shadows shifted beneath my weight felt like walking on clouds—almost as though they were about to give out underneath me but supporting me nevertheless. Raven-black clouds.

I blinked at the stream of light radiating in a long gap at the end of the path.

As I walked closer and closer to it, the mist around me slowly gave way to deep-brown wooden walls. It seemed as though I were inside a wooden box of some sort. The stream of light came from a small crack in between the walls. I halted in front of it. Recognizing it as a door, I pushed it slightly open and glanced through the small gap into a brightly lit room.

A kitchen. It felt oddly familiar with its purple curtains and dark-brown floor.

A jovial laugh resonated behind me, tearing my attention away from the kitchen and back into the wooden box.

It was only when I turned around that I became aware of all the different colored clothing hung up around me. The path of shadows had led me straight into a wardrobe; not a wooden box like I'd thought at first.

My gaze fell to the source of the sound I had just heard. A small child sat at my feet inside the wardrobe. The clothing around us rustled with her movements. The long stream of light fell right onto her, illuminating her gleeful face. The child laughed again. She seemed completely unaware of me.

I followed the girl's eyes to the darkness around her. The shadows. She was playing with them.

They stroked through her hair like the wind touches the leaves. She giggled at the caress, the sound carefree and so very light.

The girl looked down at her own shadow. I observed the shadows around her form a man's silhouette. He had his hands hidden behind his back. The girl's eyes went huge as she watched how the shadow-man moved forward and bowed deeply in front of her own shadow. He then extended both of his hands to her shadow. He held something in his hands. Once I realized what it was, a sudden sense of tenderness overcame me. He was offering the child's shadow a crown of mist and darkness. When he straightened, he moved to the girl's shadow and, reverently, put the crown on the shadow girl's head. The girl giggled and, in an effort to touch her own shadow, leaned forward. But as soon as her small fingers touched the shadow-crown, it decayed into smoke, leaving the crown-less shadow of herself behind.

A small, black dot at the girl's wrist caught my attention.

A mole.

"Cassiana."

Both the girl and I jerked our heads up at the wrathful voice of our father. Suddenly, the darkness around her swelled, surrounding her in a cocoon of mist and shadows, making her invisible.

Protecting *her.*

"Cassiana!" Our father's voice boomed again.

I jolted with every one of his heavy footsteps. Very slowly, I turned around, peering out of the closet. My dad's face was crimson-red in anger, his wrinkles more prominent in his fury.

He tore open the doors to the closet.

The girl behind me whimpered in fear.

My dad didn't seem to see me. He was looking right through me.

The girl was hidden in the darkness.

My dad took in the sight. He didn't seem to see the girl, but he looked as though he knew *her small body was hidden by the darkness surrounding her. If I'd thought he was angry until this point, I had been mistaken. His eyes narrowed as he balled his hands into fists. "How dare you?"*

I had seen him countless times like this, and my pleading had never helped me.

He made to grab the small girl out of the shadows, but the darkness lashed out and knocked away his hands. He wanted to grab her again, but the shadows pushed him away again.

"No," the small girl yelled, her body still hidden by the shadows. "Don't hurt him."

"Come here right now, young lady!"

Reluctantly, the shadows eased back. The girl's face was filled with panic at the sight of her father's.

As soon as her arm was out of the mist, her father lunged forward. He grabbed her arm, yanking the rest of her body out of the darkness. His raging eyes burned down on her. "If you ever even think about doing something like this again, I will end you," he spat. His fingers dug into the girl's skin, his grip tightening. He shook the girl's body violently, making her head fly back and forth. He leaned forward. "You do this once again, and I will end you. End you," he repeated.

The girl whimpered, her small body shaking. Tears streamed down her face. "I didn't want to do this ... I just ..."

He jolted her again, his anger coloring his cheeks in a deep shade of red. "I do not care. You are a fucking freak. A freak.*"*

The shadows were raging with wrath, wanting to interfere, but obeying the small girl.

It was only now I spotted our mother leaning against the kitchen counter, watching her husband and the girl in silence.

The dad let go of the girl, stepping around her and starting to pace.

The girl was shaking like a leaf at her father's hateful words. She glanced at our mother, but the older woman only watched.

The father gestured to the place the little girl still stood without meeting his gaze. "That thing there is not my daughter. It's a freak."

With heavy steps, he trudged toward the girl.

I moved further back into the closet. I didn't want to see this.

I knew what would happen now.

The shadows made screeching sounds.

My father drew back his hand.

The girl lifted her arms to protect herself from the blow that was about to come down on her.

The shadows thickened around me, beginning to surround me until I couldn't see my father hitting the small girl. Nor hear her screams.

When I turned around, I spotted a window behind me. I walked over to it and peered inside. A living room.

The girl that I had just seen minutes ago had grown up. Her hair was fisted in a tight grip by a man looming behind her. His back was turned to me so I couldn't make out who it was.

"I wanted to kill you all this time. But what kind of person would kill his own daughter?" He laughed humorlessly. "I should have killed you when I had the chance."

The woman's body flinched with the words.

A knife was digging into her skin, making a trickle of blood run down her throat. The woman tried leaning away from the sharp object.

The man clicked his tongue loudly, the sound making her jump. "You think you can get away from me?" He chuckled. "No. You will not. I won't make that mistake again."

Elongating, the shadows around me swelled into a threatening force.

The man turned slightly to the side, letting the lights stream in through the window where I was observing. Dad had become skinnier, time wearing out his body. His eyes were emotionless as he stared into the girl's eyes.

The girl was losing this battle. Her eyes were dull, tired of fighting. Her body relaxed into the man's hold, accepting her fate.

Suddenly, the shadows lashed out, darkening the room into the deepest shade of black. Creatures scraped against the wall of mist, and the frame of a man stepped out of it. It wasn't a human. It was the shadows, forming a man. No. He was too broad, too unearthly to be human. The shadows had formed a monster.

He stalked toward Dad and yanked him away from the girl

with brutal force. She cried out in shock. The mist caged her in, not letting her see through the fog surrounding her.

Protecting her yet again.

But I saw everything.

Dad let go of the knife in shock. It fell on the floor with a loud thud.

"What the hell?" The girl turned around, trying to piece together what was happening, but the mist still kept her in the dark.

The shadow-man dragged Father's struggling body farther away from the young woman. The shadows swelled, building a circle around him.

The father's suddenly-panicked eyes moved over the shadows, unable to understand what was happening.

And then, all at once, the shadows darted forward. The darkness seeped into Father's nose and mouth, muffling his scream into a groan.

His body hit the ground.

The woman looked frightened. "Hello?"

Dad had become completely still, his eyes staring up, unmoving. Slowly, the darkness seeped out of the man's body. He was dead. Killed by the same darkness that protected the woman, no matter the cost.

The woman's heavy breathing was the only sound in the apartment. She stood and carefully put one foot in front of the other. When her feet bumped into the knife, she crouched down and picked it up. Her hands trembled as she extended them in front of her, careful to not walk into any upcoming objects.

She was just about to reach the door when her feet crashed into the corpse on the floor. Crying out, she went down. She kept her hands extended to block the fall, but by doing so, her right hand, which still grasped the knife, was rammed into her already dead father's chest from the weight of her body falling on top. A smacking sound resonated in the room when her weight impaled the knife straight into the body. She let go of the knife's handle and tried to push herself up, but with the living room still cast in darkness and her father's body beneath her, it was nearly impossible.

The shadows chose that instant to withdraw.

The woman stared at the rigid face of her father for a split second, unable to comprehend what had happened. Once she registered it, she let out a scream and scrambled away from what used to be her father.

The shadows slowly eased back, taking me with them into their darkness.

Gasping for air, I blinked open my eyes and met a pair of striking green ones staring down at me with fear and anguish.

"There you are." Thanatos pressed my body tighter against him. "What happened?"

My eyes darted over our surroundings without being able to process anything properly. We were still at the lake. Thanatos was holding my body cradled against him in a protective gesture. This could only mean I hadn't lost consciousness for too long.

I pushed against his hold, needing space to breathe and calm myself.

Thanatos let go of me hesitantly, not for a second taking his eyes off of me as I stood.

My heart was racing and my eyes were having trouble adjusting to the lake's brightness.

The girl. The woman.

They had been me.

Sweat began coating my skin, and a heavy knot formed in the pit of my stomach when the images resurfaced of the younger me playing with the shadows. I blinked against the dots that started to blacken my vision when the sight of my dead father flashed before me. I didn't want to be confronted with that day again, but the more I fought against what the shadows had shone me, the clearer the images got.

And the shadows—

"Cassiana. What happened? Talk to me," the King of the Dead said when I didn't meet his eyes. He stood, slowly coming closer to me. "Please," he whispered, stroking my hair gently.

My voice sounded clipped when I spoke. "The shadows. They showed me …"

Thanatos searched my face. "What did they show you?"

"My past," I whispered.

Thanatos knit his eyebrows in confusion.

Watching him, I took a deep, calming breath. I had not thought I'd tell Thanatos about that day like this—or at all for that matter. But he was the only one who might have answers. "My dad. One day, after I had already moved out," a chill let the hair on my skin rise, "he came to my home. He … he wanted to …"

Kill me.

I couldn't bring myself to finish the sentence, but based on Thanatos's hardening features, he had already figured out my unspoken words.

"But instead, I … I killed him," I whispered, staring at my

feet. The words were interlaced with pain, bitterness, and shame. But more than anything with hate. Hate and revulsion toward myself.

Thanatos kept his silence, giving me the time to gather myself before continuing.

It took me longer than I liked to admit to find the courage to proceed. "Everything was so dark. And, I— I was so sure it had been me who had killed him."

"Cassiana." Thanatos's voice was soft and comforting.

I didn't dare look at him. If I did, I feared I might not find the courage to finish telling him everything. I swallowed against the bile creeping up my throat, the sound loud in the chilly night. "But it was the shadows. They had protected me from him."

A weight I had carried for four years withdrew from my shoulders.

I wasn't responsible for my father's death.

I wasn't responsible for my father's death.

The shadows had killed him. Not me.

The shadows had protected me from the man who should have been my guardian.

To live with the knowledge of having murdered somebody had nearly killed me from the inside. What right did I have to keep living if I had killed someone in cold blood?

But, all along, it had been the shadows.

I had never understood why my family hated me. My entire life I had wondered about the reason for my parents' loathing. But now? An idea began forming on the edge of my consciousness. Could it be that they …?

I lifted my head. They had seen me playing with the darkness. They had witnessed my powers.

Now I understood.

They had been *scared* of me.

A daughter who could call the darkness.

Finally, I knew why they had acted the way they had. Why they had punished me. Every time I had made use of my powers, they had made sure to discipline me.

And me?

On a subconscious level, I must have learned that whenever I used my power, a punishment would be guaranteed, and I had therefore learned to suppress them.

And, over time, I had been taught that power meant pain. My mind must have decided to black out that part of my memory altogether as a self-defense mechanism.

I had forgotten about my power.

A tear ran down my cheek.

Suddenly, every single detail, every hint of my powers surfaced to my consciousness. My breathing shallowed. This explained why I had always felt this deep connection to the darkness.

The day Thanatos had saved me at the theatre, the shadows had slithered toward me like a friend, and I had stretched out my hand, subconsciously welcoming them back.

The way I had never feared the darkness and preferred the night over the day. How I had *relished* the night. The way the surrounding shadows sometimes seemed to react to my emotions … how I felt safe within the shadows …

When I visited the Forest of the Lost Souls, it had felt as though the nearest shadows had retreated from me, illuminating my path. But I had thought it had only been my mind playing tricks on me. Now, I couldn't be sure any longer. And that day when the nightcrawlers had attacked me, Thanatos had said that the darkness had called him for help. I couldn't be sure anymore: had it truly been Thanatos's power that had frightened the nightcrawlers away or had it been the shadows themselves that had watched over me and protected me yet again? And why had the nightcrawlers backed away from me when they had fed on me? Could it be that they had recognized their ruler's power looming within me? The hissing voice of the nightcrawler suddenly vibrated in my consciousness. *Part of darknesssssssss.*

Even the smallest details suddenly seemed to point toward the truth: when Thanatos and I had played hide and seek, I had hidden behind the curtain. I had been sure that Thanatos should've been able to see me, but a cloud had darkened the moonlight, hiding me from his view. But there were no clouds in the Afterlife, were there? Now, I wondered if it was the shadows that had hidden me from their own master. They had been playing along. Even the one person who ruled over the shadows hadn't been able to see me. And the day I had seen Thanatos walk alone in Emoh's outskirts, a shadow-man had formed behind him and waved back at me. Could that man be the same force that had saved me from my father and given me the shadow-crown as a kid?

The shadows had always been there. They had always hidden but had been by my side, watching over me nonetheless.

Thanatos recognized the sheer relief that must've been written in my face and took me into his powerful, strong arms.

"It's okay," he soothed me when I began trembling.

Four years of believing myself to be a murderer had just been ripped away from me.

Thanatos's hand stroked over my back, coming to a halt at the nape of my neck.

"Why do I remember all of this now?" I mumbled through the material of his shirt.

The King of the Dead kept quiet for so long, I wasn't sure he would answer. "Maybe your memory came back to you because you used your powers against Silvan."

I chewed on my bottom lip. "I don't understand. Why do I have these powers? Could they somehow have been given to me?" I sure as hell hadn't inherited them from my parents. Both of them had been entirely human.

A beat of silence. "It is possible. I wouldn't know how, but there's definitely the possibility the power has somehow been transferred to you …"

"But why would the same power you have be transferred to me?"

He lifted a shoulder. "That's a damn good question."

A wave of silence washed over us.

I chewed on my lower lip. "Do you know of someone else who has these powers?"

I felt him shake his head.

"Just me."

Just him.

Just him.

Suddenly, his hold didn't feel comforting any longer, but restricting. I pushed against him.

He noticed my shift of mood immediately and let go of me.

I stared at him as anxiety began heating my stomach, turning my mouth sour. I took in the very first man to whom I had started opening up. My breath got stuck in my throat as realization hit me with such a force, it almost made my knees give out beneath me.

"You knew all along," I breathed.

His eyes grew wide. "What?"

How could I have been so fucking stupid? Now that the power had broken loose, I couldn't help but think that his interest in me had something to do with it. He knew all along and he just wanted to use my powers for his own purposes. "That's it." Tears began blurring my vision, but the anger overwhelmed the pain.

Thanatos never once took his eyes off of me. "What the hell—"

I darted forward, poking my index finger into his chest. "That's why you fucking brought me here," I screamed at him, too overwhelmed to rein in my emotions in any longer. And I had been so stupid to think he had brought me to the Afterlife for my safety.

I was so fucking dumb, dumb, dumb.

Thanatos stared at me. His brows knit together. "What are you—"

I snorted at him. "You are just such a fucking liar. Telling me all about your past. Making me feel sorry for you. Having what goal in mind? Earning my trust?" I gestured wildly.

The King of the Afterlife's frame suddenly darkened threateningly, but I ignored it.

"Just so you might use it for your own sinister plans?" Just like everyone else always used me.

"That is enough," he grumbled.

I glared at him. "You do this all the time? Bringing women to the Afterlife just so you can benefit from their powers?"

"I said, that is enough!" Thanatos barked. The shadows

around him flared up into a threatening force. He took a step toward me, the mist surrounding him like a second skin. His eyes blazed in the darkness, and the shadows accentuated his facial features.

Even knowing that the shadows responded to me, too, I took a staggering step back at the sight of him. He looked every inch the King of the Dead. I wasn't stupid enough not to fear him in this state.

His eyes burned with rage when he stepped up to me. "You want to know why I saved you? You want to know why I welcomed you in my home? I'll fucking tell you." He cut through the distance between us.

My chest was moving rapidly with my accelerated breathing, but I refused to show my vulnerability by stepping away. I had to tip my head back to meet his eyes.

"I didn't save you so I could use your powers." He stopped in front of me, looking as menacing and powerful as ever. The moonlight highlighted his black hair like a halo of a fallen angel. "I saved you because you are my soulmate."

CHAPTER TWENTY-EIGHT

I searched his eyes for a sign that this was a joke. For *anything* that would disclose his lie. But I found none. Blinking up at him, I hugged myself protectively. "What do you mean?"

Thanatos leaned forward. I could almost feel the heat of his skin radiating from his powerful body. "You are my soulmate, Cassiana." His voice had become so very soft and loving. There was no trace of the menace he had shown at my outburst mere minutes ago and even the shadows around him shrunk in size.

Soulmate. Soulmate. Soulmate. The word echoed in my mind like thunder. My breathing was harsh as I stared at him. His facial features that were usually accentuated by darkness looked much softer than normal, the hardness of his gaze completely gone as he looked at me in a way nobody before him had. "What do you mean?" I asked again.

Thanatos exhaled softly. "The Norns. When I went to them to ask about Silvan's problem, they explained everything to me." He grabbed my hand and looked in my eyes deeply. "Cassiana. We are fated to be together. They were the ones who organized our interactions."

Not understanding a single thing he said, I scowled. "Well, yes. That's what they do. They are the ones to determine our fates."

Shaking his head, he cupped my hand with both of his and pressed it tightly against his chest. "No. You don't understand."

"Then explain it to me."

Exhaling, he squeezed his eyes shut. It must be something he had carried with him for a long time for it to affect him this much. Slowly, he opened his eyes. His emotions were laid bare for me to see. "It was many, many years ago." Turning my hand around, he looked down at my wrist and traced the mole on my skin the same way he had the first day he had shown me Emoh before disappearing without explanation. "I don't know if you remember it," he inhaled deeply, "but I have saved you before."

I gasped for air. What? When? How?

"It was the very first time the Norns had called me to save a life." He kept staring at my mole. "There was this little girl who had fallen in the ocean. She was drowning, and she had a small mole on her wrist. It was identical to yours."

All those countless times Thanatos had paid attention to my birthmark ...

I couldn't stop staring at him as words failed me at what he was really saying. I felt the anger that had fueled me just mere minutes ago giving way to disbelief. "That day ... it was you? You were the one who saved me?" My voice was hoarse, filled with incredulity. "I was sure I had died that day."

Thanatos's expression turned grim. "You had. I brought you

back." The sound of the glittering stardust hitting the shore encapsulated us.

So that was the reason he hadn't questioned my fear of the water when we had attempted to swim. He had known where it was coming from.

"I brought you back before your soul had a chance to trespass to the Afterlife." He ran a hand through his hair. "It felt so … foreign to save a life. Never once had the Norns commanded me to do something like this, but there's always a first. So, I forgot about it until …"

"Until they called you again to save me once more before Silvan could kill me," I concluded.

He nodded.

"But why didn't the shadows help me when I drowned? Why didn't they intervene like they did with my …" I cleared my throat. "With my father?" Why had the Norns sent you instead?"

"Because the shadows are bound to the orders of the Norns. Just like me. If the Norns decide our fate should bring us together in that precise instance, then there's nothing the shadows could've done."

Sometimes, it seemed as though the Norns were the real Kings.

Thanatos looked back at my wrist. "When I recognized the mole, I went to the Norns straight away, asking why they made me save you twice, but they refused to answer. It was only when I went back to them because of Silvan's request that they revealed the truth to me: we are soulmates. The Norns have orchestrated everything from the beginning."

"Why would they ask you to save me twice and not just take

me with you the first time? And why would they wait to tell you the truth until you asked for a second time?"

Thanatos shrugged. "Maybe you were too young? Honestly, I don't know why. Nobody gets what the Norns have planned when they set up our fates. At first, I didn't want to believe them, but I had never before felt this connection. This deep connection from within. From here." He put the palm of my hand right over his heart.

"When you stood up for me against Silvan, and you could also talk to the darkness, it was yet another reason for the Norns's decision to make our paths cross." He said, never stopping watching me. "Not only did the Norns tell me to save you, they also made sure we'd stick together. The Norns knew I was too afraid of commitment to stay close to you otherwise."

"So they made sure you did," I whispered, understanding hitting me. "Silvan."

Thanatos nodded. "They organized everything in such a way that forced us to stay together. Do you remember what your friend told you when you contacted her?"

Incredulously, I nodded. "That Silvan did not try to break into our house."

"Exactly. Silvan wasn't even trying to get to you. That was something the Norns made up so they had a reason for me to bring you to the Afterlife."

I met his gaze. "That way, we were forced to get to know each other."

Thanatos nodded seriously.

I looked at the King in front of me. It was funny, wasn't it? The Norns never interfered with people's fates directly, but in our case, they had. They must have known how broken both of us were. Even being fated to be together, they knew we wouldn't just open up to one another without needing to be forced to do so.

So that had been why the Norns said I belonged to him. He didn't own me. We belonged to each other, because we were fated to be together.

You cannot let her go. Darkness calls to darkness. The Norn's words resonated in my mind, suddenly making sense.

All of our early moments together flooded back to me. Like the way I hadn't been scared of him when I first met him and had accepted his offer to take me with him to the Afterlife. Or the way my skin sometimes sizzled at our touch. Or how Thanatos spoke to no one but Minerva, Kalira, and me, how he always seemed to sense when I was okay by his closeness, how he seemed to *feel* my emotions and seemed to understand my inner workings without me telling him, the way we shared each other's pain … How familiar he had felt from the beginning, almost as though I had met him before; how I sometimes, unconsciously, sought out his body's protection; how I felt as though I had known him forever; the way his presence calmed me, letting me feel so *whole* and *complete*… There was no way to deny all those instances.

I stared at him. "We are soulmates?"

He nodded, just the slightest spark of hope beginning to shimmer in his eyes.

Locking my jaw, I looked at my feet.

"Cassiana?" Confusion colored his voice, crowding out the optimism he had just shown.

I looked back up at him. One of the things I had always loved about Thanatos was his unwavering confidence in everything he did. Not once did he strike me as someone unsure of himself, but now, as he was looking at me, all the uncertainty he felt at my reaction shone through his dulled eyes.

Not able to bear the sight of him, I turned around and began walking away.

"Cassiana?"

I kept moving and ignored his call.

He manifested right in front of me so suddenly, I stumbled right into his chest.

"Don't you dare turn away now, Cassiana. Talk to me," he pleaded.

I glared up at him. Before I had a chance to overthink what I was about to do, I spoke, "I don't want to be your soulmate."

Thanatos shrank back from me as though I'd slapped him. His mouth opened in shock.

I walked around him before I had a chance register the hurt I saw in his eyes. It was the same pain I felt filling my own heart at my reaction. I accelerated my steps, only wanting to get away from here. Something touched my elbow and, before I could brace myself, my body was yanked back into a wall of muscles.

I struggled against his hold. "Let go of me!"

"You are not going anywhere." His voice was deep, rich with anger, and it did the most bizarre things to my core.

His left arm came around, curling itself about my waist. He didn't apply any pressure on his grip, but the sheer fact that he had his arm in such a dominant way locked around my waist reminded me of who he was.

He was the King of this realm. And I had just rejected him.

His right hand rested on my hip, digging into the flesh there.

He lowered his head on my shoulder. "I know what you are doing," he growled against my skin.

"I don't—" I stopped speaking when his teeth scraped over my shoulder.

"Oh, you damn well know what you are doing." He spun me around so fast, I barely had the chance to catch myself. Lowering his head, he brushed his cheek against my own. "You are pushing me away because you are scared of me letting you down." He didn't give me a chance to answer. Instead, he brushed his nose at my temple and inhaled deeply.

It took everything within me not to let out a soft moan. I didn't manage to hold back the whimper coming from deep within my body, though. I felt him smile against me at the sound. "I—"

He pushed his body against me, and I could feel every dip, every muscle trained over centuries pressing against me.

"Thanatos, stop," I said even though my eyes fluttered closed and my voice turned raspy.

He took a step back immediately.

My body leaned toward him, immediately missing the warmth he had granted me.

He was breathing hard, his chest pushing the defined muscles of his pectorals against the white shirt. He looked at me through hooded eyes, the shadows of his eyelashes elongating at this angle. I had never seen his eyes like this. They were blazing with so many emotions, it was barely possible to catch a single one of them.

Lust, pain, anguish.

There was everything and so much more lying in the depth of

those mesmerizing green eyes. And I wanted to know every single one of them at its fullest.

But I can't.

He stared at me, the silence stretching out between us. His facial features were underlined by the shadows.

He was the first to speak. "Look me in the eye and tell me that you truly want me to leave. If you truly, honestly mean it, I'll leave." His eyes darkened at the corners, a hopeless expression flashing in them, but I recognized his words as truth. He would go if I told him so.

I opened my mouth, only for it to shut again. Did I want him to go? To leave me?

No.

But being soulmates proposed that we were truly ... meant to be. Thanatos had looked right through me. I wanted him. God, I never had wanted anyone like I wanted to get to know him. But I was scared. So damn scared the feeling rattled my bones and chilled my breathing into hurtful chips of ice. I was scared of being rejected. Of getting hurt yet again. And I knew this train of thought was wrong. After we had opened up to each other so deeply, I shouldn't think this way any longer. It put our relationship at least ten steps back. But I couldn't help it. I couldn't fight the suffocating feeling creeping up my throat from the depths of my stomach.

I stared at the King in front of me. The King who looked at me with such passion, such hope and longing. Even though he seemed at total peace, like he wouldn't care what my answer would be, the swirling of darkness behind him revealed his true feelings.

Look me in the eye and tell me that you truly want me to

leave. If you truly, honestly mean it, I'll leave. I lowered my lashes and stared at my feet. As much as I wanted to, I couldn't lie to him. I couldn't tell him to go. It was almost impossible to admit, but the only thing standing in our way were my trust issues. Thanatos had done everything right. Over and over again, he had proven that he was trustworthy. And maybe, just maybe, it was precisely that behavior that scared me the most.

My shoulders sagged. "I can't do that," I finally whispered. "I can't tell you to leave when you are the one thing I want to keep as close to me as possible."

Thanatos breathed in a ragged, stunned breath, and then slowly stepped closer, always watching me for any indication that I wouldn't want him to come nearer. But I didn't give him any.

"Then let me be close to you," he whispered, cupping my cheek. "Allow me to worship you the way you should've been worshipped throughout your entire life."

I leaned against his hand. "I'm just scared of being let down," I confided what he already knew.

"I know, love. I know." His lips brushed my skin with his words. He tilted my head back in a way that let me feel safe. I stared into his eyes. "But I'm here. I will be here for you whenever you need me. Always. That, I vow to you." His words let my heart pump faster. The suffocating feeling I had felt mere minutes ago slowly gave way to an unfamiliar warmth in my chest. "Do you trust me?" he asked me with so much sincerity in his gaze, it made my head spin.

And then, with my body beginning to tremble, I nodded.

He didn't wait a second before he lowered his head to mine. His left hand came up to cradle my face, too. He stared at me, and he must have recognized the longing in my face, because he pressed his lips firmly against mine.

Our mouths parted at the same time, allowing our tongues to mingle.

He tasted like the sin he was.

It wasn't a sweet kiss. Oh, no. This kiss was filled with lust, hunger, and impatience. Impatience for all the times we had forced our feelings back because we had been too scared to acknowledge them. To commit to each other.

Thanatos's hand found its way into my hair, fisting it like he would never let it go.

I moaned into his mouth, and he swallowed the soft sound with a deep-satisfied growl. His hold on me tightened as he drew me closer to him, pressing my soft curves against his hard ridges. I sucked in a breath, and my fingers curled into the rough fabric covering his chest when I felt him hard and ready against my abdomen.

My blood rushed through my veins, heating my body until the only thing I felt was Thanatos's touch on my skin.

He drew back a couple of inches.

Immediately, I whimpered at the loss of him. My entire body tingled from the way he was looking at me.

"Are you sure about this? I'll not be able to let you go, love. After this you are mine." His voice was raw and deep, his question making my blood run hot.

I looked him straight in his eyes. "Yes."

His face lit up in the most devilish way. A deep, satisfied noise coming from his throat was the only warning I got before he swept me into his strong arms.

I screeched in surprise. His mouth collided with mine, our teeth crushing together with such force I had to gasp for air.

Even when he crouched down, taking me with him, he did not for single second part our mouths. He put me down on the softness of the glittering sand. His broad, powerful body came down over mine, covering me.

I shuddered at the feeling of him on top of me. He might have crushed me with how much heavier he was, but I relished the feeling of him on me. Of all this weight pressed against me in the most exquisite way.

My legs fell open for him of their own accord, like they knew that this was meant to be. His tucked-in waist pressed against my core, making me hiss at the friction.

His hands drifted up my side, coming to rest on top of my breasts before cupping them. A low sound in between a growl and a sigh made its way up my throat, the sound being swallowed by Thanatos.

I felt him twitch against me when he noticed how my nipples had pebbled against the dress. My back arched, pressing my chest tighter against his touch. Before I knew what he was doing, he leaned down and took a nipple into his mouth, sucking on it through the fabric. I inhaled sharply when every nerve ending at its tip was stimulated by his talented mouth.

I grew restless when he kept sucking, drawing the most embarrassing sounds from me. My hands ran over his side to the hem of his shirt.

I wanted it off.

When Thanatos noticed my attempts to remove his shirt, he lifted his head and watched me through hooded eyes. A smirk lifted his lips. "Patience, love."

"Fuck patience," I breathed, my accelerated breathing pushing up my breasts.

He flicked my nose. "What did we say about words?"

I rolled my eyes but couldn't contain a grin. "Could you please hurry the fuck up?" I blinked up at him innocently.

"Mouthy little thing." His gaze dropped to my lips. "You should smile more often."

Before I had a chance to answer, he pressed his mouth on mine again.

I sighed in content.

His hands found their way to the back of my dress. And then he tore.

Riiiiiip.

I sucked in a breath.

A devilish grin spread his lips as he leaned back to take the fabric off of me. Lifting my arms, he first loosened the bodice from my upper body. Then, he moved down my body to take off the rest of the dress and my underwear.

I swallowed. I was truly doing this. With Thanatos. But this was different from the times I'd had sex before, because this *meant* something to me. It was different, because this wasn't only about satisfying our carnal needs. This was about us. About our path. About our trust, laid bare to both of us.

As soon as I lay naked before him, he stood and looked down at me. An expression I couldn't possibly determine flashed over his face. When I realized that I was only wearing my panties while he towered above me still fully clothed, I felt my blood rush into my cheeks. There was something oddly intimidating about it. Intimidating, but also *arousing*. I had never been shy before, but the way the King of the Afterlife was staring at me right now made me so very conscious about myself.

My hands fisted the sand beneath me, and I knew my knuckles would stand out white from how tightly I held it.

Slowly, Thanatos knelt, draping his body over mine. His core came to rest against my own. His right hand moved up to my face, starting to follow the curve of my eyebrow before tracing my lips.

With everything he did, he gave himself so much time. We didn't want to rush this. We wanted to take our time. To savor it.

He brought his hands in between us and started undoing his belt.

Slowly, my fingers began opening the buttons on his shirt.

Thanatos stopped his movements and stared at my fingers as they worked his shirt open.

He hesitated, and I knew the reason for it.

His scars.

Without saying a word, I leaned forward and brushed my lips over his in the most tender and reassuring way possible.

When I got to the very last of his buttons, he closed his eyes and exhaled deeply. I waited for him to tell me to stop, but when no dissent came, I slowly pushed his shirt over his back.

He was all muscle and power beneath it.

Hesitantly, I let my hands run over his back, feeling the uneven skin.

He hissed when I touched the two big scars running down his lower back. He let his head rest on my forehead. His deep breaths tickled my skin. "I wish you had the chance to see them," he whispered, referring to his wings.

My touch paused on his skin. "You are perfect the way you are. With or without your wings."

I traced the calloused, broken skin at his back. I moved out from beneath him and, ever so slowly, began trailing kisses on the scars. Worshipping them. And he let me. Scars should never provoke sadness of the memory that came with the injury. The memory should make the scars' owner proud of what one had overcome.

Thanatos lifted his head and kissed my front. Gently, he pressed me back down. He stared at me for a long moment, the hard edges of his eyes softening. And then, he began removing his pants and underwear.

Very slowly, I let my eyes drift from his face lower, over his defined abdomen to the v-cut of his abs, and even lower. I swallowed at the sight of him, nervous energy filling my every vein.

He was fully erect, ready to go. Though, I wasn't sure if he'd fit.

But as soon as my eyes lifted and met Thanatos's once more, I relaxed at the tenderness I found in his features.

He nestled himself between my thighs, the crown of him nudging at my entrance. He put his right arm beneath my head, supporting and reassuring me.

The stardust washing ashore in the most beautiful twinkling was the only sound around us as we stared at one another.

"Are you ready?" he asked, looking down at me. We were so close to each other that our breaths mixed.

Putting my arms on his biceps, I nodded and smiled shyly up at him.

He pressed into me carefully, letting me adapt to his size.

I was shaking like a leaf beneath him.

He wasn't even all the way in, and I felt so ... *full.*

I gasped for air, the feeling of him inside me taking me completely aback. Instead of pushing further in, he leaned down, kissing his way from my cheek to the hollow of my throat.

As soon as he felt me relaxing, he resumed his movement.

"Ah," I moaned, and he groaned when he was fully seated in me.

He stared down at me in a so very, very loving and caring way. Thanatos searched my eyes for anything that might give away my discomfort, but since I didn't feel any, he didn't find any.

When he started moving, my breath caught.

He retreated his hips and pushed back in. His pace was slow, his movements measured.

It felt good. Really good. But I didn't want to see him in control. I wanted to see what he was like when he let go. When all that power of his was directed at me.

"Harder," I breathed.

He smiled. "What is the magic word?"

He couldn't be serious. How could he possibly be teasing me when every nerve within me begged him to get down to business. "Please," I said, rolling my eyes at him.

He looked down at me, and when he saw me grinning, he began moving. *Truly* moving.

He retreated, only to plunder back in with such a force my body jolted with his movements. I moaned in bliss. With each thrust, he touched a part deep within me that had longed to be touched by him for what felt like forever.

My breasts were bouncing from the force of his movements.

Our moans collided, our breathing harsh. I curled my legs around Thanatos's torso, drawing him deeper into me.

Both of us groaned at the new angle.

"Thanatos," I breathed, my voice barely louder than a whisper. We were as close as two people could physically be, and I loved every second of it.

Bringing a hand up to cup my left breast, he thrust harder at the need filling my voice.

I was enveloped by his smell, making my joy turn into ecstasy.

He shifted his weight slightly, and then his hand moved from my breast to the place we were joined.

He found that small bundle of nerves at the apex of my core easily, beginning to rub it in small circles.

That was my undoing.

I cried out his name.

Thanatos was watching me the entire time, a broad, *savage* smile on his face. "You like that, love?"

The familiar endearment spoken in such an intimate moment almost made me orgasm for the second time in a row. "Yessss."

Smiling, he buried his face in my neck. He thrust harder and harder, slamming into me over and over and over again, chasing his own release.

I looked up into the constellations that were so different from the ones in the Land of the Living, but that seemed so much more familiar to me than the stars back home. As Thanatos stilled in me, I listened to the fallen stars twinkling in the lake. Thanatos lifted his head from the crook of my neck and kissed me tenderly on the corner of my mouth. I closed my eyes and let myself *feel* him. It felt as though a part of me that had been missing my entire life was suddenly there, completing the puzzle. Two bodies, one soul, becoming whole.

I was so very happy. Happy lying in the arms of my soulmate, my life's partner.

Thanatos stared at me, an awed expression on his face. "You are beautiful, you know that?"

I blushed, which was a total unintelligible thing to do given what the King of the Dead and I had just done together.

His long fingers brushed a strand of hair away from my face. He was so close to me his lashes brushed my cheek with every blink. The Deathbringer's heavy body lay draped over mine, our breaths calming, our skin cooling.

Thanatos's face rested on my chest, his right hand drawing lazy circles around my nipple.

I traced the curve of his brows and his luscious lips, enjoying the feeling of his body pressed on mine. He closed his eyes in complete relaxation, clearly enjoying my caress.

I was stroking his hair, letting its soft strays glide through my fingers. "Thanatos."

"Mmm?"

"I want to learn how to control the shadows."

He blinked his eyes open.

Throughout my entire life, I had experienced defenselessness so many times. Too many times. Whenever my dad had struck me, when Silvan had wanted to kill me, when the nightcrawlers had attacked me, when I had been about to be whipped ... and every time I hadn't been able to defend myself.

Thanatos had saved me, or the shadows had helped me, in almost every situation. And as thankful as I was for their help, I hated needing to rely on it. Maybe I had ordered the shadows to help me on a subconscious level, but I wanted to *consciously* defend myself.

I didn't want to be the damsel in distress who needed a savior. I didn't ever want my safety to depend on someone else again. And, since the Norns said that *I* was able to stop the awoken council member— which I strongly doubted— I needed to be as strong and in control of the shadows as possible.

"Are you sure?"

Even though I was frightened about the extent of my powers, I wanted to learn about them. I needed to. So, I nodded.

Thanatos looked seriously at me, letting his fingers run over my temple to my chin. "Then I will teach you."

I smiled at him. "That would be wonderful."

His eyes were fixed on my mouth before he turned and rested his head back on my chest, but it wasn't fast enough for me to miss the somberness that had just crossed his face.

"What are you thinking?" I asked calmly as I resumed combing my fingers through his silken, black hair.

Thanatos stopped tracing circles around my nipple and rested his hand flat on my breast. He sighed deeply before he admitted, his voice low, "I am sad."

My movements halted. "What? Why?" I tried sitting up, but Thanatos's hold on me only tightened, preventing me from doing so.

"Because of this." He removed his hand and leaned his ear against the swell of my breast.

"Thud-thud, thud-thud." When he moved his head, his lips

brushed over the place my heart was beneath my skin before kissing the spot.

The gesture was so sweet and intimate it drew tears to my eyes.

"I haven't heard a heartbeat in centuries." He leaned on his forearm and looked down at me. The King of the Dead grabbed my hand and brought it to his left pectoral. "This," he flattened my hand against his chest, "this is everything I have ever known and felt."

I focused on the feeling of my hand on his skin. I felt the softness of it, the defined muscles beneath it, but I didn't feel what should be below.

There was no heartbeat.

He took my hand, examining the mole on my wrist. "When the Norns made me save your life twice, I was sure they must be crazy. But now," he brought my wrist to his lips and kissed the mole. "But now, I couldn't be more thankful that they brought us together."

A sad, broken smile spread those beautiful lips, his eyes' usual brightness missing. "Cassiana. Even though I am dead, you make me feel alive. You touch that part deep within me that revives me. Before you, there was only darkness. So much darkness.

"I was sure I'd be alone forever. But then I met you. And suddenly, from the very first instance I laid eyes upon you in the theatre, it felt so easy to flirt with you, open up to you. Things I had not done in centuries were suddenly completely normal when I did them with you. And now I am sure that it was because of that inner connection I felt toward you from the beginning. Because we have experienced the same."

My heart broke for the sorrow I found in his eyes. His hurt

was so deeply anchored within him that he hadn't let anyone else see it. He had been sure he'd never meet anyone worth his love.

And I understood.

I understood because I had felt the same way throughout my entire life. I had lost the hope that someone might get to love me without being driven by bad intentions. It had taken me this long to find someone who would prove my beliefs wrong. Thanatos had shown me that there was good in this world—or at least in the Afterlife. He had shown me that a sense of partnership did exist.

But what he hadn't done was open his own eyes to the fact that *he* was worth being loved.

Tears began forming in my eyes, slowly streaming down my cheeks.

He saw them and moved up my body. His waist nestled between my hips as he leaned forward, starting to kiss each tear away.

"Thanatos," I whispered.

His eyes fluttered closed, as if in pain.

I cupped his face. "Thanatos, look at me."

His eyes opened, staring down at me. I stared back at him, taking in every detail of his unearthly beauty. The beauty that had hidden the deep hurt he had to live with every day. The hopelessness of it.

But it wasn't his physical appearance that fascinated me about him. It was what lay beneath all this external beauty.

My voice was hoarse. "I see the darkness in your eyes. It matches my own. It calls to me, begging me to be able to touch it, feel it. And there's nothing I would love more than that." My voice grew low. "Even before you revealed that we are soulmates,

I knew that something was different about us. I tried denying it. But now I see it. We are kindred spirits."

A tear left the Deathbringer's eyes at my words. He squeezed his eyes shut, his breathing becoming ragged.

Suddenly, I understood for the Norns's reason for binding us together: by understanding each other's pain, we were able to heal and connect to each other.

The Norns hadn't brought us together because we shared the same powers. Or because we were soulmates. They had brought us together because we needed each other. Both of us had endured so much, it was only a matter of time before we'd have broken. But we had found each other. We had recognized the deep pain underneath our skin. The pain that would eventually become so much more. Affection, respect, devotion.

We had saved each other. And the Norns had made sure of that.

I let my fingers trail down his jawline, caressing the soft skin and savoring the way he leaned into my palm. "You are the anchor to life that keeps me going," I whispered. "And I am so happy you brought me here with you."

He opened his eyes, tears glimmering in them. A thin layer of stardust moistened his skin, making it shimmer under the moon's light. "I love you."

My breathing stopped.

He had said those words to me before. Back then, I had thought he had said them because of his fever. But now?

"I love you not for being my soulmate but for the person you are," he said, making my heart ache. "The way you always want to protect others who need help even though you might endanger yourself by doing so is beyond me. The boy in the theatre, the two fae women in Emoh, when you defended Kalira for bringing you to the Forest of the Lost Souls, when you were brave enough to seek the witches in the Forest just so you could calm your friend. Even though you hurt from inside, you are selfless when it comes to the safety of others. Those are the reasons why I love you."

Tears were streaming down my cheeks when he leaned to kiss me tenderly. How many years had I hoped to hear those precise words? My parents' lack of affection was what drove me to the acting industry. I had tried with all my willpower to get recognition for someone who wasn't me. *Get skinnier, eat less ...* Only so I'd be appreciated. But what Thanatos had just said to me was so much more than I could've wished. He appreciated—no, *loved*—me for who I was. For the things I did. Not for who he wanted me to pretend to be.

Thanatos watched me closely before whispering, his voice throaty, "When I brought you here, at first, I had regrets for tearing you out of your former life, but the more time that passed, the more I hoped for you to never leave my side again. And when we knew that Silvan wasn't looking for you in the Land of the Living, I couldn't let you go. I wanted you to be here. With me. By my side. It probably makes me a selfish bastard, but the mere thought of losing you made the darkest shadow shine bright in comparison to what my life would've been without you."

An all-consuming sob emerged from the depths of my throat. I pressed my lips on his. So that was the reason he kept reminding me that the span of my stay in the Afterlife depended on him: he wanted for me to stay with him. Suddenly, I wondered if everything about the debt and its repayment for saving me had been a scheme in an effort to keep me close to him.

My words were raspy when I said those four words I had been

sure of never voicing. "I love you, too." Affectionately, my fingers trembling, I traced the jaw of the man who put everything past him in order to save others. "I will keep loving you until there are no more dreams to spin off the stars, until the entire sky is dark, with not a single star to illuminate it anymore," I whispered against his lips. "Because you are the brightness in my darkness."

I held Thanatos pressed tightly to me as his body began shaking with ragged sobs. As did my own.

Thanatos pulled slightly back, watching one of my tears slither down my cheeks. Carefully, he lifted his right hand to his face, catching a tear that just left the corner of his eyes with his index finger. Then, with the same finger, he prevented my own tear from streaming down my cheeks. Smiling at me, he closed his hands around the two drops. When he opened his hands again, a light as bright as the sun itself lay on his palm.

I gasped.

A star—*our* star. The representation of both of our deepest shared dream coming true: finding someone to trust, even to love.

We watched in silence as the light slowly elevated into the sky, joining its brothers and sisters in the heavens.

"That is our star, carrying our history, love."

Smiling, I squeezed his hand. "The brightest star in the night's sky."

As we lay beneath the sky, the stars twinkling above us, I knew I was right where I had to be. I felt the presence of the shadows and darkness retreat, letting us enjoy the company of one another.

I knew there would probably be some kind of revenge coming from Silvan for kicking him out of Emoh and that the council member would presumably become a problem we'd need to deal with in the near future. And there were all these questions circling around my head about the origin of my powers and why the Norns believed I was the key to stopping the council member … but for now, I was happy right here. I snuggled closer to Thanatos, his warmth and smell enveloping me. Yes. This was right where I wanted to be. At the side of the Deathbringer.

My King.

My beautiful, broken King.

My soulmate.

My world.

EPILOGUE

That night, I woke to the sensation of a sudden weight on my chest. I blinked my eyes open. I didn't immediately know where I was until the memory of Thanatos's tender touch on my skin reminded me. Smiling, I turned around to him. I was sure it was his touch on my chest that had woken me, but he was lying on his side, his sleeping face turned toward me.

His hands rested on my hip—as though, even in his sleep, he wasn't able to stay away from me for too long.

I lifted my hand and brushed a strand of his silken hair from his face.

I froze as I again felt the pull that had initially woken me. Careful not to wake him, I pushed myself up into a sitting position and listened.

A small breeze went through the tree's leaves, letting them whisper as they rustled against each other. My eyes darted to the lake. The stardust glimmered under the water's surface. But there was something beneath the water …. Squinting my eyes together, I tried making out the golden, glimmering object that stood out next to the thousands of bluish stars. My eyes fixed on the water, I stood.

Thanatos's arm fell from my hip onto the glittering sand with a dull thud.

I started moving slowly toward it. The sound of my steps was muffled by the softness of the sand. I didn't stop when my feet touched the water. The stardust started to cling to my skin like a mermaid's scales.

The golden object was only a couple of inches away from me, but the water was already beginning to reach my waist. As I was about to reach it, the object was pushed up from beneath by the darkest shadows I had ever seen.

Next to the obscurity of the shadows, the metallic object shone in brightness. Stardust clung to the damp metal, and water droplets ran down the rough surface.

It was a crown.

A regal, golden crown, still covered in stardust.

Even before I reached out to it, I knew that power lay within the object.

Even today, I can't explain it. But I instinctively knew it belonged to me.

My hands did not shake as my skin touched the metal. I knew it wouldn't harm me. The water of the lake ran down my arms and left a sheen of stardust on my skin as I lifted the crown high above my head and brought it down.

As soon as it rested on my head, I exhaled slowly.

Suddenly, as though they had only waited for me to put on the crown, shadows erupted from within me. They moved around me in circles, bodies beginning to form out of mist and darkness. The silhouettes dashed out.

I turned around toward the waterfront.

Thanatos, now awake, stood at the beach, the shadows looming behind him.

The three Norns appeared next to him, walking out of the forest. Their black eyes were gleaming like the sharpest of all nightmares. They approached the shore, a low lullaby leaving their parted lips. "Everything worked out just like we had planned."

The Deathbringer's gaze locked on the crown resting on my head. For a split second he seemed unable to grasp what he saw.

But once he did, without hesitating, he fell to his knees in front of me, his right arm over his heart.

The shadows and the Norns followed suit, each one of them bowing before me. Thanatos looked up at me through his thick lashes before inclining his head. His words thundered over the water's surface, making them heard in his entire realm. His eyes flared as we locked gazes. "The Afterlife has chosen its queen."

To be continued.

AFTERWORD

Dear reader...

When I first started working on *Symphony of the Fallen Stars*, I was inspired by the myth of the changelings. That idea has developed drastically throughout the process of actually sitting down and getting to write the book. Honestly, I could not love anything more than writing. I write for you. For each one of you. There isn't a job more fulfilling than to spread joy as you get lost in my stories and forget everything around you. I truly hope, with all my heart, to have achieved this.

I would really appreciate it if you could leave a **review on Amazon & Goodreads**. The series is not yet finished. But in order for me to release the following sequences, it depends on your help to spread the love for this story.

Thanks for purchasing this book!

ACKNOWLEDGMENTS

Papa, Mama, Theo: thank you for always supporting me, no matter what. You were the ones who always, *always* encouraged me to follow my own path and were there for me whenever I needed you. I owe you everything! I love you!

Jesu: thank you for always helping me figure out my plot holes in the middle of the night and getting frustrated with me—sorry for that—and Fine: thank you for being the very first person to read one of my stories and inspire me to pursue this passion! A special thanks goes to Tammy for making the time to read through my manuscript in a most definitely too short amount of time. Ariel & Nicole, thanks for helping me polish and bring out the best of my book!

Thank you to Laura Thalassa. Your courage to go into self-publishing encouraged me to take action and work toward my own dream.

And—yet again—thank *YOU* for purchasing *Symphony of the Fallen Stars*!

ABOUT MARIE LAU

Marie has always been lost in thought about bloodthirsty vampires, brooding elves, and glittering fantasy-lands. Late-night writing sessions and spending time with her family is what makes her happy.

When she isn't writing or daydreaming about her next story, she can be found reading a good book. She's still waiting for her prayers to be answered and to be turned into a vampire overnight (no kidding: she literally prayed for it when growing up).

Get in touch with me!
Instagram: @authormarielau
Mail: authormarielau@gmail.com
Goodreads:
www.goodreads.com/author/show/22314993.Marie_Lau
TikTok: @authormarielau
Pinterest boards: @authormarielau
Spotify playlists: Author Marie Lau

Printed in Great Britain
by Amazon